I0553803

FLIGHT
OF THE
MAGNUS

A Project Waypoint Novel

L. S. Roebuck

SHADOWLANDS PRESS
Tyler, Texas

Flight of The Magnus
© 2018 L.S. Roebuck

ISBN 10: 0-9986090-2-1
ISBN 13: 978-0-9986090-2-7

1.3

All rights reserved. No part of this publication may be reproduced or transmitted in any form or by any means electronic or mechanical, including photocopy, recording or any information storage and retrieval system now known or to be invented, without permission in writing from the publisher, except by a reviewer who wishes to quote brief passages in connection with a review written for inclusion in a magazine, newspaper, website or broadcast.

Published by Shadowlands Press
3706 Woods Blvd.
Tyler, Texas 75707
www.shadowlandspress.com

For Cherissa, for everything

And with gratitude to Mom and Dad for cultivating my love of the great space opera. I nearly wore out Mom's VHS Star Trek movie collection, and one of my favorite childhood memories is when Dad took me and my brothers in the summer of 1980 to see the Empire Strikes Back at the Razorback Theater in Fayetteville, Arkansas.

And thanks to Julie, Amy J., Laura, Rebecca, Matt, Paul and Andy whose joyful feedback on Waypoint Magellan *inspired this book.*

Special thanks to Johanna Musgrave for her invaluable feedback.

In memory of Lt. Commander Eric Murray.

PROLOGUE

MAGNUS (LATIN) — LITERAL MEANING 'GREAT.' MANY EARLY
KINGS INCORPORATED THE WORD INTO THEIR NAME (SEE MAGNUS
I, KING OF NORWAY AND DENMARK C. 1050 A.D.)

*Waypoint Cortes, January 13, 2603, Earth date, three months
after the battle of Magellan.*

Perspiration rolled from Arvin's forehead into his eyes. It
stung. He wanted to wipe his eyes, but was afraid to loosen his grip
on the gun clutched by his unsteady hands. He pointed the
firearm down the empty, brightly lit, yellow-walled hall. Just
around the corner, some 30 meters from where he stood, was the
Waypoint Cortes Commons, a marketplace for foodstuffs and
imported goods, with nearly a dozen restaurants providing
entrees for a wide variety of ethnic palettes. Usually the Commons
was swarming with sizzles and smells, people chatting and eating,
enjoying the company of friends. Now it was *nearly* silent.

Arvin, straining to listen to what he could not see, heard a
child crying, then a man pleading. Next, calm voices explaining
how the condemned should not be troubled, their sacrifice was for
the "greater good."

Arvin had decided that no matter what happened, he would
go down fighting. He wasn't wired like a Marine, but since war
had broken out, he found he was quick with a gun and could move
freely within the waypoint undetected.

He was now just 10 meters from rounding the corner and
exposing himself to the Commons.

"Delton, please," a man's voice said. "Spare my wife and my
child. Please. How could killing them be for *any* good?"

Arvin knew Delton, a piggish merchant who was quick with
an insult, but Arvin couldn't believe, even with all his flaws,
Delton was capable of murder.

The young child started to cry loudly, and Arvin heard a
woman's voice start to sing an unknown lullaby. The child calmed
down.

An almost robotic, monotone female voice spoke. "Your

family is everything that is wrong with humanity. You oppress your spouse with child rearing, a burden that should be carried on all shoulders. You selfishly teach your children to honor your family name over the state, over the common good. That tribalism is evil that must be extinguished."

"I am *not* oppressed, you bitch," the woman who had been singing said. "We should have exiled you Chasm trash when we had the chance."

Arvin's back was to the wall. His gun was raised as he prepared to intervene. Several weeks ago, the thought of taking someone's life was completely foreign. He'd never even held a stun gun before, much less a lethal bullet weapon. The gun he had now was given to him by a dying Marine who had sacrificed his life to save Arvin and his older sister, Olana.

More than a year ago, Olana, a news aggregator, had started reporting her theory that a secret organization code-named Chasm that was planning to take over waypoints *Cortes*, *Marquette* and *Magellan*. All other waypoints were to be destroyed. At first the public dismissed her reports as some fantastic conspiracy theory. But then she uncovered some secret communiques between a shadowy figure called the Chairman on Arara, a planet hosting humanity's first colony, and Falcon One, the alleged leader of a Chasm cell on *Cortes*. The waypoint authorities started to wonder if Olana's theory could be true.

With Olana's latest revelations, a group of well-respected *Cortes* citizens — including Marines, teachers and government officials — revealed themselves to be members of the Chasm organization. They suggested Olana's theories of Chasm conquest were just sensationalistic drivel to improve ratings, and in reality, Chasm was a society that quietly studied theories on how to improve humanity. Claiming they were being made scapegoats of traditionalist intolerance, the Chasm group announced an open meeting to explain their work and show how this shadowy organization was really working for the common good.

More than 1,000 people, including most of *Cortes*' leading citizens, showed up for the presentation at the historic Barack Obama Auditorium, located in the heart of the waypoint. The meeting was a ruse; Chasm operatives detonated a bomb that incinerated the auditorium, its occupants, and started chain reaction fires spreading across the waypoint. That was more than a dozen 28-hour-long days ago. Chasm operatives, which numbered nearly 10 times the original group that came forward, moved to seize control of *Cortes'* command center. A motley group of traditionalists and progressives who opposed the totalitarian control, including Arvin and his sister, launched an armed resistance to Chasm.

Waypoint Cortes was one of 18 space stations distributed evenly in the 8.5 lightyear gap between Earth and Arara, each an interstellar oasis where ships making the decades-long trip would make port and resupply. The waypoints were like floating cities, with permanent populations between five and fifteen thousand. Known collectively as Project Waypoint, the greatest engineering achievement of mankind enabled humanity to live among the stars indefinitely. For the adventurous souls leaving Earth for the Arara colony, the waypoints made the 20-year journey a little less lonely.

Chasm had spent the last 60 years plotting to take over or destroy the waypoints and to end the connection between Earth and Arara. Chasm meant for Arara to be its platform to build a utopian society, unhampered by a traditionalist Earth. That plan was coming to fruition before Arvin's eyes.

Arvin breathed heavily. He wasn't a coward, but he was finding it hard to resist his instinct to flee the scene to avoid a confrontation with Dalton and his mysterious female counterpart.

"Jonathan, you must understand that the old things must pass away to make way for the new. I'm pretty sure that's in your scriptures somewhere," Delton's familiar voice spoke evenly. "But I am not without mercy. I will spare you the pain of seeing your wife eliminated. You will die first."

"No!" shouted the mother's voice.

As Arvin rounded the corner, a gunshot rang out.

Arvin recoiled at what he saw. The wife jumped in front of Dalton's outstretched weapon to save her husband, and the bullet lodged in her head.

"Shawna!" Jonathan knelt by his wife, who was dead before she hit the floor. The child, Arvin guessed was just over one Earth year old, started to cry again, drawing the attention of its father,

Delton and the highly armored woman, a Chasm shock trooper, who accompanied Delton.

Arvin took advantage of the distraction to aim and let loose a volley of bullets at the shock trooper. "For *Cortes!*" he shouted as he advanced, emptying the small clip in his gun. The force of the bullets pushed the trooper to the floor, causing her to drop her assault rifle, but her armor held fast. Delton turned from the crying child to the rapidly approaching Arvin, and aimed his sidearm at Arvin's chest, but before he could shoot, Delton was suddenly thrown to the ground.

Jonathan was a small man, but in his rage, he was able to knock Delton to the floor as he reached to take the Chasm operative's gun. Delton and Jonathan both had two hands on the gun as they wrestled on cold steel.

"You killed my wife, you murderer," Jonathan fought with rage. "I am going castrate you and make you eat it! Then I'm going to throw you out the airlock."

Delton, struggling for the gun, just laughed. "My death doesn't matter. I will be honored in the new Araran order, remembered forever by a perfect people."

Arvin, shaking, struggled to reload his gun. The shock trooper had regained her footing and her assault rifle, squatted behind a dining table for cover, peered over and carefully targeted Arvin's head. "One bullet is all I need. No need to waste ammo," the trooper said to no one in particular.

It was her last thought, as a bullet from another gun blew through the trooper's brain.

"I couldn't have said it better myself," said a woman who looked to be in her early twenties, appearing on the far side of the Commons. She regarded Arvin. "Are you okay, brother?"

"Olana!" Arvin looked at his sister, who was standing with a smoking sniper rifle. She wore a black jumpsuit, and her short, dark hair was pulled into a ponytail. She stood confidently tall.

Had Chasm never existed, Olana would not have discovered that her best element was war. This was a war that Olana, writer-turned-warrior, was determined to win.

From the struggle on the floor, three shots discharged. Jonathan's body now slumped on top of Delton, who managed to get the close-quarter shots off into the recent widower. Jonathan looked at Arvin with an eternal sadness in his eyes. "Don't let them have my girl. Save Nora." Then he died.

Olana ran up to Delton as he was pushing Jonathan's carcass off of his own body in a vain attempt to escape. She gently touched the heel of her boot to Delton's cheek, and then gave a mighty thrust from her muscular leg.

Delton's body relaxed and his eyes went glassy as life left him.

The baby girl, along on the floor, continued to wail.

Olana reached over and picked up Nora, clutched the baby, tears flowing from her eyes. "Shhhhhhhh, little one. Everything is going to be alright. Arvin and I will take care of you."

"Another orphan," Arvin felt compassion. "Come on, let's get back to the Mexican Quarter and see if there is anyone in the resistance who will take care of Nora."

"No," Olana said firmly, handing the baby over to Arvin. Arvin awkwardly took the girl in his arms, not sure how to hold her and ultimately deciding to face her into himself with her head leaning on his shoulder.

"No?" Arvin said, as Olana recovered her handmade sniper rifle.

"It's now a suicide mission, something Chasm is calling 'scorched earth.' They are going to destroy the whole waypoint. We have to get off."

Arvin couldn't wrap his head around what his sister just said. How could they get off *Cortes*? Where would they go? In what? There were no deep space ships within at least a light year. The smaller vessels didn't have anywhere near the operational range to travel the half a light year distance to *Magellan* or *Marquette*, the nearest waypoints.

"You mean we are going to steal a ship?" Arvin protested. "That's certain death."

"No," Olana said with a little too much game in her voice. "That's *almost* certain death. Staying on this waypoint is certain death. Now let's get moving. There is a storage unit on the far side of the Tube station that we need to break into and grab as many rations as we can haul. Then get onto the hanger."

"Wait! I don't know how to pilot a runabout. You don't know how to pilot a runabout," Arvin stated. "Do you?"

"No, no."

"Well then who is going to run the ship?"

"Tomas."

Ugh, Tomas, thought Arvin. He didn't approve of his sister's flyboy boyfriend. But he *could* pilot the ship.

"What about her parents?" Arvin said, indicating the deceased. "Shouldn't we at least bury them at space?"

"No time. Their souls are in a better place," Olana. "Now let's move."

Arvin followed Olana in the direction of the tube, with Nora peering over Arvin's shoulder at her mother, motionless on the floor.

"Momma," Nora cried the only word she knew how to say.

On the command center platform stood Falcon One, leader of the Chasm Triumvirate on *Cortes*. Chasm had taken full operational control of the waypoint nine days ago. The command center was a large oval room lined with double balconies in full circumference. On each balcony was all manner of operational stations and control terminals, each with its own magnetic resonance screen, and a loyal Chasm operative inputting a litany of commands at the direction of their leader. From the center station, Falcon One had a line of sight and could issue direct commands to any of these stations.

Falcon One was a code name for Franco Romero, a 42-year-old futures trader, who joined the Chasm movement only five years ago. Romero was born on *Cortes* and had never been off the waypoint. He was an average height, and sported a muscular build. His light brown skin was flawless, and his dark eyes were energetic. He ran his delicate fingers through his thick, black hair, a tell that he was frustrated.

Romero was a man of ambition, and he wanted to be the absolute master of *Cortes*. When he barely lost the election to become *Cortes*' governor to an establishment candidate from a wealthy trading family, a Chasm Hawk named Igland, a harsh, solid man, saw an opportunity to recruit Romero to the utopian cause.

The Chasm Hawks were a deeply secretive sect of an already secretive movement. They swore allegiance in a blood ceremony to execute the will of the Chairman, Chasm's leader on Arara, and made sure that other operatives did the same. These were the truest believers in Chasm's dream of a utopian society built on Arara, completely split from Earth, where the common good triumphed over crass individualism and family tribalism.

Romero's ambitions and attractive charisma helped him quickly rise among the shadowy ranks of Chasm, and now he was master of Chasm on *Cortes*, and soon Chasm would have complete control of the waypoint.

Romero ran both hands through his hair and sat back in his chair, sighing loudly. He knew his life quest was about to come to an explosive end, and he couldn't figure out any way to stop it. Or even save his own life.

His communication officer, Sari, a portly woman with curly blonde hair, stepped into the center ring of the command center.

"The communication packets for today have arrived," Sari said with an air of hopelessness in her voice. "I've decrypted it. There was no rescinding the order. Scorched Earth is still on."

"I can't do it," Falcon One said aloud to himself. "I can't kill everyone on board *Cortes*."

Suddenly the command center grew quiet, as the half dozen Chasm officers and nearly dozen operatives turned and focused on their leader.

"It's what you are all thinking," Romero shouted, as the pondered the reality of impending death. "Are we really going to commit suicide for Arara?"

A nervous silence hung over the *Cortes* command center. Sari slid two fingers under her collar and pulled outward. Even though the room was climate controlled at 22 degrees, sweat started to bead in a line above her blonde eyebrows.

Ryder, a member of the Chasm Triumvirate charged with running the clandestine organization's intelligence apparatus, finished sending a message using her infopad, set the device down and stood, clearing her throat to draw everyone's attention.

"Franco, my friend, our fearless leader, where is your courage now?" the spymaster said with a sultry cadence that had an attractive melody, but a menacing harmony. Like always, she was dressed dramatically, wearing a tight red dress that matched her blood-colored lipstick.

"No, Ryder, listen to me now," Romero attempted to take

emotional command of the room, but instead he sounded desperate and seemed to shrink. "We have all worked so hard to liberate *Cortes* from the shackles of Earth. Why should we have to destroy this waypoint? That wasn't the plan."

Ryder sauntered toward the center platform where Falcon One stood, pushing her flowing dark hair back as her dark eyes flirted with several nervous male troops positioned near the command center's primary access portal.

"Apparently plans change," Ryder said, as she absentmindedly ran her fingernails across a platform safety rail, letting her long, red fingernails gently scrape against the rutted carbon polymer. "Are you questioning the wisdom of the Chairman? Did she err when she made you Chasm's leader of this waypoint? I don't blame her. You don't look the coward's part."

"Why should the Chairman be deciding our fate? Look, I've never even met her," Romero said, glancing frantically around at the rest of the bridge crew. "Listen everyone. We, the citizens of *Waypoint Cortes* we can figure out a way to survive without Arara or Earth."

"So, this is how it is," Ryder was now standing face to face with Romero. "You care more about yourself than you do about perfecting humanity. You used Chasm to further your own selfish goals. Tsk, tsk. How selfish, letting your own petty ambition convince you to thwart the common good. Perhaps it's time to step down and let someone else lead this glorious revolution. If *Cortes* could be saved, you know the Chairman would have saved it. But we've known Scorched Earth protocol was a possibility for six months. Something has gone wrong on *Marquette*."

"A possibility yes, but why should we blindly follow commands from some mythical figure a light year away, when we could survive," Romero replied, his voice trembling slightly. His eyes followed Ryder's attractive form as she rounded the command center platform.

"No, we must start the chasm here, now. There is no mistake. We threaten everything we have worked for now if we lose our resolve because we are worried for our own individual lives. It's time to end *Cortes*, for the greater good."

"Forget it!" Romero said, finding a little courage in his ripped gut. Physically, he was nearly 20 centimeters taller than Ryder and though both were in top athletic shape, Romero had a wiry strength Ryder would never possess.

"You can't destroy *Cortes* without me. I'm the only one with the access codes. No one else can overload the antimatter reactors except me."

"You have a point, Falcon One," Ryder addressed Romero by his code name as she turned her back to him and considered the armed troops. *Why isn't he here yet,* she thought, as she continued to stall. "Let's put it to a vote. All those in favor of stopping now, right at the finish line, signify by saying—"

Ryder felt a metallic tube end pressed into her back. Probably a stun gun; but maybe even the more lethal weapons that used bullets for ammunition. She raised her arms slowly in the air and delicately turned around to face Romero.

"We don't vote," Romero said. "This isn't a democracy. I am in charge here, and I have half a mind to airlock you for treason."

A deep, accusing voice came from the door. "The only one committing treason here is you, Romero." *Finally,* Ryder thought.

The blood drained from Romero's face. Igland the Hawk had come to the command center to do his job: assure that the will of the Chairman was followed without question or regard for any other concern. Igland didn't appear armed, but Romero knew not to underestimate the old man. He approached Romero from across the room with haste and confidence.

"I'm glad we are all going to die," Igland said as he closed the distance between him and Romero. "I would hate for the Chairman to know about my failure in recommending such a limp man to lead us. Time for me to rectify my error."

"Igland! Stop this madness before it is too late. Captain Milo, order your men to shoot Igland, now! Shoot him."

Instead, the captain waved off his troops. "We choose to die like good soldiers. For Chasm! For Arara!" The cultist troops cheered along with their commanding officer.

Igland was nearly to a full sprint and would be on top of Romero in seconds. "Death comes for us all, Franco. Looks like it comes for you first."

Panicked, Romero aimed the gun away from Ryder and pointed it at the Hawk. The instant the weapon was not pointed at Ryder, the she-spy struck out and snatched it from Romero's hand.

Nearly as quickly, Igland had grabbed Romero's now empty outstretched arm, and with an impressive display of strength, had flipped Falcon One over and pinned him leaning into the primary command control panel. Romero tried to use his free arm to give him some leverage, but Igland had rendered Romero immobile.

"Let me go!" Romero whined. Many of the troops laughed, but the officers seemed nervous and unsure what to do.

"I have a better idea, Franco," Igland replied. "You shut down the coolant lines to the antimatter reactor. Put the code in now, and you can have an extra half hour to live. Otherwise, I'm going to break your neck now."

"No! I don't want to die. I didn't sign up for this," shouted an officer named Apta. The tall woman with short brown hair was in charge of supply logistics for Chasm. "Don't give them the code, Falcon One! Igland, let him go or I'll shoot."

Apta had pulled a small holdout pistol from her pants pocket and pointed it at Igland. Several of the troops looked to Captain Milo, as if to ask if they should intervene.

Before he could respond, a shot rang out, and Apta fell to the floor, bleeding out from the abdomen. Holding out the smoking gun that she had just swiped from Franco, Ryder looked pleased at her lethal handiwork.

"You're next if you don't input the destruct code," Ryder pointed the gun at Falcon One's head. "Three — two — "

"Okay, okay," Franco said, desperately trying to figure a way out of his certain demise. His only chance now was to input the destruct codes, and then hopefully find a way to free himself from this Hawk, then to countermand his own order before the half hour or so it would take for the antimatter core to go critical. *I just need to keep a cool head*, Franco thought. *I can figure this out.*

"*Cortes* command, prepare to received override. Delta-Two-Charlie-Five-Tango-Tango," Franco spoke audio commands to the central computer's virtual intelligence, or VI.

The computer spoke back. "Please present exposed skin for DNA verification." Igland forced Falcon One's bare hand onto the DNA scanner, which began to illuminate the subdued man's digits. "Verification accepted, Commander Romero."

Ryder pressed the gun forcefully into Franco's head. "Give

the command."

"*Cortes* Command, override the safeties on the antimatter coolant system and shut it down."

"Are you sure you want to do that?" the computer said in a pleasant voice.

Franco paused, and considered the gun jammed into his forehead. If he didn't say yes, he knew he would be dead within seconds. Ryder wouldn't bluff on this, Franco reasoned.

"Yes. I'm sure," Franco said.

"Commencing shut down. Warning: If the coolant flow is not restored, catastrophic reactor overload could damage this waypoint," the VI warned.

"Excellent," Igland smiled.

"I've done what you wanted," Franco said, dejected. He knew his time to countermand the lethal order was short. "Now let me go, so I can die in peace."

"Die you shall," Ryder said as she emptied a few rounds into Franco. As the ex-commander of *Cortes* chasm expired, the last words he heard was the sultry spy whisper, "Your reign on *Cortes* was already too long."

Arvin pushed a large freight cart piled with rations and other supplies, as much as could be carried. The cart levitated above the textured steel corridor floor by using the reverse of the artificial gravity technology on *Cortes*. Squatting on top of the cart with her sniper rifle at the ready was his sister Olana. She clutched with one arm the newly orphaned Nora. Nora pulled forcefully at Olana's ponytail, and the woman winced.

They were close to the docks now. Olana had hoped her boyfriend Tomas was able to procure the last functioning Valkyrie on *Cortes*, the *C.S.S. Iron Star*. The *Iron Star* was military grade, equipped with explosive torpedoes and large vacuum-capable chain guns. The main hanger and most of the ships in it had been decimated in the skirmishes when the Chasm counter-insurgency began.

The cart rounded the corner, 100 meters from the primary entrance to the dock. Two Chasm troops were sitting at a checkpoint, charged with securing the critical facility, but instead playing a game of chance to pass the time.

Olana pulled the trigger of her silenced sniper rifle once, and one of the guards slumped over in his chair, his head splashing into a pile of credit chips and playing cards.

"Hey, stupid dirt licker," the other guard said. "What's the big idea?"

Then she saw the blood leaking from a hole in his head. "Dirty hell!"

Her profanity was interrupted by another shot from Olana, and the second guard fell backward over her chair.

Arvin never could get over his sister's bloodlust when it came to dispatching Chasm operatives. They did try to ruin her life when she was trying to expose the undercover operation. Still, Olana wasn't normally a vengeful person. *Now Chasm was trying to ruin everyone's life*, thought Arvin. *What if she is wrong about them trying to destroy the waypoint?*

As if on cue, the station wide automated alert system came on. The VI that made the ship's announcements spoke with programmed urgency. "Alert! Attention *Cortes* residents. I have detected a critical heat buildup in the antimatter reactor. Estimated 15 minutes until catastrophic failure of all reactor safety systems."

Olana hopped off the cart and looked to Arvin, worried. She took Nora into her arms and slid one of the dead guards off of the control desk so she could access the controls that would allow them into the hanger. "I didn't think we'd have this little time."

The cool blue metallic doors that connected the hanger to the rest of the station slid open with a slight grind, and Arvin immediately pushed the supply laden cart in as soon as there was enough clearance. "Come on, Olana!"

Olana looked back down the corridor they just traveled and muttered to herself. "Where is he? Come on, Tomas."

Olana's personal communicator, sewn into her glossy black sleeve, crackled to life.

"Olana!" a deep voice rolled from communicator.

"Tomas," Olana said, relieved, as she entered the hanger, and surveyed the several hundred yards of twisted steel, burnt out corvettes and other miscellaneous waypoint rubble. Her eyes fell on the *Iron Star*, a red Valkyrie-class runabout, and she knew that was their only chance of survival, however slim. She spoke into her sleeve. "Did you make it to hangar control? Can you get the space doors open?"

"Yes, love," Tomas replied. "Listen carefully. I am going to force the space doors open, but I have to do it from here. As soon as I do, the safety protocols will seal off the rest of hangar and the atmosphere will vent, so I won't open the doors until you are on the ship."

"Wait! How will you —"

"Don't worry, I know you can't pilot the thing, so I have a vac suit I'll put on and walk out to you. Just be sure to let me into the airlock when I knock. The vac suit here doesn't have a helmet radio."

"Okay, Arvin is loading the supplies now, and I'm getting on board," Olana said as she sprinted as fast as should could toward the *Iron Star* carrying Nora with one arm. Nora didn't like the sudden motion and responded with a sharp wail.

"What's that?" Thomas asked.

"We've had a baby, obviously," Olana smiled in the face of impending destruction.

Three minutes later, Olana was on the bridge of the *Iron Star*. Arvin was talking to his infopad, reading instructions of pre-flight preparation on a Valkyrie class ship.

"Are you sure you have to bring up main engine power before life support?" Arvin said, frustration in his voice.

His infopad VI, Max, spoke back in equally frustrated tones, "Of course I'm sure, Master Arvin. I have access to the primary user database—"

"Alright, Max, alright," Arvin said, then turned to his sister. "Where's Tomas?"

"He has to open the space doors from the control tower," she replied.

"What? How is he going to get here once the doors are open?"

"Vac suit."

"Oh..." Arvin said. "I think we're ready to go. We're out of time. Let me take her to the back and see if I can find a place to secure her." Arvin took the baby girl from her sister and exited off the bridge down the main corridor toward the crew quarters in the back of the small ship.

Suddenly, a loud whoosh sound reverberated throughout the *Iron Star*, and then eerie silence. Olana looked out the portal and saw the atmosphere sucked into space, along with a lot of metallic flotsam and jetsam.

The waypoint AI came on over the *Iron Star* ship wide comm, issuing another warning. "Alert. Five minutes until reactor meltdown."

"Come on Tomas," Olana muttered as she dropped through the main hatch into the lower deck, where Arvin had loaded the supplies and where she could open the airlock for her boyfriend.

She had waited just a minute at the airlock controls when she heard a pounding on the exterior hull. "Tomas!" Olana punched open the airlock's exterior door and peered through the interior door's small viewport to see a bulky suit walk in. *Just in the nick of time,* Olana thought.

Another minute later, the airlock had pressurized, and Olana opened the interior door.

The vac suit walked forward. "Let me help get you out. You have to fly us out of here," Olana said as she furiously worked to take Thomas out of the airtight suit. She pulled off the arms and gasped. These were not the strong arms of her beloved, they were delicate female arms.

"Come on, help me out!" a woman's voice came from the suit. "We're running out of time."

Olana, somewhat shocked, complied. "Where's Tomas?" she said as she freed the woman completely from the suit. The woman had dark hair, dark eyes and blood red lip stick.

"Where's Thomas? He has to pilot this ship!?" Olana was frantic.

"No worries, I am a pilot," Ryder said as she strode toward the hatch to the main deck.

Olana was dumbfounded. She looked to the airlock, and back to Ryder. "Where's Tomas!?" she yelled.

"Tell me, do you believe in God?" Ryder said as she gracefully climbed the ladder up. She stopped halfway and considered Olana, who appeared to be following her up.

"Yes. Now tell me, where's Tomas!"

Ryder pulled up her tight dress slightly, revealing a holstered weapon. She drew the small pistol and pointed it at Olana.

"Arvin! Help!" Olana shouted.

"Ask God where Tomas is. Heaven? Hell? How would I know?" Ryder shot Olana several times in the legs, and the journalist-turned-freedom fighter fell on the floor, crying out in pain.

Ryder turned and proceeded up the hatch. When she emerged from the top, she found who she assumed was Arvin.

"Who are you?" he asked.

"I am your only hope of survival, unless you know how to pilot this ship," Ryder said as she moved to pilot's seat on the minimalist-designed bridge.

She pointed her gun at Arvin and indicated the navigator's chair. "Sit down, it's going to be bumpy." Arvin complied.

"Where's Olana?"

"The woman? I put a few holes in her." Ryder had activated the *Iron Star's* thrusters and began to pilot the ship toward the open space doors.

"You shot my sister? Is she dead!?!"

"Was that your sister?" Ryder said, matter-of-factly, glancing in the direction of the hatch. "My apologies." Ryder was careful to dodge the debris that had been sucked out of the *Cortes* hangar when the space doors opened. "If she dies, we will live at least 30 percent longer than if she lives and eats her share of rations."

Ryder looked at Arvin as her fingers instinctively danced over the *Iron Star's* controls. He wasn't much to look at, she mused as she accelerated the ship to put distance between the *Iron Star* and *Cortes*.

A bright flash attracted Arvin's eyes to the starboard viewport.

A shockwave rippled through *Waypoint Cortes*, buckling the five-kilometer long saucer until its bulkheads could no longer take the strain. Arvin saw the station rip into several dozen jagged pieces, spewing atmospheric gasses, boxes, furniture, equipment, aluminum wall fragments and people into the cold silence of space.

Flashes of fires, quickly consumed by vacuums could be seen twinkling though out the floating fragments. Then suddenly, the new field of space junk that was once a proud waypoint was dark, save for a few emergency lights blinking.

Tears poured out of Arvin's eyes. He looked at Ryder in rage and stood up to strike her.

"Go ahead, kill me, Arvin," Ryder said. "Yes, I know who you are. It was my job to know everything and everyone. No more. But I figure we have a five percent chance of meeting someone heading this way from *Magellan* ... if you have someone who knows how to pilot this ship."

The sound of Olana crying out in pain echoed onto the bridge. Alarmed, Arvin started to move for the portal to help. He eyed Ryder's pistol and hesitated. The woman's hand absentminded twitched near the trigger. "I need to go help my sister."

"My dear," Ryder looked on the boy with hollow sadness. "Let her die. With three, the supplies would go too quickly."

"There is a baby in the back, orphaned by your Chasm comrades," Arvin said with spite, backing toward the hatch. "Do you want her gone too?"

"Arvin, that child is practically dead. We are all."

"Are you going to kill the baby, too?"

"Babies don't eat that much," Ryder considered. "She won't materially impact our chances of survival."

"So, I eat. A lot," Arvin said, defiantly, almost over the hatch now. "Why don't you kill me, too?"

"If you were dead, it would increase my chance of intercepting a rescue ship a few percentage points," Ryder said, pondering. "I can't go back to Arara. Wouldn't make it anyway. Even if we did, Chasm would kill me for my cowardice. So, *Magellan* it is. And it's a half light year to *Magellan*. Too far before I'd run out of supplies. I can't kill you. Not worth it."

"Why not?"

"I don't want to die alone."

CHAPTER ONE

Waypoint Magellan, November 11, 2603, Earth date, 13 months after the Battle of Magellan.

Waypoint Magellan was broken and desperate. Though victorious, *Magellan* proved the axiom that nobody wins a war.

Scars remained. The topside gardens, once a glorious, open breadbasket of fresh vegetation, was now withered, fragmented with debris. The lush orchards and tall green fields were no longer viable. The sealed cracks reminded the farmers of when the Chasm enemy rammed a Valkyrie-class runabout into the plexiglass exterior. Cubic meters of precious atmosphere and one of the most valuable and rare substances – soil – were sucked into the great void before the hemorrhaging could be stopped. Now, the people of *Magellan* could count on only a fraction of the food once grown here.

Fortunately, *Magellan* was designed to synthesize most of the food needed from raw elements. But this required enormous amounts of power, and *Magellan's* antimatter reactors, also victims of a kamikaze attack, were operating at a third of their former capacity. Like food, power was rationed. *Magellan's* engineers did not have the parts to fix the destroyed cells, nor the materials from which to manufacture the parts.

Water purification, air scrubbers, climate control all required more energy than could now be produced, and to many the interstellar paradise that was *Magellan* had turned into a living hell.

Waypoint Magellan's civilian governor, Thor Rillio, had proven himself to be an adept survivor. In the last year, he had rallied those who had not taken passage on the *U.S.S. American Spirit* headed to Earth, or the *U.S.S. Magnus*, headed in the opposite direction to put down the inevitable rebellion on the colony planet, Arara.

"Hope is the only thing of value now," Rillio would say time and again as the station slowly recovered. "Without hope, everything else is meaningless."

Magellan might as well be officially at war with Arara, 1.5

light years away. Regularly scheduled supply ships would come from Earth bringing relief, but seven light years distance from Earth meant those ships were infrequent. If the schedules were correct, the next supply ship was still two years out, having left Earth 12 years ago.

The station could be repaired, supplies could be restocked, but so many souls were lost forever. Nearly ten percent of the station's population perished in the initial battle, and half that many died from insufficient medical resources and various lethal system malfunctions as the people of *Magellan* struggled to bring their critical systems back online.

But even in the shadow of death, new life brought hope.

Twenty-year-old Amberly Macready held a months-old red-headed baby boy gently in her arms. Alroy, named for his grandfather, had the distinctive round headedness that identified him as a part of the Macready clan. The baby Amberly cuddled was a star of joy in the dark space that had followed the Battle of *Magellan*. Amberly was still haunted by the revelation that Amberly's own mother, Kimberly, architected the attempted destruction of *Magellan*.

However, the most painful wound Amberly endured was the loss of her good friend North, who joined the crew of the *Magnus*, as the vessel headed to Arara to confront and subdue the broader Chasm rebellion.

Alroy began to fuss, so Amberly rocked the baby.

"Shhhhh. There, there. Your mother will be here in a few minutes," Amberly attempted to soothe the baby. "And not a moment too soon."

Amberly enjoyed babysitting her nephew while her sister Kora, a nurse, worked at the Science Quarter medicenter. However, after ten hours of changing diapers and mixing formula, she was glad to pass off the baby to Kora. As Amberly sat on her bed, she pointed out the viewport into deep space.

"See that star over there," Amberly said to an oblivious Alroy. "That is Viapos. You can't see it, but orbiting the star is Arara. Your grandmother always told me she'd take me there, but, well, she's gone now. I'll have to tell you that story when you are older. Much older."

Alroy cooed.

Amberly thought about her mother, tossed out an airlock by a vengeful mob after Kimberly's unsuccessful attempt to destroy *Waypoint Magellan* a year earlier. When she was a 13-year-old girl, Amberly practically worshipped the strong, intelligent woman of science. That same year Kimberly disappeared, thought to be lost in space. Amberly was reunited six years later with her mother, who had been hiding in self-exile, waiting for the right moment to either take over or destroy Amberly's home.

If not for the heroics of North the Marine and the mysterious Chasm defector Dek, Kimberly would have won and 10,000 souls would have been extinguished in the vacuum of space. For a time, Amberly had thought that she could love Dek. But he was exiled on the *American Spirit*, headed on a decades long journey to Earth for his role in planning the attack on *Magellan*. In the end, Amberly wasn't willing to give up the only home she had ever known to go with Dek.

Dek and North were heading in the opposite directions, both now a half-light year away, and thinking about the two covered Amberly with a pronounced loneliness. She held Alroy, who had now fallen asleep, a little tighter.

The door chimed, and the baby launched into a half-hearted effort to fuss.

Amberly pressed open the door, expecting to see her sister Kora and brother-in-law, Trot Wilder, returning from their work shifts. Instead, she saw the odd pair of Skip and Lydia, holding hands and smiling broadly. The two immediately realized their entrance had woken the child, and Lydia, a tall, muscular blonde with a Nordic face, blushed in embarrassment.

"I'm so sorry, Amberly," Lydia released Skip's scrawny hand and moved forward to embrace her friend and colleague, awkwardly reaching around the baby Amberly held. "I forgot you were babysitting Alroy today."

Lydia turned her attention to the red-headed child, and gently put her finger on his nose. "Oh, you are so cute. When you grow up, I bet you are going to be a lady killer."

"Great," said Skip, half sarcastically. "Now I have to compete with a newborn for your affections."

Lydia rolled her eyes and addressed Amberly, "Isn't Skip charming?" The pair completely stepped into the semi-rare two-bedroom apartment and the exterior access port slid closed.

"Are you coming to Rick's tonight?" Skip said, his sour expression melting into a smile as he considered the baby. "I promised Skylar Trigs I would do everything in my power to get you to come hang out with us tonight." Rick's was a café bar that was a favorite of Amberly's for its live jazz music and creative assortment of both alcoholic and non-alcoholic drinks. With the current shortages plaguing *Magellan*, the booze was a little rough. Since she rarely drank, this specific luxury loss didn't bother Amberly. The set-up with Skylar did.

"Skylar Trigs?" Amberly whined. "Really? He's your boss, right?"

"I think he's pretty handsome," Lydia said. "And charming. He'll be governor someday. He certainly has the ambition – and the smarts for it."

"Technically Skylar's not my boss anymore, not since I enlisted," Skip reminded Amberly. After the battle of *Magellan*, in a rare bout of patriotism, Skip joined the Marines. He still monitored interstellar transmissions at the communications center, just for the military instead of the civilian government. "And he is my friend, so I told Skylar I'd try. Please come, Amberly. North always said the only sure way to make sure you don't enjoy a good party is to not show up."

Lydia poked her boyfriend for bringing North up.

"Ouch!" reacted Skip, then he looked at the suddenly crestfallen Amberly, her head bowed, red bangs hanging over her eyes, and said nearly inaudibly, "Oh."

Nearly a year of time and space had passed since North had left on the *Magnus* to find war, but the wound Amberly had received from her once-protector still felt fresh. North had not forgiven Amberly for her unintentional role in helping Chasm to nearly destroy *Magellan*. Many of the Marines North commanded died in the battle Amberly's actions enabled.

Amberly knew it was foolish to think about North like she did. But she thought about his broad shoulders, his dark brown hair, his kind brown eyes. Her longing for the selfless Marine, now executive officer and second-in-command aboard the most powerful warship ever built, had no logical end. He was gone to fight the Chasm rebellion and most likely she would never see him again.

"Any word from the *Magnus?*" Amberly asked Skip.

"I'm sorry Amberly," Skip said. "I miss North, too. I mean, he *was* my best friend. He was really my only friend until Lydia came around."

"Yep, you owe me one," Lydia teased, sliding her hands around Skips torso into a cozy embrace. "Amberly, don't you worry about North. He's a survivor."

Amberly knew that according to plan, *Magnus* should be arriving at *Waypoint Cortes*, just a half-light year from *Magellan*, any day now. For security reasons, *Magnus* had been running radio silent for some time now. Because of the transmission lag that accompanies distances measured in light years, the last message *Magnus* sent was received three months ago.

She knew the *Magnus* would break radio silence once it reached *Waypoint Cortes*. But if they reached *Cortes* this day, any message would take half a year to get back to the *Waypoint Magellan*.

North might as well be 100 or 1000 light years away, Amberly thought woefully. If he survived, returning to *Magellan* would take years, and North made it clear at Amberly's trial what he felt. She was acquitted of treason, but North believed she was a manipulative turncoat, just like her mother. North would never have her now.

Her brain knew she needed to get over North, but her heart held on tightly to the memory of the Marine. Today, her head won.

"Okay, Skip," Amberly smiled softly, pushing her hair out of her face. "I'll go with you and Lydia."

Alroy let out a soft whimper, and fidgeted in Amberly's arms.

"Well, as soon as my sister gets back," she said, gently bouncing the baby on her knee. "How did you know I was here anyway?"

"We went by your place first, and we just asked Verne," Lydia said, referring the Amberly's virtual intelligence construct.

"I must adjust his privacy setting," Amberly sighed. Amberly sat down on the in-wall bench.

"You guys want something to drink?" Amberly motioned to the food prep area on the wall opposite the main door. "I'm sure

Kora and Trot won't mind."

"Too early for me," Skip said.

The door slid open and Kora and her police officer husband stepped in.

"I guess we found the party," Trot said. He nodded to Skip and shook his hand, then stepped forward and reached for his son. His sister-in-law handed Alroy over and stood up to give her sister an embrace.

"Hey, sis," Kora said.

"We're going out to Rick's tonight," Lydia said to Kora. "You want to come and get some drinks?"

Alroy started to fuss, and Kora took him from her husband. Alroy grabbed at his mother's long raven-black hair and pulled. "Alroy isn't up for it."

"I can watch him if you want to go, sweetheart," Trot said reaching for the baby. "We can have a guys' night in and watch old war vids."

"I couldn't do that to you, honey," Kory protested. "You just got off work, too."

"You *must* come, Kora," Lydia smiled mischievously. "Amberly is coming."

"Reeeeally," Kora looked squarely at her sister. "Well, that's news."

"Yeah, I am trying to set her up with Skylar," Skip interjected.

"Shhhhh!" Lydia chastised her boyfriend. "Amberly is going to change her mind."

"Skylar Trigs. Easy on the eyes. Great prospects," Kora winked at her sister. "I approve."

Amberly blushed a little, absentmindedly pulling on a twirled red lock. A year ago, this sort of attention would have made her uncomfortable and even angry. But through the Battle of *Magellan* and the hard months following, these friends proved that they cared deeply for Amberly.

"Will you be my wingman?" Amberly mock pleaded to her sister, showing pathetic wide eyes with a few extra blinks.

"Go ahead, sweetheart. I'm totally fine with Alroy... at least for one night," Trot again encouraged his wife.

"Okay, I'm in," Kora said, walking across the two-meter-wide living area into one of the bedrooms. "Just give me a minute to get changed and freshen up."

Skip smiled and grabbed Lydia's hand. Trot sat down on an in-wall bench and fished an infopad out of a bench pocket with the arm that wasn't holding Alroy. Kora called over her shoulder as the door to her room slid closed.

"It will be just like old times, before Chasm," Kora said, her voice muffled through the wall.

North is gone. We'll never have old times again, Amberly thought.

The four friends hopped on the Tube after a decent walk from Kora's apartment. The apartment, a desired two-bedroom flat with station-exterior windows, belonged to the Macready family when Amberly was growing up. When Kora married, Amberly moved out. As a girl, she shared a room with Kora and her parents used the other. When Alroy and Kimberly Macready allegedly disappeared into space, the girls had the space to themselves.

The Tube was a pneumatically-powered mass transit that completed a circuit through all four quadrants of the five-kilometer long *Waypoint Magellan*: Church, President, State and Science. Each quadrant represented an institution that the forbearers of Project Waypoint, those who engineered the series of 17 interstellar rest stops between Earth and Arara, believed were foundational to civilization. Amberly remembered the reasons from her elementary schooling: Church was a nod to the moral codes organized religion gave mankind; President referred to the great leaders who brought humanity together in some of history's darkest times; State was named to acknowledge the pluralistic organization of society that was protected by government; and Science recognized how applied knowledge improved the human condition.

Tube cars held up to six people on two facing benches. Amberly sat next to her sister and across from Lydia, who was leaning into Skip. Visually, Lydia and Skip were an odd pairing. Lydia was tall and muscular and formidable. She kept her blondish hair short, and preferred to wear practical khaki jumpsuits. Skip was thin and a half-dozen centimeters shorter than his girlfriend. Before the Battle of *Magellan*, Amberly thought Skip quite disagreeable and avoided him when possible.

Because both she and Skip were good friends with North, she saw more of Skip than she would have liked.

The battle changed Skip. He didn't take himself so seriously anymore. He had been an ideologically rigid progressive, cheerless to a fault — in many ways, the opposite of his friend North. *Perhaps the trauma of war made Skip understand what was truly valuable*, Amberly thought, as she observed him offering affection to Lydia. *We are all changed.*

Well, her sister Kora's personality and character hadn't changed much, Amberly considered. She just made some drastic decisions, which actually was consistent with Kora's past behavior. Kora married Trot Wilder just a month after the Battle of *Magellan*, and Amberly didn't approve. She had no qualms with the character or worthiness of Trot, but rather she thought the attachment was much too fast, and probably just Kora's need to manufacture some emotional security in the wake of so much sudden loss.

More importantly, Amberly's once deeply held position that marriage was just a tool of social oppression still held sway in her heart and mind, even though she saw she absorbed that value from her traitorous mother. *Maybe Mom went about things the wrong way*, Amberly thought, *and clearly, she took things way out of proportion. But was she, at the base level, wrong in her thinking?*

Amberly had moved into her own place, a small studio flat, not far from the *Magellan* hangar and the science labs. As she watched her sister gab with her friend, Amberly realized how much she had naturally grown apart from Kora. Immediately following the battle, the sisters were closer than they had ever been. They had gone through so much trauma and loss together, and all they had left was each other. But then Kora married Trot, and soon after she became pregnant with baby Alroy. They were still close, but Amberly was painfully realizing that while Kora was her only family, Kora had a new family of her own that came before her little sister.

In the months following Kora's wedding, Amberly threw herself into her work at the Science Corps. She singlehandedly repaired and restarted the stellar radiation laboratory. The information from the stellar lab, which tracked all sorts of dangerous space radiation, was especially critical with *Magellan* in a state of disrepair, much of its cosmic radiation shielding compromised. The seven billion zettabyte database of Milky Way radiation sources provided timely information for *Magellan's* short-range thrusters to maneuver around approaching solar flares and other disruptive or even lethal burst of radiation. She found she had a knack for organization and leadership, as well, helping to fill a talent vacuum created from the battle.

As the Tube car quietly zipped along on a current of air, Lydia and Kora gabbed about the latest juicy gossip. Amberly wasn't paying attention to their conversation, but noted that she and her sister were wearing the same dresses they wore the day she met Dek, and the Chasm conspiracy started to unfold. She wore a black sleeveless number, and Kora had on her beautiful self-illuminated red dress. She was headed to Rick's back on that fateful day, also.

After a short walk from the Tube station, the trio entered Rick's. Skip saw Skylar had already arrived and was seated in a booth at the edge of the café. Skylar waved them over. Lydia and Skip slid into one side of the booth, and Amberly sat next to Skylar. She had a flash of mixed feelings – it was awkward sitting next to him, but she did find him, as Kora had said, easy on the eyes. A waiter came and took a drink order.

Rick's was the most popular bar on *Waypoint Magellan*. The watering hole and café was themed after the famous 20th century vid, *Casablanca*. On the walls, magnetic resonance screens showed images of the Moroccan desert, faux-neon fedora outlines, and ancient, propeller-driven Earth aircraft.

The idea of flying wasn't entirely foreign to Amberly, even though she was born and had lived her whole life on *Magellan*. She had been out in space several times, both in the two-man corvettes and the larger runabouts, sometimes called Valkyrie. She imagined that navigating those ships in three-dimensional space was similar to flying an aircraft planetside on Earth or Arara. She had studied the principles of lift as a part of the engineering courses required for her to join the Science Corps, but atmospheric flight was abstract to her. Unlike children growing up on Earth, in her youth Amberly never looked up at a bird with envy.

Amberly swirled her topis, a faux-tea, and stared alternately at the image of the ancient passenger plane and the hat. She imagined North, in civilian clothes, wearing a black fedora. She thought about when he piloted the *Clare De Lune*, one of *Magellan's* public corvettes, to take her on a romantic retreat to the Shard Caves on a Spencer Belt asteroid. She conflated the images in her mind, and imagined North piloting the airplane.

"So, have you been enjoying your promotion? Finding the new job challenging?" Skylar Trigs asked Amberly. The redhead snapped out of her daydream.

"I'm sorry, what was that?"

"Skylar wants to know what's it like being the Science Corps research director now," Skip repeated. He picked up his glass and took a swig of his beer. After the brew had cleared his throat, he shook his head a few times in rapid succession. The beer, completely synthesized from raw molecular materials, had no organic origin and tasted, Skip imagined, like piss. "I miss the old ale. Curses on Chasm."

"There certainly is a lot more stress than just working on my own stellar research," Amberly replied, looking into Skylar's bright blue eyes. Skylar was a middling height, with a healthy build — not overly muscular, but not flabby. Amberly liked his blonde hair. The curly crown gave him a care-free feel, and after the heaviness of the last year, the no-worries attitude had a certain appeal. Skylar had a charismatic smile and a square jaw, which Amberly also liked, even though it reminded her of North. "I wish I could go back to be just doing research, but we all have to do what we have to do now."

In the aftermath of the Battle of *Magellan*, Amberly had been promoted from lab analyst to research director for *Waypoint Magellan's* Science Corps. She now reported to the waypoint's Chief Science Officer Owais Memon who reported directly to the governor. For a 20-year-old to be research director was unprecedented. The previous research director had perished during the Chasm conflict, and the assistant director could not cope with harsh post-Chasm realities. She killed herself by consuming a sodium hydroxide solution.

Not unlike her off-the-charts genius mother, Amberly possessed a truly gifted intellect. This combined with the fact that

Governor Thor saw Amberly as a hero of the Battle of *Magellan*, made the path for Amberly's promotion obvious. Thor's bet on Amberly was a good one, though it was met with some resistance because of her unintentional role in the Chasm plot. She was a natural leader, and her skills in identifying threats from stellar radiation had become invaluable.

"We're lucky to have you keeping things together in the Science Corps," Skylar said as he signaled the barkeep, Kato, for another drink. Kato, who had been slouching behind the bar reading a novel on his infopad, sprung up and started filling a glass.

The bar felt empty to Amberly. These days, the bar was never crowded. Half of the furniture was gone, the metal from barstools and tables having been used for critical repairs. *And absent friends make Rick's feel all the emptier*, Amberly thought.

Kora felt Amberly's distance, and her older sister's intuition confirmed her redhead sibling was pining for their long-gone Marine friend. She jumped in to fill the gap in the conversation.

"So, Skylar," Kora said, "I've read the rumors that you may be running for a seat on the Waypoint Council. Is that true?"

"I've been meaning to ask you about that as well," Skip said. "As long as you don't get too traditional, you'll have my vote."

"To be completely honest, I haven't made up my mind yet," Skylar said, as Kato walked up and handed him a fresh glass. "I've been talking with Commander Moreno about getting her endorsement if I do run. If I have her support, that would help tip the balance in favor of running."

Marine Executive Officer Rita Moreno, a sharp-featured olive-skinned woman in her early 40s, took command of the waypoint during the Chasm attacks, and she was largely credited with saving the waypoint from annihilation. Because of her war-hero status, her endorsement would almost ensure a victory in a popular election. Although Moreno did not relish the role of king maker, she didn't shun it either, trying to make sure that calm heads and Earth-loyal hearts filled the 10 seats on the council. Anyone with any ambition had to work to curry favor with Moreno.

Kato picked up some empty glasses off the table where the friends were sitting. "For my good customers, I wanted to let you know next week we'll have our first keg brewed partially from barley grown in the topside gardens."

"Count me in," Skip said, pushing away his unfinished glass of synth beer. "Where does the line start?"

"Skippy, be grateful for what you got," Lydia said. "We're alive, and at least we have something to drink."

"And since we have drinks," Skylar lifted his glass, "I say we toast."

Amberly caught a joyful glint in Skylar's blue eyes. He caught her gaze and smiled broadly. "What do we toast to then, future Councilman Trigs?" Amberly asked.

"To Earth, to our forbearers who made *Magellan*, to our fallen friends, and to the heroes of *Magellan* – most specifically to you, Amberly Macready, heroine extraordinaire – and to our loyal Marines on the *Magnus*, Captain Obadiah and XO North, may they bring the Chasm uprising to heel!"

"Hear, hear!" said Skip, pounding his glass on the table. "To North! The best damn friend a guy could have."

"To North!" Lydia agreed, and pushed her glass into Kora's.

"To North, the bastard!" Kora said. Kora didn't require too much alcohol to get inebriated, and she was clearly starting to get buzzed. She stood and moved next to the bench where her sister sat, took her sister's head in her hands, and hugged her into her bosom. "You know, it wasn't right what North did to you little sister. I mean, North's a good man. North's a real hero. But he should know that you didn't betray us."

"Kora, please, not now," Amberly broke from her sister's embrace and smiled weakly.

"North should know better! No. No. No. Amberly, you are not like Raven One. Chasm was trying to kill us all."

Kora's intoxicated indignation on Amberly's behalf was embarrassing Amberly. Not because she was ashamed of her sister, but because she believed, at least in part, that there was some truth in what North said.

Sensing Amberly's discomfort, Skip decided to intervene. "We were all desperate and hurt. We should all give each other a little um… grace. I think seeing so many of his men die, that … broke North in ways we don't understand."

Lydia looked over at her boyfriend. She was beaming with

pride at how Skip was speaking peace and comfort. *The battle may have broken North, but it helped Skip become a better man*, Lydia thought.

Kora leaned over and kissed her sister loudly on the forehead. "Don't worry. North will love you forever, my cute baby sister."

Amberly wanted to become invisible.

Kora stood up and wobbled. "I'm sorry everyone. I've had a bit too much to drink. I'm not feeling well. I better head back to Trot and baby Alroy." Amberly and Lydia sprung up to support Kora.

"I'll walk you home," Lydia stood up. "Amberly, you want to come too?"

"No," Amberly said, wanting some more time to reminisce in Rick's. "I think I'd like to stay."

"Okay Skip, take care of Amberly," Lydia said and then looked over to Skylar. "Good to see you again."

After seeing Lydia and Kora through the exit portal, Amberly looked over at Skip and Skylar and started wishing that maybe she should have left with her girls. She took a deep breath, composed herself, and walked back to their booth.

"So Amberly," Skylar said through a half-friendly, half-wicked smile. "Are you a fan of live music? I happen to have the last two tickets to the Waypoint Philharmonic concert at the Hoover Hotel commons. Would you be interested –"

A shout from across Rick's interrupted his thought.

"Hey! Skylar," said a Marine who was across the bar. Amberly recognized him as Eli Wong, one of the enlisted men who had served in North's strike force. "What are you doing hanging out with that redheaded Chasm harlot?"

"Excuse me?" Skylar stood up. Skip followed suit. Wong paced the bar to meet them face to face.

"I'm sorry, what did you say?" Skip asked as a challenge.

Wong was followed by Leo Kendrick, also a veteran of North's strike team and Wong's commanding officer. Leo stood a pace behind Wong. Amberly stood and moved around her bench to the opposite side of the booth.

"Wong, let it go man," Leo tried to pull Wong back to the bar, but the officer was too intoxicated himself and only grabbed air. Wong jerked the table towards Amberly, spewing obscenities.

"You should be dead, Amberly Macready. You should be touring the cosmos as an icicle with your mother. They are all dead because of you. Synder. Anderson. Twig. Jindal. Topez. You killed them. You killed them all. Dirty traitor!"

Skip jumped in front of Wong to protect Amberly. He did not expect Wong to backhand him with enough force to knock the wiry Skip on his butt.

Trapped between the table and the wall, Amberly moved to escape, but could not before Wong flung the table between them out of his way. Wong got his hands around a tuft of Amberly's hair and yanked her toward the wall. Amberly tried to pull away and landed some untrained blows on the Marine with her flailing fists. Wong just intensified his grip on her hair and pushed her face against the wall – the shock of pain made Amberly yelp.

Wong whispered to Amberly under his alcohol-thick breath, "You betrayed North, you bit—"

The hard fist of Skylar Trigs kept Wong from completing his sentence. Wong recoiled and growled in surprise from the punch, but did not release Amberly.

Kato and Skip now had entered the scuffle, and together both attempted to pull Wong off of Amberly and force him to give up his grip on her hair.

"Wong, let her go," Leo shouted. He had moved over to the scuffle. "That's an order!"

Wong complied, collapsed to the floor, and began to sob. Amberly recognized the bitter sadness in his tears; she had shed them many times herself. She pushed herself on the floor away from Wong, and Skylar swooped down to support her. He held her as she started to cry.

"North's probably dead, too," Wong blustered. "We're all broken. We're all dead."

"Dammit Wong, North's not dead! Nothing can stop him," Skip said angrily. "The *Magnus* is probably docking at *Waypoint Cortes* by now."

"*Cortes* went dark! North *is* dead!" Wong wailed, and started heaving. "You killed them, Amberly. You killed everyone on *Cortes*, too. You and your evil mother." Kato and Skip had Wong fully restrained now.

"Hey, Macready, are you okay? You want me to call the

coppers?" Kato said. "We can have them throw Wong in the brig."

The whole café seemed to spin, as Amberly felt again in the middle of a tempest of humiliation and shame for her misdeeds. She should not have come out tonight. Amberly appreciated her friends defending her, but the truth she saw in Wong's pain reminded her of her deep guilt.

"No. No. He's right. I am … responsible," Amberly softly spoke in resigned confession, hanging her head.

Kato and Skip pulled Wong to his feet. "You get the hell out of my bar," Kato said to Wong. "I don't want to see your dirt-licking mug in here again."

Leo took his fellow Marine by the arm. "Your grog is piss anyway," Leo mumbled under his breath as the pair left. "It's a wonder it can even get a man buzzed."

"Get out of here. The both of you," Kato thumbed toward the main door as the Marines exited.

Skylar turned Amberly's head toward his, steeled conviction in his eyes as he gazed solidly into hers. He placed her hands softly on his shoulders. "Amberly, you are not responsible for the evil of Chasm. Moreno knows it. The governor knows it. I know it."

"North didn't blame you Amberly," Skip said, and then remembered the trial. "Okay, well, he did at the trial, but he didn't mean it… I mean, I know what he said, but —"

A robotic female voice programmed to speak in an ancient Irish accent piped up through the comm unit on Skips shirt sleeve. "Excuse me, Master Skip, I have an urgent—"

"I told you not to call me Master Skip in public," Skip spoke back to his VI, Mayflower. "And this isn't a good time. Bye —"

"Yes, but you did tell me if I ever received a transmission from the *Magnus*, I should interrupt you no matter what."

"Mayflower," Amberly addressed the VI directly, "You received a communication from the *Magnus*? They broke radio silence."

"Yes. The transmission is four months old."

"They must be close to *Cortes* now," Skyler surmised. "But this had to be transmitted well before they were close to *Cortes*."

"Well, who was it from? What did it say?" Skip asked impatiently, his voicing spiking with excitement.

"I don't know what it says," Mayflower replied. "It's from

Magnus Executive Officer North, and it has been encrypted with a key that is owned by Amberly Macready."

"Send that to Verne!" Amberly shouted and she ran out of the door. Skip, Kato and Skylar were left standing in her wake.

"So, Skip, how do you feel about the Philharmonic?" Skylar shrugged. "I may have an extra ticket."

CHAPTER TWO

U.S.S. Magnus, en route to Waypoint Cortes, July 7, 2603, Earth date, nine months after the Battle of Magellan.

After months of the tedium, something different happened on the bridge of the *Magnus.*

"Are you sure, ensign?" Captain Obadiah challenged the *very* junior officer.

"Yes, Captain," said Ensign Rhodes, who had a bad habit of speaking loudly. "It's weak, but I'm definitely getting a short-range distress signal!" Rhodes, just 16, was born just one year after the *Magnus* departed Earth with its secret mission to stop the expected Araran revolution. Her parents were both military intelligence officers, experts in insurgencies. Her mother, Darla, had even written a book theorizing what forms a waypoint rebellion might take. Rhodes' pale face was framed by her dark, medium-length, bob-cut hair. Her blue-green glowed with her hyperactive, youthful energy.

Rhodes was one of a half-dozen children born *en route* who were now part of the junior officer corps. Rhodes had dreams. If they didn't get caught up too long in Arara, Rhodes figured she would be in her late 30s when she first set foot on the homeworld. She would be old enough to be an executive officer, perhaps even captain. It was not unheard of for a captain to be under 40 – but on much smaller ships than the mammoth *Magnus.*

"What's the estimated distance to the source?" the captain asked.

Magnus' virtual intelligence, Condi, answered the question with an artificially smooth, female voice. "By my calculations, the source of the signal is just under two million kilometers away. Unfortunately, we'll need a three degree change in our trajectory to intercept."

Traveling at nearly half of the speed of light, *Magnus* required a significant amount of time and power to slow down the vessel enough to divert course.

Rhodes punched some inputs into the magnetic resonance three-dimensional screen floating at her station. She turned to the captain. "If we execute a course change now, we will overshoot the ship by 325,000 kilometers. That's not too much back tracking, correct? We're going to find out what this is, right?"

Condi's disembodied voice chimed in. "That would delay our arrival at *Cortes* by 13 Earth days."

"That's 13 more days for Chasm to destroy or commandeer *Cortes*," Obadiah mumbled. "Raven One's warning would have reached Cortes two months ago. We get there in four months. Every moment we give them to prepare –"

The thought of finding a ship, lost in space so far out from a waypoint thrilled Rhodes. She *had* to convince the captain to make the detour to investigate. Cruising at a time-shortening velocity for hundreds of days was mundane and exceedingly boring. The Battle of *Magellan* had awoken a need for adventure in Rhodes; with one hit, she had become a junkie.

She had read many novels and seen plenty of deep space movies depicting desperate souls on derelict ships holding out for salvation. *I am living in one of those adventures*, Rhodes thought. The thought brought a smile to her face.

"What are you smirking about?" the captain said, eyeing his most junior bridge officer.

"Sir, what would a Chasm-controlled *Cortes* be able to build that can stop the *Magnus*? What does it matter how much time they have to prepare?" Rhodes pressed. "Our tech is decades ahead of anything they are even aware of, and even more so than anything they possess."

That is a fair point, the captain considered, as he stroked his grey beard. But he knew never to underestimate human ingenuity, especially when necessity demanded it.

"Ensign Rhodes," the captain said, in a tone more like a grandfather offering a life lesson than a commanding officer, "the people who first came out to populate the waypoints, and Arara herself, they were the best – the best – humanity had to offer. The brightest, most capable, most ambitious people. No doubt their offspring have benefitted from both the genetic advantage of their parentage and have been nurtured for greatness as well. There is great peril underestimating the resourcefulness of our adversary."

"But we have a charge to save people," Rhodes spouted rapidly. "There could be people near death, with us being the only hope of their survival. We are the only ship out here. We have a moral obligation to help save these lives."

"A handful of lives for the 15,000 people on *Cortes*?" Obadiah had grown impatient.

"Maybe we can save them both?!" Rhodes spoke even more loudly, stood up and took a step toward her captain. He glared at her, and she shrunk back and choked out her next word. "I think it's worth the risk. Sir."

"What do you think, North?" The captain sat back in his seat and swiveled toward his executive officer and Marine commander.

North was in prime physical shape. He let his thick brown hair grow past regulation length, but this far out in space, no one seemed to care. He pushed his bangs out of his deep brown eyes, leaned against a bulkhead, and studied a large tactical display on the opposite side of *Magnus'* bridge.

Rhodes looked over at North, his strong arms and broad shoulders, and realized he was quite attractive. She had only known him for eight months, but he had been generous in helping her complete her junior officer training. *He's okay for an old guy*, the teen thought. North was generally a good-natured and easy-going man, but the Battle of *Magellan* had left him both physically and emotionally scarred. He lost too many men. And had been betrayed by one of his closest friends and dearest loves – Amberly. The general good will of his younger self had given way to an edgier, darker cynicism.

Obadiah saw this hardness as a positive quality that wouldn't make North a better person, but would make him a better solider for what seemed like a coming, unavoidable war. To win a war, one needed hardness, Obadiah believed, which led him to recruit North to be his second in command on the *Magnus'* top-secret mission to destroy Chasm forever.

"This ship – if it is a ship – is from *Cortes*. There are no other ports near enough from which it could make berth," North said. "We've had radio silence from *Cortes* for months now. Could be Chasm is jamming transmissions like they did to *Magellan*. Could be that *Cortes* is gone. Either way, radio silence almost certainly means Chasm is in control. My guess is that the people on that ship know – if it is a ship and not some floating debris, and if the people who started transmitting the distress signal are still alive."

"Or their ghosts will tell us," Rhodes piped in. The captain cleared his throat and ignored her. Rhodes persisted. "Metaphorical ghosts of course. You know, vid recorders."

"I'd say it's worth the time lost," North said. "That ship, or even logs from that ship, could give us a tactical assessment of what we are going to face when we arrive at *Cortes*. Help us cut through the fog of war. We won't have to go into battle blind. I agree with what Ensign Rhodes noted, we have the technological advantage. Let's see if we can have an intelligence advantage as well."

"Very well," the captain sighed. "Let's have a look. Condi, set course for the origin point of that distress signal. North go ahead and assemble a boarding party. Take Sparks with you — she may prove to be valuable if these people are Chasm. And I'd say it's about time that Ensign Rhodes got off this ship, too. Have her run your comms."

"Yes, sir!" Rhodes smiled.

"Definitely a ship," said James Goldsmith, a tubby Marine, with growing excitement in the Valkyrie-class runabout, *M.S.S. Prime*. "We'll be in visual range soon. Heh. We found a ship. Here in the middle of nowhere. What are the odds?"

"*I* found the ship, James," Rhodes corrected, as she squinted in vain through the exterior plexiglass port.

"Why don't you chill and turn the volume down, *Ensign*," The 37-year-old James said with a bit of disgust tossed in for good measure. Rhodes didn't really like James much, but she chose to not respond to his insult because she aspired to live peacefully with all her shipmates.

Goldsmith left Earth when he was 19 to join the Marines at *Waypoint Drake*, running away from a gambling debt that was getting unhealthy. Even though he was more than a light year away from Earth on *Drake*, James was still paranoid that one day his past would catch up with him, so he looked for an opportunity to go deeper into space. Rhodes wasn't yet three years old when Goldsmith signed onto *Magnus* during its stop at his waypoint. James was 24 at the time. He was a horrible Marine, but Capt. Obadiah took pity on the young man and signed him up for their top-secret mission. With no gambling on *Magnus* to feed his addiction, James turned to food, packing on the kilos. Obadiah had hoped to leave the overweight and underperforming James on *Magellan*. But after the battle of *Magellan*, the captain feared he could not spare even Pvt. Goldsmith, so he put North in charge of James' physical fitness. James has lost 10 percent of his weight under North's exercise regimen, but the private could still afford to skip a meal or twelve.

North, who sat in *Prime's* pilot's chair, thought about chastising James for speaking to an officer, even though she was young, in such a disrespectful manner, but held his tongue. Sparks, on the other hand, did not hold hers.

"Why do you have to be such an asshole, *private*?" Sparks shot. The insult smarted James, because he was keenly attracted to the athletic and shapely Sparks. As a civilian, Sparks had no uniform requirement, and thus wore her favorite form-fitting rubberized jumpsuit, jet black with bright violet accents. Her dyed raven-black hair was perfectly trained, not a strand out of place. James decided to cope with his pent-up frustration by insulting Sparks back.

"You should shut up, too. You are lucky you weren't airlocked, traitor," James said to Sparks. He meant to be menacing with his tone, but by the time he got to the word "airlocked" he was trying to swallow his own words, and he immediately regretted saying them.

North didn't let that one slide. "Private, that will be all," North said deeply and evenly, almost under his breath. "I would hate to see you have a four-hour shift on recycling sort duty … again."

Sparks snickered through her nose.

Still, North knew James' words were true: Sparks was a critical member of the rebellious Chasm leadership during the Battle of *Magellan*. She rammed a runabout not unlike the one they were floating in now into the *Magellan* gardens, effectively ruining *Magellan's* natural food supply. Sparks did surrender at the moment when it mattered most, halting the death of several thousand people, for the offer of amnesty and under duress with a gun trained on her torso. In the aftermath of Chasm's surrender, an angry mob immediately tossed most of the Chasm leadership into space, including their mastermind, Kimberly Macready, estranged mother to Amberly. Sparks escaped that fate because of the luck of her physical proximity to Amberly, and the fact a lowly deliveryman – Midas – recognized Amberly. In the end, Amberly's testimony saved Sparks at the military tribunal from the execution that ended many of her colleagues.

Sparks, addicted to adventure, quickly took North's offer to travel with him on the *Magnus* into the battle as an expert on Chasm intelligence and security. The only other option was to spend more than a decade on the trip back to Earth. For the first few months, she felt sick over her betrayal of the cause for which she had dedicated her life. Chasm was going to create a perfect world – no war, no hate, no greed. Humanity could be perfected, if the smartest and brightest could be uplifted to guide them, Sparks had believed. And if anyone could lead that brave, new future, it was Kimberly Macready and the Chairman. But in the end, Macready for all her genius, had failed.

For Sparks, seeing her icon martyred by a mob, broke her faith in the cause. Her cohort brother and co-conspirator, Dek also failed, easily manipulated by the wiles of a woman – the young Amberly Macready at that. *What a tool,* Sparks thought. She thought of Dek's messy brown hair, his grey-blue eyes, and pictured him spending the better part of the next two decades detained in the brig on the *American Spirit*, headed back to Earth for final judgement.

I was a fool to think Dek was any different than any other weak man, Sparks mused. Kimberly Macready had taught Sparks how to manipulate men to do her bidding, not through instruction, but by example. Macready justified the trail of destroyed men, even her husband, with her religious devotion to the cause. With Sparks' ties to Chasm gone, the only cause that mattered to her now was herself. She was ready to do whatever it took to have whatever the galaxy could offer her ambitious heart. She wasn't even sure what she wanted, but she smiled as she looked over at the chiseled North. *He'll help me get it,* she thought.

Pvt. Goldsmith peered into the visual scanner. "I see her. Red hull. I can make out the registry… *C.S.S. Iron Star. Iron Star!*"

Rhodes didn't wait for the order from the XO. She immediately opened a radio channel with the Magnus. "*Magnus,* this is *Prime*. We've confirmed contact with the *Cortes Spaceship Iron Star*, please confirm and advise."

A gravelly voice replied. "Confirmed *Magnus*. Captain wants to know if you are receiving any additional communication now that you are in visual range?"

Rhodes looked over at James, who shrugged.

"Negative, *Magnus*," Rhodes said. "Just the same generic distress signal."

"I'm going to bring us around to *Iron Star's* portside to get a better look," North said as he eased *Prime's* thrusters to match the speed of the derelict Valkyrie. "Sparks, go below and have Advika and Mateo gear up. And prep the airlock for boarding."

"You make me do all your dirty work, North," Sparks rolled her eyes, offering a faux whine. "They're your Marines. I'm just a civvy."

"I see a light coming from the bridge viewport," James said, motioning to get everyone's attention. "Look, someone's flashing a light from the Iron Star's bridge."

"Is it Morse code?" Rhodes asked.

"No, it seems… random. Probably just a malfunctioning emergency light," Sparks said, as her heart jumped. The code wasn't random at all; Sparks recognized it as a Chasm code. Clearly, someone on that ship wanted to covertly connect to any Chasm operatives on the *Prime*. Sparks forced herself to conceal her excitement. Was there hope that somehow Chasm could be saved? *Could I save the Chasm operation? Should I?* Sparks quickly processed the possibilities. If the Chasm operative on that ship could help her commandeer the *Prime*, could she somehow put North under duress so he would help her take over the whole *Magnus*? What a prize if the greatest instrument of war Earth ever created could be used against the mother planet, to separate Arara?

Sparks pushed those thoughts out for now. She had to get more information, bide her time, assess the new situation. The *Iron Star* could be a trap. Earth loyalists could have learned the code, and are using it to expose Chasm turncoats. *I'm getting paranoid now*, Sparks thought as she headed for the lower deck portal. *Who am I kidding? I've always been paranoid.*

"Well, let's see if anyone is still alive on that boat," North said.

He looked at the young, female officer. "You have the ship, Rhodes."

North looked at the older enlisted man, then frowned "Don't give her any trouble, Goldsmith."

"Yes sir," Goldsmith returned the frown.

Sparks, privates Advika and Mateo, and XO North moved single file through the flex-polymer gangway that connected the *Prime* and the *Iron Star*. Once the four of them were in the gangway, North turned to seal the *Prime*'s airlock. Although it was extremely unlikely that pressure would have built up in the *Iron Star* as the derelict floated through space, caution was in order. When they opened the airlock on the *Iron Star*, if the ship was hyper-pressurized, gasses could tear through the gangway through an unsecured *Prime* airlock, causing catastrophic hull damage.

"I hope they haven't locked us out," Sparks said into the radio transmitter embedded into her helmet.

"If these people wanted to be saved, they left the door unlocked," North's voice crackled over the radio in reply.

"Commander," Pvt. Advika addressed North by his rank, "Why don't we just tow this bird back to the *Magnus* hanger? Seems like it would a lot safer than what we are doing now."

North punched in a manual opening on the *Iron Star's* external keypad. The indicator light that confirmed the interior airlock was closed illuminated to a pale green.

"People could be dying? Could be a bomb? We don't want to accidentally expose the *Magnus* to dangerous elements? Have you ever heard the story of the Greeks and the Trojan horse?" North asked. Advika didn't respond, but nodded through her helmet. North put up two fingers and pointed toward the airlock – indicating for his marines to draw their weapons – energy weapons that stunned human life — and be ready when he opened the door.

Sparks sighed over comms. "What do you think you are going to find in here?" She stepped in front of the Marines, pushing North out of the way and pressing the open button.

"Wait! You don't know –" Mateo panicked as the airlock opened, exposing an empty interior airlock.

"Sissies," Sparks said, and walked inside the *Iron Star*'s airlock. The moment she crossed the threshold, she began to float.

"No power to the artificial gravity unit," Advika said the obvious. North slid into the airlock, and looked back at the Marines, still standing in the gangway. "You two stay here. See if you can plug *Iron Star* into the *Prime*, get this poor girl some juice."

Mateo felt as though he would wet his pants. Having to wait out in what looked like an aluminum foil tube in the middle of the infinity of space made him woozy. Sure, *Prime*'s powerful computers could scan and chart the trajectories of the billion closest chunks of space debris. The ship would automatically dodge or incinerate most of them, Mateo reasoned, but what if one got through and blew a hole in the connecting tube while he was still in it? He could get sucked out into space. His suit would sustain him for what, maybe two or three hours?

"Hey, I don't want to wait in this aluminum tube," Mateo whined. "This is a death trap!"

"The only dead things here are probably the poor souls that have perished on this ship," North said.

"At least you are safe on a ship," Mateo continued, "not with only a few millimeters of flex material between you and the cold fingers of space."

"Quit being so dramatic," Sparks sighed as she punched the control closing the exterior airlock door again, sealing the Marines outside the ship.

"But… wait," Sparks heard Mateo over her radio.

Looking at her fellow Marine, Advika shook her helmet-covered head. "Sparks is right Mateo. You *are* a sissy. Go pull the power transmission cable and let's get to work."

The interior of the *Iron Star* was nearly pitch black. North produced a multitool and flipped the flashlight on. He started scanning the cargo hold, and saw hundreds of empty ration containers bouncing around, weightless. Sparks floated up behind North, pressing her body next to his and draping her arm over his shoulder. With her eyes, she followed the trail of light cast by North's multitool.

"Eerie."

The VI Condi spoke into North's helmet with a pleasantly smooth, deep female voice. "Gaseous readouts put O-2 levels at 10 percent. Safe to breath, XO, but not for too long. No toxins detected."

North reached up and pulled off his helmet. It started to float away, but he quickly secured it with his free hand. "Don't you be going anywhere, I still may need you."

Sparks followed suit and took off her helmet. The air smelled like death marinated with fecal juice. She resisted the urge to vomit.

"Let's go topside," North pointed his light toward the ceiling, looking for a ladder and portal.

Sparks lifted her sleeve toward her mouth, and spoke into the small embedded comm unit. "Hey, sissy, how is that power transfer coming. I am tired of floating. Let's get this artificial gravity tuned on."

The radio crackled back at Sparks. "Don't call me sissy," Mateo was perturbed.

"Truth hurts," Sparks offered a sly smile no one could see.

North found a ladder and floated towards it. His radio sounded. "Rhodes here. We've got remote command of *Iron Star*, and she's plugged into our battery. You want me to turn on the gravity?"

"Yes. And turn the lights on," North said.

"The air scrubbers seem to be operational. I'll get those running," Rhodes said over the radio.

"How about firing up the climate control, too," Sparks said. "It's freezing in here."

The ship lights flicked on, and North had a queasy feeling as the artificial gravity grew. Empty packages all around him fell to the ground. North stumbled a bit as he was pulled to the floor.

Then behind him, he heard a thud.

Both Sparks and North swirled around to see a human body, female, wearing a dark jumpsuit. She was clearly dead; her ghostly pale face was crowned with dark hair pulled into a pony tail.

Sparks walked over to the body, considered the emaciated form, and pointed to the right leg.

"Looks like someone shot her multiple times," Sparks said, as she drew her stun gun. "With bullets. These holes are patched. She probably died of something else."

North smirked at Sparks pulling her weapon. "Surely everyone on here is dead, Sparks. Who are you going to shoot, their ghosts?"

Sparks hadn't forgotten about the Chasm code she saw; obviously from someone still alive. An armed Chasm operative wouldn't hesitate to put a bullet in both her and North. An operative would have no way of knowing that she is … was… a Chasm officer.

"There is a reason I am still alive North," Sparks said as she followed him toward the ladder leading up a deck.

"Because of the word of Amberly Macready?" North offered, matter-of-factly.

"No. Because I am a survivor," she said, and nodded her head toward her weapon.

And then they both heard what they least expected: The cry of a young child.

North quickly moved up the ladder through the round portal to the upper deck. "This is Commander North, *Magellan* Marines," he shouted down the topside corridors. Sparks quickly came up the ladder and flanked North. There were six portals which North assumed were crew quarters and perhaps a mess hall. He forced open the powerless door to the first room, creating a hiss as the pressures between the rooms equalized.

The air felt stale and a rancid odor dominated the thin atmosphere. The room was indeed a mess, as North surveyed a filthy food preparation area and various dishes scattered around a small dining table, bolted to the cold steel floor.

"They must have sealed off the room, to save energy and reduce the workload of the CO_2 scrubbers," North called back to Sparks. Sparks didn't follow him in, but instead, weapon still drawn, moved to the next room, a dormer. The bottom bunk was empty, but had obviously been used. In the top bunk, something human-sized was covered in a blanket tied down to the bed with grey polyflex belts.

"North!" Sparks shouted, and the Marine quickly paced the few meters between them.

Sparks indicated the bundle on the top bunk with a wave of her sidearm. North reached over put his hand on the bundle.

"It's warm," he said, with a bit of the grimness melting from his face. He and Sparks both went to work untying the belts. North flipped down the blanket and saw an emaciated, unshaven man, asleep, he thought. His dark hair was ratty and he wore a torn jumpsuit.

North looked at Sparks. "Do you have the portable medicenter?"

Sparks shrugged. "It was in Advika's loadout."

"North to Prime – Rhodes, send Advika in here with the medicenter. We found an unconscious man, looks like he hasn't eaten in weeks."

"She's on her way to through the gangway now," Rhodes reported.

The baby cried again, and this time, they could clearly hear the sound coming from the bow of *Iron Star*, probably the bridge.

"I'll go check it out," Sparks said. "You stay here and wait for Advika."

C.S.S. Iron Star was a mid-sized runabout, not designed for deep space travel, so the trip from the crew quarters to the bridge was less than 20 meters. The bridge door was closed, and Sparks half expected to have to force the door open, but upon her approach it opened automatically.

The bridge was arranged in a typical three station format, navigation, communication and command, with swivel chairs facing the main viewport. Sparks could see a dark ponytail draped over the headrest of the command chair. Sparks raised her stun gun as the chair spun around slowly.

"Who are you?" Sparks asked, but she already knew. "And whose is that?"

In the chair, a painfully thin woman with sullen dark eyes, sat. She wore an ill-fitting red dress and poorly applied red lipstick. In her left hand she had a gun – one that shot bullets – trained on Sparks, and in the other arm, she held a young child. Sparks hadn't much experience with children, but she suspected this one was just at least a year old, maybe two.

"This is Nora," the woman said slowly. She lost strength in her arm and dropped the gun to the floor. Sparks reached forward and grabbed Nora as the woman tumbled out of the chair and onto the floor, coughing. She tried to sit up, but didn't have the strength, so she smiled wryly. The woman spoke weakly. "So good to see you, Sparks."

"Ryder? Is that you? are you still with –"

Sparks heard North's footsteps approaching and cut herself off.

"North. Two survivors in here," Sparks called over her shoulder.

North burst into the room. "Advika says that man is in a coma," he said, then looked at Ryder and Sparks, holding Nora.

North leaned over to help Ryder off the floor, and the feeling of human contact, strong arms lifting her off the ground, sent a wave of endorphins through her body. North sat her back in the chair, and she looked into his eyes.

"You have lovely brown eyes. Do you have something to eat?" Ryder asked as she passed out.

L.S. ROEBUCK

CHAPTER THREE

Sparks was conflicted.

She paced quickly down the corridor toward the *Magnus* sick bay. She didn't know if she should give up Ryder as Chasm, or keep her old comrade's secret. If Sparks didn't let the captain or North know about Ryder's past, and the truth came out later that *she knew,* she could lose her clemency. That forgiveness saved her from a traitor's execution. Ryder had something on Sparks — she could out herself and reveal that Sparks knew all along. But that would run a huge risk for Ryder as well. Captain Obadiah certainly would have the legal authority, if he knew Ryder's role as an intelligence officer for the enemy, to toss her out an airlock.

Even though *Magnus* was a vastly larger ship than the *American Spirit*, the hallways were much smaller, tighter and constricted. *Magnus* was not designed for comfort. It was designed for war. Piles of ammunition, reserve batteries, escort fighter wings and a combat training center all took up the space that would have otherwise been allocated for creature comforts on a civilian ship. Sparks had only spent a few weeks on *Waypoint Magellan* before Chasm's thwarted attempt to destroy that critical link between Earth and Arara, but she had already grown accustom to the much larger and open spaces found in the five-kilometer-long space city. Here, she felt cramped.

Arriving at sickbay, Sparks conferred with the nurse on duty and slipped into a large suite at the end of the medical corridor. Two beds were divided by a mess of medical gear, various fluid bag and IV tubes connected to the two patients. The comatose man she and North had discovered on the *Iron Star* seemed to be resting peacefully. He didn't look so ghastly now that he had been pumped full of nutritious fluids and who knows what other pharmaceuticals. The orderlies had shaved and bathed him as well, so he smelled better. He lay uncovered in a loose-fitting blue jumpsuit, with pant legs that ended mid-calf. Sparks thought his legs were muscular, especially considering the little amount of exercise and nutrition he must have as the derelict *Iron Star* floated through space.

The man was tall, perhaps close to two meters, though it was hard for Sparks to tell since he wasn't standing. She didn't find him traditionally attractive, but she thought he had a kind, peaceful face. She couldn't be sure, but she thought perhaps the man had a familial similarity to the dead woman they found in *Iron Star's* cargo hold.

In the second bed, Ryder suddenly opened her eyes and sat up.

"I wondered how long it would be before you showed up," Ryder said. "Is this room … secure?"

Sparks ignored the question and tilted her head towards the sleeping man. "Who is he?"

"Some *Cortes* civilian named Arvin," Ryder said. "He and his sister were," Ryder chose her words carefully "… escaping *Cortes*. Instead of becoming space debris, I hitched a ride at the last minute."

"So, Scorched Earth then?"

"Secure?" Ryder asked again.

"As far I know," Sparks shrugged.

Ryder, always the spymaster, was paranoid about being spied on. Back on the waypoint, she had an arsenal of anti-spy measures that could ferret out clandestine monitoring devices. But she had to leave those behind. She didn't know if she could trust Sparks, so she would have to probe a little to get more information.

"What about *Magellan*? What happened?"

"We failed. We failed to capture *Magellan*, and then we failed to destroy it."

This Ryder already knew. While they were floating in hopelessness toward *Magellan*, she received the desperate transmission sent from Raven One, also known as Kimberly Macready, perhaps the greatest mind in the Chasm ranks. Of course, the message had been traveling at light speed for three months before she decoded it. It warned of the unexpected arrival of *Magnus*, the warship designed for one purpose, to put down the Chasm rebellion. And now, here she was, on the ship that could end the grand plan to create a perfect society – with no greed, no hate, no gods – only the state and the common good. *If I could corrupt this ship, or even destroy it, I could save Chasm*, she thought. *But is Sparks my ally?*

Ryder did not feel the need to reveal that she received the

warning from Macready.

"How could you fail? You had Raven One!"

"It wasn't her fault," Sparks said regretfully. "It was the weakness of men. Joti, Järvinen."

"I rather liked that old man," Ryder thought of the former captain of the *American Spirit*. She had spent considerable time with him when the deep space ship had been in port at *Cortes*, though they were not romantically involved. "He didn't seem like a weak man."

"Heh. I find all men are weak," Sparks smirked. "He killed himself after he was captured in a failed offensive to take the command center of *Magellan*."

"What about this North, is he weak? He doesn't *look* weak," Ryder said, with just a hint of lust rolling off of her lips.

Sparks tensed slightly, and the highly attuned Ryder noted the shift in her friend's temperament. "Oh, is North your mark?"

Sparks realized she had a reaction of defensive jealousy over North. She didn't love North. She didn't believe love was real. North really was someone she was using and planned on using. He was sinfully attractive. Their budding friendship took the sting off of her cavernous loneliness, and she believed she could manipulate him to help her achieve her ends — whenever she figured out what her ends were.

Sparks reasoned there was no use lying to Ryder; Sparks trained with her on Arara. The spymaster would see right through any lie. Ryder may have had the upper hand psychologically, but Sparks was the better warrior. Letting Ryder know here and now the consequences of crossing her was best.

"There is no fooling you," Sparks said. "North is *my* mark. Don't interfere."

"Really," Ryder seemed amused, "or what?"

"Dear sister, I think you know what I am capable of," Sparks said. And Ryder did. Sparks had just enough crazy that she would kill, and she was well trained in that art.

Ryder decided to change the subject to another man.

"What happened to Dek?"

"Dek turned on Chasm … on us … because of her, because of Amberly," Sparks said. "Raven One had a daughter. She's quite amazing actually. Something the Chairman didn't count on, I think. Or North. The roots of tradition are strong. But, by the looks of it, you carried out her wishes. You followed the Chairman's Scorched Earth protocol?"

"It was glorious," Ryder said. "To see the *Cortes* rip itself into pieces. And it was horrific. Random pieces of bodies floating in space."

"And what about Falcon One? What about Franco? Did he go down with the ship?" Sparks asked, picturing the charming Franco in her mind's eye.

"Well, he was already dead when the antimatter core went boom," Ryder said. "I had to kill him myself. He went jelly in the end. When we received the Scorched Earth orders, Franco balked. He thought we should keep *Cortes* for Chasm and defy the will of the Chairman. Igland was there to make sure the will of the Chairman was followed, and siding with a Hawk is always the right play."

"So, the Hawks are real then. Wow. I thought the program was just a ruse. Igland was one? But you didn't sacrifice yourself for Arara. You tried to escape," Sparks pieced together. "Why?"

"A baby. The last throws of maternal instinct not bred out of my DNA, perhaps?" surmised Ryder. "I found a brother and sister, attempting to escape with just minutes before *Cortes* went critical. They had a baby — was not related to either of them, orphaned in the battle to control *Cortes*. I knew we were all dead anyway – there was really no hope of rescue for us with nearly a half lightyear to *Magellan*. It was just luck that we ran into *Magnus*. Maybe. In the end, I suppose I wanted to save the baby."

"You saving a baby?" Sparks said. "Huh."

"When you found us, I hadn't eaten for weeks. I was saving the last foodstuff for Nora. I thought I was going to die anyway, so I tried to figure out what was the common good for that moment. It was Nora."

The two women sat in silence for a moment, both emotionally overwhelmed at the impossible turn of events. Ryder broke the silence.

"How is it that you haven't been shown an airlock, Sparks?"

A light went on in Sparks' head. "You *knew*. You knew we failed at *Magellan*. That's why you headed away from Arara and not towards it. If Chasm found you, they would probably figure you for a coward unless you were able to lie your way out."

"Of course, I could lie my way out, Sparks," Ryder said, stepping off her bed, speaking forcefully and feeling defensive. "I'm a professional liar. But the chances of us being found before we starved was almost nil, no matter if we headed toward *Marquette* or *Magellan*. The fact that you found us almost makes me believe in fate. But you didn't answer *my* question. A Chasm officer in a failed mission of high treason: Why are you not only alive, but free?"

"My new sister, Amberly Macready saved me. She saved Dek, too."

Captain Obadiah had convened a meeting of his senior officers. Wing Commander Okapi Nyota was an unusually tall, dark woman with strong facial features and a buzz cut. She carried herself in a powerfully feminine way, and she almost always wore an athletic cut jumpsuit, which easily fit under her flight suit. XO North, who held the rank of commander, had the primary duty to keep the Marine assault force of more than 200 trained and ready. As the executive officer of the *Magnus*, he was second in command to the captain and was also tasked with heading up the intelligence operation of chasm.

Lt. Commander Cho, short and sharp, was North's right-hand man, tasked with doing the grunt work of intelligence, and was considered a senior officer. Cho also ran the junior officer training program. Lt. Commander Alicia Blight was the *Magnus'* chief operations officer. The pale woman was a fake redhead and ran all the support areas — the medical bay, laundry, janitorial, commissary, entertainment, clerical, housing — that made life on the *Magnus'* long journey bearable. Chief Petty Officer Bollard was the chief engineer, responsible for the maintenance of *Magnus'* antimatter core, propulsion and deceleration engines, life support, corvettes and runabouts. Bollard seemed to have personally tapped into nearly unlimited energy of the antimatter core — he was perpetually fidgeting, tapping and swaying. His energy wasn't nervous, just excessive. He looked over at Rhodes and flashed a brilliant white smile framed by his bouncing dreadlocks.

Ensign Rhodes was hardly a senior officer, but she was often invited to senior meetings to perform clerical duties or fetch faux coffee.

"To come all this way and be too late. Dirt! Dirt! Seventeen years. Dammit," Obadiah slammed his fist on the textured aluminum alloy table bolted to a floor of the same material. The captain stood at the table's head. North leaned against corner wall of the windowless meeting room. Rhodes was seated to the right of the captain, and Bollard to the left.

Bollard reached over and put his hand on Obadiah's shoulder. "Boss, we saved *Magellan*. That's gotta count for something?"

Cho tweaked the magnetic resonance screen, replaying external video surveillance recovered from the *Iron Star's* flight recorder. The images of the remains of *Cortes*, suspended in cold, weightless space, was haunting. Two bodies, a man and a woman, locked forever in a frozen embrace floated toward the *Iron Star's* camera. Rhodes failed to stifle her tears.

"Not too late, I think, to kill all those Chasm traitors," Nyota said through clenched teeth. "But do they know we are coming? Did they get Macready's message?"

"Macready was committed to the mission. Almost certainly," North said. "But it doesn't matter. How can they stop the *Magnus*? We can bombard the surface of Arara from space. We can deflect and evade well enough. And even if they were to get a shot on us, the *Magnus* can take a hit. We're rated to take a nuclear blast and walk away."

"I wouldn't recommend it thought," Engineer Bollard jumped in.

"Do you think they've already destroyed *Waypoint Marquette*, too?" Blight asked, nervously pulling on her hair. Two waypoints? That would create a gap of a full light year between Arara and the closest waypoint."

"That was the point," North reminded. "They want to physically separate themselves from Earth."

Rhodes used the back of her hand to wipe a tear off her right cheek, then the left. "Would we have just let them leave if they asked? Why did 10,000 people have to die?"

"I promise you, not everyone on Arara wants to sever ties with the mother planet," North said. "My dad, for one. I'd find it hard to believe that many people want a … chasm."

"History is full of elite minorities imposing their will on common majorities," Cho explained, with a professorial voice, as if giving a lecture. "We knew of Chasm's plan three decades ago because some faithful patriots on Arara sent us a message 40 years ago. These were not people who were compromised. We believe those who tipped us off were silenced, but we have no reason to believe that Chasm knew that Earth knew of their plans."

"If Chasm knew *Magnus* was coming, Kimberly Macready would have been … ready," Sparks, who had entered the room unobserved, offered. Cho jumped out of his seat and spun around, surprised at Sparks sudden presence.

"Some spy *you* are," Sparks scoffed.

"I'm not a spy," Cho protested. "I'm an intelligence officer."

"Well, on that point you did have me fooled. Good job," Sparks retorted.

Cho smiled, then frowned. "Wait. What?"

The captain ignored the exchange and began to quiz Sparks, who he previously dispatched to sick bay to see what information she could find out. Sparks was a little crazy, but she was detail-focused and methodical, qualities the captain appreciated immensely. "What is the status of our guests? Did you learn anything?"

"Why is that traitor allowed here?" Blight questioned the captain. "I don't like ex-Chasm operatives being present at need-to-know meetings."

"And I don't like officers overstepping their area of authority," the captain shot back. "North is tasked with our intelligence operations, and it is his call to clear Sparks for service. As it is, North made the right move earning Sparks' trust, considering the amount of Chasm insights she has provided. We've been litigating that choice for more than eight months, and I've decided to support North's judgment on Sparks. Period. I'm tired of my authority being challenged."

"Just because you are captain doesn't mean we shouldn't question your judgment," Blight argued back. "Sparks' actions led to the deaths of hundreds, maybe thousands of innocents. She wasn't acquitted. Her sentence was commuted. There's a difference. She should be locked up on the brig of the *American*

Spirit heading back to Earth."

"You are talking like I am not in the room here," Sparks said, deadpan. "But you are right. I should be jailed, or frozen body floating in space. But I received, what do you call it North, um… *grace*. I received grace from Amberly."

The mention of Amberly made Blight even more angry. "Amberly Macready? *Amberly Macready*? The daughter of the mastermind of *Magellan's* destruction? Really? She's just as bad as her mother and just as responsible for the deaths of so many. She should have been shown the airlock with her mother."

North stood suddenly, angrily and took a step from the corner towards the chair where Blight was sitting, pointing a finger toward her face. "How dare you impugn the integrity of Amberly Macready? You need to—."

"You … you … hypocrite," Blight fired back, standing up. "At her trial you voted for her death. What is the matter with you, North?"

"Careful, Blight," the tenor of North's voice indicating he was working hard to stay calm.

Blight did not relent. "I see absence makes the heart grow fonder. How can I trust you'll have my back when we go into battle against Chasm? Your feelings oscillate like some emotional teenage girl."

"You question Amberly's integrity. Now you question my resolve?!" North burned with anger. He knew that his rising emotions would make Blight believe her thesis was correct, that he was emotionally compromised and unbalanced. "You know nothing of the pain I've been through. The friends of my mine who are dead at the hands of Chasm. You know nothing of the sacrifice —"

"Sacrifice? Sacrifice!?" Blight was now face to face with North. She was about 10 centimeters shorter than North, but the way she was projecting strength made her seem just as tall. "I have given up the best years of my life for this service. Spent nearly 18 years trapped on this tin can, on this suicide mission, leaving the people I love behind on Earth, probably never to see them again. When I send them a message to say I love you, I know it will be 10 years before they'll even read it. They may as well be dead. For all intents and purposes, I've lost them."

"Now you listen, Lt. Blight —" North said almost pressing his nose into Blight's forehead.

"No, North. Listen to me! It's you! You are the spoiled rich military brat, who has never had to give up anything, had a perfect life, who knows nothing. And Amberly. The spawn of our enemy. Even with her nearly a half light year away, she still has you thinking with your pants. She played you, North. She played everyone! She still is. She is an evil person who deserves to die for the suffering she caused. And you are giving her safe quarter in your heart!"

"Careful, Alicia, North has been known to punch fellow marines for dissing his friends," Sparks said dryly, with a smirk of delight rolling over her face. "But he's a traditionalist, so I don't think he hits girls." The captain seemed to be ignoring the conflict, seated, with his elbows on the table, holding his head in his hands.

"That's his mistake then," Blight said, seething now, eyes burning holes through the tall marine. Then in one quick motion she brought up her right fist and buried it between North's jawline and neck in a powerful uppercut. Caught by surprise, North fell back into the wall, making a thud as his 85-kilogram body collided with the cold metal. Blight pulled her right fist back again to take a second swing, but Nyota and Rhodes both jumped for her, each grabbing an arm. Blight instinctively flailed at being restrained, and her left hand broke free of Rhodes and unintentionally nailed her in the eye socket.

"Dirty hell! Ow —" Rhodes stepped back and put her two hands over her eye.

Blight looked at Rhodes and was immediately ashamed for accidentally hurting the younger woman in her rage, the tension instantly draining from her body. "I'm sorry, Rhodes."

Cho stepped for the door. "I'm going to get a freeze pack for that."

North straightened himself, then ran his hands to straighten his uniform. The pale Blight had gone bright red with embarrassment. She knew her conduct was unbecoming of an officer and was preparing for a rebuke from the XO, whom she just struck. He could throw *her* in the brig for assaulting an officer. The captain looked up a North, but said nothing.

The silence was getting awkward, which Sparks couldn't

stand. She was about to fill the air with some sarcastic quip when North spoke. "You are right, Alicia. I have no idea what you have given up to come and defend the freedom of people on Arara whom you've never met, with little hope of ever seeing home again. I'm sorry."

"Sir... I," Blight stammered.

"Sparks stays. We need her intelligence," the captain said with an air of finality.

North rubbed his chin. "I know I deserved this, but maybe next time a slap? You could break a bone with that hook of yours." North smiled weakly and sat down at the table.

"Yeah, but I didn't deserve this," Rhodes said, as Cho returned with a medicated freeze pack. The teenager placed it over her throbbing eye.

"I'm so sorry," Blight said, putting a hand on Rhodes' shoulder, and both of them took seats at the table.

"You'll be fine, Ensign," North said.

"Well, now that you are done behaving like children, let's get back to the business at hand," the captain said, hoping the incident had vented the appropriate amount of steam.

"Yes, let's," Nyota agreed.

"Sparks, what did you find out from our new passengers?"

"The dead woman and the comatose man — his name is Arvin — those two are brother and sister. The baby doesn't belong to either of them. An orphan from the battle. The other woman's name is Ryder, and we don't have any records on her. She seems to be exhibiting signs of shock. Ryder told me that Chasm took over *Cortes* after murdering most of the waypoint's senior leadership. Not surprisingly, the Chasm operatives on *Cortes* received the same Scorched Earth command we did on *Magellan*. Obviously, they were successful where we failed."

"How can you say that with no remorse, Sparks?" said Blight, her blood pressure increasing.

"Oh, let's not start that again," Bollard griped.

"That's enough, Alecia," the captain said. "What I really want to know from Sparks is if she thinks Chasm has already lit *Marquette?*"

"The Chairman believed the waypoints were valuable, and if she thought she could save one and still break away from Earth, then she would," Sparks explained. "I'd give even odds that *Marquette* is still alive and well."

"Then we make for *Marquette* with all haste," Obadiah said. "If we could capture *Marquette* intact, staging our assault on Arara would be much easier."

"Shouldn't we go and see if we could salvage supplies, water and fuel from *Cortes*, or what's left of her?" Bollard said. "If *Marquette* is gone, too, that means a full one and half-light years of no re-supply before we get to Arara, and there will probably be no welcome port there for us."

"What will that cost us in time, Condi?"

"Staying on present course to the likely location of *Cortes*, will take an additional two months over making a direct line approach to *Marquette*," the *Magnus* computer voice spoke.

"Add however long the operation would take to recover what was salvageable," North said. "Time is of the essence. We have enough supplies to miss several waypoints. We'll make it to Arara fine."

"Yeah, but what about the way back?" asked Rhodes. If we can't resupply at Arara, things could get pretty dicey on before we could get back to *Magellan*."

North stood up again and paced the short room. "Let's be realistic. If we don't win, we are not going back."

North turned to the operations officer. "Blight, you are right. I'm a hypocrite. I lived in a perfect world that was shattered by Chasm. I had no idea what evil was. But I do now."

"Steady, North," the captain held up his hand to his first officer.

"We may die, Rhodes, or we may make it back to *Magellan* someday, but there *is* no going back for me," North said. "The *Magellan*, my home I loved. The people. That life. It's dead. Gone. Chasm destroyed it, even if the waypoint is still intact. All I have left is the fight. All I want is to take from Chasm what they took from me: Everything."

Sparks relaxed on a glossy black couch in the executive officer's suite. She scooted her body down the couch back, and friction from the polyvinyl material of her pants rubbing the couch's artificial patent leather made a high-pitched screech.

North jumped in response, and Sparks laughed at the Marine.

North's quarters on the *Magnus* were actually larger than his apartment on *Magellan*. As the number two in command of the powerful warship, North enjoyed nearly 40 square meters in what would be his home for at least the next four years. The only decor on the slate-grey walls were three pieces of art he had taken with him from *Magellan*. North was not a man for excessive sentiment, but he did harbor deep feelings.

Sparks looked at the three framed images, and considered their significance to North. The first, framed in a rare, ornate oak frame, was a portrait of his father Ogdin, and his mother, Anne, who had died from the Araran sweats. The sweats were one of the few illnesses that evolved after humans left for space. The couple was young in the photo, standing in a golden field of ripe Araran ligrans, a genetically-engineered cross between lupins and lentils.

Growing up on Arara as part of an experimental "cohort" of test-tube children, Sparks never had cause to travel the smaller agrarian continent of Ingram. Instead, she trained with her cohort brothers and sisters to become future leaders of Arara in the cities of Carmenica, the larger, more populous of Arana's two continents. The only other major land masses on the blue green planet were the Lewis Islands, where Kimberly Macready had grown up.

Sparks could see the clear family resemblance of North to his parents. For a moment, she felt a flash of jealousy and wondered if she had any physical resemblance to the man and woman who contributed the genetic material to start her life. She would never know.

The second image hanging on the wall was that of a night skyline of an old Earth city. North had told her it was Vancouver, Canada, and the picture had been taken around the year 2000. Tall buildings, lit by hundreds of windows, jutted into the darkness through wispy fog that Sparks understood to be common on Earth. North said the photo was a gift from his grandfather, who received it from his great grandfather, an early settler of Ingram who was born in Vancouver.

The third image was an abstract painting of three crosses. Sparks knew it had some religious significance, probably related to North's faith. As a humanist, Sparks didn't give religion much heed, but thought perhaps studying North's religion might be helpful in future manipulation of the Marine. She made a mental note to ask him about the meaning of the painting at a more appropriate time.

North opened a small cabinet Sparks knew to contain rare liquors. He pulled out a bottle of what looked like whiskey and poured a stingy splash into two glasses. He handed one to Sparks, who barely had time to wonder where North got his stash, as she downed the shot. She reveled in the burn on the back of her throat.

"What does a girl need to do to get another?" Sparks laughed.

North frowned, and looked at the half-empty whiskey bottle. Instead of pouring Sparks a second shot, he simply handed her his glass and put the bottle away, securing the cabinet with a biometric lock.

Sparks didn't down the second shot, instead she judiciously sipped it. North sat down in a plain aluminum chair.

"So, let's get to business, then," Sparks said. "What I am about to tell you I thought to be propaganda or Chasm myth, stories told to keep the rank-and-file undercover Chasm operators on the waypoints under control. It's imperative that you get this information to my sister."

"To Amberly," North corrected.

"That's what I said," Sparks responded. "I wouldn't want any harm to come to her because she didn't know."

"Okay, I'll bite," North said, still incredulous about the dramatic "secret" that Sparks was about to tell him.

"The Chairman allegedly had super-secret undercover operators, called Hawks," Sparks eyes seemed to reflect a childlike fear as she said the name.

"Hawks?"

"Yes. Their identity was known only to the Chairman. The only purpose of the Hawks was to make sure the will of the Chairman would be done. If a triumvirate —"

"The three-headed command group of a Chasm cell?" North asked.

"Yes, like Dek, Järvinen and I were the triumvirate for Chasm on *American Spirit*," Sparks continued. "If any of us grew soft, or decided to defy the Chairman's orders directly, a Hawk was the silent enforcer to make sure either we complied or were eliminated."

"But this whole Hawk thing could just be a bluff, right?" North pressed.

"Could be, but why risk it?" Sparks admitted. She knew however, that the Hawks were real, based on what Ryder had secretly told her about the last days of *Cortes*. If any Hawks survived on *Magellan*, then they may try to finish the work that Raven One had started, and destroy *Magellan*, and Amberly Macready along with it. And because Amberly had saved her life, and because Amberly was the closest thing she had to a family, Sparks wanted to protect her so-called sister.

"Look, I know you care about Amberly," Sparks said as she stood. She reached a hand forward and gently slid it over the stubble on North's cheek. "She means a lot to both of us. Just tell her to be careful. Send her the message."

North looked at Sparks. He had no reason to not trust her anymore. This Hawk thing couldn't be some sort of coded message, North mused. Sparks had been an unlikely confidant and friend. She didn't believe in the Chasm cause anymore. Or maybe she was just playing them all, North wondered. If so, she was more dangerous than anyone would have guessed.

Sparks leaned over the seated North, quickly kissed his lips and whispered in his ear, "Thanks for the drink." North stared dumbly as she walked out his door.

North and the captain had already agreed now was the time to risk sending *Magellan* an update. Most importantly, they needed to pass on the news that *Waypoint Cortes* was gone, but they also wanted to send a quiet warning to Moreno and Thor that deep sleeper agents could still be operating on *Magellan*. But what if the agents were plugged into the comm networks? Where better to hide then as a communications officer? Skylar and Skip surely were not Chasm, but a half-dozen other techs worked to decrypt official messages, and North didn't know any of those well enough to trust them.

Use a personal channel, the captain had suggested. Most personal messages didn't have great encryption. Fortunately, Amberly had sent a special encryption key to North before he had left *Magellan*.

"Condi, begin a video message to send to Amberly Macready on *Magellan*," North spoke to the VI. "Please encrypt with this key." North pulled out the key and touched it to his infopad. He looked right into the info pad's camera.

"Hey Red …"

L.S. ROEBUCK

CHAPTER FOUR

Waypoint Magellan, November 11, 2603, Earth date, 13 months after the Battle of Magellan.

She had never run faster in her life. Amberly had already stripped off the heels she borrowed from Kora, her feet painfully pounding the cold alloy floor with abandon in her mad spring home. Her new apartment was farther from Rick's than the apartment she once shared with Kora.

After North was outvoted in a military tribunal that declared Amberly's innocence, but before he left on the *Magnus* mission, North had refused to see Amberly. She resorted to sending an encryption key via a trusted courier, Kora, to let North contact her confidentially should he ever change his mind on the *Magnus*.

Physically, the key was a nondescript plastic chit. But if one encoded a message with the key, only its mate, which Amberly had, could decode it. Amberly knew in theory the key could be cracked with brute hacking force, but that would take years of using *Magellan's* main computing processors, if one could even get permission to have that resource allocation.

Why would North only send a message back to me? Was he sorry? Did he regret his vote? Or worse, has North grown more bitter and broken? Amberly thought. She pushed herself, her lungs felt like they would burst, and her stomach felt a little queasy.

She had to pass through the promenade that connected the Tube to the Marine HQ and main hanger. This section had been significantly damaged in the Battle of *Magellan*, and in an effort to erase the horror from memory, or perhaps just prove *Magellan* could rebuild stronger, the area was one of the first repaired. This entertainment district gleamed with a sleek, modern design, filled with cafes and retail stores and even the new Snyder Memorial Art Gallery. The broad hallway was lined with shops that were relatively busy.

As she passed by Chinatown, one of the open-air restaurants that survived the battle, her mind was distracted by her memory of the night when she followed North there. It was that night she began to deceive him, not knowing that she herself was being deceived by Chasm. Chasm had promised her information about her dead mother, Kimberly Macready, if only she would steal a pass card from North. Chasm did deliver — Amberly found out more than she wanted to know. Specifically, Kimberly was not dead, and she was leading the murderous insurrection.

If only she could go back and not go to North's apartment, and undo the Judas kiss she gave for that dirt-forsaken pass card. *I would have never known my mother was a psychopath*, Amberly thought. *Ignorance would have been better. I would have remembered my mother as a strong, caring powerful woman who taught me to seize my own destiny. Or maybe I would be dead, and mom would have succeeded without my involvement.*

SMACK.

Amberly ran full-speed into Midas, the courier who had protected Amberly during the final moments of the Battle of *Magellan.*

"Owwww!" Midas cried out in surprise. "What the dirt licker! Why don't you —"

Amberly had bounced off of the bulky man and fell onto the floor, the shoes she was carrying in her hands unintentionally flung forward a half dozen meters before sliding to a halt.

People dining in Chinatown gasped at the spectacle of the petite young woman colliding full boar into the older, larger man. The shock in Midas' expression quickly melted into a smile when he recognized the redhead who was trying to stand up. He offered her a hand.

"Amberly Macready," he said, with a big smile. "Sorry about that. Hey, how have you been? I heard you got a big promotion at the Science Corps so that's why I don't see you when I'm making the rounds—"

"Sorry, Midas, I ... gotta... run," Amberly croaked out. Her lungs were on fire, but she forced her body back into a sprint towards her house.

"Amberly... wait," Midas called after her but she didn't look back. "Have you heard from Sparks?"

Midas smiled again. *Young people, always in a hurry*, he thought. He absentmindedly rubbed his face, and felt something odd. He looked at the hand he had hoisted Amberly off the floor with — his fingers were smeared with blood. Not his, he surmised.

Amberly must have cut herself, he thought. *Hope she takes care of that.* Then he proceeded on his way to catch the next Tube car.

Amberly opened the in-seat cabinets in her small living/eating area. She stored most of her valuables there. She quickly tossed a blanket she had crocheted for her late father, Alroy Macready, out of the bench and onto the table. She pushed aside a stun gun. The weapon was confidentially given to her by Commander Moreno and Governor Thor in case she needed to defend herself from vigilantes who had never forgiven her Chasm trespasses.

"Where is that encryption key?" Amberly asked herself as she rifled through her possessions.

Verne, her VI — which normally lived in her infopad but when at Amberly's place, transferred into the living space computer unit — heard the question and answered. "If you are referring to the key whose pair you gave to Commander North, then you'll find it in the lower drawer of your vanity." Verne and the infopad it called home were a gift to Amberly from her father on her 13th birthday, the last gift he gave her before being allegedly murdered by his wife.

The vanity was on the opposite side of the small suite. In one quick motion, Amberly bounded over to the vanity, pulling a chair from the eating table and sitting down. She was bending down to open the drawer when she caught sight of herself in the mirror screen. Her face was blotted with blood. She noticed a small laceration over her left ear. Once she saw it, she felt it.

"The first aid kit is in the top drawer," Verne offered, predicting her next question.

Instead, Amberly grabbed a towel, reached over to the sink and moistened the artificial-fiber cloth before pressing it to her ear. She pulled the lower drawer fully open, retrieved the key, and set next to her info pad on the main table. Immediately, the infopad sprung to life, as she saw a waving bar on the screen indicated the decoding progress.

"Thanks Verne," Amberly said. "How long to decode?"

"Just two minutes," the VI said.

Amberly hoped that the message would be in video — that she would be able to see the face of North, the man she scorned, the man she used, and now the man she couldn't get over. However, the focused narrow band "tight beam" burst interstellar transmission protocols were usually thrifty, in order to accommodate maximum data, at least during normal operations, so a text or voice message was more likely.

Verne interrupted Amberly's thoughts, "Video message from North confirmed, sent nearly 120 days ago, July 9, 2603, Earth standard date. Shall I play it now?"

"Yes, yes, yes," Amberly said. She saw North's face fill the screen. First, she noticed a five o'clock shadow on his normally clean-shaven face. Second, her heart fell when she saw that he wasn't smiling his charming smile. His eyes were focused, but weary. Maybe even angry. She looked for friendship or love in those eyes, but she could detect none. Instantly, sweet, lonely tears began to run down Amberly's face. The video buffered, and then began to play.

"Hey, Red. Long time," North said, with a note of familiarity. "It's been a hell of a year here on the *Magnus*. I know you are a survivor and believe in my heart you are well. I hope you are keeping an eye out for Skip. First of all, if you are not watching this alone, please ask everyone else to leave. This message is meant for your eyes only."

Amberly knew she was alone, but still looked around her small flat, irrationally expecting to see someone who snuck in. The confidentially request was unexpected and confusing.

"Amberly," North continued after a moment, "I am glad you gave me this encryption key. It was the best way we believed *Magnus* could communicate confidentially with *Magellan* leadership. Based on some intelligence we learned from Sparks, we believe that there could still be deep, deep sleeper Chasm agents on *American Spirit* and *Magellan*. Please share what I am about to say with only Commander Moreno and the civilian leader, who I assume is still Governor Rillio. Sparks believes that Chasm may have someone in central communications able to monitor official transmissions with military encryption access."

The thought of Chasm agents still being active on *Magellan* made goosebumps crawl on Amberly's arms and neck, and any feeling of security she had mustered in the last year seemed to be suddenly sucked into the vacuum of space.

"Although I'd love to hear the news from *Magellan*, please do not transmit back information unless absolutely necessary. The risk of Chasm knowing of the flight of the *Magnus* is too great, even with message encryption. Now, please listen very carefully and only share this with Rita and Thor. Don't share this with anyone else, not even Skip or Kora, until Moreno has cleared it."

Amberly reached out and touched the screen of the info pad, running her finger down the image of North's chiseled cheek. She smeared a mixture of her tears and blood on the screen. "Oh, North, I'm so sorry," Amberly ached aloud.

The recorded message continued. "Amberly, *Waypoint Cortes* is gone. Chasm destroyed it. By a miracle of God, we were able to recover three survivors from a runabout headed towards *Magellan*. Everyone else on the waypoint was murdered. I've attached the video we recovered from the runabout and am playing it now."

Images of the utter destruction of Chasm were now on the display. Complete brokenness. Floating death. "Stop playback." Amberly shouted to Verne. "Stop playback!" Amberly couldn't take it. Wong was right. *Cortes* was gone. Was she responsible? The amount of death was unthinkable. The emotional impact of the destruction of a waypoint was abstract up to this point for her. For someone who had spent her whole life on a waypoint, seeing a waypoint's death was tantamount to an existential crisis of faith.

"Playback paused," Verne complied.

"Send an urgent message to Moreno. Tell her it's North, and tell her it's bad."

The trio decided to meet clandestinely in Rita Moreno's apartment. Governor Thor Rillio had just left a meeting with *Magellan's* legislative council, and wore a rare orange formal jacket with buttons and blue ascot. Moreno, a petite, sharp featured, olive-skinned woman, was off duty, and she wore a floral-patterned yukata. She stood across the bar, which divided her living area and private kitchen, from Amberly and Thor. Amberly hadn't seen the governor in a while, and noticed that he had lost a significant amount of weight. Apparently, the synthetic food most of *Magellan* was forced to eat during the rebuilding of the garden dome was not as appetizing to the rotund man.

"Holy God," Thor muttered under his breath, as he watched the footage North retrieved from the *Iron Star* and had shared with Amberly.

Once Moreno had heard that North had secretly contacted Amberly, she immediately summoned both Amberly and Thor to her place. Meeting in Marine HQ or at the government offices could have drawn unwanted attention.

Moreno knew that public opinion had to be manipulated, to be engineered, in order to govern effectively. Rillio was no political novice, and under normal circumstances, was more than adequate for leading a waypoint. But times were not normal, and Thor was content to follow the cues of Moreno, whom he knew in his heart to be his superior in many ways.

Amberly hadn't even stopped to clean her face before leaving. Her eyes were puffy red, tears had streamed through the blood caked on her face.

Moreno set two ornate tea cups on the bar in front of Thor and Amberly. "This will help you calm down, Amberly," the officer said, as she filled each with hot water from an instatherm pitcher. Moreno's pitcher was much fancier than Amberly's; not only would it instantly heat water to the exact specified temperature, but it could also lower the temperature to near freezing. Then Moreno produced something which Amberly had not seen before — a real tea bag.

"The cups were passed down from my great, great grandmother. She was from Mexico City before the war. My mother told me the cups were the only things her great grandmother was able to save before the capital was laid waste." Moreno explained as she dipped the tea bag into Amberly's cup. Amberly looked at the intricate gold-plated baroque design, unlike anything she had ever seen before.

"The tea is Darjeeling from Arara," Moreno continued. "A small luxury I afford myself whenever traders have bags available. I probably have fifty or so bags left. They may be the last bags I'll ever have if *Magnus* can't right things with the colony."

Moreno pulled the bag out of Amberly's cup and slipped it into Thor's. "Mother said back on Earth, they would use the bag for only one cup, and then throw it away. *Throw it away.*" Moreno produced a third cup, and then after bobbing the bag in Thor's cup a few more times, slipped it into the empty cup she placed in front of her place at the bar. She punched in a much higher temperature on the instatherm than what she poured in Amberly and Thor's cup.

"I like my tea scalding," she explained.

Amberly took a sip of her tea. It tasted agreeable and did have an unexpected calming effect, Amberly thought. She felt the rare porcelain's sheen under her fingers, and the warmth seemed to conduct through the cup into her body.

As if she could read Amberly's thoughts, Moreno responded. "You see Amberly, this is what we are fighting for. The beauty of Earth – the cup – and the industry of Arara – the tea – and how much better they are together. Synergy. The cup gives you no pleasure without the tea, and the tea cannot be enjoyed without the cup. We are partners, Earth and Arara. Chasm doesn't understand that the legacy of the cup enhances the tea, makes it superior, gives it power. Nothing you can measure, but real all the same."

Amberly nodded, feeling her youthful inexperience. "I understand," she felt compelled to say.

"So now that we know what Chasm is up to, doesn't that mean it will be easier for us to stop them, if they even have sleeper agents here? I mean we're looking for them," Thor suggested, also now sipping his tea. "Then again, what if this Sparks is lying to North. Just trying to cause trouble or keep us off balance?"

Amberly stared into her cup. "I think we can trust Sparks. I have this feeling about her. When she gave up and stopped the *American Spirit* from ramming *Magellan*, I think she really knew it was over for Chasm. She's one of us."

"You did have a gun pointed at her," Thor reminded Amberly.

"And a good thing, too," Moreno chimed in. "Your actions saved us all. Too many people have forgotten that."

"So, what does this message mean, besides we should all be praying for *Magnus* and her crew?" Thor asked.

"Thomas Paine once said that eternal vigilance is the price of liberty. This has never been more apt. We have to be ready should the *Magnus* fail, and Chasm take control of Arara. We have to be ready if they return to finish the job that your mother started,"

Moreno looked to Amberly. "It's time for us to think outside of the box, or perhaps, outside of the waypoint."

"What do you mean?" Amberly was curious.

"We hardly have enough resources on this waypoint to rebuild the damage caused by the bombardment of the *American Spirit*. There is no way we can make what we need to defend ourselves against a Chasm warship. We need materials to fix our antimatter reactors, to build military defenses. We need materials we don't have on the waypoint."

"Do you think Chasm has a warship?"

"Until we hear back from a successful *Magnus*, we must assume they will create a weapon to finish severing Arara from Earth," Moreno said. "We have to prepare for that eventuality. We know they are willing to destroy an entire waypoint. A handful of corvettes with chain guns may not be enough to defend our home."

Amberly, Thor and Moreno all awkwardly took a slurp of tea at the same time. Moreno smiled, then set her cup and saucer down.

"Thor, North's message proves we need someone we can trust to lead this project," Moreno said, taking another sip. "And that the project needs to be conducted in a clandestine fashion. If Chasm finds out about the project, we'll lose the element of surprise at best. At worst, a Chasm agent would sabotage the whole project."

"What project are you talking about?" Amberly felt like all she was doing was asking questions and getting no answers, recalling when Chasm operatives Dek, the now deceased Joti, and Sparks lead her on with teases of secrets of her mother. This time, however, she wouldn't have to sell her soul for the answer, because Moreno was quite forthcoming.

"Amberly, Thor and I would like for you to lead our secret efforts to establish a resource colony in the Spencer Belt. We want to reopen Fuentes Station, with you as the outpost commander."

"Me? I'm a scientist. I don't... I couldn't... I'm only twenty!"

"Youth. A fault that everyone is cured of eventually, too soon, I think, my daughter," Thor said. Amberly didn't like the way he said *daughter*. It seemed condescending and patronizing. And yet, what they were asking her to do was not the task assigned to a child.

"*Trust* is the most important quality," Moreno said, walking around the bar and taking Amberly's hands into hers. "Everything else you can learn on the job. You have *million-watt brightness* in your genes. But *trust* you either have or you don't. And I trust you, Amberly Macready. I trust you with my life. And so does the governor."

Thor smiled at Amberly. "You're a true hero in my book. But you know that. More importantly, *North* trusts you."

"Hah," Amberly chortled sarcastically. "North doesn't trust me. How could you even say that after what he said? After what he did?"

"Simple. North sent *you* the message," Moreno said. "Why would he do that if he didn't believe that you were on the side of the good guys?"

Amberly smiled slightly. She didn't have answer for that.

"Amberly, you've shown remarkable leadership this past year, helping to keep the Science Corp together, leading that team through tremendous loss, in helping us remember what we are all about, as Magellans, citizens of our waypoint, our home."

"You'll need to assemble a team of people who are absolutely loyal to you, people who are capable and innovative under pressure. People who are willing to cut themselves off from those they love in the short term."

Amberly was beginning to understand. "What are you suggesting? That we fake my death to cover up the project?"

"You see, Thor, she does catch on quickly," Moreno smiled again.

"We're figuring it all out," Thor explained. "You have about a month to quietly put together your team. Then maybe we'll stage your demise – well I guess your whole team's demise – by year's end. Then you'll have a few years to get the station operational."

"We have the tech advantage over Chasm," Moreno followed. "They are right to think Waypoint and Colony Command on Earth isn't sharing all the good stuff. Fortunately, Captain Obadiah left us specifications, designs and training data so we can create the long-range beam weapons that made the *Magnus* so effective in thwarting the *American Spirit* attack.

"Once you have Fuentes Station operational and collecting

critical resources – ores, water, you know – from the Spencer Belt, and we are confident we can defend the new operation for Chasm saboteurs, we'll bring you back from the dead."

"I don't know. Lost in space. Fake death? Hiding out at Sonnet? Sounds strangely similar what my mother did," Amberly rubbed her brow.

"You have been to the Spencer Belt? To Sonnet?"

Amberly thought about the last time few times she went to the Spencer Belt, a group of a thousand or so charitable asteroids orbiting the low mass stellar object known as HD 238921 or Spencer Minorum. She was on a date gone awry with North at the Shard Caves on Sonnet, the largest asteroid in the belt.

"You'll have a window of about 12 months to get established. Fortunately, with the drive core upgrades that came on *Magnus*, our runabouts have enough increased range and speed that expand the accessibility window," Thor explained. "What do you say, Amberly, do you want to be the next commander of Fuentes Station?"

Amberly thought of the last commander of Fuentes Station, who was murdered three decades before she was even born. *Magellan* hoped to dominate her neighbors economically with the raw resources of the Spencer Belt. But hardship drove one of the pioneers mad, and she sabotaged the asteroid base by killing everyone on Sonnet, including herself.

"Amberly, if we can bring Fuentes Station back in play, up to operational status, it will make it that much harder for Chasm to win. Fuentes Station will help reinforce the chain between Earth and Arara. It will help ensure the viability of *Magellan* now that we've most certainly lost Arara as a supplier," Thor continued.

"You know how hard things have been since the attack," Moreno made her case. "A productive Fuentes Station is hope. You could really help bring things back to normal."

Normal. That is an unlikely fiction, Amberly thought. *We'll never have normal again. But getting closer to normal, even a small amount, would be good.*

Moreno pressed. "Amberly, *Waypoint Magellan* needs you to be a hero again. We need you to lead this mission."

"With all due respect, I am no hero," Amberly said, and then after a long pause continued. "How long do I have to decide?"

"How long do you need?" the Governor said. "We don't have a backup plan."

L.S. ROEBUCK

CHAPTER FIVE

Waypoint Magellan, November 22, 2603, Earth date, 13 months after the Battle of Magellan.

Amberly learned in her high school civics class that major political campaigns on Earth took months. She was grateful waypoint campaigns were much shorter. With fewer than 10,000 voters, candidates needed little time to introduce themselves and their platforms to the electorate. *Magellan* council at-large position number five was up for grabs, and two candidates had put their names in the helmet, including Skylar Trigs.

Before the Battle of *Magellan,* the waypoint was roughly split between progressives and traditionalists, but since the Chasm rebellion, progressives were entirely out of favor. The current elections represented a battle between moderate traditionalists like Skylar Trigs and more conservative traditionalists like Ixar Marve, an engineer who owned several micro-factories. Also running was Li Cali, a nurse who worked in the same medicenter as Kora.

Normally, Amberly didn't like the organic confrontations generated by the political process, but after the Battle of *Magellan,* Amberly felt it was her patriotic duty to the waypoint to be involved in the process. Also, Moreno decided to endorse Skylar and had personally asked Amberly to help his campaign.

Amberly followed Skylar on the campaign trail, recording voter sympathies in real time, as he met with groups of micro-factory laborers, school teachers, Marines and others. Amberly was impressed with how well Skylar understood the needs of each group. He had a rare gift to make these interest groups believe he appreciated them without plying them with undeliverable promises. His empathy was *palpable.*

Yesterday, Amberly had accompanied Skylar to meet-and-greet campaign stops at the Church and Science Commons, some of the largest, open areas where shops, restaurants, arcades and other retail spaces opened onto multi-story plazas. He'd spent hours meeting with hundreds of inquisitive and demanding voters. He was complimentary without being patronizing, and he was erudite without being elitist.

Each *Magellan* quadrant, President, State, Science and Church Commons also had an expansive public cafeteria.

Early today, Amberly and Skylar were at the State Commons, and now they were at his final campaign stop at the President Commons. Amberly had been taking opinion surveys on behalf of Skylar's campaign, but now just sat quietly in a corner and watched Skylar in action, receiving a group of voters a half-dozen meters away.

The world has always needed great leaders, Amberly thought, as she looked at the portraits of American commander-in-chief's that served as décor for the President Commons. The United States had been the primary builder of *Magellan*, and its residents, should they ever return to Earth, would have citizenship in with that nation. Amberly recalled her history classes and recognized most of the portraits: George Washington, the first president; Abraham Lincoln, who kept America together from coming apart during the Civil War; Nikki Haley, the first woman elected to be president; Tatiana Brown, who successfully prosecuted the great Islamo-Occidental War. Many historians argued Brown's leadership saved humanity.

Great humans do rise above to lead us all, Amberly thought. *People like Skylar, maybe.* Amberly thought about what she had been taught from a young age about leaders. Strong leadership was one of the four pillars of waypoint society: morality from religion (church), advancement from technology (science), collective good from government (state), and human exceptionalism through incredible leaders (president). *I wonder what caliber of leader Skylar will be,* Amberly thought, *if he gets elected. Of course, he's going to get elected.*

She watched Skylar treat everyone — from the most important business owners to the lowly sanitation workers — with respect, as if they were his equal. *Skylar knows how to connect emotionally with people. We need people like him,* Amberly thought. *I need people like him. I wonder, would he come with me to Sonnet?*

She watched Skylar listen to the concerns of Katie Higginsworth, a 102-year-old retired navigator, who had been to Earth, *twice.* She couldn't hear what they were saying, but when they were done, the old woman pulled Skylar into a hug. He kissed her cheek, and she walked away.

Skylar looked over to Amberly, saw Amberly had been watching him, and gave her a big smile. Amberly smiled back as Skylar turned to engage the next person waiting to tell him their government ills.

"You think I should vote for him?" a woman asked, surprising Amberly enough to make her jump.

"Holy dirt, Flora! I didn't hear you walk up," Amberly said to her former teenage rival, Flora Dillington. Flora did similar work as Amberly, only Flora's job was in the private sector for the Waypoint Research Group, the largest for-profit research company off-planet. The women were similar in size and appearance, except Flora was a dirty blonde.

"Sorry, Amberly," Flora gave a tight smile. "So, what do you think? My brother is voting for the conservative slate, but I am thinking about moving to the middle. Should I vote for Skylar?"

Amberly turned from Flora and looked back at Skylar. She enjoyed watching his flowing blonde hair bounce about as he shared his ideas with voters in an animated fashion.

"Skylar. He's great. He's not really political, you know. I love that he looks at our problems and figures out how we can work together to benefit the most people, a real utilitarian – not hung up on the sort of ideological dirt that brings us war. He seems so… real. He just wants to take care of people, to take care of *Magellan*."

"So, is he 'taking care' of you?" Flora asked with a tinge of teenage giggle in her voice.

"Oh, we're not like that," Amberly blushed. "We're just friends."

"Sorry," Flora said too innocently and too quickly. "I was just sure you had eyes for him. I guess I misread the situation."

Dirty slut, Amberly thought. *She's going to go after Skylar just because she thinks I am interested in him. Some people never change.* Even still, Amberly felt jealous. *I am not romantically interested in Skylar Trigs,* Amberly needed to reaffirm that fact in her head. *Maybe. Oh, dirt! Change the subject.*

"I guess you did. So, how's your brother?"

"Mac is doing okay, I guess," Flora said as both she and Amberly tracked Skylar as he walked across the commons to visit with another cluster of voters. "He misses Commander North. But who doesn't. I know I feel less protected now that his is gone. Hey, I heard a rumor that North sent *you* a message. Why he would send you a message, I can't imagine, after how he treated you at the tribunal. Disgusting. You must hate his guts. I would if he said those dirty words about me. To think he fancied you."

What the hell did Flora know about North's message? Amberly thought and forced herself to not panic. Someone was leaking confidential information, and Amberly started running through her mind who would have told Flora. *If a Hawk got wind of the message, it could ruin everything. Wait, what if Flora was a Chasm Hawk?*

"Message? The *Magnus* is running silent. How would I get a message from North?" Amberly asked.

"I suppose you are right," Flora said, nonchalantly. "You know how people like to make things up. Who even cares about North, lightyears away, when you have *that*?" Flora winked at Amberly as she tipped her head in Skylar's direction.

"It's *not* like that," Amberly insisted.

"Right," Flora said. "I'll see you around, Amberly. Drop by the lab sometime. I've developed a new radiation identity resolution algorithm I'd love to get your take on."

"Sure. See you," Amberly said, watching as Flora went toward the lift to the retail row a floor up. Amberly instinctively brushed her hands down her clothes, as if to wipe off Flora's presence, as her fellow stellar researcher walked away.

She turned back toward the center of the commons to see Skylar approach, smiling broadly.

"All that's left now is the voting," Skylar said to Amberly. "I'm pretty sure I've shaken every hand and kissed every baby on *Magellan*. I enjoy people, but I need peaceful time to recharge. Interested in a quiet dinner at my place? I'll cook up some of my famous double ligran soup. We could wait for the election results, there."

"What about your campaign manager and the rest of the elect Skylar team?"

"I sent them home already. I told them we weren't going to have a watch party. I'll see them tomorrow night. We'll save the victory festivities for the Thanksgiving Election ball."

Amberly looked into Skylar's eyes. She was like him, enjoying groups of people, but only in small doses. After two days on the campaign trail, a secluded dinner for two sounded perfect.

Amberly sat beside Skylar on the in-wall bench in his living room. The metallic alloy table in the center of the small room was decorated with two bowls of steamy ligrain soup. Amberly picked up the bowl and tipped it to her mouth for a sip. *Surprisingly savory*, Amberly thought. The bean broth made her tongue dance and warmed her belly.

Skylar looked at Amberly, waiting for a reaction. "Well?"

"Wow. Forget about politics. You should open a restaurant. I'd come every day."

"I wish we had the ingredients we had back on Arara," Skylar said. "If you like my soup, you would have loved my dad's recipe."

Skylar's infopad started to project a vid feed of the official results. Amberly recognized the *Magellan* Council chambers shown in the vid, an ornately decorated room where most legislative and many civil judicial functions took place.

The governor was at the speakers' podium reading the results.

"Final results for the at-large position five. Science Quadrant precinct: Marve, 1218; Trigs, 923; Li, 212."

Amberly was pleased. They had only projected Trigs would earn 700 votes, so now Skylar didn't have to over perform in the other quadrants.

Thor started reading again. "Final results for the at-large position 5. State Quadrant precinct: Marve, 1502; Li, 501; Skylar, 480."

Amberly looked over at Skylar, who frowned. They both had expended him to at least place second in the State Quadrant. "Don't worry. The crowds in the President Quadrant ate you up. You'll pull it out."

"I don't know," Skylar said, looking at the tallies on the screen. "That's 2,720 to 1,403. Marve almost has a two-to-one lead on me. Looks like it's over."

Amberly took Skylar's hand. "Don't give up yet. I believe in you. Besides, if this council thing doesn't work out, I may have something else for you to do."

"That's interesting and unexpected," Skylar said, gently

squeezing Amberly's hand. "What sort of thing?"

"Shhhh! Here come the next results."

"Final results for the at-large position 5. President Quadrant precinct: Trigs, 1922; Li, 501; Marve, 110."

"Woot!" Amberly jumped up, uncharacteristically excited. You're up, 3,325 to 2,830! I knew the President's Quadrant loved you." She looked at Skylar, pulled him up by his shoulders and hugged him. "I'm proud of you. You are going to be a *councilor*!"

"Don't count your supply ships until they are in port, Amberly," Skylar said smiling. "The Church Quadrant is where I have been polling worst. And it's Marve's home quadrant."

"That's just means they know what a real dirt licker he is," Amberly said.

"My, my, such language," Skylar chided.

Thor's voice came through the vid. "Looks like the we have final results for the at-large position 5. Church Quadrant precinct: Marve, 1222; Trigs, 756; Li, 201."

Amberly had done the math in her head before the vid announced the results: Skylar, 4081; Marve, 4052.

"You did it!" Amberly spurted. "You won, Councilor Trigs!"

"*We* did it," Skylar said, putting his arm around Amberly and leaning back into the couch. "Thanks for seeing me though. I'm glad Moreno twisted your arm to help. I'm pretty sure I would have lost without you."

"Go Team Trigs!"

"I only have one question," Skylar said with a charming smile. "Do you have a dress for the Thanksgiving Election Ball?"

"Why are you so nervous?" Kora asked her little sister. "You look *mmm mmm*." Amberly and Kora were hiding in the shadows in the crowded ballroom of the Hoover Hotel. The Thanksgiving Election Ball was one of the more elegant affairs of the year on *Magellan*.

Amberly fidgeted in her slightly-too-tight, deep blue, velvet halter neck dress. The gown fell to her ankles, elevated in her matching blue heels. "I feel a little *on display*."

"Don't worry. The display is great," Kora said. "I knew that dress would look good on you. That's why I had it fabricated."

"Thanks, I think. No. No thanks. How did I let you talk me

into getting dolled up like this, again?" Amberly said, as she looked at her sister's elegant black trumpet dress which beautifully flowed off Kora's body. "I like *your* dress. It leaves a little more to the imagination."

Trot stepped up next to the sisters, drinks in hand.

"I hope I don't have to use my imagination for too long," Trot ogled his wife. "Amberly, club soda as ordered. Kora, forget drinks. I love this song. Let's dance." Trot handed Amberly both plastic flutes.

Kora gave Amberly a what-can-I-do glance over her shoulder, as Trot, in his police dress uniform, pulled her onto the dance floor.

Amberly stood alone, watching the dance floor in the ballroom of the Hoover Hotel. The classic doo-wap power ballad, "Love Me or Airlock Me," by the Asteroid Belters, a fusion band that charted on several waypoints circa 2550, played. The song prompted lovers and would-be lovers to get handsy as they danced.

Amberly finally saw Skylar Trigs on the other side of the hall. She had been looking for him in the packed ballroom for nearly an hour. He wore a blue tuxedo, and he was talking to – Flora Dillington!

Flora was wearing a bright orange-red pushup sheath dress that didn't even cover her knees. Her blonde halo braid matched Skylar's golden mop. She leaned over and whispered into his ear, and he nodded.

Why should I care if Skylar is into Flora? Amberly argued with herself. *I'm sure he's just being nice to her anyway. That's what's amazing about him. He makes everyone around him feel comfortable. Hmm... Skylar looks so good in a tux.*

Flora pulled back from Skylar's head and appeared to giggle. Amberly felt blood flowing to her face. *I am not jealous of Flora. I am not – oh, he's looking at me.*

Skylar noticed Amberly standing alone at the other side of the ballroom. He smiled at her and turned back to Flora, and put up an excuse-me-a-moment finger. He started to walk to her.

Amberly felt panicky, set the flutes on a bistro table, and smoothed her dress.

"Hello, Director Macready," Skylar looked into Amberly's

green eyes. "You look, wow, um… stellar."

"Councilman Trigs. That has a nice ring to it. That tux does you justice." Amberly's face beamed, but her eyes darted to the dance floor and back. *He's going to ask me to dance. Do I want to dance? Yes. No. I can't dance. He's going to get the wrong idea. I'm going to get the wrong idea.*

"Amberly, would you do me the honor?" Skylar extended his hand.

Dirt. No thanks, I'm not ready for this, Amberly thought about saying, but then her mouth said, "I'd love to."

She stepped out onto the crowded floor, the smooth harmonies of the Asteroid Belters inspiring the dancers. Skylar took one of her hands in his and settled his other hand on the small of her back, pulling her close to him.

The pair swayed to the sultry beat. The gentle but firm pressure from his hand on her back guiding her steps unexpectedly excited her. *Oh no. Get control of yourself,* Amberly thought, but then leaned her head on his shoulder. *Dirt! Dirt! Why did you do that, Amberly!? Stop it! Pick your head up right now.* She took a deep breath through her nose. Skylar smelled fresh.

"I'm excited about the future, Amberly. We're going to do great things together," Skylar spoke to Amberly as they danced. "We're going to fix the damage Chasm caused, you and me. And we won't stop there. You know *Magellan* has so much more potential."

"You think we have potential? *Magellan*, I mean." Amberly asked. She loved that Skylar had a mind for something bigger than himself. She thought about North, who couldn't see past the status quo until Chasm shook him up. And Dek's devotion to Kimberly Macready seemed to just transfer to foolish infatuation with her. *I'm being too hard on North and Dek,* Amberly thought. Still, she was impressed that Skylar saw a greater picture and was doing something about it.

"After all *Magellan* has been through, it's not enough to just improve the quality of life. It's time to really improve the human condition out here in deep space. I think we're on the cusp of a real revolution."

As the music played, Amberly liked the sounds of Skylar's platitudes, but they sounded too good to be true. Still, his words watered the ambition of greatness planted by her mother when Amberly was not yet a woman. There was so much to learn, so much to discover, so much to add to the body of interstellar scientific knowledge. Everyone was so busy trying to survive, they needed someone to show them there was more to life than just living to the next day. Maybe she and Skylar could do that ... together. Amberly's lofty thoughts were interrupted by the music's inane lyrics.

"Our love is off the clock," the Asteroid Belters' female lead sang, "You knocked me off my block/I see you're done with me/Your heart has ignored my plea/Time to take a long walk/With my broken heart out the airlock."

A guitar rift faded as the song ended. Skylar looked in Amberly's eyes. He clearly wanted to go another round. But Amberly was afraid of the look in Skylar's eyes. She worried about how this budding undefined romance and Skylar's big picture ideas could distract her from her secret mission. *Maybe we can change the waypoint for the better. But first, I have a job to do. We can revisit this, whatever this is, later.*

Before her body betrayed her mind, she winked and said, "I'm sorry Skylar. I need to go. Congratulations on your win, councilman. Let's get together soon."

Skylar nodded, but before he could say anything else, Amberly had retreated.

Over the course of several weeks, Amberly had come to enjoy the company of Skylar Trigs.

At 28 years old, he was mature enough to be taken seriously and be elected to the *Magellan* Council in the Thanksgiving Election, but he still projected a boyish charm that helped Amberly find Skylar ... fun.

Amberly welcomed the diversion. Working in secret to assemble a team to recolonize the Spencer Belt had been more stressful than Amberly had anticipated. So much was riding on her to repair things. She saw this new project as a means to redemption; that maybe, just maybe, if she was successful, she could right the wrongs that she caused. *Maybe even North would forgive me*, Amberly thought.

"Look, our first new crop of corn," Skylar pointed to a section of the topside garden that had once again begun to produce fresh food. Over the past month, the pair took regular strolls in the topside garden. Before the Chasm uprising, Amberly had little access to enjoy the greenery of the gardens. But Amberly the War Hero was afforded many privileges, some that made her feel indulgently guilty. As a Freshman member of the Waypoint *Magellan* Council, Trigs enjoyed perks as well.

Amberly's eyes followed the crop line toward the topside garden's transparent dome. She winced when she saw the now-repaired dome, recalling where, during the Battle of *Magellan*, Sparks had intentionally crashed her runabout. Amberly had nearly died leaping from a spacecraft through that now-sealed fissure to the surface of the gardens. To see so much life-sustaining soil and plants sucked out in space reminded Amberly how bad things had gotten, and just how much damage Chasm had caused – damage for which she had been partially responsible.

Skylar noticed her discomfort as she looked at the sealed dome, and took her hands into his.

"Amberly Macready," he said softly as he gently turned her to face him. "I know what you are thinking. Look at me. This wasn't your fault."

She did as he asked and inclined her head toward his. Looking into Skylar's blue eyes as he pushed back one of his long yellow locks somehow made her forget the horrible things. With well over an Earth year since the battle, her scars were starting to heal. Skylar's gracious and charming attention was an emotional balm. She needed a friend, and he was there. Alone, at night, she wanted a more-than-friend, a companion, a committed something. But she felt like she was too screwed up in the head over North and Dek. Letting someone else in, someone like Skylar, would be unwise. And she was doing everything she could to keep herself from plunging into the unwise.

At first Amberly thought that her wall-building was her mother's wisdom guiding her, but later she came to own the decision. *Keep some emotional distance from Skylar,* she scolded herself. She couldn't blame her mom forever. Kimberly Macready was gone.

"No, it *is* my fault," Amberly said. "Maybe my mother would have been able to attack us without my help. But the point was she got my help, unwitting though it was. I helped her. That's what happened. Not some *maybe*."

"Did you ever think that if you hadn't have gone along with the Chasm plan, you wouldn't have been able to stop Sparks from destroying *Magellan*?"

"That's what Commander Moreno thinks. And the governor."

"And me," Skylar filled his voice with all the tenderness he could muster. He tilted his head and kissed Amberly's red crown.

"I've been meaning to ask you something, but it is strictly confidential," Amberly said in an unusually hushed tone, as she pulled Skylar close to herself. "You can tell no one."

Skylar seemed amused. "Okay, Amberly. You can trust *me*," he said with a bit of false hurt in his eyes.

"I'm serious, Skylar," Amberly said with a hard look. "If you tell someone else, it could be treason."

Skylar started to snicker at the absurd statement, but then he saw the seriousness in Amberly's face and stifled his reaction. "OK, then. I understand. I won't tell a soul."

"And I do trust you. But more importantly, Moreno cleared me to talk with you. I'm going away, and I want you to come with me," Amberly said, as she sat down on a water tank at the edge of the crop field. The corn covered about a half square kilometer, but because of the stalks' height and the curvature of the dome, the rows seemed to go on forever.

"Going away? Where? How? There are not deep space ships coming from Arara, and who knows when the next ship from Earth will get here?" Skylar didn't try to hide his confusion.

"Sonnet."

"The Spencer Belt? Why?"

"Moreno has asked me to assemble and lead a secret team to reboot Fuentes Station, to gather the materials needed for defending *Magellan* should *Magnus* fail."

Amberly was surprised that Skylar's first reaction was anger.

"Why didn't she tell the Council about this?" Skylar said crossly. "Martial law is over. This is a representative democracy, not a military dictatorship."

"We think that there are still Chasm operatives in deep undercover that would sabotage the effort. We can't go public with this, and we don't know if we can trust the Council. They could be compromised by Chasm."

"What? Chasm? No way," Skylar said. "We airlocked half of them. The rest we exiled. Why would you think that Chasm is still around?"

"You remember that encoded message from North," Amberly explained. "He said–"

"Wait. If there was anything but personal information in that message, you should have informed the Council. *We* are the voice of the *people*."

"Would you shut up and listen to me?" Amberly raised her voice. She hadn't thought so before, but now Amberly was wondering if the prestige of sitting on the *Magellan* Council had gone to Skylar's head. Skylar's countenance shrunk immediately as Amberly's own anger blossomed; Amberly made a brief mental note that this was the first time she had ever seen Skylar Trigs back down to anyone. "Apparently sometime in the past few months on the *Magnus*, North has flipped Sparks. She told North there were deep undercover Chasm agents – Hawks she called them – who answered directly to the Chasm Chairman and whose sole purpose was to make sure the will of the Chairman was followed absolutely. Secret lethal enforcers. No one in the Chasm ranks were supposed to know who the Hawks were, until Chasm had control of a waypoint."

"You mean, before the plan changed and they decided to try to blow *Magellan* and the others to kingdom come?"

"Yes. That is why we must keep this secret. Not even the Council must know we are rebuilding Fuentes Station. No one must know until we know for sure Chasm has been put down for good."

"Amberly, this whole Hawk thing," Skylar shook his head, "are you sure Sparks isn't just playing us. Trying to wind us up or just have a little fun at our expense? It all seems so cloak and dagger, loaded with drama and probably little truth."

"Thor wondered the same thing," Amberly conceded. "But I know Sparks, well sort of. We have, I don't know, some sort of a bond because both of us at one time worshipped my mother. Sparks once said that made us like sisters. I thought she was crazy then, but over time, I've come to feel like she was right."

"Your mother was impressive, but now she is influencing operatives from the grave? That's sort of weird, Amberly," Trigs protested.

"Well, it's weird when you put it like that, but I trust Sparks is telling the truth. Call it sister's intuition."

"I have a sister on Arara, but I never had any sixth sense that helps me know whether she is telling the truth or not," Skylar offered. "Chasm agents or not, I don't understand why we are so worried," Skylar said, trying to force the conversation into more sane territory.

"Why do you think this threat is real enough to keep things from our duly elected leaders?" he asked.

"It really doesn't matter what I think," Amberly said.

"Of course, it matters what you think!" Skylar protested, growing angry again but he was not sure at whom.

"Skylar, *Waypoint Cortes* is gone."

"Gone? What do you mean, it's gone?"

"Chasm won. They followed Scorched Earth protocol. Everyone is dead. I've seen the vids."

Skylar was silent for a second, his face went blank. He stared at the corn stalks for a few moments. Amberly let Skylar process the horrible news.

After a minute, Skylar's eyebrows rose, and he quietly mumbled, "How did you see the vids?"

"About six months ago, *Magnus* found a derelict runabout, the *C.S.S. Iron Star*," Amberly explained. "It had escaped *Cortes* just minutes before an antimatter reactor core overload explosion ripped the waypoint into pieces. Amazingly, there were three survivors on board, including a year-old kid."

"That video was in North's message?" Skylar said. "Wow. That sort of thing could incite a panic. Very clever of the Marine to encode it in a private message outside the watchful eyes of central communication."

"I know," Amberly said, "I had kind of hoped that North would send a message to…" Her voice trailed off and she felt awkward, turned away from Skylar and blushed. She was embarrassed that Skylar might pick up how she was foolishly pining for North.

"Why would you want me to come with you? To Fuentes

Station? You're asking me to give up my seat on the Council, my job as the director of central communication."

"Maybe you'd give up your seat. Maybe not. Skylar, I'm giving up a lot, too," Amberly said. "Hopefully, it's just temporary. But this is important. We have to be ready, and we are too weak after the last Chasm assault. I need a good communications officer who can also be a part of the leadership team. I need a second in command, someone who I can trust. You can help this mission be a success. Together, we can secure the future."

Skylar turned to face Amberly directly, looking deeply into her bright green eyes. He considered her soft red hair, her button nose framed by her symmetrical face. He liked what he saw. He spoke slowly, deeply. "That's the *only* reason you want me to come?"

"Isn't that enough?" Amberly said. She knew what he was hinting at, but didn't expect it and wasn't prepared to respond. She was trying to get over North, whom she rejected first, and then he harshly, publicly rejected her at her trial. She also thought she could have a future with Dek. His perspective on life was much closer to hers than North's, perhaps because both she and Dek were heavily influenced, like Sparks, by her mother. But while there was some chance of North returning to *Magellan*, however slim, Dek was exiled, never to return.

Her heart and head were still tangled from that emotional trauma, and though she had been growing in friendship with Skylar, somewhat of a balance of Dek and North, she wasn't ready to advance with Skylar, even though that seemed to be what she wanted in the moment.

"Well, I was hoping it was because …," Skylar chose his words carefully, "… you'd like to have the company of a good friend."

Amberly smiled. Skylar had become a good friend, a good male friend, when she needed a male friend. She had Lydia and Kora, but there was something about the strength only a male friend could provide, she thought. She recoiled slightly that she had the thought, the ghost of her mother's male antipathy echoing between her soul and mind. Then she grabbed the out Skylar had graciously given her. "Skylar, I want you to come because I'd love to have the company of a good friend."

"Great," Skylar said, "I'm in."

"You're in?"

"I'm in," Skylar repeated.

Amberly instinctively threw her arms around him in a firm embrace. "Thanks."

"Definitely in," he squeezed her in return.

"I wish you and Trot would come with me," Amberly said, as she sat eating artificial eggs – some reconstituted protein powder – in her sister's apartment. "We are still trying to fill out our medical staff. We could use a good nurse. And your police officer husband could handle security for us."

"No way," Kora said as she placed dishes in the sanitizer. "Are you done with that?" Amberly considered the remaining "eggs" on her plate an pushed it over to Kora, who scraped the scraps into the recycler, and then placed the plate into the sanitizer and closed the door.

"Come on, sister, what happened to your sense of adventure?" Amberly teased.

Little Alroy started crying in the other room. "That is what happened to my adventure."

"Kids," Amberly said. "I'm never having one."

"Never say never," Kora called out as she passed into her bedroom, only to return holding her baby boy. "This little man is a whole new adventure. It may not be as dangerous as leading a secret mission, but an adventure all the same. He's worth it. Aren't you worth it, my little baby boy?"

Alroy responded with a slight coo and a bit of spit up.

"What am I going to do without my best friend?" Amberly looked at her sister.

"So, I am your best friend, now that you need something," Kora teased. "What about Skylar? You've been spending a lot of time with him. Maybe he'll be your new *best* friend."

Amberly blushed a little. "Our relationship is purely platonic," she said defensively. "Besides, I am not sure how ethical it would be for me to have a romantic relationship with someone who would technically report to me."

"Oh, so you'll have Skylar at your beck and call. That's sort of a turn on."

"Kora!"

"Okay, but technically you are everyone's boss on this mission, right? So that means if you stick to the rules, you are going to be very, very lonely. Poor Amberly, all alone on that cold rock. With only your memories of North to keep you company as you take lonely space walks in the Shard Caves. Or would you be thinking of Dek?" Kora pressed her index finger against the lip of her closed mouth, and rolled her eyes up. "Hmmmmm?"

"Good grief, Kora. Quit that!"

"Okay, sorry. Not helpful. Let me see if I can think of someone who can be your security chief, because you can't have my Trot. You need someone undeniably loyal to Earth? What about Private Wong?"

"That drunken reprobate?" Amberly snapped.

"Well, there isn't exactly a bar on Fuentes Station," Kora said. "And Wong was one of North's most trusted strike Marines. And there is no questioning that he is truly loyal to Earth. Zero percent change that guy is secret traitor. He's loyal to a fault."

"You have a point," Amberly said. "But do you think he would work for *me*? He holds me personally responsible for the death of his friends."

"Well, if this mission is as important as you say it is," Kora reasoned, "then I bet Wong could put aside any misgivings has to serve homeworld and waypoint."

"You may be right."

"*May be* right?" Kora smirked. "Little sister, you owe me a finder's fee."

The Marine Commander's office was intimidating to the uninitiated. First off, it was especially large for a waypoint. At nearly four meters wide and eight meters deep, the office was even larger than the governor's suite. Near the door was a plain metal conference table – like everything else in the room, dark grey in color. The table was surrounded by a half dozen uncomfortable-looking chairs made from the same alloy as the table. At the far end of the room was a desk, illuminated by only a small lamp. A large, worn upholstered red chair sat behind the desk, and behind the chair, was a floor-to-ceiling plexiglass viewport showing the eternity of space.

Millions of stars, moving slowly as *Magellan* rotated, became the magnificent backdrop to those who had an official audience with Rita Moreno. The commander ascended to high office after her previous boss, Commander Anderson, was gunned down in this very space. A pair of faux-leather guest chairs sat in front of the desk.

Anderson's portrait, along with the twenty-two other Marines who perished in the Battle of *Magellan*, lined the right-facing wall as one entered the office. Each portrait was individually lit and the wall had the aura of a shrine. On the left facing wall were 37 portraits, hung upside down, with a dramatic red mark struck across each one. The mark looked like splattered blood. These were the faces of the government officials and Marines who were a part of the Chasm conspiracy. The convicted traitors to *Magellan* were now exiled or executed. This wall was in perpetual shadow, though the ambient light made it easy enough to make out faces as one passed by. Platinum letters below these portraits read: Never Forget Eternal Vigilance Is The Price Of Freedom.

Private Wong, wearing full dress uniform, entered the office. He had not yet received an official reprimand for his assault on Amberly Macready and figured this was the reason for his summons. On the one hand, he regretted his drunken behavior, that was so unbecoming of any Marine. On the other, he blamed Amberly for the death of so many good men and women. He was troubled that not only was she walking freely around the waypoint, but also, she was considered a war hero and received an honored place in the civilian corps.

The door slid closed behind Wong, and he looked across the room to the desk. He could see Moreno seated in her red chair, silhouetted against a glorious star field. And in one of the chairs in front of the desk he saw the unmistakable scarlet hair of Amberly Macready.

"Private Wong, reporting as ordered, ma'am," Wong said as he brought his hand into a salute.

At the salute, Moreno surprised Wong by standing, and then she returned the salute.

"At ease, Wong," Moreno said as she fell back into her chair. "Won't you please join us?" The commander waved a hand toward the empty chair. Wong started to cross the room, scanning the portraits of the fallen. He saw Snyder's portrait, along with Wing Commander Jindal, and in the center was Anderson's. He turned to the other wall, and immediately recognized the upside-down portraits of Strike Commander Johnson and Chief Jurist Adams. The last picture on the wall, also hung upside down, was that of Kimberly Macready. The red mark cut across her face, covering her mouth and cheeks. It did not obscure her glossy black hair, which inspired her Chasm code name, Raven One, or her piercing green eyes, which seemed to be staring back at Wong.

Although Raven One was not a member of the military leadership or elected civilian leadership, she was a top researcher in the Science Corps, the government-run research group. Her daughter had followed in her footsteps, and thanks to Raven One's destructive plan, had effectively murdered everyone in the way for Amberly to be corps' director, Wong thought as he turned back to the desk and Moreno's gaze.

"Please, Eli, sit," Moreno indicated the chair again. Wong did as he was told.

"Mission Commander Macready and I wanted to offer you a promotion and an opportunity to serve our homeworld on a dangerous adventure," Moreno said as she folded her hands together and leaned forward, resting her elbows on the desk.

Wong shook his head. "Come again?" he said, leaning forward as if he couldn't hear Moreno. "A promotion?"

"Yes. Should you accept this assignment, I will be promoting you to staff sergeant to command a Marine unit dispatched to support the mission," Moreno said.

"Ma'am, I am confused." Wong was bewildered. Staff sergeant represented a jump of three ranks, when Wong was expecting demotion or, even worse, dishonorable discharge for assault. "I thought I was going to be disciplined for conduct unbecoming of a Marine with regards to Miss Macready." Wong looked at Amberly's face for the first time since arriving, trying to guess at what was going on. Amberly's soft face had a youthful glow of energy and vitality, but her brow was furled. Wong didn't read anger, but rather intense focus or even fear.

"I don't think Mission Commander Macready chose to press charges, though I would encourage you to stay away from the bottle in the future," Moreno said, leaning back in her chair, absentmindedly rubbing a newly minted silver lock in her otherwise shoulder-length brown hair.

"Yes ma'am, but what mission?"

"What you are about to hear is highly classified. I'll let Mission Commander Macready brief you," Moreno said.

Amberly proceeded to explain about the message from North, the desire to create a survival contingency should Chasm return in force, and about the likelihood of secret Chasm Hawks still operating on *Magellan*.

"The threat is real," Amberly explained. "Wong, *Waypoint Cortes* is gone."

"What?"

"Show him the video, Amberly," Moreno instructed. Amberly pulled Verne out of a grey satchel. Verne played the footage recovered from the *Iron Star*. Floating fragments of the waypoint superstructure mingled with broken furniture, micro-manufacturing equipment, toys and suddenly-exposed-to-the-vacuum-of-space flash-frozen bodies. Wong saw both fully intact people and limbs torn from adults and children gracefully float in an eternal dance with the flotsam. His clenched right fist trembled, as a single tear escaped his left eye.

"We can't let Chasm win," Amberly explained. "We must protect the people we love on *Magellan* and honor those we have lost by being prepared. An active Fuentes Station that Chasm doesn't know about will give us the advantage."

"And it will help keep us indefinitely viable with supplies from Arara not forthcoming," Moreno said. "We used to be just one and a half light years from *terra firma* – three years of travel. We must assume that Arara is ether cut off from us now, with the destruction of *Cortes*, or worse, that Chasm has or will soon have control of the planet. The closest safe ground is eight light years away. Sixteen years from a home."

Wong looked troubled, and Moreno could read him like an infopad. "Speak your mind, Private."

"My misgivings about Miss Macready's character aside," Wong turned to Amberly, "no offense," and then back to Moreno, "why would you put someone that young and inexperienced in charge of a such critical mission?"

"Well, if she even has half the talent of her mother, she'll do well. I've seen Amberly in adversity, and I've seen her slow and steady servant leadership helping us rebuild *Magellan*," Moreno said evenly. "But more importantly, I trust her, and because she is a daughter of *Magellan*," Moreno said, waving her finger at the ceiling and walls. "She's loyal to this place. *Magellan* is her home."

"*Magellan* is *our* home," Amberly said firmly, a carefully measured correction to Moreno. "Wong, I need someone I know is loyal to Earth and *Magellan* to provide our security and lead the Marine detachment. No one is more loyal to Earth than you."

"North trusted Amberly with his critical message. You should trust her, too," Moreno looked hard.

Wong stood up, which prompted Amberly to do the same. Moreno remained seated. The Marine stuck his hand out in front of Amberly. She reciprocated, and Moreno smiled slightly as the pair shared a firm handshake.

"Mission Commander Macready, I'm in," he said.

"Good," Moreno interjected. "Because I was going to order you to help, anyway."

Wong ignored his superior officer, and still holding Amberly's hand, pulled the petite woman closer. His gaze hardened. "If you betray us again, I promise I will follow my moral duty to put a bullet in your head."

Amberly didn't flinch and pulled Wong even closer through the handshake. "Your moral duty," Amberly said sternly, "is what I am counting on."

Lydia sat at Amberly's vanity, while the redhead stretched out on her bed. The last three weeks had been long, full of secret meetings, supply level simulations, ore processing lessons and contingency planning. There seemed to be no end to the list of potential bad things that could happen, and Verne, Amberly's VI, had been expanded with some military-grade protocols to help Amberly be prepared with the hundreds of "what if" scenarios.

"Lydia, it was downright macabre," Amberly sighed. "I mean, Verne kept coming at me with scenarios: What if the food supply was contaminated? What if an uncharted asteroid fragment crashed into Fuentes Station and destroyed half of the living quarters? What if a team member goes crazy and starts shooting everyone?"

"Shooting everyone?"

"Yes, that's what ended the last attempt to colonize Sonnet," Amberly rolled over on her front side, facing Lydia and propped her head on her arms.

"I must have skipped that day of history class," Lydia mused. "How has the rest of your recruiting been going."

"Skylar is locked in to be my administrative lieutenant and communications officer," Amberly said.

"Ha! It's so sweet to think that cutie is going to be answering to you," Lydia joked.

"Sweet? How is it sweet?"

Lydia just smirked a reply. Amberly sighed, sat up and continued. "Midas is going to be facilities manager. Mars and Maria Dino are coming as well. He'll head up the mining operations; she's in charge of the mess. I am not sure if you know any of the others well. You could come, too, you know?"

"My dear friend, we've been through this a dozen times. It's tempting, but I would get too claustrophobic on Fuentes Station. It's not that big," Lydia said. "Also, I don't think the Science Corps could take losing you and me. Your people are going to freak out when they find out you are gone. Has Moreno and the Governor told you who is going to replace you when you leave as director?"

"No, and we still haven't figured out a good cover story to explain our sudden disappearance. The best idea they had was a fake death," Amberly said.

"Really," Lydia said, reclining on the bed next to Amberly. "Like your mother?"

"Honestly, with 28 people leaving, I don't know how we are going to keep people from finding out what is really going on. It's going to be hard to keep this secret from any Chasm agents that may be hiding among us."

"Did you get your security team put together?" Lydia said. "Did you really ask that crazy Wong after what he did to you?"

"Yes, several weeks ago in Moreno's office," Amberly recalled. "You should have seen the look on his face."

"Did he say yes?"

"He did," Amberly answered. "He also said he would personally put a bullet in my head if I 'betrayed' *Magellan* again."

"I don't know, Amberly, maybe Moreno is wrong and

bringing him is a bad –" Lydia was interrupted by the door chime.

"Verne, who is it?" Amberly spoke to her VI.

"Skip is here to see you, Amberly."

"Oh, my man is here," Lydia said, with a hint of sarcasm in her voice.

"Things not going well with you and Skip?" Amberly stopped moving to open the door.

"It's fine, who knows, I don't know," Lydia said. "This is why you date, right, to find out if you are compatible for better things."

Amberly shrugged. "I wouldn't know. Ask Kora."

Amberly looked at the green light next to the portal, indicating air pressure on the opposite side, and pressed the open button, to reveal a flush Skip, who had obviously been running.

"Amberly! You've got to –" Skip interrupted himself, "Lydia, I didn't know you were here."

"Skip, you don't have to always know where I am," Lydia said firmly.

Amberly thought she felt a chill from Lydia's direction. "Skip, what's up?"

"You won't believe this. You'd better sit down," Skip said excitedly.

"Won't believe this. Better sit down? Quit being so dramatic, Skip," Lydia chastised her boyfriend.

"Fine. Whatever," Skip turned his attention to Amberly. "We just received a transmission in Cencomm from the *American Spirit*. The ship is derelict. Chasm launched a coup."

"*How? What happened?!*" Lydia gasped.

"Apparently the coup failed, but not before Chasm managed to destroy to the antimatter drive and kill most of the bridge officers, including Captain Eaton," Skip continued.

"Oh no… April," Amberly said, barely audible.

"Moreno is calling her officers together now to see if we can stage a rescue," Skip explained. "I'm on my way over to Marine HQ, but Amberly, I needed to tell you in person."

"No. No-no-no," Amberly said as an emotional shock hit her system. She immediately thought of Dek. The rogue who had *almost* won her heart. The romantic revolutionary that just wanted to make everything perfect, and then betrayed everything he valued for *her*. She had tricked Dek, a good man who believed in a new, better order.

She sat down on the edge of her bed and called out after Skip, who was already heading out the door to Marine HQ. "Wait, Skip. Who is in charge of the *American Spirit* now?"

CHAPTER SIX

The American Spirit, Deep Space en route from Waypoint Magellan to Waypoint Gilbert, August 10, 2603, Earth date, 10 months after the Battle of Magellan.

Sweat dripped from the woman's short more-pepper-than-salt hair. She wiped at her face ineffectively with her red-gloved hand, and the sweat made her eyes sting. At 160 centimeters, she was at least a third of a meter shorter than the young man she was squaring off against, Chavez Ortega. Ortega handled civilian and bridge communications on the *American Spirit*. Ortega smirked with bravado as he took a swing at the woman with a broad left-hand stroke. The woman stepped out the way and Ortega's glove only tasted air. With Ortega off balance, the woman extended her left leg in a sweeping motion that made the man lose his footing entirely, and Ortega fell to the cushioned floor of the netted arena.

Several onlookers laughed at the sight of the boisterous Ortega kissing the mat.

"Nice one, captain!" The woman recognized the voice of Duke Todum, *the American Sprit's* ghostly pale chief engineer's mate, emanating from the spectators' booth.

Captain April Eaton was a competitive woman. At a half-century old, she regularly beat members of her bridge crew half her age in the *American Spirit's* sparring arena. Eaton was born on the *U.S.S. Texas*, the largest deep space cargo carrier ever built, just two years after it made berth from Earth carrying a cargo of Corvette and Valkyrie-class spacecraft, seed, livestock, and rare minerals (needed for antimatter core maintenance) among the nearly million tons of supplies.

Eaton moved quickly across the black mat to attempt to put a finishing pin to end the match. Ortega's pride spurred him on, and he scrambled up just before Eaton threw herself into Ortega.

The communications officer avoided the pin, but he was shoved up against the net, where Eaton was able to get in three successive punches to Ortega's head. The third punch knocked out his mouthpiece, which caused Eaton to drop her hands. Ortega put up one of his gloved hands to indicate a time out while he recovered his mouthpiece and placed it in his mouth."

"You spat that out to get a rest, didn't you?" Eaton said with a smirk through her own mouthpiece. After Ortega had replaced his mouthpiece, he dropped into an athletic stance and put both his hands in front of his torso to indicate his readiness to proceed.

Eaton quickly went at his head again and Ortega raised his mitts to block. But the upper body strikes she was signaling were feigns, and she tried another leg sweep. Ortega anticipated the sweep, however, and hopped over to flank Eaton. He landed a mean punch into her shoulder blade and followed by throwing his whole body into hers, flinging her face-first into the net. She ricocheted off the wall and onto the mat.

Eaton was a teenager when her family settled on *Waypoint Magellan*, and she had pursued a career in the academy. She spent her 20s at the Waypoint University on *Gilbert*, where she gained notoriety for her research and groundbreaking theories on the unique aspects of organizational leadership in deep space. How does the psychological impact of years of confinement on an interstellar ship impact leadership ability? What organizational structures worked best to ensure the mental health of deep space voyagers? Eaton literally wrote the book on the subject.

Nearly face down on the mat, Eaton knew Ortega would attempt to make a pin, so she randomly rolled to the right hoping to get some space between herself and the young man.

Eaton moved back to *Magellan* when she was 36 to care for her aging parents. On the year-long return trip she met and married an asteroid minor, who perished in an accident in the Spencer Belt two years later. Subsequently, she became the superintendent of education on *Magellan* and made friends with Kimberly Macready, mother of one of the waypoint's brightest students, Amberly. Macready introduced Eaton to a Marine officer friend of hers, Rita Moreno. Macready and Moreno were workout partners, and they also enjoyed playing competitive strategy games like chess and go. Eaton fit in, and for many years, the trio were inseparable. Eaton became particularly close to Kimberly and her husband, Alroy, when Eaton's parents both died within a few months of each other. She was especially fond of the Macready's precocious older daughter, Kora.

The captain's roll maneuver didn't buy her much time. She was still on her back and Ortega was about to bring his significant weight advantage to bear. Using only her legs and torso muscles, Eaton flung herself upward from her laid out position, landing on her two feet, and immediately headbutted Ortega.

"Mother of dirt—"

Ortega was disorientated, and Eaton leaped and tacked him to the mat, with one knee grinding into his torso, while her second leg provided leverage to force him down on the floor. She quickly seized his wrist, and though Ortega buckled, he could not overcome Eaton from her position of strength.

"Someone, grab me the dye pen," Eaton said. The chuckling Todum had it with him, and started to reach through the net and hand it to Eaton.

"Say it," Eaton laughed at Ortega.

"Awww crap, how did I lose again?" Ortega resigned and stop resisting. "Uncle."

The small group of onlookers gave cheers and laughs as Eaton took the dye pen and scribbled a red 'A' on his forehead.

"I love it when she brands them," a Marine onlooker told Todum. "A for April's bit–"

An artificial male voice came over the intercom. "Captain Eaton to the bridge. Priority beta. All bridge officers report for duty, priority beta."

"Well, I wonder what that's all about?" Eaton said, as she stood up and offered Ortega a hand. "You heard the VI. Let's get to the bridge and see what the trouble is."

Eaton was still hot and sweaty by the time she had ascended the five decks up to the bridge from *American Spirit's* gymnasium. "You had to interrupt my sparring victory? What's the situation?"

"Ma'am, security is reporting some sort of ... hostage situation," said Von Bumble, the pale-skinned 24-year-old Ensign who had the current command shift on the bridge.

"How do you have a hostage situation on a deep space ship?" said Ortega, who had trouble keeping up with Eaton.

"Can you route the security feed to my infopad, please?" Eaton asked her communication officer. He complied and within a few sections she was able to see images of a small exterior port she knew to be the toward the stern of her ship. She saw one of her security officers with his stun weapon drawn, pointed to the opposite end of the room. At the other side of the room, she saw Alan Martinez, a school teacher she vaguely recognized, and he held the hand of a young girl, maybe four or five years old.

Eaton's eyes widened when she saw Martinez had his hand on the port access button, and it was primed to open. Adrenaline hit her.

"Get me audio, dammit," Eaton growled. "He's going to blow them all out into space."

"How is that port door even able to be opened? Isn't it only accessible when connected to a gangway?" Von Bumble asked, seeming not as impacted by the situation as Eaton.

"Shut up and get down there with a Marine squad," Eaton shouted.

"Yes ma'am," Von Bumble straightened up and headed for the bridge portal. As he exited, the *American Spirit's* executive officer, Snodgrass, entered the bridge.

"What's this beta alert all about?" Snodgrass asked, scratching the back of his neck through his long black hair.

Eaton didn't answer. "Where's my audio, Ortega?"

"You're hot now, captain."

"Alan. This is Captain Eaton," April's voice was instantly carried over the intercom into the aft portal room. "Alan. I need you to let the girl go and then you need to step away from the portal."

"Captain Eaton, good. Good," Alan spoke into the air, knowing that the *American Spirit* surveillance systems would be relaying his message directly to Eaton.

"I'm glad I have your attention. Let's negotiate."

"There's nothing to negotiate, captain," Martinez said. "If you do not agree to my demands fully and immediately, I will release the portal and myself and the girl will be sucked out into space."

"Howzabout I stun you and take the girl," Eaton heard the security guard saying. Eaton rubbed her temples.

"I think you would find that quite fatal, because you too

would join us in space," Alan said to the guard.

Eaton quietly signaled her XO. She whispered to him, "I don't know anything about Alan. Pull everything we have on him. Find me someone who knows him. I'm flying a little blind here."

Snodgrass started executing the captain's orders, and Eaton spoke again with the hostage taker.

"Alan, you know that door cannot be opened. It has a failsafe mechanism and is sealed from the bridge," Eaton said, calmly. "Why don't you surrender the girl and let's talk."

"If the door can't be opened why are you scared to come and take the girl," Martinez said. "Is it because you know I have it? You know I have Macready's slicer."

A few seconds passed by. Eaton didn't know what to think. Kimberly Macready, her good friend turned traitor, now dead, was a genius code breaker. She had done the impossible during the battle of *Magellan* – hacked the master security codes on a waypoint. She had made code slicing devices and distributed them to her clandestine minions. The Marines intelligence had thought they had accounted for all the devices in the aftermath of the battle, but clearly, they had not. *Unless Alan is bluffing,* Eaton thought. *But why?* Even though Macready was gone, she was still haunting Eaton.

When Kimberly was thought to be lost in space so many years ago, Eaton's heart was broken. The loss of her husband, her parents, and her friends Kimberly and Alroy almost broke Eaton, and she withdrew from everything in her life except her work. Moreno tried to reach Eaton, but the Marine was also busy with her new promotion to Executive Officer and second-in-command of the Marines on *Magellan*.

"Nothing to say? Well, let me spell it out for you: The will of the Chairman will not be averted. You will free the Chasm operatives imprisoned on this ship. You will turn the *American Spirit* around and take us back to *Magellan*. Or this little girl will end up floating dead in space, like so many of my Chasm comrades you condemned. It's for the greater good."

"What, Chasm? A sleeper? How?" Snodgrass blurted.

"Hush," Eaton put a hand up in the face of her executive officer, then continued her discussion.

"Okay, Alan, as a show of good faith, I am going to ask the

security officer to lower his stun gun, then we can talk. Officer, lower your weapon."

The guard complied begrudgingly. The skinny girl seemed to relax some as the weapon was lowered. Eaton studied the girl's face. She didn't recognize her. The girl was really calm for a hostage, but perhaps too young to understand the peril of the situation, Eaton thought.

"Okay, Alan, now you know I can't turn this boat around," Eaton said, trying to recall some books she had read on the art of negotiation.

"Of course, you can. Let me be clear, if you don't issue the order in the next five minutes, I'll drop my hand from the release button, and the girl, your security guard and I get to become space debris. My hand is stuck to the release with some pretty powerful adhesive, so if you stun me, probably we go into space also. You turn off the gravity, I float up, and probably also trigger the door open. It's that simple."

"There's no way he's sliced the codes," Snodgrass said. "He's bluffing."

"Let me come down to you," Eaton said. "I'll trade myself for the girl. You can have me as a hostage."

"No, that doesn't work, Captain," Alan said. "You and I are alike. We'd easily sacrifice ourselves for what is right. You'd order your XO to flush us both out to space. But this girl, you wouldn't want her to go into space."

"Daddy, I don't want to go into space," the girl turned up and looked at Alan.

"Don't worry dear, this is for the greater good," Alan said, his voice wavering now. "We will be remembered in a perfect society forever. Now you be still like a good child."

Eaton's eyes sizzled with rage when she realized who the girl was. "Sick dirt-licking bastard. Your own daughter!"

"Now you see how much I am willing to sacrifice, captain," Alan said. "That is why I am going to win. I am willing to give up everything in order to fulfill the will of the Chairman. She will bring about the perfect order of humanity on Arara. My life, and Holly here, her life, are a small, small price to pay. Don't you see? The individual is not as important as the community. And even the community itself must at times be sacrificed for the State. The individual is nothing! Did not the Christian god even sacrifice his own child for his love of humanity? *Magellan* must be purged. We must go back."

"You are insane," the security officer said. "Don't you love your daughter?"

"I love her, but no more than all the daughters of the glorious revolution who will live and love in peace forever because of what I am willing to sacrifice today. Such a small price."

"You won't go through with it," Eaton said.

"I will," Alan said. "Because if I don't, then you won't believe the threats of the next one who follows, or the next. Holly's life now depends on you, captain. Turn the ship around. Free my comrades."

When Marine Commander Moreno offered Eaton the captaincy of the *American Spirit*, Eaton thought she would live some of her twilight years in peace on the long cruise back to Earth, then to retire to the beaches of Florida, perhaps. She never thought she would be negotiating with terrorists. And she had no idea what to do. There was no way she could comply with this madman. But she couldn't live with herself knowing that she indirectly allowed this four-year-old girl to die. *There must be another solution*, Eaton thought.

Suddenly a squad of marines filled Eaton's screen next to the security guard. She counted eight, half of the *American Spirit's* military complement. She also saw Von Bumble with them. They had their weapons raised and trained on Alan.

"Escalation? Really Captain Eaton, I had thought much more of you," Martinez said, as he held Holly tight. "You will be the death of this girl, captain. You are responsible. Choose your next move correctly."

Even from the dead, Kimberly Macready is playing chess with me, Eaton thought.

Von Bumble genuflected and reached out to the girl.

"Holly, honey, you need to come with me now, so I can take you home," he pleaded as evenly as he could, but nervousness still tainted his voice. "Your daddy is sick, and he may hurt you and we want to help you."

"All lies! All lies," Alan started to frantically yell. "It doesn't matter. Your time is almost up."

"Daddy, please don't be angry," Holly said. "I'm sorry. I will be good. Daddy, don't be angry."

Von Bumble scooted himself toward Holly. "Come here sweetheart. Let's get some ice cream. You like ice cream?"

"Daddy, can I go have some ice cream?" Holly looked at her father again.

"I'm sorry sweetheart, maybe tomorrow," Alan said, a tear running down his face, as he looked at a timepiece on his wrist. "At last. Time to be free."

"What is going on Alan? Alan?" Eaton shouted over the intercom.

"Don't you see, Eaton, you've been played. I knew you would never turn this ship around," Alan said, tears now flowing heavily. "But now you've been distracted and you are about to lose half your military force. I've bought the time my comrades need. The *American Spirit* will serve Chasm again."

"Von Bumble, get out!" Eaton shouted. The Marines looked to Von Bumble. The thought of fleeing flashed through Von Bumble's mind, but he knew the right thing to do was to risk his own life even for the chance of saving Holly.

"Come on, Holly," he pleaded, reaching his hand out to the girl. "Please we have to go, now." Holly looked confused. She held her father's hand tighter and leaned against his leg.

"I love you, dear," Alan said to his daughter.

"Get out!" Eaton shouted again. "That's an order!" The captain's voice echoed and the Marines started to back out of the portal foyer.

Von Bumble ran toward the portal in an attempt to make a grab at Holly.

"So long," Alan closed his eyes and opened the portal.

The vacuum emptied the chamber so fast that the intercom picked up none of the sound of the man, his daughter and Von Bumble being sucked out into space.

The bridge was silent. Eaton fell to the floor, dropping her infopad. She believed that she was leaving the conflict behind when she agreed to helm the *American Spirit*. She wanted to live her life in peace. Instead, like a dormant virus, they carried the Chasm infection with them, and a new conflict was festering a putrid puss. Her knees dug into rutted metal floor as she leaned against the command chair.

The faces of her Marines flashed through her mind, as she tried to sum the loss. She felt paralyzed and emotionally overwhelmed. And then she thought about Holly, the daughter of Martinez, who had been all but invisible to Eaton these past seven months. *How many more like Holly will die if I don't pull myself together*, April thought. She stood so swiftly she felt light headed.

She strode to an oval counter-height navigation table and summoned the other bridge officers on deck: Communications Chief Ortega, XO Snodgrass, and Engineering Chief Himari Grace. As they assembled, Security Chief and Marine Commander Shreya West entered the bridge, with a bullet rifle attached to a ready pack she wore on her back. Himari could see tear streaks on West's dark face, and she gently put her hand on her broad shoulder to comfort him.

They stood around the table, and though only a few moments passed, to Eaton, it seemed like hours of slow-motion heart ache. What would she say? How could she make this right? *Information first, action second, mourning later,* she remembers her own treatise on crisis leadership.

"Okay, let's get this situation under control. Then let's try to figure exactly who Alan was buying time for? A diversion? For what?" Eaton asked sternly. "Grace, what is the status of the hull and atmosphere on the Deck 3 portal foyer?"

Himari's black eyes scanned her infopad. "We lost minimal atmosphere – maybe 200 cubic meters of air, and the foyer is sealed. I've dispatched two techs to reseal the portal and they are onsite now.

"Good," the captain said, and then struggled to ask the next question. "Commander West, how many Marines did we lose?"

"All eight, and Ensign Von Bumble," Shreya said, choking back tears. "How in Hades can we fight these guys? If they are still hiding among us? I say we airlock Chasm exiles now. Clearly, if there are other Chasm sleepers on *American Spirit*, they feel they could free the exiles, they believe they have enough people to control the ship. We have no idea what they have planned, but we can't–"

Ortega interrupted the Marine. "We can't just summarily

execute those people. They were tried in a court of law. Besides, maybe Alan was just crazy and there are no other sleeper Chasm agents on board. Or maybe he was just bluffing."

"Maybe," the Captain mused. "We need to make a ship wide statement before the word of this terroristic act spreads too far. Ortega, start composing a message of reassurance to calm everyone–"

A soft rumble shook the ship.

The bridge crew exchanged worried glances.

"What was that? Was that what Alan was stalling for?" Grace said slowly, as she nervously pulled at her silky black hair. She grabbed her info pad off the table and called up a status report.

"Captain," she said, suddenly panicked, "explosion in engineering!"

"Snodgrass, you and Grace get a response team over there right away. Stay in constant communication with me. Use your personal scrambled radio and stay off the ship wide comms. I want a damage report ASAP."

"Yes, ma'am," Snodgrass replied and started for the door with the engineering chief in tow.

"Dammit. What the hell is going on?" Eaton muttered. "West, have your most trusted Marine report to the bridge armed in case we need security, and then go down to the brig and bring me somebody who can tell us how real this new Chasm threat is."

"Aye, captain," I'm on it.

CHAPTER SEVEN

Amberly did not come.

Dek Tigona remembered the last time he saw the object of his obsession. She had visited him at his cell on *Magellan*, when she told him she couldn't leave her home, not now when *Magellan* needed her so much.

Most of the Chasm agents and troops who were caught during the Battle of *Magellan* were ordered by the military tribunal to be executed. Nearly two dozen, however, had surrendered themselves before the battle ended in exchange for exile instead of termination.

With no hope of ever seeing Amberly again, Dek knew he'd have some rotten nights ahead. He wondered if he would ever get over the redhead. Did it even matter if he did pine for her until he died? Dek figured he would be in effective solitary confinement for the next few years – *something* had to occupy his thoughts.

He hoped of course, that he could petition the captain for more freedom soon. For now, Dek forced himself to be patient, not stir crazy. And thinking about Amberly — her soft face, her piercing green eyes, her petite figure, her dizzying intellect — seemed to calm him.

Dek often thought about the choice, when he had the brawny Marine North dead-to-rights at the business end of an assault rifle during the battle of *Magellan*. What would have happened if he filled the marine with lead instead of responding to Amberly's plea to spare the Marine? Would Chasm have won? Would he instead be a hero on the *American Spirit*, at the right hand of Raven One, heading not to Earth, but the promised land on Arara? Would he even still be alive?

If Chasm hadn't won, and he hadn't surrendered, Dek knew would surely be a floating body in space with so many of his compatriots, executed instead of exiled. Would that have been so bad?

Instead, first he lost the respect of his mentor and idol, Kimberly Macready, and then he lost his leader to the great void. Then he lost his love, the only woman who was amazing enough to make him rethink his worldview about the nature of men and women. Could the sexes be complementary when they embrace their intrinsic identities instead of shun them?

He looked around his grey cell, measuring a mere two meters by two meters. A bed hung on one wall, with storage for clothes, a supply of washcloths and a few personal artifacts. A fold out table hung on the opposite wall. In the corner, a cool metal commode and sink provided his only access to personal hygiene. The third wall had a portal with a food tray transfer door. Opposite the door was a pull-up bar, his primary means for exercise.

He did have access to a detention infopad. Unlike almost all other electronic devices, this infopad was entirely self-contained — no communication or network capacities. On it was a full library of books in almost every language, as well as a collection of nearly every movie and vid made, dating back to the 20th century. He'd recently watched the movie *Casablanca* for the first time, his interest piqued by the naming of the bar, Rick's, back on *Magellan*, where he had first met Amberly.

He probably watched the movie twenty times. He wondered who he was? Was he Rick Blane, the mercenary turned patriot? Or was he Victor Lazlo, the French resistance fighter, romantic and revolutionary? If he was Victor, why didn't Amberly come with him, like Ilsa went with Lazlo? If he was Rick, why couldn't he go to join the battle?

The infopad also had a word processor, and Dek had taken to writing critiques of the movies he would watch. Casablanca *is a timeless film, with themes that still stir the heart 600 years later,* he opined. *The popularity of the* Transformer *series of films makes me question how humanity survived for so long. I have been inspired, however, to watch the children's fables that are the source material for the films,* he wrote in another entry. Nearly a hundred times, like today, he had started to write a letter to Amberly – should he ever be allowed to send it – but couldn't get past the first sentence. Even after seven months alone in space, he couldn't find the words.

Dek put his info pad beneath his bed and started his daily clean up routine. He disrobed, grabbed a dry cloth from under his bed, moistened it at the sink, applied sanitizer and began to wipe down his body. His upper body mass had increased significantly during incarceration, owing to the endless pull-ups he would do. His arm muscles were taught and well-defined. He rinsed and wrung the cloth and repeated the process.

As he was putting fresh clothes on, his door chimed.

"It's Ramos," the man on the other side of the door said. "Would you like a visit today?"

Pastor Ramos, a thin, balding brown-faced man, had come again to see Dek. While Chasm traitors were not allowed to interact with each other in their confinement, they were allowed visitors. Ramos, was pastor of an evangelical congregation of about 35 that would meet on Sundays in one of the smaller common lounges. During the week, he would spend his time visiting as many of the Chasm prisoners as possible.

"Ramos," Dek said, "Come in."

A guard who had escorted Ramos placed his palm on a DNA scanner and entered a passcode. The door slid open as Dek pulled a clean blue shirt over his torso.

The guard looked at Ramos. "Punch the comm button when you are ready, preacher," he said as he locked the door.

Dek indicated the bed for Ramos to sit down, but the 60-year-old man declined, instead sitting cross-legged on the floor and leaning up against the wall. Dek shrugged and sat down on the bed.

"Would you ever help me break out of here?" Dek said dryly.

Ramos smiled. "No."

"Here is what I don't understand about God," Dek picked up from a conversation they left off on two days ago. "What purpose does he have for me here? Locked up in this space for the best years of my life?"

"Well, you can pray. Prayers are powerful. You know back on the waypoint, among the believers we had this popular little saying, 'the only thing that travels faster than the speed of life are prayers.'"

"Do you think that's true?"

"I dunno. I'm no physicist. I don't even have a theology degree. Maybe all God wanted was to give you a timeout so you would believe in him," Ramos said. "Do you think you would still be an atheist if you had won back on *Magellan*?"

"Do I believe God exists? I admit I would not have had so

much time to ponder the question as I have these last six… seven months," Dek said. "I'm not really sure that I believe that God exists. I mean, I want to believe, but how do I ever really know for sure?"

"That's what faith is about, my friend," Ramos replied, rubbing his hand on his bald brown head.

"That's an easy answer," Dek snapped back.

"Just because it's easy, doesn't mean it's not true," Ramos remarked. "You know, I think Amberly was a bad influence on you. If she would have come, maybe we wouldn't have become friends. She and her mother weren't exactly faith-friendly."

"Well, her sister and dad were religious," Dek said. "But yes, she wouldn't be too keen on my new religious… study. And that's why I am not sure if I believe, Ramos. I mean, I want to think there is more to my confined life then pull-ups and old movies. Maybe I believe because I want so much right now for it to be true."

"Maybe," Ramos yawned. "I could use a cup of coffee." Ramos looked around the room, but knew that prisoners had no personal food service of any kind. Just three meals delivered daily.

"This is why I know I don't believe. Because if Amberly were here right now, and she said she would never visit me again unless I disowned God, then I would disown God. How could anyone turn down the love of a real woman for the love of an invisible God?"

"You might surprise yourself," Ramos said.

"Or not," Dek said as he reclined on his bed. He abruptly sat back up and looked Ramos in the eye. "Why are you here? I mean, you are going to die on this bird if you don't get off on a waypoint along the way."

"Oh, I am going to die on this bird."

"But why? Why didn't you stay on *Magellan*?"

"Because I believe in God and his infinite love," Ramos said. "When I was younger, I was foolish and full of doubt. But I was blessed to have good friends in the faith along the way – Alroy Macready, ironically, was one."

"I don't get it," Dek said, turning to face the wall. "You didn't answer my question."

"God gave me the people I needed to carry me in my doubt, and now God has called me to do the same to others. That's what

I am doing here on the *American Spirit*. Freely you have received, the good book says, freely give. Someday, after I'm dead and my body has been cast to the stars, God will give you the chance to bless someone else. Maybe someday soon."

"God *called* you? You mean you heard God's voice? Or had some sort of a feeling?"

"Well I did have a feeling. But feelings can be deceptive. But God did tell me. It's right in the book. 'I was naked, and you gave me clothing. I was sick, and you cared for me. I was in prison, and you visited me.' Well, he called me to visit prisoners, and here I am," Ramos smiled and opened his arms wide.

"Sometimes I wish God would just... you know... give me a sign," Dek said.

"You don't need a sign, you have the good book," Ramos said.

A loud rumble shook Dek's cell, and the men exchanged inquisitive looks.

"That could just be a coincidence," Ramos said.

"Or it could be a sign," Dek stood up. "You should call the guard and go see what is going on. Come back and let me know!"

"You're probably right; I should go," Ramos said as he stood up and hit the intercom button.

A disembodied voice came through the speaker. "We're on our way to get you, Ramos," the guard said.

"Read through the book of Jude before I come tomorrow," Ramos said as he prepared to leave, "I'd like to see what you think about –"

The door slid open, and both Ramos and Dek were surprised to see three Marines, heavily armed. One of the Marines pointed his firearm at Dek while another cuffed his wrists. They all looked angry and crestfallen.

"Dek Tigona," the third Marine said. "Captain Eaton wants to have a few words with you."

After months of peaceful monotony, the bridge of the *American Spirit* was anxiously active.

The youthful zeal Ortega saw in Captain Eaton's eyes when she punished him in the sparring arena had transformed into a somber gaze. Eaton felt like she had aged 10 years in the past hour.

"Ortega, sound a general curfew. All crew and passengers,

except essential personnel, are confined to quarters until further notice," the Captain ordered. She turned to security chief West. "Pair off your civilian officers and have them patrol the ship, reporting back to you every fifteen minutes. I don't trust our electronic surveillance – it could be compromised. Kimberly Macready apparently gave her cult followers all sorts of toys to play with. If Chasm is attempting to sabotage *American Spirit*, we need to restrict their movement."

"Engineering Chief Grace is calling," the ship VI, Jefferson, interrupted the captain.

"Grace, what's going on over there?" Eaton asked as she sat back in her command chair.

"April, it's bad," Himari's voice came over the internal comm. "The explosion busted a crack in the antimatter housing and the core vented out into space. I've lost two people. My second lost her arm; I'm getting her to sick bay. We're lucky the whole ship didn't go up – the bomb wasn't powerful enough to bust the internal casing and the antimatter mix chamber."

"By design?"

"Hard to say."

"Are you sure it was a bomb, and not just a coincidental accident?" the captain rubbed her temples.

"We found traces of ammonium nitrate, so probably a bomb," Grace replied. "Captain, if our bomber was trying to disable rather than destroy us, they knew exactly what they were doing, exactly where to bomb."

"But why would they disable us?" the captain asked.

"If we find out who, we'll know why," West said. The main portal to the bridge slid open, and XO Snodgrass had returned. The captain shot him a look as a silent question, and he replied by shaking his head once.

"Bad news, April," Ortega looked up from the magnetic resonance screen at his post. "We've been knocked off course about point zero, zero two degrees. If we can't get navigational power back, we are going to miss *Waypoint Gilbert* by, I don't know, maybe several million kilometers now, assuming we can even slow down."

Eaton punched her engineer on the ship's comms. "Himari, can we get back on course?"

"I'm not sure, Captain. I'm still picking up the pieces here," Grace said over the bridge PA. "It's possible the reserves don't have enough power to redirect us and slow us down."

Eaton looked at her navigation chart. "Himari, so based on the vectors I'm seeing here, were going to be better off using our power to dead stop now, and rotate our heading to make a run for *Magellan*?"

"That sounds right, captain," the engineer said. "But I'll have to confirm those calculations. Let me get this fire put out captain. We'll figure it out."

"Copy," Eaton said. "Get engineering buttoned down, but be careful; I need you now more than ever."

"Without main power, we could limp back to *Magellan*, but it would take us four or five years," Snodgrass said. "No main power, it's hard to say how long we'll keep food synthesis running, much less life support. Captain, there's a good chance we're all dead already."

Everyone on the bridge fell silent, absorbing the news. Ortega started to sweat. West bowed her head and fingered her rifle.

"Unfortunately, I concur with the XO's position," Grace said over the comm.

"Understood, Himari," Eaton said. "Please immediately put the ship on minimum power consumption protocol. Only essential operations are to be powered at this point. And let's keep the artificial gravity on for now, too. Otherwise, any exceptions to be approved by me."

"Yes ma'am; Grace out," the engineer said.

"Options, ladies and gentlemen. I need options," the captain surveyed her bridge crew.

"Our best bet is going to be trying to make it back to *Magellan*," Snodgrass said. "I haven't read Ortega's latest transmission report, but there is no ship *en route* to *Magellan* that is close enough to have any hope of rendering aid. And we'd never make it to *Waypoint Gilbert* with enough power to slow us down, at least not with many of us alive."

"No one would be alive," West snarled. "We'd waste our power getting us in the right direction, and we'd just keep sailing by at half-light speed."

"But we don't have enough power to make it to *Magellan*

without the antimatter rectors either," Ortega said.

"Like I indicated, we're almost certainly all as good as dead," Snodgrass said. "But if we turn around now, and we get a message out to *Magellan*, they could send us some help. A runabout outfitted for custom range, maybe?"

"To fit a everyone on the *American Spirit* for months of space travel? Unlikely," West said. The door to the bridge silently slid open, revealing a bound Dek and his Marine escort. Ramos was also in tow, standing to the side.

"But they could send supplies and personnel to repair our antimatter core," April smiled. "Maybe. Still, I feel we are being tricked into going back — that Chasm has set us up to return to *Magellan* to finish the job. You all heard what Alan said. Are just playing into one of Macready's contingency plans?"

"I wouldn't put it past her," said Dek. The entire bride crew looked up, surprised by his presence.

"Reporting with the prisoner as ordered, captain," the Marine escort leader reported.

"Dek Tigona, condemned traitor, what do you know about this?"

"Nothing ma'am," Dek said, matter-of-factly. "I was unaware of any continuing Chasm activity."

"Liar," West seethed. "Maybe we should see if throwing him in an airlock will loosen his tongue?"

"Yeah, that would kill me," Dek rolled his eyes. "Then I'd be a great help."

"Now, West," Eaton sighed, literally putting a hand up to keep her top military officer from bounding across the bridge and physically hurting Dek. "Let's hear him out."

Eaton nodded to Dek, and he continued.

"Well, as you were speculating, Chasm always operated with contingencies. One of them was the Hawk program. Chasm Hawks were deep undercover, hand chosen by the Chairman herself, completely loyal to the will of the Chairman, and they were supposed to make sure, should a Chasm cell like mine fail, that our mission would still be carried out. No doubt Alan Martinez was a Hawk," Dek explained.

"Why didn't you tell us this a long time ago?" Snodgrass

demanded. "Withholding this information does give us grounds to rescind the commutation of your death sentence –"

"Whoa... wait a minute," Dek became defensive. "I always thought the Hawk program was a bluff or rouse or something to keep us in line. Just something the Chairman cooked up to scare us. And part of the point was that Hawks were completely anonymous, not supposed to reveal themselves until Chasm had full control of a waypoint, which we never had at *Magellan*, despite the best efforts of Kimberly Macready."

"Pastor Ramos, you are a good judge of character, is this traitor lying?" Eaton looked at the bald man.

"Well, um, I didn't want to get involved, I was just... visiting Dek in his cell when your Marines came, and –"

"And yet here you are," Eaton said. She quickly paced across the room and put a hand on each of Ramos' shoulders. "You know Dek as well as any of us. And if I can't trust you, I can't trust anyone. So just tell me your honest judgement."

"I don't think Dek is lying," Ramos said, looking Dek in the eyes.

West's eyes were wild with anger. "Well I think Dek is full of dirt–" A loud warning klaxon sounded, and immediately both Snodgrass and Ortega moved to their stations.

"What now?" Eaton looked to Dek.

Dek shrugged shook his head "no" and then brushed some of his brown locks from his eyes.

"Captain, low power mode disabled the cyber-warfare processors. Those guys suck up a lot of power applying encryption algo–"

"I know what they do, Ortega," Eaton was hot. "What is the alert?"

"Captain, it looks like someone was waiting for the hacking defense to go down," Snodgrass sighed. "And lookie. They've unlocked all the doors."

"The Chasm exiles!" Eaton steamed. "Kimberly! Dammit! We keep playing into her hands. Anyone else have any bad news?"

"Kimberly Macready is dead, Captain Eaton," Dek said.

"Then why is she still taunting me?"

The *Magnus* bridge VI Jefferson's disembodied voice spoke

through bridge speakers, "I am sad to report the Armory VI just told me it has been compromised. Several assault rifles have been stolen."

"This is not going to end well," Dek warned the captain. She gave a look of understanding back to Dek.

Two of the remaining Marines entered the bridge, both had their weapons drawn and were out of breath.

"Captain," the shorter Marine panted, "They're out. Chasm. They overpowered a pair of civilian security officers and they have weapons."

"West, secure the bridge," Eaton said, then looked around at the bridge crew. "They are coming for us."

"Captain, the doors won't lock," West replied. "The whole system is haywire."

"Barricade them," Eaton commanded. "They have the be physically on the bridge to set course. We have to keep them from finishing their plan, whatever it is."

Eaton looked to the console next to the command chair. "Jefferson, please reengage the cyber warfare security measures."

"I'm sorry captain, I've been locked out of all systems, as of two minutes ago," Jefferson said.

"On whose orders?"

"Yours, captain," Jefferson said. "You made them non-rescindable."

"I did no such thing. Oh, dirty hell," the captain swore again. She looked over at the junior tech officer, a twenty-year-old who looked green with nausea. "Caddo, shut down all automated systems with bridge manual override. Cut us from the ship network. And turn off Jefferson. He's compromised."

"What? I am noooooooottt...." Jefferson went silent.

"How many Chasm detainees do they have?" Ortega asked.

"There were 15 of us," Dek said.

"Will they all really try and take the bridge?"

"Of course, they will," Dek replied to the communications officer.

"West, bring me my sidearm," Eaton said.

The security chief opened the bridge reserve armory and distributed pistols to Ortega, Snodgrass, Eaton and Caddo. She offered Ramos the last gun.

"No thanks," the preacher said. "Give it to Dek. He knows how to use it."

"Captain?" West indicted the last gun and Dek.

"I am a pretty good shot," Dek said to Eaton. "I betrayed Chasm. If they get control of this ship they will kill me. I am with you."

The captain nodded her head, and West handed the firearm to Dek.

"That was a mistake," Snodgrass muttered.

Caddo and Ortega had unfastened the tactical conference table from the floor and flipped it on its side, blocking the main sliding door. A rarely used hatch was the only other method for accessing the bridge. Snodgrass broke a chair arm and stuck it through the hatch wheel so it could not be turned.

"What else do we have to secure the barricade?" Snodgrass asked the room.

"If you pry that panel off, there are some reserve oxygen tanks," Caddo said, pointing to a surface between bulkheads on the opposite side of the bridge. "Those are heavy."

"Until someone turns off the artificial gravity," Dek commented.

"Well, let's get them," Eaton said, and several of the bridge crew members went to work on the panel.

"What good will it do to hold them off? I mean they can just wait us out," Ortega asked.

"Hopefully, we can organize a counter-resistance," Eaton said. "As long as we hold the bridge, and we have the automated controls shut down, we have the power."

A loud series of pings resonated from door.

"Gun fire. They're here," West said.

"I've almost got the panel off," Caddo said.

"You know, putting oxygen tanks into gunfire might not be a good idea," Dek said, as he joined several of the bridge officers in taking up defensive positions against the door.

Caddo screamed.

"What is going on, Caddo?"

"Bomb! Bomb! Bomb!"

Underneath the panel was something Eaton clearly recognized as an explosive device.

"How long has that been there?" Ortega said. "Who could have planted that?"

"It must have been planted when Järvinen had control of the ship before the battle of *Magellan*," Dek said.

"You knew?" Eaton demanded.

"No. No," Dek said, putting his hands up defensively and slowly. "This is clearly the work of the Hawk or Hawks."

Some more gunfire hit the door, then it was forced open, only leaving the barricade between the bridge and Chasm attackers.

Snodgrass and two Marines rushed to hold up the barricade, which was still little more than the tactical table and a few flipped chairs.

"Ortega, can you deal with that bomb?" the captain looked at her communications officer.

"What? I don't have explosives training?"

"But you have basic electronics training," Eaton said. "See if you can find the power source for the detonator."

The flipped table began to slip a little. A voice shouted through.

"Captain Eaton, surrender the bridge or we will kill everyone on this ship," a young woman's voice carried from the other side of the barricade. Dek recognized the voice of Maria Alton, a small *tour de force* and a Chasm true-believer.

Eaton saw the Marines straining against what she figured were Chasm prisoners pushing on the other side. "You have one chance."

"Forget it," Captain Eaton snapped.

"You are making a big mistake, Captain," Maria said. "We have the power to end you now, but why do more people have to die? Let's save lives. Surrender the bridge."

Eaton waved at the bridge officers and crew, signaling them to ready their weapons. She made eye contact with Snodgrass, and her executive officer understood. He signaled to the Marines helping him prop the barricade. She looked over at a confused Ortega, and he looked back at her and shook his head. The bomb was still hot.

Eaton stood tall in the center of the bridge, stepped into an athletic stance, and drew her sidearm, aiming it right at the barricade. The others followed suit, until nearly a dozen firearms were aimed at the portal.

"You made the mistake. We know about the bomb," Eaton said. "This will only end one of two ways. Either we all die today, or you die. Either way you will die. So, prepare to meet your maker."

"How do we di–" Maria sputtered, but before she finished, the Marines holding the barricade suddenly dropped it down.

A spray of bullets filled the space where the barricade once stood, and soon after pocked the flesh of nearly a half-dozen Chasm exiles in the corridor. Misty blood drifted in vaporous clouds, and the muted moans of the dying filled the air.

"That was for Holly," Eaton said calmly.

"And Von Bumble!" Snodgrass shouted.

The sound of rapid footfalls projected up the corridor.

"There are more coming," Dek shouted, as he took a step toward the door to get a better view down the bridge access hallway. "Get ready."

Dek stepped into the hallway, his back to the bridge crew, gun drawn, and shouted. "Stop and surrender, now. It's over."

"Dek, what are you doing?" Ramos said between gritted teeth. "Eaton is going to kill all these guys. Stay alive!"

"Surrender, please, my Chasm friends, and beg for mercy," Dek said. "Let's stop the bloodshed now."

A person Dek did not recognize appeared in the hallway with his hands up. His face was scarred, and Dek figured from his thinning hair slight hunch that he was in his sixties.

"Dek Tigona," the man said. "I am one of two Hawks sent by the Chairman. She would be so disappointed in you. I'm sorry Alan had to die, but he knew the price of perfection. Come to me now, and you will be spared. Help us perfect humanity."

"Dek, I don't have a clean shot," Eaton said. "Get out of the way. There is no mercy that will tame this insanity. Dammit. Move!"

Dek was torn. He wanted to do the right thing, to end the bloodshed. He thought that God, if the deity existed, would not want him to murder an unarmed man, and hoped that Eaton and her crew would not kill unless they had to. *Maybe I am naive, but this is what I believe,* Dek thought.

"Just stand down," Dek said.

"Didn't Raven One tell you the legends of the Hawks?" the man said, stepping closer to Dek. Dek's gun was trained on the Hawk's forehead. "Didn't she tell you we will do anything to win?"

The Hawk smiled mischievously. And then Dek saw it. A remote detonator on the Hawk's sleeve. "Forgive me," Dek said, and he pulled his trigger.

Dek's aim was precise, and he put a hole in the middle of the Hawk's forehead. His eyes rolled back, but his smile became more twisted and bigger as he fell to the ground, his fist dropping the depressed trigger.

"Noooo!" Dek said, but his words were swallowed by the sound of the explosion.

A fireball expanded through the bridge, and the force of the blast knocked the Dek to the ground.

CHAPTER EIGHT

Dek woke to the sensation of being dragged across the metal floor. The rivets scraped his skin. He choked on an acrid haze. His eyes burned. Ramos was pulling the 70-kilo man toward the bridge. Fire suppression systems had already engaged, and XO Snodgrass handed Ramos and Dek emergency filter masks.

Dek's ears were ringing as he looked around, trying to get his bearings. He couldn't see much through the smoke and haze. The Hawk was dead, but Dek cursed himself for playing the fool and thinking he could show mercy. *Was everything lost because of my naïveté?* he asked himself.

"How bad?" Dek asked Ramos.

"Bad," Ramos said, through his mask as he rubbed his bald head.

Dek sat up and rubbed smoked from his eyes, trying to assess the situation. Snodgrass clutched a bloody arm to his chest. Dek could see bone and sinew protruding from what used to be the XO's elbow.

"Caddo, take this and make sure no one comes on the bridge," Snodgrass winced from pain as he indicated the sidearm in a holster on his hip. The tech officer reached for the gun and went to the main portal.

Dek stood and cringed as second-degree burns on his neck and arms smarted. The bridge lights flickered in sync with a pounding in Dek's head. Fragments of twisted metal and various carbon polymers littered the once orderly command deck. Dek look to the far side of the room, and his heart felt like it had been punctured. Two bomb-mutilated bodies rested near the hole torn open in the interior wall by the bomb. Dek didn't even try to hold back his tears as he recognized Captain Eaton and Communications Officer Ortega, both dead.

My sins revisit me, Dek thought as he strode over to the officers. *I will never be able to escape the evil I have brought.*

A Marine whose name Dek did not know was sobbing in the corner. Dek went up to the young woman, who he thought couldn't be much older than Amberly Macready, maybe 21 or 22. Her eyes were swollen from smoke and grief. She looked up at

Dek.

"Why?" she asked, as Dek pulled her into an embrace of support.

"It's difficult to explain," Dek spoke softly as the Marine collapsed into his arms, fully in shock. "But we are going to end this."

Dek looked over to Snodgrass. "There are more. They still need the bridge. They will come." Dek's eye was drawn to a firearm on the floor, half hidden under a charred wall panel. The gun was probably Eaton's or Ortega's.

A tapping came from the floor hatch. Caddo pulled his infopad off his utility belt and checked the bridge surveillance video feed. "It's Engineer Grace!"

Dek pulled the stick that had jammed the hatch, spun the wheel and pulled the heavy door on its hinge.

Engineering Chief Himari Grace, emerged from the hatch. Her white jumpsuit was stained with hydraulic lubricants and fresh blood. Her dark hair that had been pulled back was now loose and chaotically arranged around her face. Her eyes were dark and devoid of hope. Dek secured the hatch.

"I came back as soon as I could; I had to get my assistant to the medicenter," Himari said, looking to Snodgrass. "There is a force of about a dozen people, my guess Chasm, who are armed in the Starboard command deck observation room. So, I had to go around and down a deck and come up through the hatch."

"I'm so glad you are here, Himari," Snodgrass said.

"What happened here? Where is the Captain?" Grace said, scanning the room.

"There was a bomb... and," Caddo said.

"Oh, my Lord, no," Grace exhaled, reaching an arm out. West caught it and steadied the engineer. "What is this all about? What can we do?"

"I have a plan to end this once and for all," Dek said to Snodgrass, "but I'll need your guns."

"Not a chance you are getting our guns," West said. "In fact, I think your terrorist friends just forfeited your amnesty." West pulled his assault rifle and pointed it at Dek's head.

"Stand down, West," Snodgrass said, still clutching what was left of his elbow. "That's an order. I'm in charge now."

"How's that Snodgrass?" West replied, and took a step towards Dek. "There is no law out here anymore. It's broken. You have no power. I am going to do what needs to be done. What should have been done back on *Magellan*. Any last words, Chasm traitor?"

Ramos stepped between West and Dek. "No, this isn't right."

"Get out of my way preacherman," West said. "I am not afraid of God."

Dek placed his hand on Ramos' shoulder and nudged him out of the way. "Ramos, step aside." The pastor hesitated, so Dek more aggressively stepped around him, and was now less than a meter from the end of West's rifle.

"If you think it will make things better, West, go ahead," Dek said, raising his hands slowly and pressing his forehead into the barrel of West's gun. "Go ahead. I deserve to die. We all do. But... I can end the Chasm threat on *American Spirit* once and for all if you just trust me."

Tears rolled down West's eyes. Snodgrass slowly flanked West, let his injured arm fall to his side as he recovered a gun and pointed it at the insubordinate security chief. "Auuugh. Drop it, West. Drop it. Stand down, now."

"No!" West shouted at Snodgrass. "You'd really kill me to save this worthless sack of manure?"

"No, he won't," Dek said. "Snodgrass, lower your weapon. I'm ready to die, if West wants to kill me, let her. It will be all right."

"I *am* going to kill you, Chasm bastard." Sweat beaded on West's forehead as she felt the hard curve of the metallic trigger beneath his finger.

"West, listen to me," Ramos pleaded. "God forgives. We can, too."

"No, we can't," West said. "Dek Tigona, traitor to the *American Spirit* and *Magellan*, Chasm, now *you* die."

Dek closed his eyes and recalled something he'd read in the Hebrew scriptures about death, and recited it in his mind. *For I know my redeemer lives, and at last he will stand upon the earth; and after my skin has been thus destroyed, then from my flesh I shall see God.*

A shot rang out, and West dropped his rifle and clutched at

her heart, and then she fell to the floor, blood gushing over her hands. "What? Who…"

Caddo dropped his gun and ran to West and kneeled beside her. "I'm so sorry. But you were going to kill–"

"You," West coughed some words out, spitting in the direction of Caddo. "Curse you, Caddo. Someone kill Dek… so I can kill him again … in the afterlife." The light left West's eyes.

"Dammit," Snodgrass cursed as his mind reeled. As XO he would have to assume command of the *American Spirit*, a job he didn't want, especially without a security chief. He was at the emotional brink already.

Dek exhaled slightly. He was happy to be alive, but with Chasm not contained, the loss of West's skills would be felt. "I'm so sorry."

Dek looked at the people remaining on the bridge. Snodgrass, Caddo, Grace, Ramos and two Marines, whose names he didn't know. Everyone else was dead. The living were scared, and in Dek's estimation, Snodgrass was not up to the task of keeping the survivors on *American Spirit* alive.

Caddo looked over to Snodgrass, the implications of what he had done starting to sink in. "I… had to shoot West. She disobeyed a direct order… and she was going to shoot Dek."

"And what of it? I would have much rather of had Chief West than that Chasm prisoner if I had to choose," said one Marine. The other Marine, whom Dek had comforted over the loss of Captain Eaton, wiped tears from her eyes, and asked, "What if West was bluffing?"

"To what end? No one else had anything to fold," Caddo argued.

"You just shot the security chief, Caddo," the first Marine said. "You should be court martialed!"

The Marine pulled for his stun gun and aimed it at Caddo.

"XO, permission to stun and incarcerate this murderer," the Marine asked Snodgrass.

"I don't know…" Snodgrass said. Dek looked at the XO to give him a stop-the-madness look, but Snodgrass' gaze was distant, and he was trembling.

"He's in shock. Someone have his wound treated," Dek said. "Everyone, listen. I have a plan to neutralize Chasm. We must stay calm. Once we have eliminated the threat, I will return to the brig. We will mourn our dead after we survive this."

The other Marine grabbed her stun gun as well – only she pointed it at her follow trooper. "We follow orders. Put your weapon down until the XO says otherwise."

"XO?" The first Marine said, "What are your orders?"

"I … don't … know," Snodgrass said, as he sat down on the floor.

"Oh, he's losing it," Grace said. "Okay, everyone, stand down. I am invoking Deep Space Maritime Code 2.4. I'm captain now."

The Marines knew what Code 2.4 was. The Engineer was claiming that Snodgrass was incompetent, and she was taking command.

"Sir," Caddo looked to Snodgrass. "Are you okay with that?"

"Two… four. Yes. Sure, sure," Snodgrass said, growing more distant and focusing inward, wrapping his good arm around his legs while a Marine started bandaging his wound. "Listen to Himari."

"Okay, please put your weapons away," Captain Himari told the Marines. "Dek, what's your plan?"

In the Starboard Command Observation Room, the eleven remaining Chasm exiles, who had been incarcerated and isolated for seven months, gathered to plan their next move.

"Both the Hawks are dead. We don't know what we are doing," said Philonius Marcher. The Chasm agent, who was an assistant to Kimberly Macready for nearly a decade when she was working undercover in *Magellan's* Science Corp, was having second thoughts about the Chasm operation to take over *American Spirit*. "I mean, the Hawks busted us free like what, just over an hour ago. We were following their plan. But they are both gone."

"They both killed themselves so we could complete the mission," said Mirandi, a tall blond woman who had a menacing look that made Marcher shrink. "This is our chance to redeem ourselves. To succeed where Raven One failed us!"

"If Raven One couldn't finish the task, why do we think we can?" Marcher asked, dubious. A few of the others threw some comments of support.

"What choice do we have now?" Mirandi said, as she lifted her assault rifle off the ground. "We should storm the bridge while they are reeling from the bomb. Let's stick with the plan. What is the alternative? Surrender? Do you think they will just quietly put us back in our cell?"

"This is it then? So, we fight and die."

"No," Mirandi said, "we fight and win. The new world is destined. Let's bring it."

The observation room's comm systems crackled to life.

"Mirandi? Are you there? This is Dek Tigona on a secure channel from the bridge," Dek's voice projected from the speakers.

"This is Mirandi. Authentication codes, please."

"Tango, delta, three, beta, beta, four, zeta, alpha."

"Dek! The Hawks are dead, but we are armed and free. Join us, brother. Shall we complete what Raven One could not?" Mirandi asked rapidly. Already wired on adrenaline, the chance to be rejoined with Dek Tigona, favored disciple of Kimberly Macready, elevated her excitement.

"I have good news for you, sister. I have captured the bridge," Dek announced. "Captain Eaton is dead, and I have the first officer as a prisoner, along with the rest of the bridge crew. I have secured their firearms. But it will only be a matter of time before Earth loyalist reinforcements arrive. How many of us are there?"

"Eleven, sir," Miranda beamed.

"We'll need everyone here on the bridge now," Dek said through the speaker. "I have five people held at gunpoint, so I'll be compromised if I have to take my attention off them to face loyalists. So please hurry."

"*En route* already. We're just a minute or so from your position," Miranda replied. She raised her rifle and looked at the others. "We don't need the Hawks. We have Dek. Let's go."

"But Dek betrayed Chasm," Marcher said. "Can we trust him?"

"None of us is pure," Miranda said. "We all pleaded innocence or ignorance, which is why we are exiles and not among the executed. Dek did what he had to do at the Battle of *Magellan*. So did we. And now we have a chance to make it right."

With nothing left to do, Marcher raised his weapon and

followed Mirandi out of the observation room.

When she arrived on the bridge a few minutes later, Mirandi liked what she saw. A pile of weapons, mostly sidearms and a few assault rifles were in a pile on the command chair. Between the chair and the starboard side of control stations were a pair of Marines, Executive Officer Snodgrass, Chief Engineer Grace, and another officer she did not recognize. All were kneeling, with their hands clasped above their heads.

She saw Dek, his messy brown locks seeming more dramatic than the last time she had seen him – more than nine months ago, with his arm outstretched and a stun gun in hand. Across the bridge, she saw several bodies – one she recognized as Capt. Eaton's. Mirandi smiled.

"Is this everyone?" Dek asked, as Mirandi led the Chasm group on the bridge.

"Yes, yes," Mirandi said. "We're all here. Do you have a plan to turn us back to *Magellan*?"

"We can probably get ourselves pointed in the right direction, and if we get our calculations correct, and we leave an AI active to do last minute thruster corrections, we can use *American Spirit* as a sub-light missile to decimate *Magellan*, once and for all," Dek said.

"That's not going to happen," Himari said, clenching her fingers tightly over her head. "You'll never get me to cooperate, and I'd like to see you get this bucket of bolts turned about without a chief engineer."

"I think we'll manage," Dek said flatly.

"There's no way," Himari said again, her face flush. "I swear, I'll blow this whole thing sky high as soon as –"

Dek pulled the trigger of his stun gun, and Himari Grace slumped to the floor, passed out.

"Don't think I won't shut the rest of you up," Dek said, and then briefly took his attention off of the bridge crew he held at stun point to look around at the eyes of the Chasm exiles. He could tell they were ready to follow his command, to the death. He knew Kimberly Macready would want him to take advantage of his position, to destroy *Magellan* and make the chasm between Earth and Arara, once and for all. But Raven One was dead. Dek used to believe there was no afterlife, but now he wasn't so sure.

Would the spirit of Macready be trying to influence his thoughts? Would she try to control his actions from the undiscovered country?

"We're probably all dead," Dek said. "Without the antimatter core, life support and food generation systems will fail. We'll all be dead well before we reach *Magellan*. But since I intend to use this ship as a missile – what our lost Sparks failed to do – and destroy *Magellan*, we will die anyway. We just won't be alive to see the glorious conclusion of the final voyage of this grand vessel. But time is short. We must move quickly – every minute we have less power to get our grand work complete."

Dek could almost hear Kimberly Macready's voice resonating the words coming from his mouth. "Now, let's secure a perfect humanity."

The group of rebels nodded in agreement, and the four remaining un-stunned *American Spirit* crew grumbled as Dek's stun gun threatened them.

"Okay, everyone, please each of you take a control station, and I am going to tell you what to do." Dek motioned to the control panels, five on each side of the bridge, and the Chasm conspirators slowly fanned out across the bridge.

"First, we need absolute control of *American Spirit*. These have all been locked down by passcode, and we need to enter the correct code, simultaneously to unlock them. If we don't do it with the correct timing, it may take us months we don't have to manually take control of all the ship's system. We don't have months."

Mirandi noticed Ramos in the shadows.

"What is the preacherman doing here?" Mirandi said, leveling her assault rifle at Ramos.

"An innocent bystander," Dek said. "He was visiting me when the first Hawk, Alan, sacrificed himself. Then Capt. Eaton over there stupidly summoned me to the bridge so I could tell her all the Hawk's Chasm plans – so they made Ramos come along, too. He is a neutral player and will stay out of our way."

Marcher the assassin spoke up, also aiming his assault rifle at Ramos. "I don't trust him."

"Quite frankly, Marcher, it doesn't matter if you trust him or not," Dek said. "I am in command here, and I have decided to let

Ramos meet oblivion the same time the rest of us do, not before."

"God will decide who dies and when," Ramos said, somewhat defiantly, with his arms crossed.

"Let's not delay destiny any longer," Dek said. "Grace here," Dek pointed at the stunned engineer on the floor, "thought she could slow us down by putting a little unlock puzzle on the control panels."

As the Chasm agents took their place in front of each terminal, the magnetic reconnect screens came to life with two sets of numeric keypads, spaced on the far side of each screen.

"Okay, this is important," Dek said slowly. "I am going to give you the code, four pairs of numbers. Each pair has to be entered on each screen – one number for each number pad – within one second, or we have to start over."

"What happens if we get it wrong?" Marcher asked, as he set down his assault rifle in front of the console and hovered each hand in front of a keypad.

"I'm not sure, but my guess is that too many wrong tries will lock the system down," Dek replied, eyeing Marcher's rifle. "Okay, is everyone ready? On my mark, enter the first pair of numbers: two-seven. Counting down, five ... four ... three ..."

The Chasm conspirators, facing away from the center command chair, needing both hands to enter the codes, all begun to set down their rifles.

"...two... one."

The group all frantically punched in the numbers, and at the same time, Dek raised his stun gun and shot Mirandi. She cursed as she hit the floor hard.

Several Chasm agents started to flip around to see what happened, and Dek quickly put two more of them into a shocking sleep.

"What the heck!" Marcher flicked his assault rifle up with his leg, caught it and started to take aim at Dek's back. But before he could pull the trigger, he also sank to the floor, caught in a stun beam.

Two of the agents looked over at Ramos, who held a small stun gun forward. Ramos clearly had never used a stun gun before was shocked as he saw Marcher writhing on the floor. Both the Chasm rebels simultaneously started reaching for the rifles they had been tricked into setting down. Before they could reach them, they fell unconscious as well. This pair had been taken out by stun bolts from Caddo. At the same time, Snodgrass has also pulled out his hidden stun gun and put three other Chasm operatives into a deep sleep.

Dek flipped around and stunned two more, and soon, there were 11 Chasm operatives with slight convulsions, sleeping unpeacefully on the floor with Grace.

"Did you have to stun Grace?" Caddo asked, with an annoying amount of whine in his voice.

"I had to sell it," Dek said.

"Let's airlock the chasm traitors before they wake up," one of the Marines demanded, as he looked over at the dead captain. "They surely deserve it."

"No," Dek said, a natural authority resonating in his voice. "No more death today. Zip bind them and lock them up."

"We don't take orders from you," the other Marine growled.

"Now you do," Snodgrass said. "As XO, I am placing you under Dek's command. If we are going to survive this, Dek is the guy to lead us. He's got the stuff."

"Are you serious?" the first Marine asked. "He is a Chasm traitor."

"No," Snodgrass said slowly. "Actually, he betrayed Chasm... twice. He's in command, at least until Chief Grace comes around. I mean *Captain* Grace."

Dek felt sick to his stomach. The inertia dampeners always made him ill, and they had been on for five Arara 28-hour days as the *American Spirit* slowed to a full stop. He sat in the command chair that had been piled up with decoy weapons just a week earlier. Dek watched as some of the maintenance crew worked to repair the damage caused by the Chasm Hawk bomb. He was amazed at how quickly the scars and char from that blast had been erased, almost as if the horrible, desperate Chasm gambit had never happened.

"Grace to Tigona," the comm unit crackled to life.

"Dek here, go ahead Captain," Dek replied. As the new XO of *American Spirit*, Dek had come to be trusted by Captain Grace. The captain respected the roguish turncoat as being both resourceful and cooperative. With the Chasm sabotage thinning the command ranks, Grace knew she needed to take advantage of natural leaders if they were going to survive. Now doing double-duty as chief engineer and captain, Himari found herself needed off-bridge, instead leaving Dek in the command chair while she oversaw the efforts to shore up the batteries and backup generators. They were going to need every watt of power to have any hopes of getting in range of a *Magellan* rescue team before the batteries drained and life support failed – and they all froze or suffocated in the nothingness of deep space.

Dek beamed. He didn't know if Ramos' prayers had inspired divine intervention or if everything that had transpired was the product of infinite randomness, but he was now heading in the direction he wanted — toward Amberly. While his chance of survival was worse than a coin-toss, his chances of ever seeing Amberly again had improved astronomically. Dek would have risked even more, betrayed deeper, sacrificed all, he knew. *For the love of a woman*, Dek thought. *No, for the love of one very special woman.*

"Okay, XO," Himari said through her comms. "Confirming spacewalk to begin the manual conduit bypass from cell bank C to cell bank D. This should buy us at least another month of life support – if we can tap into the D bank."

"It's too dangerous, Grace," Caddo said loudly over Dek's shoulder. Caddo was acting Security Chief now, though promotion was not his ambition when he killed the previous chief.

"It's no problem," Grace said. "Believe me, in six months, you are going to be glad we did this. I got this." Her words and steady voice did not betray her anxiety.

"Spacewalks make me nervous in the best-case scenario," Caddo said. "One snag on your suit… or exposure to antimatter residue… or…"

Because of damage from the first Chasm bomb, Grace knew her space walk through jagged and twisted steel fragments and shards was risky. The sabotage assured there was no internal access to many of the batteries — the only way to get there was by going out a nearby airlock into space and maneuvering over and through the gaping hole in the side of the *American Spirit*.

"Are you sure there isn't another engineer who could install the conduit," Dek asked, "you know, someone more expendable?"

"Leadership 101, Dek," Grace said. "Don't ask someone to do something for you that you would not be willing to do yourself. That's what April taught me."

"Yeah, I read her book, too," Dek sighed.

"I'm a go," Grace said to Dek. She then spoke to the *American Spirit* VI. "Jefferson, please begin visual scans and loop the XO into your report. Open the airlock."

Caddo nervously looked over at Dek. "Maybe we should have asked Ramos to pray?"

Captain Himari Grace. As she rolled the phrase in her mind, she chuckled audible. *Who would have thought?* For a woman who had little ambition, the fact she was now master of the *American Spirit* seemed absurd. Her breathing echoed in her helmet.

As the airlock slid closed behind her, she reached out and attached a carabiner to a handle on the exterior door. She let herself float for a second, free of the artificial gravity created by the *American Spirit*.

"Whoa," Grace said aloud.

"Is everything alright, Captain?" Dek's voice projected from the speaker in Himari's helmet.

"Fine, fine," she replied, "Just getting used to the weightlessness. I suppose we'll have to shut the artificial gravity off at some point to save power. Soon you'll be 'whoa-ing' too."

Pulling herself arm-over-arm she ascended the dorsal fin midway to the open wound inflicted on *American Spirit* by the first Chasm bomb.

Suddenly, she felt her suit get snagged hard by a jagged piece of ripped hull obscured by shadow. Grace stilled herself as her heart rate jumped. The sharp metal would have torn through most materials, but Grace's suit was made of advanced flexible polymers, capable of withstanding significant puncture pressure. She freed herself from the snag, pushed her self away from the ship, and examined the damage close up.

"I'm so sorry baby," the engineer spoke softly to her ship. She peered into the dark hole. "Activate headlamp." Grace calmly asked Jefferson. The light flicked on and she gasped.

"Captain? Everything OK?"

"I'm fine. Things are not OK. Both cell banks C and D are leaking. Rapidly." Grace reached for her supply pack to find some space-worthy adhesives. She didn't expect to have to do a patch job.

Jefferson offered some unsolicited perspective. "Captain, the damage to the inertia dampeners in this area of the ship has created ruptures on the batteries. We are fortunate you are out here to catch this problem now."

"Jefferson, analyze the leakage and calculate the impact on the return to *Magellan*." The engineer moved to pack D, and very carefully worked to avoid the acidic fluids erupting from the power cells.

Jefferson answered her question in his calm, nearly monotone artificial voice. "Captain, at the current rate of loss, each minute reduces the viability of the *American Spirit* in maximum conservation mode by roughly two days."

"I'm patching D now," Grace said. She expertly applied emergency adhesive to the poly-patch, careful not to accidentally stick it to her suit. If she did that, she'd never get it off.

"Please use caution captain," the Jefferson said. "The battery fluid is highly corrosive."

She pressed the patch down quickly and it sealed, but not before a spirt of acid shot in her direction. She threw herself out of the way into space, and for a second wondered if she had attached her safety cord.

The sharp jerk of the cord when it had no slack left to give comforted her, and she pulled herself back to the ship on the two meters of cable that had extended. The force of the pull seemed to have agitated the leak in the C bank, and now it was gushing acid.

"I'm moving to patch C," Grace said dryly.

"Please be careful," Dek said.

"No time, no time," Grace said. She didn't have to ask Jefferson to know they were losing weeks of power.

Reaching back into her pack, she produced another patch, and applied the adhesive.

"Patching C now," she reported.

She pushed down on the leak, and managed to seal three sides of the square patch, but fluid continued to escape from under on corner of the patch in a misty spray. She frantically punched down on the corner and the leak sealed.

"Now I just have to connect the conduit," Grace talked through her next task. The misty acid had formed a crystalline cloud in space. Grace eyed it nervously, and pulled out the conduit. The cloud was drifting toward her.

"Come on, come on," Grace grumbled as she stretched the power cable between the two battery banks. "C connected."

Jefferson triggered an alert inside Grace's helmet. The acidic cloud was dispersing, becoming wider, but less caustic.

"D connected."

Grace could hear the cheers from the bridge.

"Great job, captain," Dek said. "Come on home."

"Wilco," the captain said. "Dek, I may have a problem."

The menacing acid cloud was less than a meter from Himari now.

She jumped to avoid the hazard, pushing off the hull with her legs – but didn't clear as much distance as Grace hoped. Her safety chord was tangled in twisted metal. The acid crystals hit her suit, and heat escaping from the suit immediately melted the crystals. Quickly a thousand micro holes were burned through the polymers. Grace knew she had seconds.

"Dek, I'm out," Grace said. "I'm sorry."

"Grace, what is going on?" Before Dek had finished his question, half of Grace's suit had dissolved. She tried to respond again, but didn't have enough air left to speak.

Jefferson spoke through the bridge comms. "Himari Grace's suit has been compromised."

"No! Grace!" Dek said. "Grace! Talk to me!"

"Captain Himari's vitals have flatlined."

Everyone on the bridge looked to Dek Tigona, the new captain of the *American Spirit*.

CHAPTER NINE

Waypoint Magellan, December 13, 2603, Earth date, 14 months after the Battle of Magellan.

To Amberly, Dek Tigona looked as if invisible weights were crushing his beautiful soul. His brown hair was gloriously messy; his lovely grey-blue eyes seemed dim. Her heart ached for him, and she wished she could reach through the vid and hold her mysterious one-time suitor in her soft arms. His arms looked *hard*, and his pinched face made her think he had lost a few kilos since she last saw him on the eve of his exile.

The recorded visage spoke with a positive energy that seemed anachronistic considering the desperate circumstances of the *American Spirit*. "This is Dek Tigona, captain of the *American Spirit*. This will be our last tight-beam transmission, as we hope to conserve power to keep life support alive long enough that any rescue effort launched by *Waypoint Magellan* will find people to save, and not just equipment. Jefferson has finally finished the navigation calculations. Our path will take advantage of gravitational impacts and keep us at a velocity that could be matched by rescue vehicles. All the data is in the attached nav chart. You know where we will be and when we will be there."

Amberly did some quick math in her head. This transmission was sent, traveling at light speed, more than three months ago and if the *American Spirit* was traveling at top speed, roughly four-tenths the speed of light, it wouldn't have even covered half the distance to *Magellan*. And the *American Spirit* wasn't traveling at top speed. How long would the reserve power last? She tried to calculate how much time they had to rescue Dek and the survivors on *American Spirit* before life support gave out. She didn't have the right data to do the math, but once she saw Jefferson's navigation chart, she'd know the odds of success.

Dek's recording continued, "We'll try to keep everyone alive until a rescue team – should you decide to send them – brings us what we need to repair the antimatter generator. We've taken all non-essential systems off line, including artificial gravity. We've deployed our stellar radiation panels, but there isn't much sun in this nowhere patch of space. Our lives are in your hands now, and we have faith that *Magellan* will live up to its purpose."

Amberly looked around at the assembled *Magellan* leadership in conference room adjacent to the Command Center. The *Waypoints* were built to serve the deep space-farer traveling the light years between Earth and Arara – and provide hope that help wasn't too far away if things became critical. Everyone in room had been taught that this was the fundamental reason of existence of every waypoint. They had said oaths to that effect as early as grade school.

Moreno had seen Dek's last transmission already, so her focus was on how others would react. Gov. Thor Rillio, whose own family had died when an antimatter accident put their ship out of reach decades ago, was struggling to hold back tears. Lieutenant Boro, a veteran who had seen some of the most intense combat during the battle of *Magellan* and who was briefly aligned with Chasm before betraying them to *Magellan* authorities, was less moved. *Dek cannot be trusted*, he thought. Although he had been fully pardoned, his own guilt consumed him. *No one who sided with Chasm should be.*

Officer Trot Wilder had a stone face, masking the mix of excitement, stoic duty and fear that turned in his thoughts. He was tapped by Thor to lead the rescue flotilla of three Valkyrie-class runabouts to save *American Spirit*. If Jefferson's calculations were correct, the flotilla would intercept the *American Spirit* in about a fourth of an Earth year. There was no margin for error. Without accurate data on the deep space ship's supply levels, number of survivors, and power drain, it was hard to know if the flotilla could reach the *American Spirit* in time. If they were able to make repairs, and get the *American Spirit* up and running to full power, they would load the flotilla on the massive cruiser and be back in *Magellan's* safe harbors in six to nine months.

Because of the deadly risk, Trot had wanted to leave his beloved Kora and baby Alroy, but Kora insisted that they come. Trot remembered her argument. "I've lost so much family letting them go without me," Kora had said, tears streaming down her face. "And now Amberly is leaving for Sonnet. I will never leave your side. Alroy and I will follow you wherever you go. Your duty is our duty, and we will face it together as family, do you understand?"

Moreno examined the features of Councilman Skylar Trigs. He had trimmed his golden locks in favor of a more practical haircut. He'd also grown a beard. Trigs was going with Amberly to Sonnet, and he was sweet on Amberly, Moreno knew. She worried that if Trigs and Amberly became romantically involved, and such an involvement did not hold fast, that the fallout could jeopardize the whole Spencer Belt operation. Sonnet had an unhappy history for love lost. Still, she was glad to have that overly ambitious-if-not-charismatic glorified radio operator off her waypoint for a while.

As the video of Dek continued, Amberly thought about how she had lied to Dek, just over a year ago, when he was in a *Magellan* cell waiting for exile on the *American Spirit*. She told him she loved him – because she didn't have the strength for the truth. She had taken advantage of his love for her to save *Magellan*. She used Dek, just like her evil mother used people, manipulating them through deceit. Only, her ends justified the means, she thought.

What ends? She thought about her beautiful sister with her flowing black hair holding baby Alroy. *New life. We endure. Even here in the middle of deep space. Those ends justified the means.*

"One final message, which could be our last," Dek continued. "As the last captain of the *American Spirit*, I'll use my prerogative to make it a personal one. Amberly Macready, I know the odds are against us, and I will probably never see you again. Still, the glimmer of a chance has become a bright flame of hope."

Maybe I should have warned Amberly about this, thought Moreno as she remembered Dek's public profession. *Oops.*

"Amberly," Dek said, looking directly in the camera, "I will do everything in my power to get us to *Magellan*, to home, and if I make it there, I am never leaving again. There's no one from Earth to Arara like you. Your brilliance. Your beauty. Your amazing capacity to love and inspire love. All my heart, Amberly. See you soon, *Magellan. American Spirit* out."

Amberly had gone beet red. Standing next to Amberly, Trigs, her aspiring beau, shifted his weight uncomfortably. Lydia stood on the other side of Amberly and leaned toward her ear to whisper, "That was a little overdone."

Trigs heard the whisper, and awkwardly said, "He's right, Amberly. You are amazing."

Thor, somewhat ignorant to the romantic positioning going on, but one of Amberly's biggest supporters – who never stopped reminding everyone that if it weren't for Amberly, her mother's evil plan to destroy *Magellan* would have succeeded – raised his fist in the air. "Three cheers for Amberly, hero of *Magellan*." The assembled crew awkwardly followed the governor's suggestion.

Amberly wanted to die. Lydia took her friend's hand. Amberly looked for an exit from the Command Center to escape this unwanted attention when Boro spoke up with a *non sequitur*.

"This plan is crazy," Boro said. The Marine, dark-skinned, tall and muscular, expressed his doubts. "Even if we make it to the *American Spirit*, there is no guarantee we'll be able to revive the *American Spirit* antimatter reactor. And we'll have no margin of error without an antimatter reactor ourselves."

Boro was leading the security detail for the *Elcano* flotilla, named for the captain of the only surviving ship from Ferdinand Magellan's historic circumnavigational voyage around the Earth. He also was serving as the command officer for the *M.S.S. Firebird*.

The flagship of the flotilla was *M.S.S. Nautilus*, commanded by the mission leader, Wilder. The third Valkyrie, *M.S.S. Palomino*, was commanded by a young *Magellan* engineer, Kuuku Akachi. Just 25 years old, Akachi had already proven herself as particularly resourceful during the rebuilding of *Magellan*. She shored up critical radiation shielding by recycling polymer compounds from large fragments broken off the topside garden's viewport during the Battle of *Magellan*. As an engineer's mate, she had worked for *Magellan* Chief Engineer Zelma overseeing maintenance on the waypoint's antimatter reactors for nearly four years.

Akachi sported an attractive figure, standing just over one and one-half meters tall with a smooth asymmetrical cut for her dark hair. She had striking, deep brown eyes that drew attention to the smooth copper skin of her face. She rarely smiled, but when she did, she lit the room.

"Boro," the young engineer countered, "we are here to save lives. To be an island of salvation in the Great Spaces." She considered the Marine, who was in his dress uniform for this final top-secret mission briefing. "If you are going to command the *Firebird*, you must believe in the great purpose of the waypoints. This is it."

"Kuuku, my child," Boro spoke slowly, mixing his words with a hint of condescension, "you are idealistic, but you are young and naive. I was once as you are—"

"Lieutenant," Rita interrupted her recently commissioned officer. "*I* am neither young, nor am I naive. Akachi has the spirit we need for this mission to succeed. She is correct. If you do not believe in the mission then perhaps we should find someone else to take your place."

"No, Commander," Boro's tone became humble. "My apologies. I am ready to do my part to save the *American Spirit*, even if that means we don't return."

"We're coming back, Boro," Wilder said. "We've run the simulations. We've done the math. We know the *American Spirit* trajectory."

"I know what we know, Trot," Boro said, putting his hands up to stop his friend from continuing. "What I am worried about is that we don't know what we don't know."

"You better come back," Moreno said to Wilder with a modicum of jocularity. "You are taking Skip, and Amberly is taking Skylar. Those are our best communications techs. Who will I have to decrypt those love letters for Mission Commander Macready I keep getting?" Moreno smiled, and her display of soft emotion put the assembled team, except Amberly, at ease.

The Marine commander stepped four paces across the Command Center to where Amberly was standing. She took both of Amberly's hands, and the older woman squeezed them. "I hope we rescue the *American Spirit*, but your mission is the one that must succeed, my dear Amberly. My instincts tell me Chasm will be back. You'll make sure we are ready."

Amberly and Moreno's preparation to secretly launch a team to establish a permanent base at Fuentes Station had only one flaw – how to keep it a secret when the supplies and contingency of nearly 30 engineers, miners, biologists, Marines and others were leaving *Magellan*.

The distress call from *American Spirit* presented the perfect cover. Amberly's team would take a Valkyrie, the *Magnus*-berthed runabout *Liberty* and a pair of corvettes pretending to be part of the rescue flotilla. And then when they were well out of visual and most signal ranges, the secret Spencer Belt team would part ways with the *Elcano* fleet, and any deep Chasm operatives would be none the wiser.

Once again, Dek Tigona, your timing is impeccable, Amberly thought. Part of her wished she could go with her sister and her brother-in-law, but she knew she was the best candidate for this mission. There was no one else with her talents. And as Morneo had said, harvesting new resources from the Spencer Belt was essential to the long-term survival of *Magellan*. Amberly wasn't particularly vain or egotistical, but she was self-aware that she had amazing problem-solving skills, not unlike those of her mother.

Moreno looked as though she was about to give a motivational speech as she surveyed the leadership teams for both expeditions. Instead, she took a deep breath and kept it brief. "You know your jobs. Shove off in six hours. Get to work."

"We'll be praying for you," the governor said.

At 20 years old, Amberly felt weird sitting in the command chair of the *Liberty*. Alone on the bridge, she looked out the viewport into the endless inky blackness of space. Off the bow of her ship, the darkness was broken up by the white blooms generated by the propulsion units on the *Palomino*, *Firebird* and *Nautilus*. Their engines were powering up for weeks of acceleration.

The thruster's ambient light illuminated barge containers the *Palomino* and *Firebird* had in tow. Essentially a steel lock box made in space, these barges had no propulsion ability or life support. Inside one barge was extra batteries, emergency oxygen, food and other supplies. If that barge were lost, the flotilla would have to turn back.

The second barge held repair tools and supplies to fix the antimatter chamber on the *American Spirit*. If the chamber could be repaired and restarted, the amount of energy generated would be more than enough to ensure a safe return for the cruiser and the *Elcano* flotilla. Kuuku had engineered the rigging between the barges and Valkyries with enough strength to ensure that any structural stress from the long acceleration would not cause detachment.

"Verne, can you bring up the aft camera view please?" Amberly had requested that her VI be installed on the *Liberty*. When they arrived at Sonnet, she would transfer Verne to help her manage Fuentes Station. She needed a VI she could trust and with which she felt comfortable.

An image of a slowly shrinking *Waypoint Magellan* covered the viewport. Amberly couldn't take her eyes off the spinning, grey-metallic waypoint. Beams of light pierced dark space from the windows and ports scattered across the exterior hull. In just a few minutes, the waypoint would be just a speck of light, and not long after that, invisible to the naked eye. *I hope I make it back, dear friend,* Amberly thought as she gazed softly at her diminishing home.

The scars inflicted on *Magellan* by the hand of her mother were not as visible as they once were. Her home was healing, and that thought made her smile.

Skylar Trigs quietly stepped on the bridge and silently leaned against the portal's frame. His eyes took in the unaware Amberly. He admired her beauty, but he was even more impressed by her intellect. Over the past few months, he found Amberly lived up to her impossible reputation. *She really does have her mother's genius,* Skylar thought. He observed her thoughtful fixation on the waypoint as it diminished in the screen. *Someday, she may become one of the greatest leaders humanity has ever seen – if she can grow beyond Magellan's small stage.*

"We'll be back soon," Skylar said. Amberly jumped out of her chair.

"Skylar – you startled me!"

"Sorry." Skyler tipped his head toward the waypoint. "Even for a short time, I'll miss her. Don't worry, we'll have a home to return to, Amberly, because you are going to save it."

Amberly sat back down and returned her attention to the viewport. She took a deep breath. She felt that Skylar understood the value of *home* the way she deeply did. To Amberly, *Magellan* was more than a mass of bulkheads and airlocks. It was more than an engineering marvel. The place grounded her. *Magellan* was her identity. Amberly suspected that her mother's longing to return to the Lewis Islands on Arara was akin to the love she had for her waypoint. *Skylar gets that. Skylar gets me.*

Skylar walked up behind her chair and placed his hands on her shoulders. "You'll complete this mission. You've got this."

"We're going to do this together, XO," Amberly looked over her shoulder and smiled at Skylar. He slipped his hands off of her shoulders and resumed his seat at the communications station.

Amberly turned her seat to look at her friend.

She hadn't gotten used to Skylar's new hairstyle, the masculine crew cut. The new look jolted her with something positive, but she did miss his golden, romance-novel style locks. His neatly trimmed beard was also growing on her. She imagined what it would be like to kiss someone with facial hair.

Besides an unfortunate smooch with the gangly and somewhat smelly Mike Opal when she was just fourteen, the only men she had ever kissed were Dek and North – both on the same day, she recalled. She believed, irrationally of course, she would learn something from the kiss with Dek, but it only left her … unsatisfied, confused. And as much as she had enjoyed the kiss with North, Amberly knew it was laced with deception, something she regretted still. *The History of All the Boys Kissed by Amberly Macready, the shortest book ever written,* she mocked in her head.

"I'm not intimidated by him, you know," Skylar said, as he checked the heading on his magnetic resonance screen.

"I'm sorry," Amberly said after a brief moment, shaking the kissing memories from her head, "not intimidated by whom?"

Skylar looked over at Amberly. "Dek Tigona," Skylar said. "I know you were … special friends."

Not this, again, Amberly thought. She remembered North's jealousy of Dek and how she felt when those two peacocks started puffing their plumage. *Why is Skylar bringing Dek up?*

"Let's just focus on the mission, okay," Amberly said, starting to get feel her face turn red from both anger and embarrassment. She wanted to end this topic of conversation with Skylar, permanently. "I made my peace with Tigona when he left *Magellan.* I wish him well, but I wonder if he'll make it back alive. He may already be dead."

Amberly hadn't considered the idea that Dek may have already perished until the words came out of her mouth. She was surprised how much she still cared. A flood of emotions hit her, and she worked to keep her composure in front of her second-in-command. The thoughts of Dek and North reminded her that she felt alone – *except when Skylar was near.* She forced the lonely feeling back down, attempting again to ignore its existence.

"But you told him that you loved him," Skylar stood and stepped toward the command chair. "Where does that leave us if he shows up at Fuentes Station or back at *Magellan*?"

Amberly stood up and faced Skylar, her blood now starting to boil. *How could Skylar presume so much?*

"Us? What *us*? You tell me. Where does that leave us?" Amberly demanded.

"Now that you ask," Skylar snapped back cynically, "why would the hero of *Magellan* and the Mission Commander want to hanging around with a lowly comm operator."

"I don't know!" Amberly raised her voice, stepped face-to-face with Skylar, piercing him with her brilliant green eyes. She was so angry at Skylar for trying to frame their relationship as something that he knew was not a good idea. But another part of her wanted him, like forbidden fruit. She was fighting that part, as she suspected he knew. *Why won't he just come out and say what he means?!* Amberly thought, then said slowly, in a more diminished voice, "Why would the oh so honorable councilman want to lower himself to slum with a red-headed lab rat?"

"Well... because..." Skylar reached his arms out and took Amberly's head and pulled her into a messy kiss.

Oh, wow. Amberly's mind raced.

She pushed herself out of his grip, her furious face still covered with conflicted emotion. Her temples pounded.

"What the hell, Skylar! That was totally inappropriate. I am your *commanding officer*," Amberly said a little too loudly and stood away. But despite her words, her impulse was to throw herself back into his arms. She was parched with loneliness. Amberly had ignored it, denied it, pretended the emotional solitude did not threaten to consumer her. Skylar's kiss was cool water on her dry pain. She could no longer avoid how real her desolation was.

And the kiss excited her, that kind of so-wrong-it's-right kiss that Kora had talked about before life got so complicated.

But she had a mission, and the wisdom of her mother echoed in her head: Romantic relationships would only serve to distract her from her destiny. She remembered the exact day her mother said it — the day Kimberly Macready left 13-year-old Amberly, presumed to be lost in space. It was a day she would never forget.

Mind over heart, that is the way it must be, Amberly thought.

"Don't stand on protocol now," Skylar whispered.

"Skylar, you are special to me, but.... I can't afford to be distracted. Not now. The mission is too important."

"Amberly, don't stop us. We're good together. You know it's true." Skylar stepped closer.

For some reason, Skylar's lovely blue eyes seemed to validate his point. She got lost in them, trying to read his thoughts, questioning her own. *Good together,* Amberly repeated Skylar's words in her head.

The pair stood silently for a few moments.

She was buzzed with confusion and desire. *Good together,* she thought again. *Maybe we are.* Amberly stared unflinchingly at Skylar as she pulled the back of her hand over her mouth.

She pushed herself up on her toes and threw her arms around Skylar's neck, plunging into a kiss at her pace, slow and powerful. Her pulse raced.

"Oh, snap, I was right," came Mars Dino's voice from the portal, lifting his infopad to snap a picture. Amberly and Skylar shoved away from each other so fast Skylar fell back into his seat. "Maria bet me that it would be at least four months before Amberly gave in. I *knew* it wouldn't take that long. And Maria says I don't understand anything about women!"

Amberly wanted to melt into the floor. Skylar was half-embarrassed, half-happy. *This is the right direction,* he thought.

Amberly sat down in the command chair and started fidgeting with her infopad.

"Friends," she mumbled. "Just friends."

"Yes. I can see that," Mars sat down at the navigator's chair and started checking for space debris.

Skylar stepped toward the door. "I'm going to go help my other *friends* with kitchen patrol." He exited.

Amberly decided she was going to pretend she was invisible for at least the next week. She knew it would take much longer to figure out what to do about Skylar Trigs.

The *Elcano* flotilla, three Valkyries towing two barges, had taken the lead from what Midas had dubbed the *Macready* flotilla – a single Valkyrie and two smaller corvettes. *Magellan* had nearly emptied itself of all its runabouts and fighters for the two simultaneous expeditions. With nearly 15 hours of travel between them and the waypoint, Amberly knew it was time to say goodbye to her sister and her family.

The *Macready* flotilla would now alter course for the Spencer Belt, and *Elcano* group would try to intercept *American Spirit* before it was too late.

"New course set, awaiting your order, Amberly," Verne spoke to its master through the bridge PA system.

Amberly tried to hold back her tears. She was looking at a live video of Kora, Trot and little Alroy in his father's arms.

"I know you will take good care of my sister, Trot," Amberly smiled at her brother-in-law through the video feed. Just then, Alroy made an unintelligible gurgle. "And my nephew, too. You are going to be so big when I see you again."

A tall, athletic blonde stepped into the frame. "Amberly, make us proud at Sonnet. I expect there to be a luxury hotel complete with swimming pool built on that asteroid by the time we get back."

"There's not enough gravity on Sonnet to hold down a pool," Amberly heard Skip's voice say off screen.

"Always crushing my dream," Lydia shook her head and smirked. "Always crushing my dream."

"Have you decided what you want me to tell Dek?" Kora asked her sister. "We're going to find him alive … and the first thing he is going to do is ask after you. Do you want me to tell him your secret?"

"Which one," Amberly asked half joking, and then nervously glanced at the rest of the *Liberty* bridge crew. She knew Kora probably meant how she left Dek thinking that she still loved him. Although she had strong emotions for Dek, Amberly believed she never really loved him. She used the pretense of love to manipulate Dek in order to save *Magellan*. The gambit paid off, but since he was exiled, Amberly figured that she would never see

Dek again. She thought it an act of kindness for Dek, imprisoned on the *American Spirit*, to continue to believe the fiction that Amberly had lingering romantic interest in the roguish rebel.

But maybe the secret Kora meant was if she should not tell Dek about the hottest gossip the flotilla had to offer — that a certain redhead scientist-commander and her charismatic first officer were seen making out in deep space.

Or the secret that she had given North a clandestine method to contact her. In the second it took for her to consider these options, Amberly panicked.

"No, no, no," she said with a bit of panic. "Don't tell him anything."

"Well, what should I tell him then?" Kora said, slightly amused, slightly concerned for her little sister.

"I don't know, you'll have at least two or three months of floating in space to figure it out," Amberly sighed. "I am going to miss you so much, Kora."

"We've never been apart this long," Kora said. "I'm going to pray every day for you. You know what North likes to say, right?"

"Yeah, prayers are the only thing that travel faster than the speed of light," Amberly remembered.

"So it's like I'll be with you every day," Kora sniffled, holding back tears.

"I'll send you regular vid updates. You guys better get going, Kora," Amberly said, now crying openly. "Go save, Dek."

"You go save *Magellan*. Again."

The Spencer Belt was not at an optimal distance from *Magellan* in its current orbit position, but it wasn't outside the range of a Valkyrie. The waypoint normally kept a rough synchronic position with Earth, enabling the city in space to be found with relatively low-tech navigation systems. So as the asteroids orbited Spencer Minorum, the distance from Sonnet, the largest asteroid, and *Magellan* was variable. At its closet point, one could travel from *Magellan* to Sonnet in less than a day in even a small, slow ship, like a corvette.

At its furthest point, it would take months for a speedy deep space ship like *Magnus*, to make the trip. Corvettes and Valkyries, unless they were towing extra batteries, just didn't have the life support range to travel when Fuentes Station was on the far side of its orbit. Instead, they would have to wait until Sonnet swung around again on its six-year orbit, riding the asteroid back into range of *Magellan*.

Nearly a week had passed since the *Macready* flotilla had parted with the rest of the *Elcano* flotilla. The ships were still nearly two weeks out from Fuentes Station. Amberly, who was naturally introverted, was already going crazy trying to find some solitude on *Liberty*. Besides the bridge crew, 15 other members of the new Fuentes Station team were riding along. She wished she had traveled on one of the escort corvettes now. Sure, they were cramped, but she would not have had been forced to interact with her team.

She had studied about the mystique of leadership, in particular the books by April Eaton. Eaton had warned new leaders about how certain types of followers tended to put their leaders on pedestals simply because of the position they held. "You'll find that some people find security in placing their faith in the leader, which sometimes leads to an unhealthy lionization and expectations that the leader can do much more that she is actually capable of," Eaton explained in her book, *The Mind of the Follower*.

Eaton also offered advice for new leaders about ambitious lieutenants in her most famous book, *The War Within*. "The worst situation is when the leader has two equally successful and talented subordinates both jockeying to sit at the right hand. Both have claim on the glory seat, and if the leader cannot figure out how to give both the glory they deserve, she will end up with at least one disenchanted human resource, and if she is not careful, the talent of both will the castrated," Eaton wrote.

Both Moreno and Thor, accomplished leaders in their own right, put great faith in Amberly's abilities. Amberly really believed that their faith was misplaced, but also felt that her duty compelled her to accept this assignment. *Or maybe it's my guilt*, she thought, ever aware of her participation in her mother's schemes. *North is right. I am responsible for so many deaths. Now I must make it up to my home waypoint. No matter what it costs me.*

Amberly sat up in her bed. There were six other makeshift

bunks that had been added to the small quarters, all filled with dozing members of her team. Unlike her fellows, Amberly was not able to sleep. She had been plagued with insomnia, and was hopeful when they arrived at Sonnet, she could rest better. But they were still ten 28-hour days out. She slipped out of bed, grabbed her kimono, and quietly stepped into the Valkyrie's upper deck hall.

She heard Skylar and Wong discussing political theory on the bridge, and though Skylar was pleasant to be alone with, the super close quarters of the *Liberty* had given her more than enough Trigs time for now. And she was definitely not interested in a conversational threesome about politics with Wong and Skylar. She'd rather walk out the airlock. Which gave her an idea.

She slid down the hatch to the lower deck. Maria Dino was reading her info pad in the mess. She looked up and gave Amberly a knowing smile and then went back to her book. *Probably another noir novel*, Amberly thought, musing of her friend's love of crime capers.

Amberly walked a few yards into the approach to the airlock. Alone at last. She connected earphones to her infopad and requested Verne play music by Claude Debussy, her favorite composer. As "Claire De Lune" played, she sat and looked out the small airlock portal into the infinite void. Spencer Minorum was beginning to outshine the other stars due to its proximity, but that wasn't saying much. This insignificant star system, along with *Waypoint Magellan*, occupied a nearly empty part of space.

She slumped down the wall, sitting cross legged with her back leaning against a natural curvature in the airlock. As the strings played, a horrible, shocking memory came back to her.

A year ago, in an airlock foyer on the *Firebird*, a Valkyrie runabout not much different than this one, she discovered her mother, Kimberly Macready, was alive. And then her mother subsequently murdered a man — Joti, loathsome in his own right — by forcing him out into space.

She wondered if that was how her mom killed her dad. Then she tried to push the thought out of her troubled head. But the thought persisted. Somewhere in space both her parents were floating for infinity

In spite of it all, I think they really did love each other, she thought. She didn't know if she really believed it or just hoped it was true. At any rate, there was no way for her to know.

Amberly finally felt familiar tiredness behind her eyes. She closed them, and her mind danced in the space between the conscious and unconscious.

Half-dreaming, Amberly imagined her dad's floating body sometime finding her mother's, reunited in the vacuum of space, reunited in love, until both their bodies floated into the gravity pull of some atmospheric planet, and then falling like a burning star, going out together in a blaze of glory.

She smiled as she fully gave into the temporary abyss of sleep.

L.S. ROEBUCK

CHAPTER TEN

U.S.S Magnus, en route to Waypoint Marquette, November 28, 2604, 25 months after the Battle of Magellan

"*Marquette* isn't where she's supposed to be," Cho told the secretive gathering of *Magnus*' top officers in the captain's conference room. Cho pointed to a blip on a scan report on the room's magnetic resonance screen. "See, this here is an antimatter signature. On the next scan, we see it moved again. *Marquette* is on the move."

"How do we know that's not an antimatter signature from another deep space ship like ours?" North asked.

"Well, it could be," Blight explained. "But the one that should be coming from *Marquette's* waypoint anchoring is gone."

"Logically," the captain said, "If *Marquette* is not destroyed, it has been moved. But why?"

Nyota blurted. "They're hiding from us. Which confirms they know we are coming with guns blazing."

"They don't know we can track antimatter signatures, because the technology was invented a few years before *Magnus* left Earth," Cho reasoned. "They must think they are hidden."

"I know we are close to *Marquette*, but these signatures are months old. Couldn't *Marquette* be anywhere?" Rhodes asked.

"Moving a waypoint is not like moving a ship," Bollard reminded Rhodes. "They have minimal thrusters for evading space debris and keeping Earth sync. The engines that pushed the waypoints from Earth to their anchorage were designed for one-way trips, and their materials were repurposed once arrived."

"I've had Condi run a constant analysis on the signature," operations chief Blight said. "Based on current trajectories, we can reasonably expect the *Marquette* — or whatever that is — to be around *here* if we plot to intercept." Bight pointed to the upper corner of the projected map.

"They don't know where we are, and they don't know *we know where they are*," Obadiah mused. "I like that tactical advantage."

"It's hard to spot us now, with their older tech, when we are traveling at half-light speed. But as soon as we get close enough and we start decelerating, they'll have plenty of opportunities to spot us, especially if they are looking. We're big enough."

"Size matters?" North asked. Nyota looked at Blight and rolled her eyes.

"Absolutely," Bollard said. "We have all sorts of electromagnetic wake that continues on ahead of us as soon as we slow down. This wake will light up their sensors."

"But a smaller ship, like say, the *Prime*, would be harder to see coming?"

"Well, likely yes. It's possible the *Prime's* wake would hit a sensor, but not likely. And it's relatively small, so it's not obvious that the signal noise was created by a ship. It could be a radioactive meteor, or something."

North smiled. "I have a thought. No, I have a plan."

The mission prep had taken several weeks, and Sparks was ready to put North's plan in action. She sat on a toolbox in the *Magnus* hanger bay. The air was chilly, and she pulled her knees to her chest, looked over at Ryder and fumed.

Ryder could tell she was getting to Sparks, and she silently smirked back. The she-spy leaned seductively against the outer hull of the *Prime*, *Magnus'* most capable runabout. Ryder pulled out a vapor stick and slipped it between her lips. Sparks couldn't tell from where she magically produced the puffer: Ryder's skin-tight red dress did not provide many opportunities for concealment. She took a drag from the stick, then blew gray vapors from her mouth and nostrils in the general direction of Sparks.

Sparks didn't like being held in check by Ryder. Ryder knew too many of Sparks' secrets. She knew that Sparks intended to hook North in any way possible and use him to achieve some unknown end. She knew Sparks was much more dangerous than any of the Earth loyalists realized. And worst of all, Sparks thought, was that Ryder knew Sparks knew Ryder's secret: Ryder was an active Chasm agent.

Sparks had the thought she should have ratted Ryder out the moment she and North rescued her from the *Iron Star*. But she didn't. And now, if she turned in the Chasm intelligence officer, everyone would ask why Sparks waited *over a year*? Sparks' own switched loyalty would be questioned, and there were more than enough crew and Marines onboard *Magnus* who were still looking for an excuse to send Sparks on a long walk out a short airlock for her destructive role in the Battle of *Magellan*.

For her part, Ryder played along as an innocent bystander. Sparks knew that Ryder didn't know her true loyalty, and that was because Sparks didn't have a true loyalty – except perhaps to herself. In the end, Sparks was a survivor – and an adrenaline junkie just looking for the next rush. Sparks was the bright center of her own universe, and progressives and traditionalists and loyalists and Chasm were just playthings for her entertainment.

Another point of friction between the two was the man Arvin, who died a few months after being brought on board. Sparks had suspected that somehow Ryder kept Arvin in a coma, perhaps by contaminating his IV fluids. But Sparks had no evidence. She also wondered if somehow Ryder had secretly murdered the one person besides Sparks who could expose her.

Sparks didn't know why she cared about the final fate of Arvin. If he had survived and exposed Ryder, there was a good chance that Ryder would take down Sparks with her. Maybe her desire for justice for Arvin was the bad influence North was having on her. If Sparks could prove Ryder did murder the comatose Arvin, Ryder would have to decide if she wanted to out herself as Chasm so she could expose Sparks' deception just to spite Sparks.

At some point the friendly fiction that Sparks and Ryder maintained would have to end. *If Ryder thought I was really with the loyalists, she would have killed me a long time ago*, Sparks reasoned. Ryder considered that Sparks had the potential to be duplicitous, but why would she be? If Sparks incriminated Ryder, Ryder would just return the favor. Mutually assured destruction. Thus, they had remained allies of necessity for the time being.

But something had created a new tension between them: North.

The Marine commander stepped out of the main port of the *Prime*. North's eye was immediately caught by Ryder, drawn to the feminine curves not-so-hidden by her tight clothes. He flashed a gigawatt smile at her, set down his equipment and pivoted to face Sparks.

"Hey, sorry I kept you waiting for so long," North shrugged. "I wanted to triple check the operational details. It's a bad habit, but—"

"Oh, no," Ryder interrupted, "I'm glad you are so thorough. So many things can go wrong. Who knows what sort of armed resistance we will find when we board *Marquette*? Let's make sure our runabout gets us there smoothly."

North turned from Sparks back to Ryder. Sparks frowned.

"Are you sure you want to come with us, Ryder," North asked, catching her dark eyes from behind her dark bangs. "There's no guarantee any of us is coming back."

Ryder twirled her vapor stick aggressively and stepped toward North, putting her pale hand on his bicep. "I don't have anywhere to go back to. They took my home, and now I want to make those bastards suffer. You didn't lose *Waypoint Magellan*. I lost *Cortes*. I am going to kill every last Chasm scumbag."

Ryder extinguished her vapor stick by pushing it into North's chest as she said the word *kill*. Behind North, Sparks rolled her eyes and stifled sarcastic laugh. Ryder was good, and Sparks reminded herself for the hundredth time not to underestimate the master spy.

"Well, when I first carried you off the *Iron Star*, I would never have imagined you to be the fighter that you are," North mused, as he recalled Ryder's nearly undefeated record in *Magnus'* sparring ring.

"You still haven't sparred with me, North," Ryder said North's name as if something sweet was passing through her lips. "Afraid I'll beat you?"

"I don't spar with girls," North shrugged. "Call me old fashioned."

"And sexist and weird. Careful, your old-fashioned prejudices might be your demise. Sparks is a powerful female. I bet Sparks could take you."

North looked over at Sparks in her trademark rubberized black jumpsuit. Definitely female. Definitely powerful.

"Well, now," North said. "I've seen her fight. She's savage. Of course, Sparks is like... family to me. That another reason not to spar with her. But she couldn't beat me." Sparks openly rolled her eyes.

"I guess we'll never know," Ryder teased.

"Please. If Sparks and I ever went mano-a-mano at the gym, I'd win. We both know that," North elbowed Sparks. "Speaking of the gym, Sparks, you still want head down to get a workout in? I need to burn off some pre-mission nerves."

Sparks smiled slyly at Ryder. She felt like sticking her tongue out at her overdressed frenemy, but she resisted the impulse. "Sure North. Meet you there in 15."

Sparks held the punching bag as North beat it with right and left hooks.

"Why don't you spar with women?" Sparks asked as she held the bag steady. "Centuries of female empowerment, and sexism is still living the good life rent-free in your head."

"I guess I respect women too much. I don't like to hurt women." He wiped his forehead and dropped to the floor for push-ups.

Sparks let the bag hang. "I'm trying to decide if I am talking to North the 'prick' or 'idiot'. You are so full of dirt. How can you not see how condescending 'I-don't-want-to-hurt-poor-petite-defenseless-damsels is?'" Sparks said, and then began to punch the bag rapidly.

"Let's go with 'idiot'. I suppose that can be seen as condescending," North said through a series of push-ups. "Still, when you consider the biological differences, sparring can be dangerous and–"

"Don't fool yourself," Sparks dropped to the floor next to North and began to do push-ups at twice North's rate. "You hurt women. Take Amberly, for example. You hurt her."

North stopped mid-push, rolled over, and sat on the floor next to Sparks. Her bringing Amberly up threw him. "Quit being cute. You know I meant I don't like to hurt women *physically*."

"You like to hurt them emotionally, then?" Sparks was getting winded.

"Of course not," North exhaled. "Why are you being an ass?"

"My natural state." Sparks stopped her push and sat cross-legged next to North on the gym floor.

North usually enjoyed Sparks' spunky nature, but she was

about to max him out.

"I did hurt Amberly," North's eyes burned with bitterness and sweat as he caught Sparks' gaze, "and even though I didn't mean to hurt her, *I was wrong* to hurt her. Does that make me a hypocrite, because I punished Amberly for hurting us all, even though she didn't mean to? I don't know." Sparks suddenly felt pursuing this line of discussion with North was not wise, and she started to look for an exit.

"You're many unmentionable things, but you are not a hypocrite. I'm sorry. Bringing up Amberly was a low blow," Sparks said with an authenticity that surprised North. Sparks was always hiding behind sarcasm; this rare transparency was … attractive.

"No foul. Don't worry about it," North smiled and leaned back on his hands, brushing against Sparks' legs.

They sat quietly for a moment.

"You know why I think Chasm will fail?" North broke the silence. "Because they live outside of reality. Take gender. Women and men are not the same. Men are physically stronger. Women are more nurturing. Men are more individualistic. Women are more communal. Men and women are *intrinsically* different."

Sparks smirked cynically. "Ah, back to misogynistic butthead status. Men are not better than women."

"I didn't say men are better. I said men are *different*. That's reality. But forget your vaporous reaction to my misogyny. What about Kimberly Macready — misandrous husband murderer? *You* followed her to hell and back. How many men did that man-eater leave in her wake?" North shot back. "Kimberly Macready modus operandi was to use, then trash, her men. Isn't that what Amberly did to me? You all do it. Ply us with your damn wiles, throw your curves at us, so we'll drool and do whatever the dirty hell you say."

Sparks didn't expect to hit something so raw. She wanted to change the subject. She reached out with her hand and gently touched North's shoulder. "Hey, I'm not perfect. I've manipulated my share of losers. But I never claimed first-class angel status."

Sparks humility cooled North again. Muted, he looked away from Sparks and continued his diatribe in little more than a mumble. "Society has been trying to deprogram the natural differences of women and men for centuries, and it never works. We always revert to the natural order. God gave humans natural order, and we keep trying to break it."

Sparks frowned as North invoked deity. She didn't respond because it was a no-win conversation, when she needed a win. She rolled away from North toward the bench with her gear pile, popped up, grabbed her water bottle and took a swig. She sat on the bench, following North with her eyes as he stood and moved to the towel rack. He grabbed two.

North sat down next to Sparks, handed her a towel, and studied her attractive, bright face. He had come to really care about her, and he wanted her to understand what he saw as the folly of Chasm ideology. "I'm just saying Kimberly. Johnson. Amberly. *You.* You think you can rewrite the universe's source code. If your dear Chairman wins, and she gets to rebuild a society that suits her warped vision, eventually nature will tear it down. Like a sand castle on the beach. The ocean always wins, every time."

"She's not *my* Chairman. Not anymore."

Sparks understood how important North's worldview on this point was to him. She had her opinions on the topic, but they didn't animate her. When she was honest with herself, she recognized her motivations had always been Sparks-centric, even when she was playing for the "common good" team. She wanted North to understand that she wasn't hung up on Chasm ideals. Not now, and not before.

After a few moments of quiet, Sparks opened up.

"I am going to let you in on a secret," Sparks said, as she pulled the rubber band off her strawberry blonde ponytail, her hair falling across her shoulders. "I never really cared about Chasm, not really. I didn't care about the cause. Chasm was always about the journey. Where is the biggest fire? Where is the brightest light? That's where I want to be. When it's my time to go, I am going to go out as the brightest flame."

North focused on Sparks' words. They felt … honest to him. She leaned against his shoulder. "You know, I never thought I'd survive this long. Maybe when this war is over, we can take a break. Maybe I'd learn to *like* peace. I once visited the Lewis Islands when I was on Arara. That is the place I think of when I picture what peace looks like."

North remembered aloud. "You know, I'd like to see the Monet Sea again myself. We should go. I may never make it back to *Magellan*, but I may get to hear the waves crashing on the eastern shores of Ingram. Or maybe not. Tomorrow may be our last."

"I'm not afraid of the coming battle," Sparks opened up. "I'm not afraid of the infinite darkness. I guess what I fear is emptiness. I'm ready to go, I just don't want to go alone."

"Sparks, you know whatever happens tomorrow, I'll be with you. Whether we make it out alive or die trying, we're in this together." North reached an arm around Sparks shoulder, and absentmindedly started playing with her soft hair. Sparks pretended not to notice, but her heart beat accelerated.

"We're going to win this thing," Sparks said, trying to make a contagious smile. She turned her shoulders and faced North. "We're going kick the Chairman's old, skinny butt. And maybe then we'll find some peace together."

"You and I, we don't get to have peace," North frowned, looking into Sparks' deep green eyes. He noted they were not to dissimilar to the color of Amberly's. "We're broken. We're the kind of broke that doesn't get fixed, I think. I'm not sure there will a place for people like us in the bright world of Morenos and Macreadys. That is the legacy of a soldier. We pay the price of war."

"Meh. Don't get all broody on me. The dramatic soldier doesn't look good on you," Sparks tried to spin the situation. She needed him to be positive; otherwise, her disposition would be to follow him downward. "I know you think Amberly and you could never love each other because you're broken. You may be right. But Amberly will never be able to love anyone else, either. Who could get over you?"

North gave Sparks an incredulous look.

Sparks took North's hand tightly in hers. "I know my sister better than you think. We were mentored by the same woman, remember? You know what else I know? I know she would want you to be as happy as you could be."

North rolled Sparks words in his mind and after a brief moment chucked, "You are *not* Amberly's sister."

Sparks gave her emotions some space to rise. She had nothing against Amberly – in fact, she respected Raven One's younger daughter, but she wanted North. What was Amberly to North anyway? Whenever she was brought up, it seemed North was either be mad at the redhead or mad for her. *For a man, he is so confusing.* North needed to let Amberly go, not just for Spark's sake, but for his, too. Sparks thought a good strategy might be to show little desperation. She knew North loved to play the savior.

"Amberly's not my sister? Why not? I'll make that fiction my reality. Why can't everyone want me like they want her? Dek wants her. You want her." Sparks suddenly turned away from North. "I'm not jealous of Amberly. I adore her. But can't broken people have some happiness, too?"

North's heart flooded with compassion for Sparks. He understood where her heart was. He was *still* hung up on Amberly, and he wasn't even sure why. Amberly was indirectly responsible for so much misery, but she was also a source of so much joy. She represented so much of what life used to be, when it was worth living. He knew he would never meet someone quite as amazing as Amberly, but so what? And frankly, that old life was dead, maybe even the North she rejected was dead too. Everything had changed. Even his devotion to faith had faltered. He felt un-tethered to anything that used to be grounding.

There was no happiness for North — he only had a mission to do. Destroy Chasm. At least his broken life could still save others. That was all that was left. Amberly had no part in this. Sparks on the other hand, was present. And hurting, like he was. *Sparks is right. Broken people deserve some happiness, too.*

North's resignation made him feel reckless.

He reached out and grabbed Sparks' head, pulling her mouth to his. A torrent of desire and confusion and frustration and loss flooded the space between them. And then, as they lingered, there was a small serenity neither had felt in a long time.

Perfect, Sparks thought.

"I love this sort of crazy," Sparks said, as she boarded the *Prime* in the *Magnus* hanger bay. Marines Goldsmith, Advika and Mateo, fully armed with multiple assault rifles and loads of explosive ordnance, joined Sparks and climbed aboard the *Prime*.

Sparks did not carry the heavy weaponry of the marines, instead opting for a pair of elegant pistols, low caliber and lightweight. They each had a shiny holster, one hugging each of Sparks' muscular thighs. Slung across her back was a lightweight staff with a dense metallic cap. If she had maneuvering room, Sparks preferred the staff in a melee fight. The weapon gave her extra reach, and she had trained enough with the staff to incapacitate or kill at her pleasure.

North stood on the deck, receiving last-minute instructions from Captain Obadiah. At his side was Rhodes and Lieutenant Kilo, a tall, quiet, thin Marine who was extremely secretive and introverted. He was also an ace pilot.

"Thirty-six hours, North," the captain said.

"Yes, sir," North said. "We'll cut of the head of the beast and have it for you on a silver platter as a welcome-to-*Marquette* present."

"Just stay alive and get us some actionable recon," Obadiah saluted North. The officers returned the salute and turned toward the *Prime*. Sparks had stuck her head and torso out of the Prime's main port.

"Why don't you double-time it, Marine," she chided North with a subtle smile. "This plan is only going to work if the timing is precise." North strode to the runabout and looked up at Sparks.

Rhodes detected a little bit of flirting from Sparks that she hadn't seen before. *Sparks and North?* she thought. *No way.*

"Rhodes," the captain looked at his most junior officer, "I'm counting on you to bring back North in one piece. Don't let him do anything stupid."

"Yes, sir," Rhodes said, smiling at the captain's jocularity, but also trying to hide her anxiety. She wasn't even two decades old, and her ambition had finally caught up with her. She knew that if she was part of a successful military operation, particularly one as crucial as the coming insertion on *Waypoint Marquette,* her command dreams would be significantly catalyzed.

She practically demanded to be on the *Prime* as it attempted to secretly deposit a group of Marines onto the waypoint. But the danger was real, and she was now afraid she had volunteered for a premature death. Rhodes had a soldier's faith — the outdated saying, "There are no atheists in foxholes," applied. But like all people of faith, doubt nibbled at the edges of her thoughts.

Ryder entered the hanger and quickly paced toward the *Prime*. Rhodes couldn't remember the last time she had seen the woman in anything but a dress, but thought Ryder wore the dark grey light armor well. Her hip holster carried small sidearms not unlike Sparks, and she also carried a Japanese-style sword in a sheath built into the armor's back. Rhodes had never seen armor like Ryder's before. It looked formidable and feminine.

"I want your duds," Rhodes said, and fell in line behind Ryder as both boarded the *Prime*.

"If we survive this, I'll fabricate you some."

The *Prime* ejected itself from the *Magnus* hanger, both vessels traveling at just under half the speed of light. The *Prime* immediately started deceleration. Rhodes felt a queasy turning in her torso as the inertia dampeners worked overtime to keep the crew of the *Prime* from being crushed against the *Prime's* bulkhead.

Who came up with this stupid plan? Rhodes thought, as she scanned the room for a receptacle just in case she was going to hurl. In actuality, it was North and Sparks who devised the insertion mission.

Assuming the *Magnus* had successfully disguised its approach to *Marquette*, the warship would purposely overshoot the waypoint, so by the time *Magnus'* wake was spotted, it would appear to be headed away from *Marquette*. If Chasm controlled *Marquette*, as nearly everyone suspected, they would be looking for *Magnus* because of the desperate message Kimberly Macready sent out two years ago at the height of the Battle of *Magellan*. All of *Marquette's* eyes would be on *Magnus*. This would serve as a distraction as the *Prime*, running electromagnetically dark, would quietly attach itself to an obscure and hopefully unguarded airlock.

Chief Petty Officer Bollard, using a modified version of the Macready hacking box, would then slice through *Marquette's* security. Using the airlock, North would lead the strike team on its two-objective mission.

First, if they were not detected immediately, North's team had to conduct rapid reconnaissance to assess to what level

Chasm had taken hold of *Marquette*. Assuming they found Chasm had substantial or complete control over *Marquette*, the second objective was to create a lot of chaos. This second distraction would allow Wing Commander Nyota to safely lead a second landing assault of nearly the full contingent of *Magnus'* fighters and transports to multiple airlocks.

Bollard, Rhodes, Cho and Kilo would keep the *Prime's* engines hot in case North's strike team needed to make a hasty retreat.

Rhodes felt like she might be getting used to the sudden deceleration, when she suddenly felt nauseous again.

North looked over at Rhodes from the command chair. "Wow. I didn't know someone could be that shade of green," he joked.

"Ugh," Rhodes replied. "My stomach feels like it's in my head. Why did we have to hit the brakes so hard?"

Bollard, who was seated behind North, looked up from his infopad. "Well, we have to go from 150 million meters per second to zero over a distance of about 10 million kilometers. You do the math."

"Math makes me sick," Rhodes sighed.

"Ten minutes until *Marquette* contact," the Condi reported. "*Prime* is rigged for stealth. All external lights extinguished, complete radio silence mode engaged. Unaided visual range of *Marquette* in five minutes."

"Time to suit up," North said with a hit of wistfulness. "Hopefully there is a resistance to Chasm on *Marquette,* and we'll have some allies to help us take control of the waypoint before the *Magnus* returns. I want to wrap *Marquette* in a bow for the captain."

"Maybe Chasm doesn't have control of *Marquette*?" Rhodes mused aloud.

"If *Marquette* was not under Chasm control, why have they gone radio silent for the last year? Why would they have moved the waypoint? The timing works out that *Marquette* would have received Macready's message one year ago. Clearly Chasm found out we were coming and decided to execute their plan to take control. There is no other explanation," the pilot said. Kilo was unimpressed; he believed Rhodes had a weak grasp on concepts like logic.

Condi spoke up over the PA system. "*Magnus* has been detected by *Marquette*."

North stood from his chair. "Cho, the bridge is yours. Keep the *Prime*, err, primed in case this goes south in a hurry."

"What does that even mean, 'in case this goes south'?" Rhodes asked.

Lt. Commander Cho took North's command chair. "Well, on a planet, south… it means, well… you know if our Marines start getting shot up."

"So, north means things are going well?" Rhodes followed up.

"You said it," North smirked.

"What in God's sweet Milky Way?" Kilo said, as *Marquette* became clearly visible to the naked eye through the *Prime's* small windows. *Marquette*, the newest and most advanced waypoint, was a beautiful seven-kilometer long saucer. The waypoint gleamed a silvery spectrum of reflected star light, with a brilliant green garden center. What had caught Kilo's attention had also grabbed North's gaze.

"I've been to *Marquette* twice, and it didn't have *that*," North pointed. "Must be how they moved the waypoint."

A large, rectangular structure stuck out from the far side of the waypoint. Ugly and asymmetrical, the tower had running lights, but at first glance had no viewports or windows. A second main structure was attached to the first tower.

"Is that a ship?" Rhodes asked.

"It doesn't look like anything docked; it looks fused to the waypoint," Cho said.

"Whatever it is, we're going to find out," North said. "Cho, wait two hours, then break radio silence and send a message to *Magnus* informing them of *Marquette's* new … appendage."

"This does not look good, XO," Kilo mused, as he shook North's hand. "For *Magellan*! Good luck." North turned to get ready for the insertion.

Rhodes stood from her chair and grabbed North's hand as the XO strode off the bridge. He stopped and look back, catching the junior officer's glance directly. He could see the fear in her young eyes. *She's worried that I won't come back*, North thought. He gave her hand a gentle but firm squeeze.

"Ensign. Rhodes. Listen," North said. "I'm coming back. In one piece. You'll see. You know what I believe: If God is for us, who can be against us?"

"Is God for us?" Rhodes asked.

"I hope so," North replied.

Rhodes leaped forward and embraced North, her mentor and big brother. "I don't know what I would do if we lost you." North returned the hug and then released her. She stepped back.

"Sorry, I'm not sure if that was sanctioned by regulations," Rhodes mumbled.

"Don't worry, Rhodes," Sparks, who had just stepped on the bridge, said. "I'll make sure North comes back in one piece. This isn't our first Tube race."

Sparks turned to North. "Well, I'm a traitor to Chasm, so why stop now? Let's go thwart the will of the Chairman."

North smiled and followed Sparks to the lower level hatch.

"One minute until contact with *Marquette*," Condi reported over the *Prime's* speakers. "No evidence of detection. The *Magnus* has begun its deceleration."

Good. The distraction appears to be working, North thought. He looked over his strike force. Sparks was stretching and jogging in place. Ryder was testing the sharpness of her blade against her gloved finger. Goldsmith looked like he was about to wet himself. Advika was putting on a brave face, but North could sense her apprehension. Mateo was double checking the charge on his stun weapon and the ammo counts in his extra magazines.

Bollard stood at the interior *Prime* airlock, ready with the Raven One-designed hacking box. "I hope this thing works."

"Of course, it will," Sparks chided him. "Kimberly Macready herself designed the thing. She was a real savant. Genius. I miss her."

"I can't believe you were part of Chasm," Ryder lied to Sparks. Sparks fought her natural eye-roll reaction at Ryder's misleading comment. "From what I hear, Kimberly Macready was something of a monster."

"She wasn't a monster. Maybe she was crazy, but she wanted to make everything perfect," Sparks told Ryder what she already knew.

From the outer hull, came a slight ping.

"Contact with *Marquette*," Condi announced the obvious.

"The slicer is working; the airlocks are connected," Bollard said with a little surprise in his voice. "It should be only another 30 seconds for me to crack the lock." The indicator light on the airlock blinked green, indicating atmospheric pressure on the other side.

"Fall in," North commanded his strike team. He was all business now. His face grew tight, and he raised his rifle and aimed it at the airlock door. *Please God*, he prayed silently, *don't let there be anyone on the other side.*

The team paired off, making a two by three column. Sparks was at North's side, with her side arms drawn. Behind the lead pair were Ryder and Goldsmith, and bringing up the rear were Mateo and Advika. Ryder had her sword drawn, making Sparks a little nervous. She wasn't interested in getting stabbed in the back, figuratively or literally, by Ryder, so she pivoted slightly to keep the spy in the corner of her peripheral vision.

"Don't forget to lock the door once we're gone," North said.

"No worries there," Bollard said. He punched in a command to the hack box. "Door opening in ten."

"Let's do this thing," Sparks bounced.

"Five, four, three, two, one," Bollard completed.

The airlock hissed, and North pushed the *Marquette* exterior airlock open, and he quickly stepped into *Marquette*. The airlock opened up into a waterworks system control center, on the rim near the "lower" side of the waypoint. Once all six members of the strike force had exited, Bollard sealed the airlock behind them.

The hall was tight, even for a waypoint, and North had to hunch slightly to keep from hitting his head. The gentle hum of water moving through pipes and being pushed through filters was the only sound.

Ten meters down the hall from the airlock, there was a left turn into what North speculated was a monitoring station.

North silently indicated that he was going to look ahead using hand signals. He ordered the rest of the team to stay hidden on their side of the corner. North swung around with his rifle raised, and saw the monitoring station – a small table with a magnetic resonance screen interface – he was expecting.

He didn't immediately see the person who was supposed to be monitoring the waterworks life support systems, because she was curled up under the table. When he did see her suddenly, dressed in a white lab coat, he was startled because he was almost on top of her. Her breath was deep and slow.

Then he heard her snoring.

CHAPTER ELEVEN

North quickly examined the woman he assumed to be a life support technician. He guessed she was probably 30, around his age. She had a relaxed ebony face framed with a short cut of shocking white hair that matched the brilliant teeth in her half-open mouth. Her cheek was moist with a trail of drool. She wore a loose-fitting khaki jumpsuit under her white coat.

North eyed Ryder and rotated his right pointer finger around his left wrist and then indicated the woman. Ryder nodded and reached into her supply sack. North pointed to Mateo, tapped his side arm, and then nodded at the snoozing figure. Mateo unholstered his stun gun and aimed it at the peaceful face.

Ryder expertly zip cuffed the snoring woman. Goldsmith tapped his rifle nervously, and Sparks punched the Marine in the arm to show her disapproval. North rolled his eyes, then offered hand signals to tell the rest of the team to keep quiet.

Advika had moved to a position five meters down the apparently deserted corridor. Condensation on the pipes lining the hall created a slow, unnerving drip. A drop fell on Advika's helmet visor. She cursed under her breath and then moved out of the drip.

"Be ready," North whispered to Mateo. He reached his hand down to the woman's face, covered her mouth with his hand, and with his free arm, proceeded to gently shake who he thought to be sleeping technician.

"Hey," North said. "Wake up. Wake up."

The woman's eyes jolted open, and her irises expanded as her heart beat with terror, glands pumping her bloodstream with adrenaline. She instinctively wanted to push the man's hand from her mouth, but realized her arms were secured behind her back. She thrashed reflexively a few times before noticing Mateo's gun pointed at her.

Then she bit hard on North's hand.

"Son of a dirt licker!" North swore in pain, withdrawing his hand. The woman and been successful at drawing blood.

"Hey, hey," Ryder said, putting her hands up reassuringly, "we're not going to hurt you."

"Unless you're Chasm," Sparks snorted.

"What? No! I'm not Chasm," the woman said. "You... You, you look like Marines. But they are... Who are you?"

North held his bitten, bleeding hand with his good one. "First things first. Who are you? What is going on here?"

"What?" the woman said, trying to sit upright against her restraints. "I'm Meliana. You guys are armed. And you are not Chasm?"

Sparks leaned over and helped the white-haired woman sit upright.

"Definitely not Chasm," Ryder said.

"Only Chasm has weapons," Meliana said as she looked at North. She noted his handsome face as he examined the hand she bit. "You should get some disinfectant on that bite. There must be a million bacteria in there. Like, I haven't brushed my teeth in days."

"You're a doctor?" North said.

"Duh," Meliana said, gesturing at her white coat. "Now who are you?"

"We'll get to that," Ryder said, her spymaster interrogation skills taking over. "What is the status of *Marquette?* Who is in control?"

"Are you with the Underground?"

"If they are against Chasm," North said, "then yes."

"So, Chasm *is* in control of this waypoint," Sparks said. "No Scorched Earth. I guess the Chairman decided to keep this one."

"*No way*. You guys are not from *Marquette,*" Meliana said. "Are you from Arara? Has Chasm taken over there, too?"

"No, we are not from Arara," North said, looking deep into Meliana's eyes. "I'm North, from the *Magellan* Marines. We beat Chasm there, and now we're bringing the fight to Chasm."

"I guess we just went straight to full trust then," Ryder disapproved. "This woman could be a Chasm spy for all we know."

"How do I know you are not really Chasm?" Meliana asked.

"We're not Chasm," Sparks sighed.

"Ryder, you could be Chasm spy for all we know," North tossed back as Sparks suppressed a guffaw into a condensed snort. "Trust has to start somewhere."

"Fine, with your carelessness, just don't count on me to pull the knife out of your back when the time comes," Ryder chastised the XO.

That's because you'll be the one putting it in, Sparks thought. She made a mental note to double her already diligent watch on Ryder. She had grown lax over the last year; Ryder played the innocent survivor well.

North waved off Ryder, and knelt in front of Meliana. He withdrew his combat knife and showed its seriated edge to the woman. "I do not abide traitors. Even those I love." North's thoughts lingered on Amberly. Then he remembered that Sparks was a traitor to her side, too.

"Um... ok," Meliana said. "A bit weirded out here."

North shook his head to clear it. "Sorry, right." Then he took his knife and cut the zip cuffs off of Meliana.

"Do you have a medkit?" Meliana asked. Goldsmith produced the red box from his pack and offered it to North.

"Please," Meliana snatched the kit and opened it up. She clearly knew her way around the medkit and found the wound-care foam. "Give me your hand, okay?"

North gave her his bitten hand she began to care for the wound.

"How sweet," Ryder said. Sparks had been checking in with Advika down the hall, and turned back to see what she thought a little too tender of a moment. Meliana was gently holding North's hand, applying foam, but she was looking him in the eyes.

"No ring," Meliana said, looking down at the hand she was massaging. "That's probably for the best."

"How is that good for North?" Sparks jumped in, almost a little too quickly.

"You know, Chasm's revolution is ugly," Meliana said as she held up her smooth, small left hand and displayed an emerald ring. "When you love someone, you have so much more to lose."

Mateo thought about his new fiancé, a sanitation worker back on the *Magnus*. "What happened?"

"They like put him and our son out the airlock," Meliana said, suddenly somber. "For the dirt-licking greater good."

"Don't cry to us. We've all lost something," Ryder said. "*Waypoint Cortez*, is gone. The whole damn dirty waypoint."

"*Hevi.* It's true then," Meliana looked at Ryder. "We heard rumors, but Chasm has all communications locked down. So sorry."

"Enough talk, we're here for payback. We are going to send Chasm to hell," Goldsmith said. "We need to take this waypoint back for Earth."

"Earth? Earth? Earth is a dream. What do they care? They left us out here. We are alone," Meliana said.

"Sister, I came all the way from Earth to fight Chasm," Goldsmith said. "We are not alone. We're packing some real firepower."

"Extra *Hevi*," Meliana's eyes lit up like a supernova. "You have been to Earth?"

Goldsmith's face lit up with pride. "I was born there."

"And now you are here, to rescue *Marquette* from these monsters. With a… ship?"

"The Cavalry is here, sweetheart," Sparks said.

"That's good, because it's going to take more than the six of you to take back this station," Meliana said.

"You are probably right," North said, "but don't underestimate us." North winked at Meliana.

"Listen Meliana, we need you to give us a sitrep," Ryder implored. "Are we secure here? What can you tell us about the composition of the Chasm forces?"

"Say what?" Meliana said. "A sit-what?"

"Situation report," North explained. "It's a military term. Bottom line is we have about 30 hours before our battleship arrives, and we need to get this place ready for its liberation."

"Chasm controls everything," Meliana said. "It's like the whole place is a machine, and the people are just parts of the machine. Strict curfew. Long work assignments. No freedom of movement. All the bars are closed. And the churches."

"And the schools?" Ryder asked.

Meliana's eyes grew wide. "The schools are all run by Chasm teachers, indoctrinating the children. They took them all from us. Once they had control, it was the first thing they did, they took the children from the parents. My man wouldn't have it. He wouldn't let them take little Barack from us. So, they took them both from me."

"I'm sorry, Meliana," North said. "What can you tell us that will help make this right?"

"Join up with the Underground," Meliana said. "And kill Queenie."

"We're not assassins," North said. "But... who's Queenie."

"Queenie is an overseer," Meliana answered. "He's the one who killed Ehud and Barack."

"An overseer?" Mateo asked.

"That's what we call the Judas scum who sold us out to Chasm," Meliana said, her eyes growing large with rage. "You see, there weren't enough Chasm to effectively manage their new slave population. So, the cowards and the greedy of those once loyal to *Marquette* were, like, recruited to oversee the rest of us. You want to help? Kill Queenie. Or maybe give me a gun and let me pop him myself. You'll have to show me how to use it though."

"That's not helpful," Ryder said growing impatient. "Tell me about this resistance, this Underground. Do they stand a chance? Could they help us catch Chasm off guard?"

"I don't care about the dirty Underground," Meliana swore. "Ehud wanted to join them. He had heard they had managed to make a secret base somewhere in the Africa quadrant. He said he knew where it was, but he didn't want to tell me, just in case he was found out."

"Makes sense," Sparks said.

"You know what? Queenie found out Ehud knew something, and they tortured the humanity out of him, but my Ehud, heck, he was stubborn as ever. So, like, they came and took Barack and put our boy in the airlock. In the *airlock*." Meliana's closed her eyes tight, as if cringing from the memory.

"Chasm dirt-lickers had no regard for children either when they lit up *Cortes*," North said, his anger starting to match Meliana's.

"Ehud, he still wouldn't talk, so they threatened to put my boy, my precious baby, out into space. Oh, God, I can still hear him crying for me," Meliana was crying now as the fresh, painful memory flooded her brain. "Ehud thought they were bluffing. Bluffing. And then Barack was gone. Snap." Meliana pounded her arms against the wall painfully hard three times.

"I'm so sorry," Goldsmith put his arm around Meliana.

"Ehud lost it; he was red, red mad. I know he couldn't bear to look at me. He went to kill Queenie with his bare hands, but Chasm had a bullet for my love. Oh, God. Oh, God. Ehud, I can't go on."

Sparks awkwardly patted Meliana's back.

"Oh Gawds, I ran and never looked back. I should have taken my chance then. I should have died with them."

"But you didn't," North said. "And now you can help us get revenge on Chasm."

"I've been hiding down here for days, praying that God would, like, give me a weapon of revenge. Now here you are. An answer to my prayer. Go kill Queenie."

"Help us find the Underground resistance, and I promise you, I will find and kill Queenie myself," North said as he clenched his fist. "We will help you, Meliana. For Ehud and Barack."

"But where could they hide on a waypoint?" Goldsmith asked. "Someplace that people wouldn't think to look."

"And someplace where heat signatures couldn't be easily detected," Sparks said. "I can't imagine Chasm not at least using heat detectors if they believed that there was a hidden resistance base on a waypoint they controlled."

"Let's see if we can find them first," Ryder said.

Noisy steps caught everyone's attention. North grabbed his rifle and aimed down the hall that led back to the runabout. He used his left hand to instruct his squad to be silent, then he brought his rifle into assault position.

A shadow moved around the corner. North's finger glided over the rifle trigger.

A loud clank followed by a familiar-voiced "owww" sounded up the hallway.

"Rhodes?" North said, putting his gun down. "What the hell are you are you doing?"

"Hitting my heads on water pipes, apparently, sir," the young ensign said.

"Why are you here?" North was angry. "You were supposed to remain on the *Prime*."

"I couldn't wait, not knowing if you would ever come back. Sparks, North, all of you are my family. I have decided if you die, I want to die with you," Rhodes said, looking at her fellow

Marines. "Besides, I was literally born for this fight. Let me come with you."

"Get the hell back on the ship, Ensign. This is not your day to die, Rhodes," North said, still angry, but feeling protective of his protégé. She wasn't the 16-year-old girl North first met and trained as part of the youth officers' program. In the two years since they had departed *Magellan*, Rhodes had become an attractive 18-year-old woman, with dark hair and a sharp wit, and also, North thought, a heart of gold. He put his hand on her shoulder. "You have got to live. Who else is going to be captain of the *Magnus* when Obadiah kicks the bucket? Besides, this is no suicide mission."

"I want to be at your side," Rhodes persisted. "I can do this." Rhodes hoisted her gun.

"Listen to old man, kid," Sparks smiled. "He knows what's best."

"I'm not an old man!" North protested. "I'm only 32."

"Please. I want to help," Rhodes said, about to tear up.

"Sorry, Ensign. Back to the *Prime*. That's an order. But since you are here, go ahead and send this message encoded to *Magnus* once you are back. Report that Chasm has control of *Marquette*, and we are attempting to contact an underground resistance. Also let them know that *Marquette* has been modified, added to in some way. Let them know about that tower monstrosity grafted on the back of this beautiful city…Wait. Hold on," North turned to Meliana. "What is that thing that is strapped to the back of this waypoint?"

"It's called *Utopia*. It came from Arara seven months ago. It was a supposed to be some sort of all-purpose vessel. A waypoint, but with mobility of a deep space ship. I've never cared much for ship stuff, but my Ehud, he was fascinated when it arrived."

"Let me guess," Sparks said. "It wasn't long after it arrived that Chasm took over."

"Did you know about this *Utopia*?" North asked Sparks. Sparks eyed Ryder nervously.

"I had heard rumors before I left Arara of a secret project, a plan to defend the space around the planet should Earth send a space attack," Sparks said. "What good would it do for Chasm to take over the surface of the planet if Earth loyalists could just bombard them from space?"

"Why didn't you tell us?" Mateo demanded.

"I mean, they were just rumors," Sparks said defensively, pulling at her hair nervously.

"So, the Chairman figured something could be coming, something that could effectively control Arara from space, like the *Magnus*," Ryder said. "She guessed, no she anticipated, the *Magnus*?"

"Maybe," North said. "Rhodes, report back to the Magnus about this *Utopia*. Go. Now. Godspeed, Rhodes."

"Yessir. The ensign stood smartly and gave a sharp salute, turned and was gone. North had grown fond of Rhodes, and thought he would have liked to have her with them, but she was too young to die. The risk was too high.

North looked at the others. "Let's get moving and see if we establish contact with this 'Underground.' We can do some reconnaissance and figure out what this *Utopia* is capable of and why did they graft it to *Marquette*. Then let's get ready to make some noise for when *Magnus* pulls around."

North pulled out his infopad and looked at a schematic of the waypoint. "Condi, can you figure out a path to the Africa Quadrant that is most likely to avoid populated areas of *Marquette*?"

"If you follow this network of capillary corridors just beneath the main tube system, you should be able to move mostly undetected," Condi said. "To get to the Africa Commons, I recommend this path. Total distance is six kilometers."

"Your computer is right," Meliana said.

"This place is *a lot* bigger than *Magellan*," Mateo sighed. "Looks like a hike."

"I'm worried about being discovered before we make it to the Tube," Sparks said. Each waypoint utilized a pneumatic tube system as a mass transport known casually as the Tube. While *Magellan's* Tube was simply a concentric ring with roughly half the radius of the disc-shaped waypoint, *Marquette's* system was more sophisticated. Besides the ring, it had tubes spurs that moved people out toward *Marquette's* rim.

"Pass out the ponchos," North looked to Advika. The Marnie pulled out the dark green, lightweight cover garments out of her pack and handed one to Goldsmith, North and Sparks. She then offered one to Ryder.

"Sorry, that's not my style," the she-spy refused the robe. "Besides, we'll look just as conspicuous wearing ponchos then in our normal garb."

"Maybe," North said, "But at least with these ponchos, we can keep our armor and weapons easily concealed. Which might buy us a little time that we need to talk ourselves out of a situation. I think that katana strapped to your back will make the locals suspicious and nervous."

"Fine, I'll cover up," Ryder sighed.

North looked hard into Meliana's bright eyes. "If you come with us, you must agree to follow my commands. Do you understand?"

"What if I don't come with you?" Meliana asked.

"Then we'll have to tie you up. We can't have you letting anyone else know we are here. I suspect you've never been tortured," Sparks replied. "We'll come back for you. If we survive."

Meliana looked at North, her eyes asking him if she was serious.

North nodded.

"Let's go then," Meliana said.

"Sparks, take point," North said. "I'll cover the flank. Ryder, protect Meliana. She's your charge."

Sparks took a quick glance at North's infopad to get her bearings and then headed toward an opening at the far side of the corridor. "Finally, action."

Thirty minutes later, Sparks was looking at a common area that served as an intersection hub for the Cook Manufacturing District where most of the prefabrication of durable goods happened on *Marquette*. In order to get to the sub-tube service corridors recommended by Condi, North's party had to sneak through the district. Restaurants on the perimeter of the hub were closed and looked like they had been for some time. Large greenhouse planters were placed near each corner of the commons. The planters had a sickly-sweet smell, with lush green and white vegetation growing in the humid boxes. Condensation caused drops of water to form on the inside of the greenhouse's translucent surface.

Sparks quietly moved from the corridor to behind the closest planter. She poked her head around the corner and saw a teenage boy, carrying a box of what she assumed were manufacturing supplies. He set the box down in the center of deserted commons and took a seat on bench next to an eating table. Then he pulled a flask from his pocket and lifted it to his lips.

Sparks threw up a fist, and the rest of the party halted. North moved to the front to confer with Sparks.

"It's just a boy taking a break. Must be a courier or something. Probably taking raw polycarbonate for manufacturing," Sparks said. "Let's test our disguises and see if they alarm him. Maybe he'll just ignore us."

"No, let's give him some time to clear out," North said. "I'd rather not risk it."

"What if he comes this way?" Sparks asked.

"Oh, you'll figure something out," North whispered. "Keep an eye on him, but stay out of sight."

"No problem."

North leaned against the cold corridor wall, and signaled to the others that they might not be moving for a while.

"North, look," Spark's hissed.

A tall man carrying stun gun and an assault rifle had entered clearing and moved to confront the teen. North hand signaled silence to his squad.

"Who said you can take a break?" the man said to the boy. His tone wasn't threatening, Sparks thought. Instead, the man sounded amused. "I'll take that," the man said, pointing toward the flask.

"Chasm trooper," Sparks mouthed to North. Sparks recognized the Arara-made armor he wore as standard-issue for Chasm muscle.

The boy, about 10 meters away from corridor opening where Sparks and North were spying from, stood up. He didn't look afraid. He took a defiant posture.

"I'll get this to weapons auxiliary before my deadline," the boy said. "I just was taking a breather. And you can go airlock yourself if you think I'm going to give you my hootch. I don't think Chasm is letting us make any more of this stuff. It's not for the *greater good*."

"Fine, fine. But you know there is a toll for passing through the Orchid Hub. How many credits do you have? I'm feeling nice today; transfer… *half* of them to me."

"I thought you Chasm people didn't care about money," the teen said, getting steamed.

"Yeah, money is meaningless, so go ahead and give me yours," the Chasm trooper said, pulling out his stun gun.

"I don't think so," the boy said. "Look, I'm not causing any trouble."

"Like I care if you are," the man said, growing agitated. "Just pull out your infopad and authorize a transfer of some credits."

"Go ahead and stun me," the teen said. "If you do, you still won't get any credits, because last I checked, an unconscious person can't authorize a credit transfer."

"Ugh, you're right," the Chasm trooper said. He pulled the trigger on his stun gun, and the boy fell to the floor, and began to flop around, as if having a seizure. Then the boy grew still, barely breathing. The trooper grabbed the boy's infopad and pulled out what North thought looked like a hacking device not dissimilar from the ones Kimberly Macready had distributed to her allies on *Magellan*. Sparks figured he would get the credits.

"Let's take him," Sparks whispered.

"No. Let him go," North said. "It's not worth the risk of us getting detected."

"A second hacking box could come in handy," Sparks said.

"Do you even know how to use —" North looked up from crouching behind the greenhouse and saw Ryder had removed her poncho and strode confidently toward the trooper. Her form-fitting flexible armor fully on display, Ryder put some extra sway in her hips.

The trooper looked up. "Where did you come from?"

"Does it matter?" Ryder said confidently, as if she owned the room. "Did you get what you wanted from the boy? If so, I want my cut."

"Who are you? What do you mean your cut?" the trooper stuttered. He put the infopad in a pocket and shifted the stun gun from his left to right hand.

"This is *my* Commons. Don't you know who I am?"

"Ummm…" The trooper was confused and more than a little suspicious. But he also found himself immediately attracted to the strong female. Ryder strode right up to the trooper, with just a few centimeters of space between them.

She leaned up to his ear and whispered. "Shhh. I'm a Hawk."

"You're dirty crapping me," the trooper said, relaxing and offering her the most charming smile he could muster.

"So, trooper, I'm impressed how you handled the boy. But I still want my cut," Ryder said.

"Why would someone like you … need money?"

"Don't question me. Hand me your infopad," Ryder commanded. "Or should we call your squad leader and discuss this? Come now. We don't have to be enemies. We can be friends. Really *good* friends. I just need my cut."

"Okay, okay," the trooper said. "I get it." He holstered his stun gun to free his hand to grab his infopad.

As the trooper presented his electronic device, Ryder reached over her back, and in one swift motion unsheathed her sword, stepped back, flung her arms around in a powerful swing and lopped off the trooper's head.

Ryder held the pose with her now bloody sword extended, as the decapitated man collapsed, his head rolling in the general direction of North. "Thanks for the cut."

"Holy hell, Ryder," North said as he and his squad came out of their hiding spot.

Ryder spit on the headless body. "Dirty loser."

"Wow, that was disgusting," Sparks said.

"He was a bullying asshole. He deserved it," Ryder said, as she wiped her blade on her poncho.

"I'm going to puke," Goldberg said.

Ryder sheathed her sword, reached down and picked up the hacking box and the boy's flask.

"Presents," Ryder smiled slyly as she handed the hacking box to North and the flask to Sparks.

"Here's to the 'greater good,'" Sparks said as she took the flask from Ryder, unscrewed the lid and tilted it up. Sparks feigned taking a swig, but did not let the alcohol pass her lips. She would have liked to enjoy the burn of hard booze on her the back of her throat, but she had to stay one-hundred percent on her game now. She was the better fighter between her and Ryder, but the spy's sudden display of swordsmanship reinforced just how lethal she could be. Sparks had no idea where Ryder's loyalties lay, and that made her even more dangerous.

"Should the doctor help this kid?" Advika asked.

"He'll be all right. It was just a stun," North said. "We have to keep moving."

"What about the body?" Mateo looked at pool of blood collecting near the exposed trooper neck. "Should we hide it."

"No time, this will all be for naught if we are–"

A man and a woman in civilian clothes walked into the Orchid Hub, startled at the unexpected carnage on display. The man screamed.

"What is going on here?" the woman demanded, and started reaching for her infopad. Before she could activate it, it shattered. The woman dropped it, and looked up at Sparks, who had pulled one of her side arms to decommission the infopad with a bullet.

"You didn't see us," Sparks said, menacing.

North frowned and looked at his squad. "Let's triple-time it for the tubes," North said as he took off for the opposite side of the commons.

"We're going to run?" Meliana asked Advika.

"Yes. Run!" Advika confirmed, as she took off after North. The rest followed.

"Wait! Are you Chasm?" the woman called after them, but received no answer.

CHAPTER TWELVE

Goldsmith was glad he had lost a score of kilos over the past year. He had resented his commanding officer's extra-exercise-and-less-food regimen, depriving him of his gluttonous pleasures and giving him the pain of extended cardiovascular exertion. 'North' had become a secret curse word for the tubby Marine. But in the tight squeeze of the service tunnel beneath the mass-transit Tube, Goldsmith could literally breathe a little easier as he slipped through.

North, on the other hand, was regretting his genetics. His above-average height combined with the hard mass of his well-defined upper torso made the "underground" corridors, lined with pneumonic tubes, water lines, fiberoptic conduits and assorted manual pressure monitors a gauntlet of poking and prodding.

"We should be under the Africa Quadrant Medical Center," Meliana said.

"Confirmed," Condi chimed in from its pocket on North's pack.

"If anyone can tell us where the Underground is staging, Dr. Lind should be able to help us," Meliana said.

"Can he be trusted?" Sparks asked.

"Does it matter?" Goldsmith asked. "I do not want to sit around in these dank tunnels. We should have just hopped on a Tube car."

"Too risky," North said.

"Risky? What's risky is opening this secure hatch and climbing into the back of the medical center, hoping Dr. Lind is there and not some Chasm trooper," Sparks said.

"Oh, you of little faith," North smirked and looked at the pistols holstered to Sparks' hips. "Just keep your friends at the ready. Goldsmith, you think you can get this hacking box to work?"

"Sure thing, sir," Goldsmith said, attaching the hacking box to the control on the hatch. The panel controlled the locking mechanism and also housed the pressure monitors. A green light indicated good, breathable air pressure on the other side. Red indicated a deadly vacuum. The indicator was green. "It's really quite simple, actually. The box tricks the locking mechanism into an all-open state."

The seven-member squad waited in silence as the hacking box buzzed and then made a slight pop.

"Unlocked," Goldsmith said.

"Sparks, on point," North said, as he prepared to throw the ceiling mounted hatch open.

"Oooh. I love being the cannon fodder!" Sparks joked as she drew her twin pistols.

"I wouldn't waste you as cannon fodder," North smiled. "You can get up the hatch faster than any of us. And you are the fastest draw. Secure the room, then I'll boost Meliana up. Ryder, head a deci-klick back and keep lookout. Chasm troopers must be close."

Sparks stepped next to North, pushed herself up on the balls of her feet, and planted an open-mouth kiss on the handsome Marine. Ryder kept a poker face, but Advika and Mateo both went wide-eyed at the unexpected, sensuous display. Sparks slid off of North and then squared herself under the hatch, poised to spring.

"If I get killed, I hope you have many rotten, lonely nights," Sparks said.

"That *may* have been inappropriate." North winked at Sparks. He was joking, but was starting to wondering if this "kissing friends" thing was going to end up badly. "Ready?"

Sparks nodded.

He put up three fingers, verbally counted down and threw the hatch open. Sparks sprung through the open hatch, leaping with enough strength to clear her entire torso through the portal. She caught herself by throwing her stomach on the ridge of the circular opening, then rolling the rest of her body on the floor of the clinic.

She sprung to her feet, looked across the medical supply room at a gaunt, bald man in a white coat who had been reading inventory on a magnetic resonance screen. He looked stunned at the sudden appearance of Sparks in his clinic. Then he noticed she had two lethal-looking weapons pointed right at his chest.

"Dr. Lind I presume?" Sparks smiled. "Don't say a word."

To indicate he understood Sparks, Dr. Lind nodded, slowly raising his hands.

"Clear," Sparks called down the hatch. With a little grunting, Meliana appeared through the portal, as she was pushed up by North. Sparks did not offer a hand to help, instead keeping both firearms trained of Dr. Lind.

"Meliana!" Dr. Lind said. "I thought you were dead." The white coats reached out and embraced each other.

"Dr. Lind," Sparks said. "Back away! We have a few questions." The male doctor did as was instructed, stepping a few feet from Meliana. Meliana shot her colleague a "I'm sorry" look.

"Sparks, give me a hand down here," North hissed. Sparks squatted down, holstered the gun from her left hand. She stuck that hand through the portal and grabbed North's up-stretched arm. Her other arm remained extended, gun at the end, threatening Dr. Lind with lethal force. She hoisted on him as he left, and North rolled into the room.

Advika's voice rose from the portal. "Ryder signals Chasm patrol on approach. They are coming. Get us up!"

North reached down and pulled Mateo up with two hands. Mateo was a relatively small man, and North tossed him clear of the portal as if he were a sack of reconstituted protein powder.

"Come on, Ryder, come on," Advika said in forced, hushed tones. She took her assault rifle and aimed it down the corridor. "They tracked us down here. They are about to find us."

North bent over and pulled up Goldsmith by his arms, straining his back and rolling the Marine away from the hatch once cleared.

Advika held her breath and took the safety off her rifle. She was ready to shoot whatever came around the corner that wasn't Ryder. North hosted the athletic woman onto the clinic floor. Although the clinic backroom wasn't particularly small, it was getting crowded.

"Where is Ryder?" North asked.

"Down here. Hurry, Chasm on our position, ETA, 30 seconds."

Then Ryder felt herself being lifted. North grabbed her by her pack and lifted her above the hatch as Mateo reached down and pulled the round door closed.

"The hacker!" Goldsmith shouted. "It's still attached."

"Shhhh!" Sparks said. "Too late. Hope they don't notice it."

"We need that box," Advika said.

"Maybe not; I have the one Ryder ... procured," North said.

North indicated for silence, leaned down and pressed his ear to the hatch. He could barely make out footfalls. For a minute, they became louder, and then the sound dissipated.

North stood up and surveyed the room for the first time. For a storage room, it was relatively open. Medical compounds were stored in vacuum-sealed containers latched into a complicated locking grid from floor to ceiling. At the end of the room was an inventory database access terminal, and a flabbergasted white-coat clad doctor.

North looked over at Sparks, who still had Lind at gunpoint. "At ease, Sparks. Dr. Lind, I am Commander North, Executive Officer of the *U.S.S. Magnus*, and we're here to liberate *Marquette*."

"You are such a tool, North," Ryder rolled her eyes. "You trust too easily. You just gave up strategic information."

"It's okay," Meliana said. "Like, we can trust Dr. Lind. He has no love for Chasm." She looked over at the doctor. "Is Pinita? Is she?"

"She's safe, thank goodness. I was able to keep her safe from Chasm, for now," Lind took Meliana's hand. "And Ehud? Barack?"

Meliana looked to the floor and shook her head.

"Meliana, I am so sorry. I should have never told Ehud."

Meliana nodded, unsuccessfully trying to hold back tears.

"Barack, too. Oh, God, I'm so sorry Meliana."

"Doctor, you need to tell us what you know about the Underground," North said.

"I've been secretly supplying the Underground with medical supplies," Lind explained. "It was too suspicious for me, with complete access to ... well to this." The doctor waved his hands at the medicines. "I needed a courier and Ehud volunteered. We sent the stuff, painkillers, stabilizers, you know, home with Meliana. Ehud runs... er... he ran a microfactory close to the secret Underground base. He would drop the supplies off on his way to work."

"Commander, should I recover the box on the bottom of the

hatch," Goldsmith interrupted. "They must be gone by now."

"Or not," Sparks said. "We have another. Well, we don't know if it works."

North waved the pair silent and turned back to Lind. "Dr. Lind, we must know where this base is. We must contact the Underground. Can you tell us?"

"That information cost Ehud and his son their lives," Lind said somberly. "Are you willing to pay that price?"

"I didn't a travel light year to play it safe," Sparks said. "Okay, let's be honest. I wouldn't travel a kilometer to play it safe."

"How can you be so easy with jokes?" Meliana raged. She wanted to slap Sparks' smug face and pull out her strawberry blonde hair. "They tortured Ehud for information. He didn't give up the location. They threatened the life of our son, and Ehud didn't give up the Underground, didn't give up Dr. Lind, didn't give me up."

Lind took Meliana into his arms. "Were you there, Mel. Did they make you see your husband suffer?"

"I saw enough. He convinced them I had no knowledge, and then they separated us for hours. They brought me back, and Ehud had been beaten to a pulp. And they had Barack in the airlock. Ehud just blubbered, 'you're bluffing, you're bluffing' and then they… oh God."

"Shhhh," Lind comforted Meliana. "They are in a better place."

"Doctor, we're short on time," North insisted. "The location."

Lind shifted his eyes around the room, then drew close to North. He lowered his voice. "If *Magellan* is designed like *Marquette*, then you're probably aware of the reserve water tanks located a few decks beneath the main hanger. They are large tanks, maybe 30 meters long. One of them was empty for maintenance when *Utopia* arrived. That's where the base is. Maybe 30 or 40 people are hiding there. Many of them injured from the skirmishes when Chasm was taking control."

"How do they mask their heat signatures?" Goldsmith asked.

"Well, first, no one expects to find humans inside a water tank," Lind said. "But our chief engineer, who survived with the Underground, built a false tank wall on the inside, like a tank within a tank, and flooded chilled water between the gap.

Eventually, I'm sure Chasm will find the cooler that has been syphoning power, but for now, the Underground is remarkably well hidden."

"Take us there," North said with an overtone of demand.

"Sorry, friend," Lind said. "I've already helped too much. Honestly, I don't know you, and I just want to do what I can to help the people who are suffering. Getting caught and tortured will not do anyone any good. What if you are just undercover Chasm?"

"If we were undercover Chasm, you'd be dead," Ryder said with a hint of finality.

"I don't think you know Chasm as well as you think you know them," Lind said. "They are not enemies. They are crazy, to be sure, but they believe they are making everything better. Chasm is the apex of humanism. They would kill you if it helps the greater good, but if your life could contribute somehow, if you had some piece of information, that was valuable... they'd ... *process* you first."

"I have found that not all Chasm are as idealistic as their leaders," Ryder said. "For example, there was this lecher whose head I removed earlier today."

Lind's eyes became wide as he noted the sword strapped on Ryder's back.

"Heh," Ryder smirked, as she pulled out a tube of lipstick and applied the cosmetic.

"At any rate, leave me out of your mad quest," Lind said, "so that I can continue to help the hurt among us without obstruction."

"That's sort of ... noble, I guess," Advika offered.

"Okay, we're running out of time," North said. "Let's make for the Tubes. Sparks, check out the front corridor to make sure it's clear." Sparks nodded and exited through the main door.

"Thank you, Lind," North bowed slightly. "You seem like a good man. I hope we meet again." Lind returned the gesture.

Sparks poked her head back in through the front door.

"It's pretty clear. Ponchos on and let's move."

The seven-member squad drew a few stares as they made their way at a decent pace from the clinic to the Tube Station.

Once they were on a Tube car, they could get near the hangar bay in a few minutes, and then hopefully, North thought, find the Underground in time for *Magnus'* return.

The corridor opened up into the Auni Mandela Commons, named for the first president of the Pan-African Alliance. The Mandela Commons' most prominent feature was the Tube station where, during normal times, people would queue up for a quick ride to all parts of the station. The tube cars floated and were pushed by highly regulated currents of pressurized air. Each pilotless, windowless car had seating for four.

The dim lighting in the commons contrasted with the brighter lighting in the arterial corridor. North's party was dramatically silhouetted for anyone watching their entrance to the commons.

North counted about two dozen people in the vicinity. *No children,* he made a mental note. Some ate quietly at a picnic area. Others headed to one of the few stores that were open. The planters, and it seemed, any other unneeded amenities, had been pulled out to make room for a make-shift dock. The whole commons seemed bleak to North, and not just because it had been stripped of its natural color. A trio of scrawny teens were loading crates into every other tube car, sending the unknown cargo to be presumably unloaded at one of the other four tube stations.

"They have turned some of the markets into ration distribution centers," Meliana explained. "Money supposedly has no value, says our Chasm overlords. But there is a black market, and no one has tossed their credit chits away, yet."

Sparks traded glances with a couple heading into a market. When the couple saw the squad, they hurried into the store.

"Don't worry," Meliana said. "Just keep walking. Like, they were just worried our group would get in line in front of them and maybe the rations would run out. They'll be glad when our group moves on."

The only person who looked military was an armed Chasm guard at the tube gate who was asking everyone boarding where they were headed. North's team made for the gate.

North signaled Mateo to walk astride him. He spoke covertly. "We have to make sure we secure a beachhead for *Magnus* to unload her troops. Once we act, Chasm will know for sure *Magnus* is attempting to inject a full hostile force. We'll try to trick them into thinking we are trying to take the hangar bay, and instead cut some doors on the hull near the tanks and this alleged Underground base, for Magnus to soft seal to."

"It's a good plan, commander," Mateo said.

"I want you, Goldsmith and Advika to board the first car, but take the tube back to the *Prime's* insertion point. I'm going to keep my comm channel open to you and scrambled, so pay attention when we make contact with the Underground in case the plans change. These loyalists may be cooperative, or not," North gave Mateo commands under his breath.

"Ha, just remember your mic is hot if you have to take a whiz," the Marine joked.

"As soon as you get back, have Rhodes encode and transmit the sitrep to the captain, and then detach and hot rod it back to *Magnus* and join the main assault force. You let them know what to expect when the board."

"Sir?"

"Just leave the ordnance with me," North smiled. "I don't need the three of you to help me plant the bombs. I'd tell Sparks and Ryder to go with you, but I don't have time to argue with either of them."

Mateo causally reached beneath his poncho into his pack and pulled out a small, translucent plastic bag holding three white orbs, small ball-like devices only a few millimeters in diameter. These were the latest in Earth explosive technology.

The bombs had micro-receivers built in and could be detonated by radio signal. A red gash decorated one side of the explosive orbs, giving access to a manual trigger. In a pinch, a fingernail or other thin tool could start a five second count-down.

"These little things are really lethal?" North asked Mateo.

"Oh yeah, no shrapnel, but nearly 10,000 kilojoules of blast satisfaction. You don't want to be near this thing when it goes."

"That's right," Sparks said, who pushed herself between the Marines, now just a few meters from the queue and the guard. At any given time, three cars were available to be loaded and released.

As they approached, a teen closed the door to the first car, full of cargo, and it vanished down the Tube. A lone rider was in the next car, and as soon as the first car was gone, the second car sucked away as well. The teens didn't even wait to fill the third car complete with cargo before sending it on its way.

Within a few seconds, a car appeared and stopped. The door of the white, egg-shaped transport opened, and North saw it was empty. Another car arrived and opened, and four armored Chasm troopers stepped out. A woman who North thought might be the leader of this group eyed his squad with obvious suspicion. Seven people dressed in ponchos was an uncommon site on the waypoint. What were they hiding under the baggy clothing?

Under her poncho, Sparks fingered the pistols she *was* hiding, but she knew a shoot-out now would be disastrous for their plan. If she were caught and identified, she knew she would die painfully after she had been tortured for every bit of information she had.

A third car sped into the station, opened, also empty. The group of Chasm troopers moved toward the market.

Sparks whispered to North, "Let me handle this, muscles."

Sparks walked up to the guard, while the rest of the group stood about two meters away.

"Destination please?" the guard asked, as she adjusted her uniform. "And who are you?"

"You don't have clearance for that information," Sparks said.

"Excuse me… I think I do, this is my job," the woman seemed to be considering whether it was worth it or not to hold this unusual group of people attempting to use the Tube. "You know all travel on Tubes is for official business only. If your business isn't official, you'll have to walk."

"We're in a hurry," Sparks said. "I'm Chasm. Former triumvirate. I can give you my confirmation code and you can call it in, but my boss is already antsy." Sparks thumbed out North.

"Wow, he's your boss," the young guard said, instinctively messing with her hair. "I want your job. Wait. How can you be former triumvirate?"

"Long story. Anyway, my boss, he is —" Sparks waived the now flush guard close to her head, "a Hawk. Let's not delay him shall we."

"I thought Hawks were just a legend?" the guard asked.

"Look at that mass of man. Doesn't that look like a legend to you?"

The guard considered North. He looked stern as he conversed with the others standing off in his group.

"I suppose," the guard said. "Mmmm."

"Yeah, he's nice when he wants to be," Sparks said, revealing her two pistols "Gave me these babies after my tenth kill, but he's a real SOB when he's impatient. And he's getting impatient. Let me just give you my code, so you can call it in. I know that will take time to verify."

"No. No, you guys are good."

North looked over and saw Sparks showing off her firearms. The leader of the Chasm trooper foursome also noticed.

"No, you guys are good," the guard said. "By the way, I'm Kayla. Nice to meet you. Can you give me..." Kayla pointed discreetly at North.

Sparks smiled slyly and lowered her voice. "I'll get you his contact handle to your infopad when we're in the Tubecar. That Hawk knows how to charge a woman's battery."

"Thanks," Kayla shrugged. "It never hurts to try, right? You better get going, don't want to keep a Hawk waiting."

Sparks winked at Kayla, turned to her group and said loudly, "Okay, the guard cleared us. You, you and you," she pointed to Goldsmith, Mateo and Advika, "into the first Tube car. The rest of you, with me."

Mateo grabbed North's shoulder, and muttered quietly, "Godspeed." The Marines boarded the first car, closed the hatch and it speed off. The third car was half loaded with crates. Ryder tapped North and nodded toward the crates. "I've figured out what that is. That's ship-to-ship ammo."

North, Ryder, Meliana and Sparks sat in the second car. As North took his seat, he winked at the guard. She giggled, then suddenly sobered up when she noticed the Chasm Trooper leader sprinting back toward the station.

"Stop that car," she shouted to the guard.

The guard looked confused.

"It' okay," the guard said to the Chasm Trooper. "He's a Hawk. Dirt! I probably shouldn't have said that."

"Wait!" the Trooper shouted.

North shrugged and pulled the door closed. Just as the door from their car sealed closed, Sparks saw the Troopers loading into the third car. North's car shot off.

"They are following us," she announced as the suction sound matched the inertia of sudden propulsion.

"Are you sure that is ammo?" North said to Ryder. A whistling sound could be faintly heard as the car was pushed along.

"Pretty sure," Ryder said.

"But what would they need ship-to-ship ordnance for? Waypoints were specifically designed not to have external weapons. The small fleet of armed corvettes was the defensive resources."

"*Utopia*," Sparks said. "It is possible that Chasm developed ship-to-ship ballistic technology."

"But *Magnus'* flack defense system could easily thwart a simple missile attack, so it would be a futile effort," North reasoned.

"We have a more immediate problem in the car behind us," Sparks suggested. "We have about three minutes until our tube stop."

"Time to make something go boom then," North smiled.

"Oh, you know that makes me happy," Sparks said. "Do you have the orbs?"

North produced the explosives pack with three thumbnail sized bombs.

Sparks pulled out one of her pistols. "Cover your ears and eyes," she told her fellow passengers. She aimed at the rear of the car, between Meliana and Ryder's head, and pulled the trigger. The bullet hole she created made the tube car wobble as the internal pressure of the car adjusted to match the external pressure.

"The car should be about five meters behind us," North said. "I've got to time this right. Condi, set the fuse for three seconds on bomb A and make it hot on my mark."

The Marine switched seats with Meliana, pulled Bomb A off of the explosives pack and wedged it in the bullet hole. He took the remaining two and gave them to Sparks.

"Hold these. Okay, Condi. Mark," North said. "Bomb A active," Condi replied.

North flicked the bomb with his finger, but it didn't dislodge.

Ryder's eyes went wide.

North immediately flicked it again, and this time, it vacated the bullet hole, and a second later, detonated.

The explosion rocked North's Tube car, but it kept sailing.

Suddenly, another larger explosion filled the Tube. A flash of heat penetrated the North's car as it was bounced through the Tube, careening until it hit the sidewall and cracked open. The four passengers were tossed hard and clear of the wreckage, onto the tube floor. Smoke filled the tube.

"Ow, mother," Ryder said. "It feels like my arm is broken. Meliana?"

"I'm okay," she replied standing up.

North was already up and moving down the tube. "That worked too well."

"The explosion must have set off the ship-to-ship missiles being carried in that trailing car," Sparks said. Her hair was being whipped about as the pneumatic pressure system went haywire from punctures caused by the explosion.

"Condi, what is the quickest way to the tank access," North asked.

"There is an emergency hatch 20 meters ahead. Through that hatch, take a left for 50 meters and you should be at tank control," the VI responded.

"With any luck, the Chasm authorities will think that explosion was just an accident," Meliana shouted over the wind.

"I doubt we'll be that lucky," Ryder said, tossing off her poncho and drawing a gun. The air current caught her poncho and blew it out of sight. "Let's move while there is chaos. If we can find that hidden base, maybe we can lie low until this heat dies down. Literally."

North nodded and the remainder of the crew followed suit. If they met resistance now, there was no hiding the squads anti-Chasm intentions.

The in-ear communicator filled North's head with Mateo's voice. "Commander, are you guys okay? We've lost pressure and we are moving out on foot."

"Yeah, we had to use one of our toys a little early," North said. "It was a little too effective. Make all haste to the *Prime*. Tell the *Magnus* about potential ship-to-ship missiles. Probably just a nuisance, but better safe than sorry. And keep this line open."

"Wilco, Commander," Mateo radioed his confirmation.

"Do you want me to look at your arm?" Meliana asked Ryder. Ryder winced, but shook her head.

"Let's move."

The hatch was easy enough to find, and within a few minutes, the foursome had stepped out of the damaged tube into the maintenance access beneath the hangar. North quickly found the corridor Condi described and led his team that direction. At the end of the tunnel, a man leaned against the wall, vaping.

North ran up to the man, who smiled when he saw North.

"How are you doing, friend," said the man, who wore baggie dirty civilian clothes and a beanie cap. He was probably 50, North guessed.

"How do you know we are friends?" North asked.

"Well you don't look like Chasm," the man said. "You're not Chasm, are you?"

"You are the lookout?" North asked a second question.

"Yes, sir," the man said, "Let's get you inside and you can talk to our Underground leader. I think she's been waiting for you."

"How did she know we were coming? And who is she? Did Lind contact her?" Meliana asked.

"Can't say that I know. Now before I let you in, not Chasm, correct?"

"With security like this, I can't believe you haven't already been discovered. The Chasm intelligence here must be really horrible," Sparks said. "We're not Chasm."

The man pushed aside a refuse collection unit, exposing a three-quarters-height door with what looked like an antique numeric keypad.

"This old tech doesn't interface with wireless protocols," the man explained. "Makes it much harder to hack."

After he entered a four-digit code, the man pulled open the door. "You guys go on in. I need to keep here at my post and make sure you weren't followed."

North crouched through the door, followed by Meliana, Sparks and Ryder bringing up the rear. The interior of the tank was pitch dark as the door swung closed behind them. North stood, and when he didn't bump his head, he instructed Condi to provide some ambient light, and the infopad complied.

They were in a small room, with the small door leading out behind them and a larger, full-sized sliding door in front. North stepped toward the door and it automatically opened. Through the door North could see what was obviously the large cavity inside the tank. It was still mostly dark, although he noticed ventilation tubes and power cords connecting to the exterior of the room. On the far side of the room was an elevated platform. On the platform was a large chair, facing away from them and towards at least a dozen red-glowing magnetic resonance screens. If the chair didn't have casters and a swivel, North would have thought it was some sort of throne. North started to approach the chair, but then he noticed human activity in the shadows all around them. Smartly dressed men and woman in grey uniforms were reading screens, whispering to each other things North couldn't make out.

This wasn't some rag-tag resistance, North thought. This seemed like a highly coordinated logistics operations center. Taking the *Marquette* from Chasm may be easier than they hoped.

Sparks, a pace behind North, was worried. The air seemed over chilled, and she tried to suppress a shudder. Her instincts drew her hands to her thigh holsters. Meliana walked next to Sparks, and behind them was Ryder, who still had her stun gun drawn.

"Hello?" North said, but the workers seemed to ignore them as they approached the elevated platform and the chair. Someone was clearly sitting in it, and various workers were walking up to that person, whispering in his or her ear, and then walking around to various stations in the tank.

"Hello? I'm Commander North of the–"

"Yes, I know who you are," a female voice came from the chair. "Second-in-command on the *Magnus*. My eyes and ears are nearly omnipresent. Nearly."

"Are you the person in charge here? Who are you?" North asked. He was just a few meters from the platform now. As if on cue, the lights around the platform brightened significantly. North could see the woman in the chair had precisely-placed silver hair pulled back in a perfect bun. Although he couldn't see her well through the back of the chair, North judged her to be a relatively petite woman. Sparks heart was beating fast, her eyes peeled wide.

The chair slowly turned, revealing what North could only describe as a frail-looking woman.

"No! It can't be," Sparks shouted as she simultaneously drew her guns, aiming them at woman and emptying her clips. The bullets seemed to vaporize before they could reach the woman. Shocked at the unexpected, sudden violence, North tried to process what he just saw. Alien tech? Magic? And while his conscious mind was reeling, his instincts already had his hands moving for his rifle.

Sparks looked at her now empty guns and the woman who seemed to be impervious to bullets.

"How the he—" Sparks started convulsing before she could finish her sentence. North reached an arm out to stabilize her, then looked behind him and saw Ryder with her stun gun drawn. North saw fear like he had never seen before in Sparks eyes, as she fell to the floor next to Meliana, who was also convulsing from the effects of a stun gun. Within a blink, both women were unconscious.

North rounded his assault rifle toward Ryder, and was about to put a bullet in Ryder's leg when the old woman spoke. "Put your gun down, North. Or I will order them to shoot."

North hesitated and noticed that every single one of the uniformed workers had drawn side arms and they were all pointed at North. He guessed there were at least 30 weapons pointed at him.

Ryder walked up to North, and holstered her gun.

"Now let's see, how did Sparks do this?" Ryder said as she went to kiss North. She pressed her lips to his. North firmly closed his mouth, as Ryder licked the Marine's lips with her extended tongue. North slowly turned his head sideways, careful to not make any sudden moves. As Ryder stepped back she took his rifle. "No taste for me? That's too bad. What can I say? I'm Chasm. I don't know why Sparks didn't tell you."

Hot blood filled North's head. He was embarrassed, shocked and growing afraid. This whole Underground tank story was a trap, probably used to ferret out those who still opposed Chasm. Was Dr. Lind a plant? He wanted to throttle Ryder's pale throat the way he did Dek, but instead turned slowly back to the old woman, hands raised in clear sight.

"You didn't answer my question," North pressed.

"Oh, yes I am most definitely the one in charge," the old woman said. "My name isn't important, but most people know me as the Chairman."

CHAPTER THIRTEEN

The Chairman stood from her chair and walked toward North. She flicked her head in his direction, and immediately two sharply uniformed Chasm officers, both blonde and burly, seized the Marine, taking his knife, sidearm and pack, before zipping his hands behind his back.

North didn't take his eyes off of the Chairman. She walked in a way that almost seemed like she was floating toward Sparks and Meliana, both sprawled unconscious on the floor. Her face was almost porcelain, and her deep-set eyes appeared to lack an iris. Instead, they were filled with large inky pupils.

She strode over the bodies toward North, looking down at the fallen through her steps. "The dark one, I do not know her. But Sparks, my heart breaks at her treachery. Was it not Dante who believed the coldest parts of hell were reserved for traitors?"

North remained silent.

"Take these two to a holding cell," the Chairman said, as faceless officers jumped to enforce her will. "Let Queenie pass judgement on the dark one. Prepare Sparks for a pre-extermination interrogation. She may have failed at *Magellan*, but perhaps she has unwittingly brought us information we can extract to benefit the common good."

"If you hurt Sparks, I'll will personally introduce you to the vacuum of space," North shouted, his fists clenched hard.

The Chairman, giving no heed to North's threats, turned to a female lieutenant. "Note the toxic emotion exhibited by this alpha male. Many have been tempted to channel this, this ... masculine energy into a powerful military force. But the risk is too great. We must engineer this out of males."

"Yes, Chairman," the officer agreed robotically.

"So, you are this Chairman I keep hearing about," North said. "Shouldn't you be on Arara, building your grand utopia?"

The Chairman ignored the question. "So, you are the handsome Marine North, whom Kimberly wrote about in her reports. Her description doesn't do you justice. You are quite the specimen."

"You knew Kimberly Macready?"

"Raven One," the Chairman said thoughtfully. "Of course. I personally selected her for the *Magellan* mission. *Magellan* was the most important. It was to be the vanguard to protect us from Earth's inevitable retaliation. *Utopia* was mean for *Magellan*."

"*Utopia*? That Frankenstein ship grafted onto this waypoint?"

"We'll, it's not exactly grafted. No matter. Kimberly was my best. But she took her undercover role to far. First Alroy. Then two daughters. When Joti told me, I must confess, I was vexed."

The Chairman suddenly swung her left hand against North's face. The backhand smarted something fierce. North resisted wincing and crying out in pain, but he wondered if his cheek bone had been broken.

"It's rather surreal to see you in person," the Chairman said calmly, as if the flash of violence had never happened, as she stood inches from North. She reached out again, making North flinch, but then she ran her cold fingers over the scar on North's chin. "Kimberly didn't like the influence you had on her daughter. Amberly was Kimberly's mistake, and she paid for it, didn't she? Killed by her own daughter. Matricide. Sick."

"We suspected you still had spies *Magellan*," North asked. "So, it's true?"

The Chairman did not respond to North and continued, "The weakness of humanity starts with the family, then the tribe. Family verses family, tribe verses tribe, nation verse nation. How much human suffering starts with the first attachment: family. The common good transcends this selfish preference for one's own blood. Family corrupted Kimberly, and then family betrayed her. Do you understand, Commander?"

"Amberly didn't have a choice," North protested. "Kimberly was trying to kill everyone on *Magellan*."

"AND WHAT OF IT!" boomed the chairman, who pulled her arm back again to strike North, but before executing the blow, she let her arm drop. She continued in a near whisper. "What of it? Such a small price to pay for the perfection that is coming. Ten thousand measly lives? Out of billions? You thought paradise would be cheap? That it wouldn't cost blood? Kimberly's life was worth more than every soul on every waypoint. Hers is a genius we'll never see again."

"You're insane," North said.

"Araran history won't see it that way. History will remember you, however, and how you tried to stop true goodness from destroying evil forever and how you failed. And history will remember the Amberly Macready, who martyred her own mother, putting her personal desires over the good of the many."

"Leave Amberly out of this," North shouted.

"Why?" the chairman asked as she paced back towards her chair. "She could have been a prince of Arara – but she chose vanity instead."

"Vanity?" North was confused.

"Yes. The young Macready was so self-centered to deny human progress because of her own desire to survive. When we arrive at *Magellan*, Amberly will realize the full error of her ways. She will suffer for her betrayal in ways she never thought were possible. She will wish that her mother had succeeded, and she was dead. Only then will she understand her true value."

"Arrive at *Magellan*?" North asked, his eyes growing hard.

"You thought we were going to just let *Magellan* live?" The Chairman explained. "No, *Magellan* will either join us, or die."

"I don't know what secrets this *Magnus* has," the Chairman looked at North as she sat back on her thrown, "but do you believe that I haven't been preparing for this eventuality? *Magnus* is coming back, we know. We'll see if she is a match for *Utopia*."

"Madam Chairman, I *do* know what secrets *Magnus* has," Ryder said, bowing low. "I've been spying on that ship for the last year. With your permission, may I confer with your tactical officer?"

The Chairman offered a thin smile. "Ryder, you have served us well. Honored destroyer of *Cortez*, and a survivor. You will have a grand appointment in the Ministry of Truth. Yes, take your leave immediately. Let's hope your information will give us a critical advantage."

Ryder rose and left the room, with several officers following her. North couldn't believe how foolish he had been, that he hadn't seen Ryder was Chasm.

"Ryder, I saved your life!" North shouted after Ryder as the door slid behind the spy.

"North, your time runs short," the Chairman said as her eyes settled back on the Marine. "And it looks like the flight of the

Magnus is coming to an end, as well."

"Whatever power *Utopia* has, it's nothing compared to the *Magnus*," North boasted. He was trying to goad Chasm, to get them to reveal tactical information.

"You speak out of ignorance, loyalist," the Chairman retorted.

"We have particle beams with accuracy for tens of thousands of kilometers that can disable your engines and your weapons. Just like we did on *American Spirit*. We have a fleet of corvettes capable of quarter-light speed that you will never be able to target. Their chain guns will shred *Utopia*. You all should just surrender now! Do you hear me?" North shook as he looked around and shouted at the officers. "What do you have against those? You will all die at the hands of the *Magnus*!"

The woman who North assumed was a second-in-command stepped up and shouted back. "Did you see that personal point defense system the Chairman used to dissolve bullets? Everyone one of our ship-to-ship missiles is equipped with one! You can't shoot our ordnance down. And some of our warheads are fusion-powered. Can your precious *Magnus* take a direct hit from a nuke, filthy traditionalist?"

Bingo! North thought. "But what about the corvettes?" North demanded, hoping the officer would give up more information.

"Stupid man! We have our own fleet of –"

A shot echoed through the chamber, and the lieutenant fell to the floor, dead with a bullet through her head. The Chairman was standing with a gun at the end of her outstretched arm.

"Idiot woman," the Chairman sighed. She holstered her sidearm, sat back down in her chair and looked to another officer. "Clean up that mess. And someone get a signal scanner on this Marnie."

A male tech officer who North guessed was barely 20, timidly approached North with what he assumed was some sort of device that scanned for EM frequencies.

North's gambit was up. He was pleased he was able to play Chasm after they had played him so well. If he was lucky, *Magnus* would finish its mission and free him before Chasm executed him. But the odds weren't good. It could take days for *Magnus'* teams to board and overtake *Marquette*. It would only take minutes for

Chasm to toss North out of an airlock, or seconds to put a bullet in his head.

"Let me save you the trouble," North said. He knew he wouldn't get any more enemy intel to his retreating Marines over the personal comm channel he and Mateo had left open. He knew the end was near, as the Chairman had prophesied, and he could only think of one person: Amberly. He had once last chance to send her a message. *No reason not to go all in,* North thought.

"Hey, Mateo, looks like I'm signing off. Hope you've been listening. Looks like I'm going to buy the farm. If you make it home, tell her... tell Amberly I love her."

"Tell her yourself, Commander," North heard Mateo's voice through the open channel on his communicator. "We're coming for you."

"Get the intel back to *Magnus,* that's an order. For the fallen, and for *Magellan,* friend."

"I understand," Mateo said, and North could hear his voice choke up with sudden grief. "Godspeed, Commander."

"North out." North then poked his pinky finger into his inner ear and carefully popped his micro-communicator and handed it to the tech who stared dumfounded at it.

The Chairman, in what seemed like an instant, sprung from her chair to the tech, grabbed the tiny comm unit from his hand, crushed it between her index finger and thumb.

"Find his compatriots! Don't let them off this waypoint," the Chairman shouted. The hidden command center immediately buzzed with activity.

North smiled, seeing he had gotten a rise out of the otherwise unflappable Chairman.

The *Prime's* engines were hot. Kilo looked over at Rhodes. "Are they onboard, Ensign?" Kilo pressed.

"Goldsmith?" Rhodes nearly shouted through the ship's intercom. "Status?"

The enlisted Marine's voice responded. "We're all on. Airlock is secure."

Rhodes pushed back her black mane. "They're onto us. Get us out of here!"

Mateo rushed on to the bridge. "Move before they launch

their corvettes."

The *Prime's* thrusters fired and the ship pulled away from the exterior hull of *Waypoint Marquette*. Kilo's hand moved through the pilot's magnetic resonance screen, commanding the runabout to full power as it sped away.

Mateo looked at the doppler. "Three corvettes have cleared the *Marquette* hanger," he said. "We're not going to make it. Rhodes, transmit our sitrep and North's comm log to the Captain and hurry. If they get to us before we can transmit —"

"Can't we fight back?" Goldsmith asked.

Advika had just made it to the bridge, eyes wide, full of adrenaline and fear.

"Transmit the message first," Mateo said. "Once we know the information is safe, then we can turn and fight."

"I'm good, but I can't beat three corvettes," Kilo said.

"We all knew the risks," Mateo said. "Let's finish the mission, then bring whatever pain we can on those Chasm bogies. Rhodes, how is the transmission going?"

Condi chimed up. "Two minutes until we are in bogie firing range."

The ensign looked at her magnetic resonance screen. "Almost there. We should make it."

"Keep running, Kilo," Mateo said. "The more distance you give us, the more time we have to finish the transmission."

"Tell me something I don't know," Kilo said. "In fact, even better, make yourself useful and man the chain gun."

"This is it, then," Rhodes said, looking to Advika. "The transmission is complete."

The ship wide comms crackled to life.

"*Prime*, this is Nyota. We're coming in full throttle. Your escort back to *Magnus* is here!"

"Wing Commander Nyota, I've never been so happy to hear your voice. We have three bogies bearing on our aft, ETA, less than a minute," Lt. Cho said from the command chair.

"*Prime*, keep your course steady. We're on them."

Rhodes looked out the bow portal and saw six growing lights heading straight toward them. Within seconds, the *Magnus* corvette wing zipped past the *Prime*.

"Awesome!" Rhodes shouted loudly.

"Alpha wing, we weren't expecting you for hours. What happened?" Kilo said into the ship-to-ship comm.

"The captain was just impatient," the Wing Commander replied. Then she addressed her pilots. "We've trained for this for years. You know what to do. Let's take out those Chasm corvettes. Weapons free and go give 'em hell."

The Battle of Marquette has begun, Rhodes thought.

Captain Obadiah had given up vaper puffing many years ago, but he thought this was as good as any occasion to relapse. He puffed on a thick cylinder protruding from his mouth, and examined the tactical screen, surrounded by senior officers and their support yeomen.

The captain blew a thick stream of smoky vapors out his nose, and then turned to the communications officer on deck. "Bring me a live link with *Prime* as soon as they are in encryption rage."

The scrawny officer, Fuego Boot, looked up from his post across the bridge. "Secure comms in two minutes; we should have the *Prime* safe in harbor in less than 10."

Lt. Commander Alicia Blight's green eyes were crossed as she intently studied the live tactical display. "Nyota is now in weapons range. The enemy corvettes must see they are outnumbered two-to-one, and they are not breaking off."

"If they are the original models transported out with *Marquette*, we should easily be able to out maneuver those dirt-lickers," Boot said. "Based on their pursuit speed, Condi reports we have a six-x speed advantage."

"Excellent," Obadiah mused. "I hope we make short work of them."

"I have the *Prime* on comms," the scrawny officer said.

"*Magnus*, this is *Prime*. Thanks for sending the cavalry," Rhodes' voice crackled over the speaker.

"Rhodes, what's is the XO's status?" the captain asked.

"We lost him sir," Rhodes replied. "Also, missing are Sparks and Ryder ... Ryder was a turncoat."

"Dammit," the captain swore. "Boot, tell engineering increase speed to point-oh-two c. Alicia, launch Beta Wing and tell the Marine squad commanders to prepare for grappling gangways."

"That's risky," Blight replied through red bangs hanging over her pale forehead. "We don't have enough on-the-ground intelligence."

"Captain, Cho here," North's second-in-command spoke through the radio. "They did not have the major waypoint corridors locked down, though the main Tube is out of order. North's handiwork. No doubt they will soon lock everything down. I think the longer we wait, the more we lose whatever advantage we have."

"I agree," the captain said as he puffed. "Execute assault plan Optima Two. If the civilian traffic is light on the waypoint, we can move faster to the command."

"Yes, it seemed that way," Cho replied. "We have you on visual now."

"Excellent," Obadiah said. "Get on board and I want you, Rhodes and Bollard up on the bridge on the double."

"Wilco, *Prime* out."

"Should we be worried about this point-defense-system?" Boot asked.

"They were developing that sort of technology on earth 100 years ago," the captain said. "But no one could ever get it to work. The computing technology and energy reserves needed are just too great."

"Maybe Chasm was able to make point-defense work." Boot suggested. "What then?"

"Then, Feugo, we have a problem."

This is going to be no problem, Nyota thought, as she rubbed her dyed-blonde buzz cut.

"Alpha-six, put some distance between you and Bogie One," Nyota gave orders as she glided her corvette, the *M.S.S. Khan,* behind the lead enemy corvette. The *Marquette's* corvette attempted to juke Nyota with some evasive spinning, but the ship's inferior speed made it impossible to get clear. Nyota matched the Chasm pilot, move for move.

"Chasm corvette, this is Wing Commander Okapi Nyota of the *U.S.S. Magnus.* You are ordered to surrender immediately or be destroyed. Power down your vessel and prepare to be taken aboard as a prisoner of war," Nyota said in a voice that made it clear she meant business.

"Wing Commander Nyota," the enemy pilot responded over the open channel, "please take your corrupt evil ways and go back to Earth and leave us alone, or we will be forced to destroy you."

"Stupid death cult," Nyota muttered and she switched on her secure channel to *Magnus*. "Wing commander to *Magnus*, I am going to turn this guy into space junk."

Blight's voice came back over the comm. "Wing commander, the captain confirms your previous weapons free order. Light 'em up."

"Confirmed, engaging. Nyota out."

Finally, you murderous bastards, it's payback time, the wing commander thought. She pulled the trigger on the manual guidance yoke and immediately the chain guns spun up, sending hundreds of rounds of explosive ammo at the Chasm corvette in her sight.

Okapi Nyota had never seen actual ship-to-ship combat, though she had done drills and simulators enough to expect quite an explosion when 50 mm ammo shredded the carbon-fiber hull and engine of a corvette.

But after nearly 30 seconds of nonstop weapons fire, Nyota had seemed to deal no damage to her target.

"*Magnus*," the lead pilot called back to her base ship, "I can't explain it. My chain guns seem to have no effect. It's like the bullets are just … disappearing."

"Nyota, this is Bollard," the chief engineer's voice filled the cockpit. "It's the point-defense system that North was able to get us a warning about. We may be able to get past it with a particle beam. Surely they can't deflect energy weapons discharging at just under the speed of light."

"Great," Nyota said. "We don't have particle beams on corvettes. Any other helpful intel you want to pass on, Bollard?

"Sorry," Bollard "Captain says to keep them occupied until *Magnus* is in rage – four minutes – or, if you can, draw them into our range sooner."

"Copy," Nyota said, glancing down at her tactical display. A Chasm ship had broken formation and was charging her stern. "Dirt!"

She rolled off of the ship she was tailing to get out of the line of fire of the second bogie bearing down on her. Her ship didn't have any magic defense system, and those bullets fired from the enemy corvette would tear her apart with ease.

Nyota juiced the *Khan's* engines and quickly put hundreds of kilometers between her and her assailant. She made a wide bank, identified a target, and attempted to get behind it.

"Anyone got anything?" a deep, male voice came over wing comm channel. "My bullets are useless. Wing commander?"

Even without the computer identifier, Nyota recognized the voice of Carlos Spike, probably her best pilot – at least in a simulator. "Everyone, stay out of their scopes. Just try to keep them tied up until *Magnus* is in range. We have the agility advantage, but our weapons seem to be useless. Unless…"

"Commander?"

"Carlos, I'm going to try something crazy," Nyota said. "I want to get the first kill."

The *Khan* maneuvered behind the same corvette Nyota had been tailing before.

"Hey, Khan," Nyota said to her ship's eponymous VI. "Can you auto pilot us to within, say three meters of the bogie?"

"At that range, we could take damage from the bogie's rear thruster," Khan replied.

"I know. Put us off center a meter on the z-axis. Please execute the maneuver."

"Executing."

At the speed they were traveling, colliding with the bogie, particularly if it adjusted speed unexpectedly, was highly possible. Nyota had to rely on the computer pilot to adjust faster than she could.

"Are you crazy, Nyota?!" Carlos shouted over comms.

"Shut it, Carlos."

The two ships were locked in a formation that almost seemed choreographed now. One miscalculation would cause a fatal collision. The Chasm pilot tried to break away, but his ship lacked the speed. Nyota imagined the enemy pilot sweating.

"We are now three meters away from the target and holding," Khan announced.

"Can you get us as close as two meters?" Nyota said.

"The possibility of my making a fatal adjustment at this speed at two meters distance is 30 percent and not advised."

"Get us closer. Two meters distance please," Nyota commanded coolly. "I want to smell this guy's butt."

"Understood," Khan replied. "Shutting down all extraneous processor tasks to devote maximum computational ability to the autopilot. Two meters and holding."

"Hey, Chasm leader," Nyota said on the open channel. "My guess is your bullet defense has to be projected, maybe three meters?"

The Chasm pilot growled, and then said over the channel, "Wait. What?"

"Allow me to be the first to welcome you to hell," Nyota said as she spun up the Khan's chain guns. The point defense system seemed to activate as well, and as Nyota expected, her ship was partially inside the field – specifically, the business end of her chain guns.

With no energy shield between the bullets and the Chasm ship, the vessel was quickly shredded. The Chasm pilot screamed over the open channel, and Nyota wondered if he would die from space exposure or from bullets ripping though his flesh.

Then, the Chasm ship exploded.

Debris from the fireball immediately slammed into the *Khan*, sending the ship in a rapid, uncontrolled spin.

"Chairman, our corvettes in pursuit of the runabout have been engaged what looks like a complement of *Magnus*' corvettes," a grey-clad officer hastily spouted, clearly out of breath. "Somehow one of our fighters was destroyed by ballistic attack."

The Chairman struck North again with the back of her hand, slopping blood from the Marines lacerated mouth onto the otherwise meticulously clean floor of the Chairman's secret headquarters. She eyed the blood splatter and licked her lips, momentarily distracted from the Marine.

"How many corvettes are on *Magnus*?" the Chairman refocused on North.

North smiled, "A million."

"I don't have time for this," the Chairman said, turning from the bound Marine. She started barking orders at her entourage.

"Launch *Utopia*, and tell Captain Niki to nuke the *Magnus* as soon as that ship is in range. If *Magnus* retreats, pursue until destroyed. That ship is the only thing that can stop *Marquette* from taking up watchdog orbit over Arara."

"I don't understand," North said. "Why do you need a watchdog?"

"Simpleton. Resistance on the planet takes far too long to subdue with traditional forces. From space, we can just bombard resistance. There is nowhere to hide. And there's no way to disable or take out a waypoint from the surface of Arara. *Marquette* is the ultimate enforcer. We will watch over the beloved community from on high."

"And only *Magnus* could take out a weaponized fascist waypoint?" North surmised.

"Fascist? Such an outdated term. Such slander," the Chairman said. "You have nothing to offer the common good, therefore you are nothing, Commander North. Good day to you."

The Chairman pointed to her two brawny bodyguards. "Put the commander out an airlock. Immediately."

Sparks sat up with a start. She was lying on some sort of metallic bed or gurney, soaked in her own sweat. *The Chairman? Here! Dirt!* Sparks thought. Her head buzzed worse than any hangover she'd ever known. *I've been stunned!*

She looked the around the poorly lit space and realized that it was Dr. Lind's clinic. She peered across the room and saw, on another gurney, Meliana, unconscious. Sparks forced herself to stand, her temples throbbing, and she walked over to Meliana.

"Hey, Meliana, get your ass up!" Sparks shouted, and Meliana slowly opened her eyes, reached her arms above her head and rubbed her bleached white hair. "We've got to get out of here."

Sparks saw a plastic tray with a half dozen rainbow colored stim injectors, evenly spaced out. "Do you know what those are?" She asked Meliana, who was struggling to sit up.

The door swung open, and she saw a tall, dark curly-haired man, with a gun strapped to his hip. Sparks thought he looked surprised to see her up and about.

"Queenie!" Meliana shouted.

"What the—" Queenie said, expecting his victims to still be

stunned.

Sparks grabbed the tray and flung it into Queenie's face, injectors flying all over the room. Queenie went for his gun, but instead collapsed when his femur cracked with a loud snap under the pressure of a leaping kick from Sparks.

"Auuughgths!" Queenie garbled in intense pain.

Sparks grabbed the gun – a loaded pistol, she guessed by the weight – and aimed it at Queenie.

"Get on the gurney," Sparks commanded, waving the gun in his face. "Now!"

"I can't even walk," Queenie cried.

"Oh my, oh my. You let them kill my husband," Meliana had picked up the tray and slammed it into Queenie's head. "And my baby!" She hit him again, and this time, the corner of the tray ripped a chunk of skin off Queenie's face, blood surfacing quickly.

"Wait! Wait!" Queenie said.

"Just pull the trigger," Meliana said. "By gods, be done with him."

"Slow down, Meliana," Sparks said. She wasn't afraid to take a life, but to kill someone who had been neutralized gave her some pause.

Sparks back was to the door as it slid open again. Dr. Lind came barreling through, throwing the full force of his body into the petite woman. She dropped the gun as she fell, and it slid into the hands of Queenie.

"Lady, get back on the table now, and let Dr. Lind do his work," Queenie said, as he forced himself in a sitting position against the wall. He aimed the gun plainly at Sparks.

Sparks put her hands in the air and slowly backed away.

"Do you know how cross the Chairman would be if you are not properly interrogated?" Queenie asked. "Meliana, you need to sit down as well. I was going to spare you torture. But since you decided to rearrange my face, maybe I'll let Dr. Lind take a turn on you, too."

Meliana spat at Queenie as she slowly backed up and sat down on her table. Dr. Lind had gathered up the injectors.

"Lind, how could you side with Chasm?" Meliana said as tears welled up in her eyes. "You led us into a trap. What about Barack? What about Ehud?"

"I'm sorry Meliana," Dr. Lind said. "It was me or them. Join or die, they said. I joined."

"What about Pinita?" Meliana asked.

"She made her choice. She wouldn't join," Lind replied. "Out of my hands."

"Coward! Damn dirty coward!" Meliana shouted angrily.

"Maybe, but I may get to see this paradise Chasm is building."

"You idiot," Sparks snorted. "There is no paradise. Just slavery to the Chairman."

"Get it over with, Dr. Lind," Queenie said, waving the gun. "And then get my leg patched up. It hurts like the living hell. And I'm gonna need some stitches on my face."

"So, the first one is an intoxicant, the second is a hallucinogen, and this orange one essentially reduces your inhibition to zero," Dr. Lind said, indicating the three injectors he was palming. "Please lie down, Sparks. Queenie will shoot you if he has to."

"Believe it, bitch," Queenie smiled a mouth full of crooked teeth.

Sparks laid down on the cold metal, and reached her hand slowly into her front left-hand pocket, and fingered two small orbs.

"Please don't," Sparks quivered.

A shot rang out, putting a hole in the wall just a few centimeters above Sparks' head. "If you say anything else, it will be the last thing you say," Queenie threatened.

Sparks put her fingernail into a slot in one of the orbs of her pocket.

Dr. Lind pulled out the small intoxicant injector. As he bent down to inject Sparks neck, she reached her hand out of her pocket and shoved the orb deep into Dr. Lind's right nostril.

"Wow!" Sparks said as she grew flush from the injection.

Queenie tried to shoot Sparks, but Dr. Lind had stumbled between them, crying out in pain and clawing at the orb imbedded deep in his nasal cavity. The two unused injectors fell to the floor.

"Get out of the way, Lind!" Queenie leaned forward to try to get a clear shot on Sparks who was climbing over to the far side of the gurney, but he couldn't stand up for the pain in his broken leg.

Meliana eyed the injectors, and in a split second, scooped

them both up and lunged at the distracted Queenie. She pushed both injectors into his neck.

"Dirty ho!" Queenie said, and he dropped the gun.

"Get down, Meliana!" Sparks said as she flipped the gurney on its side and crouched between it and the wall.

Dr. Lind had nearly clawed his nose off.

Too late, sucker, thought Sparks.

Dr. Lind's head exploded, the bomb essentially vaporizing his brains and skull, while large fleshy torso fragments flew across the room. The force of the explosion pushed the gurney into Sparks and shoved her up against the wall. A fire had broken out, and pink retardant started spraying, covering everyone and everything in the room.

"Mel- mel- anna," Sparks struggled to say, "Are you okkkkkaaay?"

"I'm fine, I think," she responded. She looked down at Queenie. She couldn't tell if he was unconscious or dead. She looked at the blob that was Dr. Lind. Definitely dead.

"If get you to a pod, will you take me back with you to *Magnus*?"

"He he he he he," Sparks giggled. "I am soooooooooo lit."

"Great, let's scoot," Meliana said. She picked up the gun and was about to hand it to Sparks.

"Oooohhh, a gun," Sparks said. "I miss my guns."

"On second thought, I'll hold onto it. I think I know a pod we can escape on."

"No... nooo.... rrr... no."

"No? Why not?"

"Nooo. Not no... Norrth. We have to get North. I can't live without him. I loooove him."

CHAPTER FOURTEEN

"Action stations," Captain Obadiah tossed his empty smoker on the command table. The bridge had grown hot with human activity. "Rhodes, get me Nyota on the horn. Weapons station, report."

"Suri, reporting in sir," the gunnery chief's voice projected over the bridge speakers. "All tubes ordnance laden. Particle beams one fully charged. Two is powering up – three minutes until charged."

"Rhodes, do you have Nyota?" the captain said.

"Negative, sir," the teenage officer said in an unusually quiet voice.

"See if you can have Carlos get us a visual. I want my wing commander back. Put me on ship wide."

"Yes sir," Rhodes said, swallowing each word.

"Attention, this is the captain. We've traveled for 18 years and eight light years for this moment. Our lives were meant for this. Fulfill your destiny. We will liberate *Waypoint Marquette*, we will defend *Waypoint Magellan*, and we will avenge *Waypoint Cortes*. We have this strong ship, our friend, the *Magnus*. But don't count only on our particle beams and antimatter drives. Count on our humanity. Our individual talents, and our voluntary love for each other. We were not forced to be here. We *chose*. We *choose* our future, and that is why we are better than Chasm, and that is why we will win. Godspeed to us all."

"Captain!" Blight looked up from the tactical display. "It's massive. The ship, *Utopia*, is debarking from the waypoint. It's headed on an intercept course."

"Full stop," the captain said. "Let her come to us."

Rhodes felt her stomach jump into her head as the inertia dampeners kicked in.

"Gunnery chief, let's see what the particle beams can do against point defense," Obadiah said as he looked around for his vape smoker. "Target Bogie Three. Rhodes: Tell Lt. Spike to get clear. And find Nyota."

Rhodes picked up her headset to comply with the captain's orders, her eyes welling with tears. The captain noticed.

"Rhodes," the captain looked at his youngest officer with compassion. "North is not your fault. Not your responsibility."

"We should not have left them behind," Rhodes said.

"You obeyed orders, Ensign. North knew the mission was paramount, and you delivered critical information. Do not grieve what isn't. We'll get them back."

"Spike is clear of Bogie Three," Blight reported.

"Blow it," the captain ordered.

Lt. Carlos Spike had nearly emptied his ammo reserves attempting to wear down the point defense system on Bogie Three. *That thing has to suck a lot of power,* the pilot reasoned. Spike had joined the Alpha Wing when the *Magnus* had stopped at *Waypoint Cabot.* When Captain Obadiah told him about *Magnus*' highly classified mission, Spike knew this was the best offer he was ever going to have to get out his mundane life defending *Cabot* from … nothing. The last seven years on *Magnus* had been equally boring until the Battle of *Magellan.* Now, two years later, he was back in action. Real action. *Of course, my stupid guns are useless,* Carlos thought.

The corvette he was tailing, designated Bogie Three by *Magnus,* hit its retro thrusters. Spike had to dive deep on the relative z-axis of his corvette, *M.S.S. Menudo,* to avoid colliding.

"Spike, this is *Magnus,*" Rhodes said over the wireless. "Do you—"

Now Bogie Three was on his tail. He pushed his hand forward through the dense magnetic resonance yoke, and kicked the manual accelerator pedal. "*Magnus,* no time to chat. I have flames licking my ass here."

Bogie Three didn't waste any time to take its shot. The corvette unloaded its own spray of explosive ordnance.

A single bullet found its target, but only shredded a cosmetic fin.

The *Menudo* spun wildly to avoid the additional fire as it accelerated. Even with the inertia dampeners, Carlos nearly passed out as 4G of effective pressure pushed him hard into his seat. The superior engines on the *Menudo* slipped the ship out of the firing range of Bogie Three.

"Yowza! That was close *Magnus.* Looks like I got nicked,"

Carlos said to the radio. "But I'm cool. I'm cool."

"I think you just made history as the first Marine pilot to be hit in a space dogfight," Rhodes said.

"Don't report that," Carlos said, dejected.

"Captain orders you to break off and find Nyota," Rhodes instructed. "We can't find her. We've got Bogie Three for you."

Carlos did a 180-degree turn, and in the process, the *Magnus* in all its gleaming glory, came into view. He had never seen the firing tubes open with its torpedo-like ordnance in strike position. He scanned about eight or nine of the fifty tubes open. He noted the *Magnus* must be at action stations, as many of the portal windows that would have normally exposed lit rooms were dark. Non-essential lights shut off during combat to make it harder for enemy ships to make a visual detection.

Suddenly, a sustained yellow streak of what could only be described as liquid light, shot from the *Magnus* and intersected with Bogie Three. The point defense system seemed to disperse the beam before it could reach the corvette, which was attempting to retreat toward the flat cylinder form of *Marquette*.

A second beam fired from the *Magnus*. The point defense system seemed to hold it back as well. The beams persisted, and Bogie Three attempted all manner of evasion, but *Magnus'* computer would not lose its target so easily.

Carlos pointed the *Menudo* at Bogie Three and began a strafing run. The last remaining corvette from the original *Marquette* dispatch was moving in to get a shot on the *Menudo*, even though several *Magnus* corvettes were showering it with chain gun fire.

"Lieutenant Spike, what are you doing? You were ordered to get clear of bogies."

"Boring," he said as he lined up Bogie Three, still being assaulted by two particle beams, in his sites. He pulled his firing trigger and found the limit of Bogie Three's point defense system.

Menudo's bullets shredded Bogie Three's cockpit, killing the pilot immediately. The point defense failed, and both particle beams sliced up Bogie Three, leading to a spectacular explosion.

"Wooo hooo! *Magnus,* is that the first space kill in history?"

"Negative, Carlos. Nyota got a kill. WHOA! Careful on your aft, you've got —"

Carlos Spike did not live to hear the rest of the sentence. The ship-to-ship missile had traveled so fast that *Menudo's* sensors barely registered it before it embedded into the ships engines and exploded into a disintegrating fireball.

Silhouetted against the lights of *Marquette*, the mighty *Utopia,* on the move, claimed its first victim.

Sparks was struggling to walk in a semi-straight line, as she followed behind Meliana. Meliana was holding Queenie's pistol out. The waypoint public address system was blaring. A shrill female voice spoke, "Residents of *Marquette*. This is a drill. Please return to your quarters and comply with general curfew rules. Failure to participate in the drill will result in your immediate termination, by order of Chasm command."

The pair were walking through a brightly lit corridor, with blank white walls and a series of portals. This section of the Africa Quarter was full of professional offices – lawyers, independent software engineers and others had small workspaces here. To their relief, all these civilians were curfew-compliant. The place was deserted.

"We're almost to the hanger," Meliana said. "Gawds, you are smashed."

"I havennnn't had a drop. Drop. Drop."

"This way," Meliana opened a side hatch which led down a small, steep stairwell.

"Um… I don't know if I can… umm…" Sparks put on foot tentatively on the first step, missed it entirely and fell down the flight to the hard metal floor.

"Owwwwwie," Sparks mumbled, sitting up sticking a finger in the air. "I'm oooooo-kaaaay."

"Are you sure?" Meliana. "That's a nasty fall!"

Sparks started to laugh uncontrollably. "I actually can't feel ennathing. I shood do thi-smore often."

Meliana looked both ways to see if anyone had seen them enter. When she was convinced they were not being followed, she closed the hatch, descended the stairs and helped Sparks to her feet.

"That was noooot fun," Sparks said.

A few minutes later they were around a corner from the

entrance to the secret headquarters.

"You think he is still in there?" Meliana asked Sparks.

"How's shooed I know," Sparks slurred. "But we better hur-hurry. Get-ty up."

Meliana rounded the corner with her gun drawn. The liar who said he was part of the Underground was still at this post, in dirty, baggie civilian clothes. He saw Meliana with her gun drawn and he just laughed.

"I guess you don't know what a point defense system is," he said. "All the elite guard have it. Go ahead, shoot."

Sparks stepped forward and pushed down Meliana's arm holding the gun. "I got this sisther."

Sparks sauntered toward the guard. "Hey cutie, you wouldn't shoot something thith... this... beeee-utiful."

"Actually," the man said, "you're kind of a wreck."

"And I'm drunk as a skunk."

"Is that so?" he asked.

"You know... know... what I like to do when eeeeeye am drunk as a skunk," Sparks said, as she licked he lips.

"No, but maybe I want to find out." The man's gaze had turned into a leer.

Sparks walked right up to the guard and started licking his ears, then his face, and his nose.

"Gross, stop," the man pulled away a few centimeters. "I can find a better place for you to use that tongue though."

"Elite guard, puuuushaah," Sparks slobbered. "Pretty laaaame. I just swiped your gun."

Sparks put two or three stun bolts into the man. Who fell to the floor, convulsing.

"Wow," Meliana said as she stood next to Sparks.

Sparks grabbed the pistol out of Meliana's hand and placed it next to the temple of the now unconscious guard. "Let's see if point defense works at pooooint blaaaank range." She pulled the trigger.

"Nope."

The main door opened, and two guards came out, both holding onto one of North's arm.

"Which airlock do we take him too?" one said as he looked up and noticed the dead man lying at the feet of Sparks and

Meliana, with Sparks literally holding a smoking gun.

One of the guards immediately aimed his rifle at Sparks.

"Drop the gun, traitor," he said. Sparks complied, slipping her now empty hand into her pocket.

"Sparks? What are you doing here?" North asked.

"I'm drunk off my ass! Woooot! And we're saving you.... because I loooooove you North. I love your hard arms and your tight bu—"

"Shut up!" the guard said.

"Ready to go booooom!?!" Sparks shouted with just a little too much crazy in her eyes.

"Holy dirt, Sparks," North swore.

Sparks pulled out the last micro-bomb, inserted her fingernail and tossed it in the general direction of the escort guards – and North!

North's self-preservation instincts kicked in, and though his hands were still zipped, he shoulder-butted the guard that still held him, knocking him to the ground. North dove to the ground himself and tried to roll away from the explosive pebble.

"What the!?" asked the guard who still had his assault rifle trained on Sparks.

Meliana jumped away, hitting the ground too and covering her head with her arms. Sparks just stood there, smirking. "Five, four, three –"

"What is it going to do, make a puff of smoke?" the armed guard said.

Wow, you are that dumb, thought Sparks as she turned around and started to walk away.

"Stop," the guard said, "or I *will* shoo—"

Both guards were decimated in the blast. The explosive force caught Sparks by the back and threw her to the ground.

Alert alarms begin to blare as a second pair of guards came out of the HQ to see what was going on. They saw Sparks on the ground, and then the smoldering pile of human flesh. North came from behind and kicked them in rapid succession in the back of the knees.

Sparks slid over the floor, picked up the stun gun and put both of the new Chasm troopers to sleep.

"Cut my zips! There's a dozen more troopers in there," North said.

Meliana started working on the cuffs.

Sparks walked up to North. "What? I saved your ass. Time for my... my..."

Sparks pushed her mouth onto North's just as Meliana freed North's hands. North put his strong arms around Sparks.

"You almost blew me up," he whispered in her ear.

"Worth it."

"Come on! Let's go!" Meliana urged.

"Captain, Carlos is gone," Rhodes said, her voice unsteady.

Cho saw uncertainty in Rhodes' eyes. He stepped over from the command table to the comm station and put a hand on Rhodes' shoulder. "Steady now," he said, softly and deeply.

"Anti-ballistic missile system online," Blight reported.

"Bring us around," the captain said as he looked up from the tactical display to the portal on the bridge. He saw *Utopia* with his own eyes for the first time. The mammoth ship was almost twice as large as *Magnus* and at least equally armed. *Utopia* was not trying to hide. The ship was brilliantly lit, with a metallic blue hue. The ship had a secondary hull which was the primary mechanism that allowed it to seemingly fuse with *Marquette*. Port and aft hanger doors slid open, and a swarm of half-sized corvettes buzzed out of *Utopia*.

"I count fifteen, maybe twenty new bogies," Cho reported from the tactical display.

"Helm, try to slip us between *Utopia* and *Marquette*. If we can't disable *Utopia*, I still want to get our Marines onboard the waypoint," the captain said.

"Wilco," the short helmsman said.

"Prepare to empty our tubes. Let's hit *Utopia* with everything we've got."

North, Sparks and Meliana were looking for an escape pod. North's plan was to eject from *Marquette* with the hope that they could get towed by a runabout or a corvette back to the *Magnus*. The pods had minimal propulsion, an emergency radio beacon, and not much else.

"Are we lost?" Sparks asked, rubbing her head. North

instinctively grabbed for his infopad from his pack, but forgot that Chasm had taken his gear.

"Let's try this way," North frowned, pointing toward what he thought was the exterior rim of *Marquette*. "You never have an infopad when you need one."

Sparks stim-high was fading, and she had descended into another headache. She signaled for her party to stop and get quiet, and listened. "Hear that," she whispered. "We're being followed."

"Over there!" Meliana pointed to an emergency direction marker. "The pod should be around the corner."

North stepped around the bend and nearly ran head first into Ryder. She immediately drew her sword and swung for the Marine's head.

"Ha! Knew you'd come for the escape pod," Ryder said mid-swing. North dove under the blade and wrapped his arms around Ryder's legs, bringing her to the ground with a hard thud.

Sparks looked behind Ryder and saw a hideous Queenie, covered with freshly burned flesh and blast wounds, hair stuck together with matted blood. His leg was splinted and braced, forcing him to limp. He held an assault rifle at gut level and immediately started spraying bullets.

Sparks jumped and rolled, attempting to get out of Queenie's line of fire. She felt a sharp pain in her right thigh. She made a show of reaching into her pocket and then flinging her hand at Queenie.

"No! Not again! Bomb!" Queenie shouted deliriously, dropped his rifle, and threw himself backward, stumbling over North and Ryder, who were struggling over Ryder's katana blade.

I can't believe that worked, Sparks thought as her imaginary bomb did no real damage. She reached for the fallen rifle.

Queenie's momentum pushed North clear of the Ryder, and North was able to kick her swiftly in the head before springing to his feet. Still mad with hallucinogens, Queenie lunged at North. The pair grappled, but North clearly had the upper hand.

Sparks was lifting the assault rifle from the ground as Ryder thrust her sword, attempting to strike Sparks' torso. Sparks used the rifle to parry with Ryder's lethal blade. Beads of sweat glistened on Ryder's forehead as she kept beating down on Sparks and the rifle, prompting Sparks to aggressively block. Sparks kept trying to get the lethal end of the rifle pointed at Ryder, but the spymaster's relentless attacks required her to keep using the gun as a shield.

North punched Queenie in the gut with so much power he was nearly lifted in the air as he vomited. Queenie forced himself to move through the convulsive expulsion of his last meal. North stepped back, and he began to draw up another punch as Queenie reached for his sidearm, a stun weapon.

He was too slow, and this time, North hit him square in the nose. Queenie began to see stars and collapsed.

Sparks ducked a full slice from Ryder. "I treated you like a sister. I protected you. And now this is how it is?"

"I have no idea what game you are playing," Ryder said.

Ryder took another swing, and Sparks leapt back. Sparks tried to train the rifle on Ryder, but she was too quick and forced Sparks to defend again.

The pair grappled, weapons locked, both pushing hard for an advantage.

"You're playing North. You're playing me. But it ends today. We're both survivors, Sparks. You just bet on the wrong side at the wrong time. You actually thought you could kill the Chairman? Ignorant."

Ryder broke the stalemate, lunged forward with her sword, and this time the blade slipped through Sparks' rifles' trigger guard. Sparks spun the rifle, and both it and the sword flew out of the women's hands.

"You used up all your luck on *Cortes*," Sparks said as she kick-boxed Ryder back a half-meter. Ryder sauntered out of range, and Sparks could see she was drawing her short knife. Sparks turned to the weapons, on the floor two meters away. She rolled into a diving handspring as Ryder expertly flung the nine-centimeter blade and charged Sparks, hoping to catch her off balance.

The knife stuck deep into Sparks right shoulder as she landed next to the entangled weapons. She came up with the katana.

"Goodbye, Ryder," Sparks said. "Survivor no more."

Sparks pushed the katana into the charging Ryder's midriff. The sword had barely penetrated Ryder's armor when the blade became stuck. Ryder struggled, but Sparks was the stronger of the two. She exerted herself, driving the blade clean through Ryder, and releasing the hilt, sticking out at her naval.

"Well done," Ryder said, a smile lighting her face as she struggled to stand, impaled with her own blade. "So, this is how it ends? Don't think ill of me, Sparks."

Ryder fell to her knees. She was still struggling remain upright, but the life was draining from her too fast now. Sparks pulled the short knife from her own shoulder and groaned. The pain made her entire nervous system scream.

"After all this, what do you care what I think of you?" Sparks growled, panting.

"I'm dying... all that remains ..." Ryder fell down on her side, and tried to prop herself up on her elbow to keep her weight from pushing the blade laterally through her torso. "Auuugh... all that remains .... are the memories of me. No one... left from *Cortes* to care. And the Chairman —"

Ryder didn't have the strength to prop herself up anymore, now fully collapsed on the floor, lying on her side as the blade twisted inside her from her own weight. Her head fell at an awkward angle. Sparks knelt beside her.

"The Chairman doesn't think highly of failures, I know," Sparks whispered. "I'm sorry, Ryder. I'm no saint. But we are not the same. I am an adopted Macready sister. What good have you done?"

"I... saved ..." Ryder choked. "I saved Nora."

"Yes," Sparks remembered. She stood as North approached.

"Don't leave me... I am not ready to go..."

North came and kneeled next to Ryder.

"Ryder. Godspeed," he said. His fury at Ryder's betrayal had waned as he saw death approach. North closed his eyes and said a silent prayer.

When he opened them, Ryder was straining her head with her last strength to catch his gaze. North leaned closer to her and gently lifted her head with one hand, and with the other he stroked her jet-black hair.

"Don't... trust ... her," the she-spy whispered nearly inaudibly with great effort.

Ryder's eyes flooded with fear. Filled with compassion, North smiled to reassure her.

Ryder went limp.

"Senseless," North said as he gently set Ryder's head on the floor. She had betrayed them, but which only made the loss of the woman he befriended over the past year on *Magnus* all the sadder. "Damn the Chairman and damn her dirty war."

"I need a med kit," Sparks said, her hand putting pressure over the knife wound. "Looks like you KO'd Queenie."

"Where's Meliana?" North asked. "Did she run?"

Sparks scanned the corridor, clutching her shoulder, then rounded the corner they came from. "North!"

The Marine followed and saw Meliana leaning up against the wall with a least a half dozen bullet holes permeating her body.

North kneeled beside the bullet-ridden woman. Meliana's breathing was shallow, and with the amount of blood on the floor, North knew her wounds were fatal.

"No! Sonofabitch," Sparks grew enraged.

Meliana coughed blood. "Did you … kill him?"

"No," North said, "I just knocked him out."

"You … promised… me," Meliana gasped.

"Meliana," North protested.

Sparks limped back around the corner, blood leaking from the bullet graze on her leg. She stood over Queenie's unconscious body, pulled on his arms and dragged him. Her wounded shoulder spiked with intensely sharp pain, but Sparks had learned how to use anger to ignore pain.

When Queenie was past the corner and in plain sight of Meliana, she dropped his arms. The jolting caused the man to stir. North stood up and stepped into a defensive posture.

Sparks limped to Ryder's corpse, and with a quick yank from her good arm, she pulled the katana from the body. She returned to Queenie, who was still lying down, but rubbing his head as he slowly regained consciousness.

Meliana looked over at Queenie, her tears mixing with her blood.

Sparks swung as hard as she could to take Queenie's head off. With her wounded shoulder, she didn't have the strength to decapitate him cleanly, so the first blow didn't kill him. Queenie shrieked in pain, and then fell unconscious again. Sparks hacked at his head a few more times before fully separating his cranium from the spinal cord.

She dropped the sword, walked over and collapsed next to Meliana.

"There you go," she said. "Now Ehud and Barack can rest in peace. And so can you."

Meliana slowly release her breath, her mouth turning almost into a smile as her gaze lost focus. Sparks closed the dead woman's eyes.

"Let's get out of here," North said, as he wrapped his arm around Sparks waist to provide her support, and then they moved around the corner. North's arm became covered with Spark's blood. He made a mental note to find a medkit in the pod.

Sparks stopped them as they passed Queenie's mangled body. She reached down and grabbed Ryder's sword. Then the pair made their way down the hall to the pod.

North opened the pod door using a brute force manual override, and then helped Sparks to climb in.

"I hope *Magnus* is waiting for us," North said. He sealed the door and started the eject sequence. Locating the medkit, popped it open and began to tend to Sparks' wounds.

With the briefest of wooshes, a burst of air ejected the pod clear of the *Marquette*. North felt the waning of the artificial gravity as the pod gained distance from the waypoint. He started to float, and pushed off the pod wall to position himself to peer out the small portal.

"Wow."

Through the window he saw two of the most magnificent war machines ever built facing off against each other. *Magnus,* at full alert, appearing to stand its ground as *Utopia,* with its asymmetrical dual hull, drawing itself toward its nemesis. In the 20 or so kilometers between the ships, several dozen corvettes were engaged in a lethal dance, against a backdrop of a billion brilliant stars. The sight was horrible and beautiful at the same time. *We're so alone out here, and we're killing each other,* North thought. *We can't stop proving our inherent depravity.*

Even with the explosive violence outside, the pod was perfectly silent. North entered his encrypted *Magnus* ID code in the emergency beacon and turned the radio on.

He pushed his weightless self against the pod hull into a sitting position, and Sparks leaned up against him, resting her head on his shoulder.

"I saw you pray for Ryder before she died. That's what you were doing, right?" Sparks asked.

North nodded. "An old habit. A good one."

"When it comes time for me die, I hope you'll pray for me," Sparks said, as she closed her eyes and rested. "It's all I have."

"You're not going to die anytime soon," North said. "We still have to find our peace together."

"Mmm hmmm," Sparks muttered. Utterly spent, she slipped into a light sleep, floating. North put his fingers slowly through her strawberry blonde hair and smiled weakly.

Then he prayed again as the pod drifted toward the battle.

Obadiah looked at the rapidly approaching *Utopia*.

"Draw back our corvettes and prepare to fire tubes one through twenty," he ordered.

"Calling back corvettes, sir," Rhodes confirmed.

"Gunnery chief reports all silos green," Blight responded.

The captain looked at the tactical display, closely watching distance to *Utopia*. "Hit them with the missiles and the follow with the particle beams. Steady. Steady. Fire."

"Let's see if *Utopia* has a point defense system that can stop 20 missiles," Bollard said.

The space between the great warship and *Utopia* was suddenly filled with a barrage of missiles as *Magnus* emptied its projectile tubes. Several Chasm corvettes were caught unaware, and brilliant explosions filled the space as missiles collided with the dogfighters. The missiles were packed with explosives and a highly expanding gaseous "shrapnel" designed to the carry the destructive expanding shockwave through the vacuum of space.

For a ship of its size, *Utopia* rolled nimbly on its relative x and y axis, protecting the small secondary hull behind the larger primary hull. *Utopia* employed anti-ballistic measures in an attempt to misguide the intelligent guidance systems – electromagnetic-charged balls that gave off decoy EM signatures. Several flak cannons also spooled to fire.

Some of the Chasm corvettes attempted to engage the missiles with their chain guns, but they lacked the speed and agility to compete with the VI's piloting the guided missiles. The wave of missiles reached the flak field, but with advanced armor, the sleek silver rocket-propelled instruments of death seemed undeterred, and *Utopia* itself was moving toward the missiles.

"Three seconds till impact," Condi announced to the bridge crew of the *Magnus.*

The bridge had grown silent in anticipation.

North watched the missiles from the window of the pod. In seconds, he knew *Utopia* would be reeling from massive damage, if not entirely disabled. The Battle of *Marquette* would be over soon.

And then, for the second time that day, North could not believe his eyes.

As the missiles closed in for the kill, they appeared to dissolve, and then explode just before hitting the target. North knew it was as the Chairman's now-dead lieutenant had promised. The same point defense technology that saved the Chairman from Sparks' barrage of bullets was now making *Magnus'* assault on *Utopia* meaningless.

Almost.

Shockwaves from the explosions, carried on the gaseous shrapnel, slammed into the *Utopia* hull, and the ship shuttered and listed. One of the ships three main propulsion drives fractured off, sending out a stream of fuel and other gasses, pushing the *Utopia* into a slow spiral. North could see *Utopia's* thrusters firing to counter the spin.

On the bridge of *Magnus*, there was confused optimism.

"Is she disabled?" Bollard asked. "Looks like they lost a main propulsion vent."

"Hit them with the particle beams," the captain ordered.

"Gunnery chief confirms both beams are now continuously streaming," Rhodes reported, at her normally too-loud volume.

"Doesn't look like we are getting past the point defense system," Blight announced. "Almost worst-case scenario."

"The *Utopia* has righted itself and is still heading toward us, though at reduced speed," Cho shouted, surprised. "They don't look very hurt."

I shouldn't let them get too close, the captain thought. "Prepare reverse thrusters, and ready tubes twenty through forty."

"Captain, incoming ship-to-ship missiles," Cho shouted. "From the port and starboard! *Marquette* is firing missiles and *Utopia* just unloaded its tubes."

Blight swore loudly. "They armed the waypoint. We should have seen that coming!"

"Count?" the captain asked.

"Eighty-five incoming."

"One minutes till impact," Condi announced. "Warning impact imminent."

"Flack cannons free," the captain told the gunnery chief over the ship comm. "Keep those things off my ship."

"Beta Wing Commander reports his corvettes are engaging the incoming ordnance," Rhodes reported.

"Particle beams set to intercept mode," Condi told the crew.

"Go get 'em, Condi," Cho said.

Outside the *Magnus*, the escape pod floated closer to the battleship.

North peered out the portal. "This is good. We're heading in the right direction."

Then, what seemed like an endless stream of missiles filled the viewport.

"Okay, I'm not sure we are headed in the right direction anymore," North said to a groggy Sparks.

Sparks lifted her head, sat up and joined North in looking out the window.

"I wanted excitement. I guess I should be careful what I wish for," Sparks said softly, as the pod drifted toward the strike path of missiles launched from *Marquette.*

"It's going to be close," North said with a simple resignation.

Sparks slipped her arm around North's waste and leaned her head on his shoulder again, taking in the view.

"I feel peaceful," she said.

Suddenly the pod jerked and accelerated, throwing the pair up against the pod wall, Sparks unintentionally pinning North, their bodies facing each other.

"Saved again?" North wondered. "Someone has us in tow." Sparks smiled and kissed North's cheek.

The *Khan* was speeding toward *Magnus*. "Nyota to *Magnus* flight control, I'm coming in hot. I have North's rescue pod in tow. Locked missiles on my six. Please disengage flack defense on my flight vector so I can come into port. Catch these demons on my tail. Thirty seconds ETA."

"Captain," Rhodes shouted. "Nyota has North in a pod. Coming in hot between us and missiles. She wants the flack down so she can land. Permission granted?"

Bollard looked at the captain. He knew they had no time, so he was brief. "Missiles will get through."

"Do it," Obadiah made his split-second decision.

Rhodes shouted in her comm. "Gunnery chief, captain orders to cease flack cannons 34 through 39 now or Nyota will die."

I hope he is holding on in there, thought the wing commander as she started to hit her decelerator. The flack fire was still up for a second or two as the *Khan* entered *Magnus'* defense radius. The *Khan* shook violently and warning signals blared. Nyota knew her ship was seriously damaged and she struggled to keep it on course. *Please stay connected*, Nyota thought about the vacuum tow cable connected to the pod.

"*Khan*, this is *Magnus* flight control. Cleared for emergency landing," Nyota heard through her comms.

"Roger," she replied.

The *Khan* entered the hanger at significant speed, hit the deck and slid to the far end crushing another corvette and erupting in flames before coming to a harsh halt. The pod slipped into the deck as well, ripped off the tow cable, and bounced around violently before rolling to a stop near the emergency atmospheric containment curtain.

I am going to be sore tomorrow, North thought as he sat up in the pod, back in a field of artificial gravity. Through the window he could see the hanger closing, and half-glanced at Sparks, smiling back at him, her hair wild and messy. Through the pod's small viewport, North saw the missile just as the *Magnus* hanger door closed completely.

"Get that flack back —" the captain shouted.

"Too late," Blight said. "Brace!"

The nuclear warhead-armed missile hit the *Magnus* just outside its port hangar door. The brilliant radiation sphere melted a large section of the outer hull of *Magnus*, and several decks immediately vented out into space. Inside the hanger, a shockwave and heatwave blasted everything, causing secondary explosions from corvettes still in the hanger.

The bright light that flashed through the pod portal burned North's eyes, and his skin immediately browned as the radiation flooded exposed parts of the hanger.

Fires jetted out all through the hanger as various gasses sprayed from breaches. Several holes in the hangar door exposed open space.

Sparks, who was leaning against the pod wall when the flash hit, screamed in pain as her skin cooked.

And then the blast was done.

"Sparks," North called. "Are you okay? I can't see. I can't see."

"Here," Sparks struggled to say, weeping and moaning with the pain of second- and third-degree burns. Her armored suit was melted and some had fused with her skin.

"Did we make it?" North asked.

"I don't know."

The force of the blast pushed the mighty *Magnus* laterally at great speed.

"Direct hit from a nuclear strike," Bollard shouted.

"Deploy damage control teams," Obadiah was on his training autopilot now. As captain, he literally had decades to plan for every possible scenario. Nuclear strike was such a scenario, and he was ready. "Blight, rapid damage situation report?"

"The port hangar took a direct hit. Multiple hull breaches. About a third of port-side decks four and six have vented into space, including gunnery command. We've lost flack defense on about a quarter of our ship."

"How are the engines?" the captain asked.

"Still green," Bollard replied.

"Get us out of here," Obadiah barked. "Rapid acceleration

permitted. Spool up and retreat. Condi, program a heading toward *Magellan*."

"Retreat?" Cho argued. "We can do this, sir."

"We're injured. We can't defend against a waypoint and a warship. We have one advantage – speed. *Utopia* is crippled and we can outrun her."

"But sir," Cho objected.

"We fly. Condi, make best speed to *Magellan*."

Condi spoke over the ship wide comms. "All hands, brace for rapid acceleration."

"Not a moment too soon," Bollard announced. "*Marquette* has launched another round of ship-to-ship ordnance. Go, go, go."

Rhodes spoke up. "We still have two corvettes out there from Beta Wing! Lieutenant Wall and Jack, sir. One minute out. We can't leave them."

The captain sat in the command chair and put on a seat belt as the force of acceleration increased to multiple Gs. Other officers also took chairs as the rapid acceleration put thousands of kilometers between them and *Marquette*.

"I'm sorry," Obadiah said. "Hard choice. Please let them know they are on their own. We can't lose the whole *Magnus*. We have to survive and prepare to defend *Magellan*. You heard the Chairman."

Rhodes struggled to hold back tears as thought of the pilots of Beta Wing who had been close friends.

"Communications Ensign," the Captain addressed Rhodes. "Please immediately send an encrypted tight beam message to *Magellan* to relay to Earth. Use the Amberly Macready's encoder. Inform them of the tactical situation, the readout on *Utopia*, and our defeat at *Marquette*."

"So that's it?" Rhodes said. "Chasm wins?"

"No, we regroup. Fall back to *Magellan*. Commander Moreno and I made a contingency plan. We'll lose a few years."

The captain looked at a screen displaying aft camera view, grateful for *Magnus*' quick acceleration. *Marquette* was already impossible to see with the naked eye.

"We'll be back."

CHAPTER FIFTEEN

Fuentes Station on the asteroid Sonnet, in orbit around Spencer Minorum, August 2, 2604, Twenty-two months after the Battle of Magellan, and four months before the Battle of Marquette.

Amberly was a nervous wreck. She instinctively went to fidget with the locks of her red hair, but found nothing to twirl now that she had an ear-length bob. The new style was a few weeks old, but she still wasn't used to the cut.

She was alone in the command center of Fuentes Station, with the main illumination off. The sparkling light from the stars outside mixed with the ambient light from various status indicators on computers scattered across the room. Dull patches of space were blackened by other asteroids that were floating near Sonnet. The floating rocks blocked the stars behind them, and reflected little light back.

She sat in the black, soft, faux-leather command chair, *her chair*. Even after six months of hard work leading this critical resource development mission for her waypoint, her command still felt surreal to her, not even 22 years old.

Her mind conjured an image of her dirty blond beau, Skylar. He had been instrumental in Amberly's early leadership success, helping her manage personnel disputes, offering a much-needed sounding board for making hard decisions, and providing a foundation of emotional support with his friendship – and affection. *Skylar believes that he loves me,* she thought. *And I love him. Or maybe I am just lying to myself. Hiding.*

Amberly tossed uncomfortably in her chair.

Every lie has a cost, Amberly thought. The hour was late, and most of the 28 souls she had brought with her from *Magellan* were asleep. Looking down through the floor-to-ceiling window from the command center's perch, she could see the lights on in the primary mess hall. *Wong and Midas grabbing a midnight snack and a game of chess, no doubt,* Amberly smiled at the comfortable patterns her team were settling into. Then she looked up, out the broad viewport past the horizon of the asteroid, Sonnet.

Amberly's lies were nibbling her soul with painful, pointed

memories. Her lies to North leading up to the Battle of *Magellan* cost her a dear friendship. After the battle, her lie to Dek — she loved him — was innocent enough, she thought. She made herself believe the lie would help him endure exile. *Ha! There's no such thing as an innocent lie.*

She never imagined she would see Dek's unconventionally handsome face again. What were the odds she would ever again have to look through his blue-grey eyes into his revolutionary soul? A billion to one? She thought he would take his devotion to her — the devotion she abused to turn the tide in the Battle of *Magellan* — millions and millions of kilometers away. Now she would have to face the lie, and the prospect of that confrontation made Amberly do something weeks ago that even Kora would probably think was rash, Amberly thought.

The repaired *American Spirit*, along with the Elcano flotilla, was due to arrive at the Fuentes Station tomorrow. Amberly made herself believe that she had not agreed to Skylar's proposal simply to have an out when Dek Tigona arrived. Now she wasn't so sure.

She stood up from her chair, secured her kimono, and paced over to the large window. Amberly stared out into infinite space, lost in her thoughts.

She jumped slightly when she felt two arms reach from behind around her waist. She recognized the familiar and somewhat pleasant smell of Skylar Trigs. She turned her head and kissed him lightly, then turned back to the window.

"Can't sleep?" Skylar asked. "Want to tell me about it?"

Amberly leaned her head back on Skylar's shoulder. "Not really, but thanks for asking."

"It's Dek, isn't it?" Skylar pushed. "You are just going to have to tell him the truth."

"I said I don't want to talk about it," Amberly demurred.

"Well, you might rest better if you come back to my room for the night," Skylar said almost as a whisper, tenderly tightening his arms around her.

"Tempting, but we've been over that," Amberly said, gently pulling herself out of Skylar's embrace and turning to face him. "I'm not ready." Amberly wasn't sure why, but something in the back of her head kept her from giving herself completely to Skylar. At first she thought it was her own insecurities, but as time progressed, she realized that it was something else holding her back. Whatever *it* was, Amberly was starting to question her decision to agree to marry Skylar when he asked three months ago. The pair had been, as Skylar promised, good together, both as colleagues and friends. But making the matrimonial promise was a lot easier than actually walking the aisle. Was the memory of Kimberly Macready whispering wisdom in her ear? Was her engagement just a latent act of rebellion against her murderous mother. Was she using Skylar to shield her emotions from Dek? Whatever the case, Amberly did not want to think about it now.

"Of course, my love," Skylar frowned. "Well, let's get something to drink, sit up watching the stars and plan the wedding."

"I'm sorry, love, but I'm not in the mood," Amberly sighed.

"Okay, I understand," Skylar said, stepping back, sitting down in the command chair and considering Amberly's lovely figure dimly silhouetted by the star field behind Spencer Minorum. He paused and then continued, "But at least let us pick a date?"

"You pick a date if that will make you feel better," Amberly snapped. "I want to wait until I have a chance to talk to my sister and brother-in-law."

Amberly took a deep breath.

"Look. I'm wearing the engagement ring. What's your hurry?" She fingered the beautiful crystal harvested from the Shard Caves, set in a simple polycarbonate band. "Why so insecure?"

"You know why," Skylar said, as he stepped to Amberly and took both her hands. "If you held the most precious thing in the universe, you would hold on to it with all your might. You know if you let it go, you may never get it back again."

Skylar released Amberly's hands and stepped back into the shadows, bowing slightly.

"Goodnight, sweet Amberly. I'll see you for the stellar anomaly review tomorrow morning. Get some sleep."

Amberly smiled warmly. When Skylar had left the room, she plopped down in the chair and flopped her head into her hands. She sighed audibly as she looked out the window again. The light in the mess hall was still on. *Maybe a snack will help me sleep.*

"Hey boss-lady," Midas looked up from the chess board and smiled as Amberly entered the mess hall, bits of protein bars stuck on his teeth.

"Hello Midas; hello Eli," Amberly said, as she opened the food storage bin and found an orange-colored carb sphere. She unwrapped the artificial foodstuff, held the orb up to her mouth and took too large of a bite.

Wong grunted at Amberly in acknowledgment, but most of his focus was on the chess board. He moved a knight to capture one of Midas' bishops.

"A fair move," Midas said. He moved his queen diagonally across the board to put the knight in jeopardy. The queen also had a diagonal shot at Wong's remaining rook.

"Well, that smarts," Wong said. "Which one should I save?"

"Now that's a good question. I'll let you figure it out," Midas chuckled and turned to Amberly. "What has you up at this ungodly hour, sweetheart?"

"How am I going to face him when he gets here tomorrow?" Amberly said.

"Dek?" Midas asked. "Well, I don't see how you could tell him anything but the truth."

Wong looked up from the game.

"Amberly," Wong looked sternly at his redheaded commander. "I'm your chief of security. And even though I didn't agree with how you got off the hook at the Battle of *Magellan*, I respect you too much to not tell you what's got to hurt you, miss. There is only *one thing* to do when *American Spirit* gets here."

"We've been over this too many times, Wong. No."

"He should have been shown out an airlock back on *Magellan*," Wong said. "All of them should have been. The fact that the damaged *American Spirit* is returning to us is proof enough of that. The exile plan was always going to end badly."

"Eli," Midas said with a little bit of threat in his voice, "Let's not be talking of airlocks. We've floated enough people in this stupid war."

"At the very least, you must not let him remain in command of the *American Spirit*," Wong pressed. "You have the authority to relieve him of his command. Maybe put Skylar in command."

"Yeah, the optics on that would look great," Amberly with sarcasm steaming off her head.

"Whatever you do, you have to be really careful," Midas advised. "The people on that ship may technically be under your authority when they get to our humble little outpost, but they may be loyal to Dek. He has led them through quite an ordeal. Even if your brother-in-law and sister and the rest of the *Elcano* flotilla are with you, there are what, ten times as many people on the *American Spirit*? I'm not saying they'd all be with Dek, but—"

"Midas, that's not what I am worried about," Amberly replied, "Dek thinks that I love him. I told him that to ease the pain of his exile—"

"Well that was a stupid idea if you were trying to get rid of him," Midas said. "Absence makes the heart grow fonder."

"But I thought I'd never see him again. For crying out loud, he was going seven light years away!" Amberly justified herself. "And maybe I don't love him, but it's not like I don't have any feelings for him."

"Pardon my saying so, but that is sort of dangerous for a woman who is getting married to another man," Midas was firm, but gentle in his admonition. "You need to straighten out your feelings, and soon."

"Amberly's feelings are irrelevant. Her duty is to Earth, *Magellan* and this mission," Wong said. "Dek is an exile. Sentenced in a legal tribunal. The one right thing to do is to incarcerate him until another ship is heading to Earth."

"That could be a long time," Amberly protested, "or never."

"Then toss him out an airlock," Wong said, his anger rising. "Don't forget who those bastards killed. Anderson. Jindel. Synder. Twig. Dek was part of that. He was as responsible, if not more so, than dozens of others we executed after the Battle of *Magellan*. He attempted to murder North. You remember *our friend*, North? Do the right thing. Don't make me regret believing you are truly loyal to *Magellan* and Earth. Because of you, North almost died—"

Midas grunted his objection to Wong's escalation.

"I *saved* North," Amberly shouted while she stood up, throwing her half-eaten carb sphere to the floor. She began tearing up with anger and guilt. "If it wasn't for me, he would be dead. Dek would have killed him. I saved him! And don't forget it was

Dek that helped save *Magellan* in the end!"

"If it wasn't for you, Dek would have never had the opportunity to knife North," Wong shouted back, anger rising in his voice. He stood and waved a pointed finger at Amberly. "You almost killed North! And now he's gone."

Midas stood over Wong and calmly put his huge hands on the Marine's shoulders. He spoke softly, "No Eli, in the end Amberly saved us all. She shot her own mother to save us. I was there. Now you've said your piece, and let that be all. Let's stay focused on the task at hand – making *Magellan* strong so we can fight back against Chasm if we must. That's what matters now."

Wong looked to the floor and exhaled slowly. "Yes. I'm sorry."

Skylar rushed into the mess, shirtless, exposing defined abs, his yellow curls wildly messy. "What's going on here? I heard shouting."

"Everything is fine, XO," Midas said reassuringly to the Fuentes Station second-in-command. "Amberly and Wong were just having a discussion."

Skylar looked at Wong and then over at Amberly and frowned. He knew what they were arguing about without anyone saying a word.

"Maybe *all* of you should get some sleep," Skylar scolded. "Tomorrow is going to be a long day. There are uncharted stellar radiation bursts to avoid and an entire flotilla of ships to integrate into our mission. We don't need anyone on a short fuse because they aren't getting the rack time they need."

Amberly walked over to Skylar and planted a short but sweet kiss on his lips. "Thank you, love," she said sincerely. "Don't worry. I'm just going to clean up here then I'll go back to my quarters and get some sleep."

Skylar stared hard at Wong, who was still in his chair looking down, then turned to give an evil eye to Midas. Midas just shrugged his shoulders and gave an innocent *who me?* look. Skylar looked over at Amberly, forced a smile and exited the room.

"Skylar's in a snit," Midas chuckled. Amberly started picking up her dropped foodstuffs.

Midas sat down, and waved his hand palm up toward the chess board. "Well, what's it going to be? The rook or the knight.

You can only save one."

"Doesn't matter," Wong said as he stood up, knocking over a few pieces. "I am done playing this game. I'm going to bed."

"Goodnight, Eli," Midas said, as his eyes followed the Marine out the door. He looked over at Amberly. "I'll clean up here. It's my job. You brought me here as a janitor, you know."

"Yeah, but I prefer you as a counselor. Or maybe a stand-in grandfather," Amberly sat down and smiled at the old man. "Midas, what am I going to do about Dek?"

"Double jeopardy," Midas said. "Just like Wong's rook and knight. You can't have them both, Dek and Skylar. You can't make both of them happy. And you can't run away from your Dek problem anymore. Figure out what you want, and then commit."

"I'm engaged to Skylar," Amberly said, but with no confidence. "I've obviously figured out what I want."

"Uh huh," Midas said. "You've figured out how to hide. Maybe Skylar is what you want. Good for him."

"Of course, he is," Amberly said softly.

"Sure, sure," Midas reassured Amberly with just a hint of patronization. "And then there is the *other* guy."

"What other guy?"

"Commander, have your dad's good looks, but you have your mother's brains. You are one of the brightest stars in the havens. You'll make the right choice. Goodnight, my dear Amberly," Midas said kindly, and then he opened up his heart. "Whatever you chose, whatever you do, know that I will have your back."

She believed him.

"North! Stop!" Amberly's voice was sharp and clear. "North, you're killing him! Stop! Please."

North looked at his hard hands encircling Dek's neck. A whitish-blue ring started to form where blood was being cut off.

"Please, North, please. This isn't you."

North breathed heavily and fought back tears as he released his grip from Dek's marred throat, shoving the transient back into the hard Magellan *corridor wall. Dek gasped as air filled his lungs.*

Dek took a long breath and then unexpectedly pummeled North with his free arm, landing a kidney punch that caused North to double and completely release Dek for just an instant. Dek had enough space to draw his short blade from its hidden sheath.

"Dek, no!" Amberly shouted.

North was already recovering when Dek, with all the strength he could muster, drove his knife into the center of the existing wound on North's arm. Dek pulled the blade out and stabbed North's torso beneath the left rib cage, and in a flash pulled it out again only to stab North's injured arm again, leaving the blade piercing the wound.

The large man cried out in excruciating pain and stumbled back into Kora, his arm immediately bleeding profusely. The blade remained lodged in North's muscle and bone as he collapsed to the floor.

"North!" Amberly shouted. She and Kora both moved to him as he clutched his arm.

"Lord, no," Kora said, "I think he hit an artery."

With the attention on North, Dek slowly reached over and picked up the assault rifle and aimed it squarely at North.

"Amberly, Kora," Dek said with a quivering voice, "Please, step away from North now."

"No!" Kora said, with tears running down her face. "He needs my help! Please."

"I don't want to, but I will kill you if you make me," Dek said, looking hard into Kora's eyes. "North will never surrender or stand down — he has to die. We've come too far, so close to perfecting humanity, to let this Marine get in the way. Death comes for us all; for North it comes today."

"Go to hell," Kora growled.

Dek lightly pulled the trigger and a single bullet rang out, a warning shot aimed purposefully well above North's head. Amberly yelped in surprise at the sound of the gunshot, but she stayed by North's side.

"You don't scare me," Kora said, turning her back to Dek and preparing to pull the knife from North's wound. "Shoot me. I know where I'm going when I die. Do you?"

"Apparently to hell," Dek mocked Kora.

"Save yourselves," North gasped. His breaths were rapid, but shallow. Both the Macready sisters knew North would soon die from blood loss. "Maybe it is my time. No reason for you to die, too. Save yourself. Be happy. Kora, you're a dish. I'll always love you,

Red."

"North," Amberly said, tears running down her face. North shook his head at her in surrender.

"Amberly, please step away from North," Dek begged.

North slowly forced himself to stand, blood trickling from his wounds onto the cold steel floor. He gently pushed Amberly and Kora out of the way and stood vulnerably in sights of his own assault rifle, which Dek had trained on North's torso.

North looked at Dek. "Kill me if you must, but promise me you'll take care of Amberly. Promise me you'll die for her." Then North closed his eyes and fell to his knees. He was bleeding out, shot up, stabbed, stunned, broken and worn out. He leaned against the wall, and slid down into a seating position, leaving a crimson streak on the wall. Dek's blade still protruded from his arm.

North smiled and closed his eyes.

"Don't you see, Amberly," Dek explained, "This is the only way for our true love to live forever. You do believe in our love, don't you Amberly?"

"Yes, Dek," Amberly watched herself tell the rogue, as she walked next to him and put her arms around his waist.

"North, I promise, I will take care of Amberly," Dek pledged. "I promise I will die for her. I really love her." Dek pulled the trigger gently, releasing one bullet into the center of North's forehead.

"Wait! That's not how this happened," Amberly saw herself scream. "I saved North! I saved North! I love North!"

A mysterious door opened and Skylar Trigs walked out. He was quietly chanting, "Amberly Macready murdered Lt. Commander North. Isn't that true, love? You lied to Dek. Shame. Are you lying to me now, love?"

A hatch on the ceiling of the hall opened, and a scantily dressed Sparks fell through and landed in a crouch. "You don't love North, you killed him, my dear sister," Sparks whispered as she leaned over and kissed the dead body. "Still warm. But not for long."

"I didn't kill him!" Amberly saw herself shout again. "I saved him. I intervened."

North's eyes popped open. "You chose Dek over me? And now you are on to Skylar? You're a maneater. Reminds me of dear mother. Like mother, like daughter."

"North, no I love you, It's just that... it's not like that—"

North's body suddenly turned to ashes, causing Amberly to cover her mouth to keep from screaming.

Something was tapping on the back of her leg. She looked over and saw her toddler nephew, Alroy, speaking in her late father's voice, "I never got to meet uncle North. He was dead when I was born."

"He's not dead. I didn't kill him. I saved him!"

Amberly saw the people gathering around her start to chant, "Like mother, like daughter. Out the airlock. Like mother, like daughter. Out the airlock."

She looked to Dek. "You lied to me! You never loved me. Float to hell with your dead mother!"

Out of nowhere, an airlock portal appeared. She recognized Joti, the Chasm conspirator, inside the airlock. "Come on in," he said. "The air is fresher in here."

"No! I didn't kill North. I saved him."

Suddenly, Amberly was inside the airlock, although she didn't remember going through the interior door.

She heard Verne's familiar voice. "Don't worry, I'll delete myself when I am gone. Or maybe I'll transfer to her."

Amberly looked out the window and saw her teenage rival, Flora Dillington. "Open the airlock, Verne," Flora said with a dismissive chuckle.

Joti smirked at Amberly. "Now you know how I feel."

"No! Wait. I saved Magellan! This isn't how it happened. Wait–"

Amberly woke from the dream. Her heart was pounding, and her gown was damp with sweat.

"What time is it?" She asked aloud.

"Oh-five-hundred hours," Verne replied. "Why are you awake so early? Your alarm isn't set to go off for another hour."

"Nightmare. Just a nightmare," Amberly told herself and her VI. "Please get me a cup of morning java."

Amberly didn't regularly drink the foul-tasting caffeinated substance that approximated coffee produced by the food synthesizers on Fuentes station. The synthesizers on the station were nearly 100 years older than the ones on *Magellan*, and as such, the food tasted much worse. Amberly had hoped the garden project would have gone better, but they had no *good* botanists on her initial team. There were several, however, on *American Spirit*, and Amberly was looking forward to the fruits of a well-run greenhouse if she could conscript the botanists.

Getting farmers from American Spirit is the least of my worries, Amberly thought.

Amberly quickly showered and donned her old Science Corps dress uniform. Professional and feminine, the familiar white pantsuit with green trim made Amberly feel comfortable and relaxed. She liked how she looked in the get up, examining herself if the small vanity above her sink. Of course, the Science Corps uniform reminded Amberly most of her mother, and right now she chose to remember Kimberly Macready as the caring, nurturing role model Amberly knew her to be during the first 13 years of her life. She did not want to think of her as Raven One, traitor to her family and humanity, architect of unspeakable evil.

"You look very sharp," Verne said. "Like your mother."

Amberly smiled at the VI's comment. It always said that when Amberly wore her dress uniform. Then Verne added something it hadn't said before, "Happy Ship Day, Red."

For waypoint residents whose reason for existing was to support inter-planetary ships passing from Earth to Arara and back, the arrival of a deep space ship was a day of celebration. "Happy Ship Day" was a common greeting on the somewhat rare occasions when ships visited the waypoints. Red was North's pet name for Amberly, but she wasn't sure when Verne picked up the vernacular.

She remembered North calling her Red, half-friendly, half-flirty. She missed North. She wanted him back. She wanted everything back. But she had gone through this with herself a hundred times. *There is no going back,* Amberly thought. She had to go forward. She believed going forward meant Skylar, but doubt nibbled on the edges of her brain.

Happy Ship Day, Red. North said those same words the last fateful Ship Day, when the *American Spirit* arrived at *Magellan* two years ago. Ship Day had come again, and so had the *American Spirit*, but it was not happy for Amberly. She wanted what she could not have, and wasn't sure if she wanted what she did have. She felt childish, ungrateful and foolish. Pining for North was *stupid.* Being good together with Skylar was *smart.* Dek being back was just *crazy.*

Amberly left her somewhat spacious quarters and headed for the research lab to find Skylar.

Compared to *Magellan*'s diameter of five kilometers, Fuentes station was tiny. But when combined with the various flotilla ships temporarily converted into housing, the permanent base on Sonnet offered more than 10,000 square meters of space for the Amberly's team to spread out — likely the least densely populated structure in space. Being a loner and hiding from others was easy. That would change when *American Spirit* and the *Elcano* flotilla arrived today, adding nearly 1,000 souls to the operation.

The door to the multi-purpose science lab slid open, and Amberly saw the senior scientist, Li, a tan 60-year-old with long salt-and-pepper hair, deep in conversation with Skylar.

"I've charted the high energy plumes. Nothing to worry about today," Li told Skylar.

"Amberly," Skylar smiled, acknowledging his fiancée. "I wasn't sleeping well so I woke up early and began downloading the new stellar radiation data from the *Magellan* tight beam. I'm glad I started early. It took two hours because asteroids kept breaking the beam."

Li looked up from her magnetic resonance screen. "Don't worry, Amberly. I've almost charted all the anomalies for the next month. Nothing headed our way. Looks like no temporary evacuations in the next 30 days."

"Did you get the batch communications from *Magellan*, too, or just the stellar data?" Amberly asked. "I haven't heard from Moreno for a while now. I wonder how long she'll want us to keep the *American Spirit* hiding here in the Spencer Belt?"

"What kind of low rent communication tech do you think I am?" Skylar joked. "I mean, I'm no Skip, but I get by. Of course, I got the mail."

"Any word from *Magnus*? They must be near *Marquette* now."

Skylar's smile turned into a frown. "Nothing I saw. No encoded messages. Just the normal stuff. Still, it's odd that we haven't gotten the situation normal report from *Magnus* for a while now. Maybe those new guys in *Magellan* comms are sleeping on the job. Maybe Moreno has decided to keep *Magnus* data on a need to know basis. Maybe something bad happened to —"

"Naw, I am sure Moreno would have tagged anything that was important," Amberly interrupted.

"Any particular reason for the interest?"

"I dreamed about when Dek and North nearly killed each other. Only in my dream I, Dek actually killed North. It felt so real. I guess I had *Magnus* on the brain," Amberly admitted.

Skylar chuckled, relieved. "More like some bad carb balls in the gut. That's why I avoid late night snacking: indigestion. I'm sure North is fine, your dream notwithstanding."

"Yes, of course," Amberly said to comfort herself.

"You can go on to the command center. I've got this," Skylar said with a smile.

"No. I can stay until you're finished."

"No need to wait for me. I still have a little work to get all the outgoing comms through the tight beam to *Magellan*. And I have one other bit of business to tackle. I'll see you there in a few."

The largest space in Fuentes Station was the Adriana Greenhouse. Not nearly the spectacle the topside garden was on *Magellan*, the Adriana Greenhouse still featured a large transparent ceiling that had a magnificent view of the Spencer Belt and, when Sonnet was in the right rotation, Spencer Minorum. Because of the lack of manpower, only about a fourth of the greenhouse was being utilized. The rest was open space, a rare phenomenon in the human habitats between Earth and Arara.

Amberly stood in front of the entire assembly of her team, 20 civilians and eight Marines. The Marines were in full dress and stood at attention with rifles in hand. She looked up at the magnificent *American Spirit,* ten times the size of Fuentes Station, floating in a geosynchronous orbit just few scores of meters above the large asteroid. The American flag decorating the hull was illuminated by spotlights from Fuentes Station. Midas, who was standing near the end of the assembly, felt a tinge of reverence at the sight. Amberly focused on lights from the observation deck windows where she first saw Dek on Ship Day at *Magellan* two years ago. So much had changed since Dek Tigona came into her life.

Fuentes Station was not designed to accommodate a ship the size of *American Spirit*.

One of the first projects Amberly's engineers worked on was designing an airlock for such a ship. The connecting point was installed at the end of the Adriana Greenhouse. The gangway had been extended from *American Spirit* to the new airlock to allow for easy transfer of people and supplies between ship and station.

A small light on the airlock door connected to the gangway flashed green, indicated equalized atmosphere on both sides of the portal.

Amberly was happy and anxious and fearful all at the same time. Happy that she was about to be reunited with her sister, anxious that she was about to face the lie she told Dek, and fearful that she would not be able to command the respect of the thousand-plus people on *American Spirit* who were now under her command. If she had *no* feelings for Dek at all, Amberly supposed the lie wouldn't smart so bad, but she *did* care.

"Verne," Amberly spoke to her VI, now installed in the station wide computing network. "Let our friends in."

The door began to slide open and made a slight hiss. Behind the door, at the front of the *American Spirit* delegation, stood Dek Tigona. Amberly's eyes locked with his and her heart filled with a mix of fear and love. Her gut churned.

Dek looked good. His hair was neatly cropped, and his upper body had gained some impressive build since she said goodbye to him. He wore a brown poly-jacket over a loose-fitting tan V-neck shirt. Amberly saw, strapped to his black pants was low hung hip holster, complete with some sort of pistol. He seemed older, as if he'd lost a lot of his youth along the way, but his blue-grey eyes were still young and brilliant.

Then she saw Kora and Lydia behind Dek, and her heart leapt with gladness. She resisted the temptation to run to hug them – debarkation of the captain was a supremely formal event on Ship Day for waypoint denizens. Still, her smile beamed off her face as she saw the people whom she could truly let her guard down. She loved those women, too, with all her heart. Amberly was excited to hear their stories of adventure rescuing the *American Spirit*.

She couldn't wait to debrief with her girlfriends, of which she had precious few on Fuentes station. And then in an instant she was horrified. *What will they think when they find out I am engaged to Skylar?* No matter. They were family. They were friends. *I don't care what people think. I'm just so glad my friends are here.*

Dek stepped out of the airlock and approached Amberly, keeping with the waypoints' custom of an arriving captain to greet the governor first.

With the comforting Kora and Lydia smiling in the corner of her view, Amberly reciprocated the smile as Dek walked up to her. Behind Dek, XO Snodgrass, Bridge Officer Caddo, two *American Spirit* Marines and Lieutenant Boro entered the greenhouse and made a smartly formed line.

"Captain Tigona," Amberly said as she extended her hand, "Welcome to Fuentes Station."

"Mission Commander Macready, on behalf of the 987 lives on the *American Spirit*, we are grateful for your hospitality. We recognize your authority on this gentry of *Waypoint Magellan*," Dek said, per waypoint protocol that was as old as Project Waypoint itself.

Dek grasped her hand, and then pulled her to him, bringing her into a full embrace and then leaning his handsome face into her soft one. Lost in the emotion, Amberly went with the passionately wet kiss for a few seconds, and then suddenly remembered where she was and *what* she was: engaged. She snapped her head away. "Dek," she breathed, and stepped back a few paces, holding her left hand to her chest, palm facing her bosom, displaying the brilliant crystal from the Shard Cave. Amberly realized she had just made things ten times worse, and she bowed her head slightly. She swallowed, her throat tight, flush with conflicting emotion.

For a brief instant, Dek didn't understand. He could plainly see the ring on her finger. Then he registered what it meant. *What did I expect?* Dek thought as he tried not to tear up in front of this group. *How naive am I? Of course, she wouldn't wait for me. I wasn't coming back. Why didn't Kora tell me?*

"I don't understand," Dek said, the opposite of what he was thinking – he understood all too well.

Amberly cleared her throat. "I'm sorry."

The greenhouse was awkwardly silent.

Breaking the quiet, Skylar Trigs, who had jealously watched the whole kiss just a few paces behind Amberly, marched forward and pointed to Security Chief Wong.

Wong drew his rifle and stepped forward with two of his Marines in tow, approaching Dek.

Dek fingered his sidearm instinctively, and the *American Spirit* Marines flanking him drew their rifles and aimed at the Wong's squad.

"Whoa!" Boro said, putting his large arms in the air and pushing down with his palms. "Let's all calm down here."

Amberly was shocked. "What is going on?"

Midas took a few steps toward Amberly, out of a protective instinct.

Trigs walked up until he was nearly nose to nose with Tigona. "Dek Tigona, as executive officer and second in command of Fuentes Station, prisoner administration falls to me. You are an exile that has returned to *Magellan* sovereign soil, in violation of the terms of your sentence. I am ordering these Marines to escort you to our holding cell until legal proceedings can decide your fate."

Caddo stepped forward. "You can't arrest the captain!"

"You are bridge officer Caddo?" Wong said. "You are under arrest for the murder of *American Sprit* Security Chief West. As an officer, you are subject to military court martial."

"What?" Snodgrass said.

"Stand down, everyone," Amberly shouted.

"No can do," Wong grumbled. "I've reviewed the applicable law with your XO. You do not have the authority to pardon or offer clemency to criminals convicted under *Magellan* tribunal law. As Fuentes Station's chief law enforcement officer, I have the obligation to arrest this murderer and this Chasm scum."

Dek looked hard at Skylar. He looked angry. He glanced at Amberly. She looked confused and torn. Amberly wanted to override Wong, but quickly decided until she could consult with a legal counsel back on *Magellan*, she had to defer to her security chief.

Skylar placed his hand on Dek's shoulder and gave it a sharp shove.

"Stay away from my fiancée," Skylar threatened as he leaned into Dek. He looked to Wong, "Take this traitor to the brig."

Snodgrass stepped forward. "Trigs? Skylar is it? Captain Tigona was duly appointed and is the master of the *American Spirit*. I am pretty sure as captain, he has, shall we say, diplomatic and circumstantial immunity from incarceration."

"And who are you?" Skylar asked.

"Executive Officer Snodgrass," he replied.

"Well, looks like you're acting captain now," Skylar said, "until Amberly appoints a new captain. Please have your Marines stand down, or I'll make sure they are court-martialed as well."

Snodgrass looked over to the Fuentes Station Commander, to see if backed her XO.

Boro spoke up, "Mission Commander Amberly, are you ordering Dek to be arrested?"

Amberly hesitated, and she knew she looked weak to her team and the senior leadership from *American Spirit*. Maybe she had loved Dek once. Maybe she had used him. But she trusted Skylar. She was going to be his wife. How could she not back him? She could feel the utter sadness from Dek now, and she could see in his eyes that he knew the truth. She betrayed him, lied to him, used him. Amberly tried to hide the shame she felt. She was about to stab him deeply, again.

Amberly started to open her mouth to speak, when Dek waved down his Marines. "Guys, my freedom is not worth bloodshed. Neither is my life for that matter," Dek looked at Wong. "I surrender."

Dek glanced at Amberly. A solitary tear rolled down her sweet face. He did his best to make a mental picture. *I may never see her again; but this was worth it. How could I not forgive her, the one I love.*

"Goodbye, Amberly," Dek smiled bittersweetly, as Wong zip-cuffed him. "I wish you and your fiancé all the happiness you deserve." He bowed slightly toward her as a Marine started to tug him away.

Another Fuentes Station Marine cuffed Caddo, who was completely befuddled. The Fuentes Station Marines escorted the pair out of the greenhouse.

Amberly's head was spinning. Suddenly everything was completely out of her control. She ran to Kora and embraced her sister, trembling.

"Don't worry," Kora reassured her, with a bit of defiance in her in voice. "We'll fix this."

Amberly stood in her small office, looking out the portal at the gleaming *American Spirit*. She knew this day would be hard. She didn't expect it would be so explosive. Facing Dek had threatened to unravel her. Skylar's independent arresting of Dek and Caddo put everyone on edge. She had to push forward with the mundane and hope that the inevitable direction from Moreno would release some of the rapidly-building pressure between Skylar's and Dek's supporters.

"I'll transfer six members of my botany team to report to your greenhouse director first thing in the morning," Snodgrass, acting captain of the *American Spirit,* promised Amberly. "Do you want to review the hydrogen dioxide storage protocols?"

"No, thank you … Captain," Amberly sighed. "I think we've covered enough territory today. I can't tell you how much I appreciate your cooperation today after the … arrest. You should get back to the *American Spirit* and make sure your people remain calm."

"Yes, we have to keep our heads when the Trigs and Tigonas of the waypoints are stirring things up."

"Are you sure you don't want the permanent captaincy?" Amberly asked again.

"No, and a thousand times over, no. Dek Tigona is the legitimate captain of the *American Spirit*. I will not betray him by taking the center seat. You have to reinstate him, Amberly. You know how bad this makes you look with your fiancé arresting Dek."

"We'll wait for the counsel of Moreno and Thor," Amberly said. "This is too delicate of a situation for boldness. The situation is unstable."

"Maybe," Snodgrass said. "Good night, Mission Commander."

As Snodgrass walked out of Amberly's office, Skylar walked in.

Amberly stood quietly until the portal slid closed.

"What the hell were you thinking, Skylar!" Amberly's face went instantly red. "You undermined my authority! You made me look weak at the worst possible time. I thought you supported me. I thought you were supposed to —"

"Do the right thing?" Skylar interrupted. He leaned on the edge of Amberly's desk. "Dek Tigona is a Chasm traitor!"

"Why the hell didn't you tell me what you were going to do?"

"I tried to tell you last night," Skylar protested. "But you reused to talk about Dek, remember?"

"That's dirty bull, Skylar and you know it," Amberly walked around the desk stood face to face with her fiancé. "That was personal. I'm talking about professional. If you can't keep your personal feelings out of things—"

"If *I* can't keep my personal feelings out things?" Skylar stood straight up. "Are you serious? You are the one who can't seem to remember to whom you are engaged."

"I'm sorry about that kiss," Amberly retreated. "It wasn't like that… it …"

"It sure looked like it was like *that*," Dek said tightly. He paused. "No, wait. Listen, Amberly I understand that things are complicated between you and Dek. That's why I wanted to talk about this last night. We have to be able to talk about these things."

"Of course," Amberly said. Skylar looked to the ground, wringing his hands.

"I'm sorry we arrested Dek without letting you know. I see now that even though incarcerating him was right, I put you in a really hard position." Skylar took Amberly's hand and gently rubbed it with his thumb. "I'm really *sorry*. And I admit, I was jealous when you were kissing Dek. Can you blame me?"

"No, I guess I can't," Amberly felt her temperature dropping to a normal level. "This whole marriage thing … You have to understand how hard this is for me. Every morning I wake up, and I remember that I am engaged, and it feels so foreign. It doesn't feel like … me."

"Amberly, we *need* each other," Skylar started to argue.

"Oh, I know I need you," Amberly smiled. "The synergy of you a me, it's perfectly logical. My head is with you. My heart is wandering. Wondering."

"Amberly, I want your heart, too," Skylar took Amberly into his arms. "I will win it."

"Skylar, you're cute. My heart isn't something someone wins. My mother was Chasm, for waypoint's sake. When my heart told me to follow North, I turned him down, because my head said, 'No.' I am Amberly Macready. My heart *follows* my head. That's who I am. My whole life, I've fought the idea of marriage. I thought my head was against it, but in reality, it was my heart."

"I made things worse by pressuring you to pick a date," Skylar said. "I'm so sorry. Sometimes I can be so insensitive. You are already stressed with the return of Dek and the *American Spirit* and with this crazy hard mission."

Amberly smiled. "You are actually one of the most sensitive men I know. I *love* how you care about every member of our team. You pay attention to their needs. You solve people's problems. You are going to be a great leader for *Magellan*. As for making it worse, we both know I couldn't do this without you."

"I *need* you, Amberly," Skylar leaned his forehead into hers. "Together, we are going to do great things. First here at Fuentes Station, and then *Magellan*. We're going to build a utopia, a waypoint that will shine brighter than any star. We have to believe in us. We can't let Chasm or Dek Tigona or Rita Moreno or anything come between our faith in each other. Amberly, you are the most capable, beautiful person I know. I believe in you. Do you believe in me?"

"You know I do," Amberly smiled as she looked into his bright blue eyes. "My head knows it, and my heart is coming along, too."

"Show me," Skylar said as he kissed her.

CHAPTER SIXTEEN

Fuentes Station, on the asteroid Sonnet, in orbit around Spencer Minorum, October 28, 2604, 24 months after the Battle of Magellan, and two months before the Battle of Marquette.

Why did I think I could do this? Amberly Macready thought, as she leaned back in the uncomfortable conference room chair. *What made me think that I had what it takes to lead this mission?*

Around the room, several arguments were going on at once. As everyone talked over one another, the noise level in the *American Spirit* officer's conference room made it difficult for Amberly to sort her own thoughts.

Amberly desperately wanted the advice of Thor and Rita on what to do with Dek and the other 11 Chasm exiles, but the tight beam transmitter and receiver had both been malfunctioning since shortly after the arrival of *American Spirit*. Skylar and Skip, both *Magellan's* communications experts, along with the engineers from Fuentes Station and *American Spirit*, could not figure out the cause of the malfunction. And in an unfortunate coincidence, the primary transmission array on the *American Spirit* tight beam had burned out, rendering it inoperative as well.

The one micro-factory on Fuentes Station had failed three times to produce an adequate replacement array for *American Spirit*. The three women who operated *American Spirit's* micro-factory were on strike until Dek was released and reinstated as captain. Amberly had thought about using force to commandeer the factory, but Skylar advised against it. A violent confrontation could explode into mass chaos and jeopardize the whole mission. Similar protest from many of the *American Spirit* crew had broken out on ship and station, and *American Spirit* crew outnumbered the Fuentes Station team about thirty to one.

She looked across the conference room at her fiancé. Skylar was involved in a heavy dispute with Midas. She had relied so heavily on Skylar's advice for the practical and political operation of Fuentes Station with great success.

She loved Midas as if he was family, but she trusted Skylar's judgement completely now. When *American Spirit* XO Snodgrass declined the captaincy after Dek's incarceration nearly three months ago, Amberly turned to the only person with the natural leadership skills needed who she could trust completely.

Skylar Trigs was the new captain of the *American Spirit* — many on the deep space ship were not happy about it.

"Quiet everyone, please," Amberly scratched out. She had been shouting so much in recent days her voice was tired, but this time, the room complied. "Let's get started."

Amberly looked at the faces around the table. Representing the *American Spirit* were *Captain* Trigs, XO Snodgrass, and Boro, appointed by Amberly as acting security chief on *American Spirit*, with Caddo in the brig. Representing Fuentes Station was Wong, her brother-in-law and *Magellan* police officer Trot Wilder, who Amberly picked as her new second-in-command. Kuuku Akachi was serving as the ranking mission engineer.

Amberly had also invited Lydia to this Fuentes Station Council meeting. Lydia represented the Science Corps. She invited Skip as well, because of his communication expertise. The expertise was particularly relevant in the present crisis — their inability to communicate with *Magellan*.

As the proceedings started, Midas left the conference room for the lobby, where he took a seat next to the waiting Ramos. Ramos did not have access to Dek, and wanted to petition Amberly's makeshift council to get it. He wanted to make sure Dek, back in solitary confinement, was doing okay.

"I'm tired of waiting for you guys to fix the tight beam," Amberly opened up, already cross because she knew the fight with her subordinate and fiancé was coming. "Since you can't seem to get your act together, I want to send a communication on an open radio channel to *Magellan* to give them a status update."

"Amberly," Skylar said, frustrated to cover this ground with Amberly for the hundredth time. "Without a tight beam to direct the transmission to only *Magellan*, we're just giving intel to the enemy. Eventually, unrestricted radio broadcasts will reach Chasm ears. We've been over this."

"So, fix the dirty tight beam," Amberly exploded. "We're supposed to be the smartest and most capable *Magellan* has to offer, and we can't even get our standard tech working!"

"I'm sorry Amberly," Kuuku sounded deeply remorseful.

"Once I get one bit of code fixed, I find another is corrupted. I think we may have to write the control software from scratch."

"I know I have been opposed to it until now, but maybe we should just let the *American Spirit* fly back to *Magellan*," Boro said. "It will take a few weeks, but at least then we can get —"

"No, no, no," Amberly said. "I've already said the *American Spirit* is not leaving until we have a full cargo of processed materials for the *Magellan* renovation. That is the *plan*. We're sticking to the *plan*. I'm tired of repeating myself."

"Amberly," Skylar said, placing his hand on hers. "It's going to be at least two years before are once again in runabout range of *Magellan*. But our deep space ship can make it there in and back in two months, three tops. We should send the *American Spirit* now."

"Don't patronize me," Amberly groused, snatching her hand away. "That will put us that much further behind."

"Amberly, you've always trusted my judgement," Skylar said, his golden locks, having mostly grown back, trembling now as he held back his own frustration. "Why don't you trust me now?"

"Captain Trigs," Amberly said, now embarrassed and angry, "you are out of line." Amberly's face grew flush, and the color of her skin more closely matched the color of her hair.

She took a deep breath, closed and opened her eyes. "Skylar, when I made you captain, it was to be the administrator while the ship was here. I need you here. With me. I assumed that when the day came for *American Spirit* to leave, we would have a new captain in place."

Her confession of need for him made Skylar smile. Wong, however, was not satiated.

"You assumed that *Magellan* would give Dek a reprieve once we communicated the situation with them," Wong growled. "Well, we haven't heard from *Magellan*, circumstances being what they are. What if Moreno tells you to pitch your ex-boyfriend out the airlock? Don't worry. I'm sure Skylar won't mind if you give your old beau a goodbye kiss."

Lydia gasped at Wong's brashness.

"Watch it, Eli," Trot threatened, protective of his sister-in-law. "Maybe we bring up those assault charges you deserve."

Wong's eyes widened. He knew the threat was hollow, but he

still sat back in his chair, crossed his arms and kept quiet as a means to show Trot he got the message.

Trot had the floor and ran with it. "Begging your pardons, leaving now is way too dangerous. The crew and passengers on *American Spirit* are way too volatile right now. Skylar, I wouldn't be surprised if they mutinied as soon as you start to spool up acceleration. And if you had any trouble, without a tight beam, you'd be forced to broadcast on open radio. If there are these Hawks on *Magellan*, they don't know about Fuentes Station's rebirth. Secrecy was always the plan. We stay silent until we are prepared."

"We don't even know if Chasm is coming back," Skylar said. "*Magnus* hasn't reported problems."

"*Magnus* hasn't reported at all," Skip said, drawing a scowl from his former boss. "Well, at least not in a while."

"We know the Hawks are real," *American Spirit's* second-in-command Snodgrass said solemnly. "We paid for our ignorance with our dearest blood. Captain Eaton. Officer Ortega. Engineer Grace. Ensign Von Bumble. And if the Hawks on my ship would have succeeded, maybe we'd all be dead."

"Why should we risk it?" Trot asked. "Let's stay together until we have a tight beam fixed."

"Amberly," Snodgrass spoke evenly to get the calm attention of the mission commander. "I too believe that sending the *American Spirit* to *Magellan* now is the wrong play. However, if *you* decide to send the *American Spirit*, I believe that the crew trusts me enough that I can prevent a mutiny. I don't think they'll go *there*, anyway. However, I have a bigger question. What will become of Dek? Will you transfer him back to solitary confinement on *American Spirit* – like the other eleven Chasm conspirators – or will you keep him on Sonnet?"

"He has to stay on Sonnet," Boro said. "If Dek is on board, I don't know if you could keep the crew from freeing him."

"Would *Magellan* just send the *American Spirit* back on its original mission to Earth?" Lydia asked. "If they sent the *American Spirit* back to us, would they just execute the exiles? I mean, they did try to commit mutiny. If Dek is actually back on *Magellan*, is he as good as dead?"

"Good riddance," Wong offered a morose smile at the

thought of Dek finally being shown a *Magellan* airlock.

"Captain Tigona is staying here, because we're not sending the *American Spirit* back. Not yet. Not till we've finished our mission and have the materials needed," Amberly said. "If the *American Spirit* shows up now, without Dek as captain, which everyone believes he is, without half the flotilla that left to rescue it, people are going to realize that there is something weird going on. They are going to wonder where I am. One of those persons could be a Chasm sympathizer. We'd blow our cover. We have to get the tight beam fixed so we can resume our confidential communications with *Magellan*. That is the only path forward. Period."

Skip raised an arm to get Amberly's attention.

"Yes, Skip," Amberly called on him.

"None of this makes sense," he said, shaking his shiny black bowl-cut hair. "I've been auditing the communication logs since I arrived, and it just feels like something is missing. I sort of have that feeling like when I suspected those encrypted files back on *Magellan* were trouble. And we found out they were for ... Dek. Only that was back when Dek was still a bad guy." Skip felt like he just put his foot in his mouth. He turned to Lydia and shrugged. His girlfriend replied with a don't-worry-about-it smile.

"What do you mean, it doesn't make sense?" Amberly said.

"Well," Skip tapped his infopad which threw up a magnetic resonance projection so everyone in the room could see. "Look at the patterns. Regular reports from Moreno for the first five months of your mission. Clockwork. Then the reports become more irregular, and then they almost disappeared entirely just before the *American Spirit* arrived."

"Maybe the Marine Commander just wasn't feeling as chatty as she used to," Wong suggested.

"Maybe," Skip said.

"Maybe not. Commander Moreno is pretty consistent," Boro suggested.

"I did notice that Rita had stopped replying to my reports," Amberly said.

"I noticed that in the log, too," Skip said. "Well, you know bandwidth is precious, so I wondered what *Magellan* was filling that unused data space, where Moreno's replies used to be."

"So, what did you find?"

"I found nothing."

"Nothing?" Skylar asked. "Skip, you are losing your touch."

"Yes, but something *did* use the bandwidth," Skip said. "I also noticed that the fake system logs we had been transferring back to *Magellan*, the ones they would use to make it look like you were rescuing the *American Spirit* with the others instead of gathering supplies here on Sonnet, had been truncated. Cut off."

"Why would that happen?" Boro asked.

"Well, the bandwidth is limited and completely spoken for. No space for anything extra. The only thing I can think of is someone has slipped an extra message in there, and it bumped the logs slightly."

"Holy God," Lydia said. "Someone has been sending secret messages back to *Magellan*?"

"A spy, here?" Amberly said.

Skip put his hands up. "Well, wait. It's a theory. I'm not entirely sure. It could be —"

"Which means most certainly there is a spy on *Magellan*, too." Skylar said. "We have to warn them. *I* have to warn them. As a member of the *Magellan* Council, it's my obligation to —"

"Skip, I want you to find out exactly what has been transmitted," Amberly said.

"I'll need mission commander clearance," Skip explained. "They don't normally let us comm officers read other people's messages just for fun."

"I'll have Verne get you my access credentials," Amberly said. "How long will it take you?"

"Well, if I had Skylar to help me review the logs," Skip replied, "it could help cut the time in half."

"Sorry. Captain Trigs needs to begin his preparations to return the *American Spirit* to *Magellan*," Amberly said.

"Wait, what?" Skylar looked at his bride-to-be. "You mean it?"

"We haven't been in contact with *Magellan* for months. Who knows what the Hawk who has been receiving info about us will think now that we've gone silent. She may be preparing sabotage or mischief already on our waypoint. Hopefully, Skip will confirm the identity of any Hawks on *Magellan* after he sifts through these phantom transmissions."

"Oh, hell," Skip said. "Sabotage. Some dirt licker must have sabotaged the tight beam. They cut us off on purpose. We may be too late. Amberly, you're right. We need to send the *American Spirit* now!"

"You won't regret it," Skylar said.

"But... I've been trying to fix... your saying someone has been deliberately corrupting the tight beam software?" Kuuku looked incredulous. "How could I not have seen it?"

"We have a traitor in our midst," Boro said, and suddenly everyone started looking around at their colleagues at the table. For the first time since the meeting was convened, the room grew quiet.

"I'll get to work rooting out the mole," Trot said after a moment. "But we'll need to keep the fact we may have a mole to ourselves. If we do have a mole, and she knows we are onto them, she may go to ground."

"Okay, we have our work to do," Amberly said. She stood up, and everyone else followed her cue. "Skip, the minute you confirm our theory, you report directly to me."

"I don't see how it could be anything else," Skylar said.

"Trot," Amberly looked at Kora's husband. "Begin your investigation. If you even suspect you have someone who is good for the crime, you have my permission to stun and interrogate. But keep this on the down low. Wong, you better stick closely with Trot and watch his back. If we have a mole, and they get wind we are looking for her, then Trot may need some security."

"Yes ma'am," Wong said.

"Skylar," Amberly said. "Get the *American Spirit* ready to fly. Keep the prep on a need-to-know basis. Don't let the crew and passengers know what is going on until the last possible moment."

"What about Dek?" Snodgrass asked.

"Grab a few Marines and transfer him to the *American Spirit* brig," Amberly said with conviction.

"Yes ma'am," Snodgrass was impressed with Amberly's command of the unfolding situation. Up to this point, he took her for someone mired with too much uncertainty, but now he saw what Moreno and Rillio saw in her.

"Wong, I am going to reassign you to be Security Chief for

American Spirit," Amberly said with a tone that made Wong realize this wasn't up for debate. "Boro, you'll take over security here until the *American Spirit* returns."

"But- I-" Boro stammered. The thought of being cooped up on Fuentes Station for months when he could be getting back to *Magellan* depressed him. "Yes ma'am."

As the room began to clear, Skylar lingered

Amberly moved to Skylar and kissed him.

"Be safe. I miss you already."

"Now that I am going, I am worried about you. If there is a Hawk here —"

"Boro is a good man. He's got my back. Don't worry about me. I'm a big girl."

"Yes, you have proven yourself. I shouldn't worry about you," Skylar smiled, as he ran his fingers though his fiancée's short red hair. "But I do."

"Hurry back. We have a wedding to plan."

Skip was almost to the main deck elevator when Skylar caught up with him.

"Skip, you are in a hurry," Skylar observed.

"You heard Amberly," Skip said. "I have all the transmissions copied to the communication workstation on Fuentes Station. And now that I have clearance, I should be able to figure who has been hijacking our tight beam transmissions."

"And what they have been saying," Skylar added. "I'm glad I caught you. I pulled all the encryption processors from Fuentes Station to see if I could figure out why the tightbeam wasn't working. They are in the captain's quarters here on *American Spirit*. You should grab them before you head back to the station."

"Yeah, okay. I'm glad you caught me, too," Skip said. "I would have hated to have had to walk all the way back up to the ship once I am on station."

"Still so lazy," Skylar joked. "Come on. I was headed to my quarters now anyway."

Midas and Ramos were waiting outside the conference room, after the *ad hoc* council had dispersed. Amberly called them in.

"Ramos," Amberly smiled at the clergyman. She hadn't really

interacted with Ramos much after her father disappeared, but knew her late father trusted him. "I need you to do me a favor. But first, I need you both to understand this conversation is confidential."

Midas and Ramos both nodded.

"With Skylar gone, I don't really trust that I can manage Wong," Amberly explained. "And honestly, I'm still a little scared that Wong will forget his promise and could hurt me. So, I'm sending him with the *American Spirit*. Boro, on the other hand, I trust with my life."

"A wise choice," Midas said. "I'm sorry you are in a position to feel that way. I wish Wong –"

"Don't have any pity for me. I deserve Wong's ire," Amberly rebuffed Midas. "But I also have a mission to accomplish."

"How can I help, Amberly?" Ramos asked.

"I need you to both to make sure that Dek makes it safely to *Magellan*. I've ordered Skylar to allow you to visit Dek again, Ramos."

"Thank you."

"Anyway, I need you both to be quiet eyes and ears for me, keep everyone honest. Midas, look after Ramos. Ramos, look after Dek. It's that simple," Amberly said and looked at both men with fondness. "Pastor, my dad really respected you a lot. He always said that you were a 'prophet preaching the truth.' I'm sorry I never got to know you better."

"You're sounding like one of us is going to die," Ramos smiled. "I don't think it's our time yet."

"A prophecy?" Midas asked.

"Meh," Ramos shrugged.

"Midas, I want you to take this message and make sure that you give this directly to Moreno," Amberly said. "Don't let anyone else see it. Not even Skylar." Amberly handed Midas a small message chit.

"Keeping secrets from your husband is not a good idea," Midas warned.

"He's not my husband, yet," Amberly reminded him, "but get back soon, because I am inviting you to the wedding."

Amberly hugged Ramos, then Midas. "Midas, we've come a long way since you were delivering parcels to me at the science lab. I felt so young and untested over this past year – it's been nice to have the old men around to help keep me on the right path. Thank you both."

Midas wiped a tear from his eye and offered a bittersweet smile. "I'm proud of you kid."

He paused, looked sideways and then said, "I'm not that old."

Ramos shot an incredulous look at Midas.

"Okay, okay, I'm that old."

Snodgrass offered his security credentials to the Marine on duty at the makeshift brig on Fuentes Station. The original designers of the outpost did not anticipate the need for incarceration. Dek had been confined to a one-room apartment, where he had only been visited by Wong, delivering him food once a day.

As the door opened, Dek immediately recognized the XO and smiled. He looked at the Marine guards with him, frowned and instinctively grabbed at his neck.

"Not yet, captain," Snodgrass told Dek. "But we are taking you back to solitary on the *American Spirit*."

"The *Spirit* is going somewhere?" Dek asked.

"Sorry, captain, that's on a need to know basis."

"He's not the captain, sir," one of the Marines corrected Snodgrass. The XO turned and faced the Marine, a hint of rage flashed in the corner of his eyes, betraying his otherwise calm demeanor.

"Who gave you permissions to speak, private piss-ant," Snodgrass said evenly.

"I'm sorry sir," the Marine said, barely able to hide his own indignation. "And the name is Stewart, not piss-ant."

"Private Piss-ant, the next time you feel the need to correct your XO in front of the captain, I'll make sure you are assigned extra recycle sorting duty for a month or two. Do I make myself clear, Private Piss-ant?"

"Yes sir," Stewart replied.

Snodgrass turned back to Dek and handed him a small plastic pouch. "Grab whatever personal affects you can fit in here and let's go. We're in a hurry. You have a date with Ramos."

"I feel like I should be excited, but I am not sure why," Dek said, and then turned to Stewart. "Don't worry about the XO, Stewart. He's all bark and no bite. And thanks for the escort."

Snodgrass frowned. Then smirked a bit.

"You know, I've never been to the captain's quarters on *American Spirit*," Skip told his former boss as they paced down the small hallway through the executive housing suites on the highest deck of the *American Spirit*. "I bet it's pretty sweet. Am I right?"

"It's sufficient," Skylar said, monotonously. The unexpected tone made Skip look over at his fellow comm officer and notice perspiration beading under the Skylar's blonde bangs.

"Are you feeling okay?" Skip asked.

Skylar stopped and looked at Skip. Skylar would have never said it, but he never really cared for the awkward simpleton. Skip was already annoying, though Skylar feigned friendliness with him for years. His growing relationship with Lydia made him more insufferable. He forced himself to smile.

"I'm fine, Skip," Skylar said. "I guess I am just a bit nervous about taking the *American Spirit* out as captain. Obviously, I've never commanded anything so big before. And I'm worried about Amberly when I am gone. I mean, there may be a mole among us, and maybe when I am gone, he'll try to kill Amberly."

"Boro can take care of Amberly," Skip reassured Skylar. "He's pretty tough."

They arrived at the captain's quarters, and after Skylar provided his biometrics, the door offered access to what Skip thought was a disappointingly modest apartment.

"I've been thinking about the mole," Skip said as he surveyed the apartment, looking for the encryption processors. He saw a small, Japanese-themed kitchen with a re-heater and a vintage beverage dispenser. Otherwise the place was unremarkable, even lacking windows. "I mean, whoever this person is, they have to know how to access and use the main communications console. They'd have to be pretty knowledgeable in tight beam protocol to be able to insert and remove data segments. I guess that would really limit down the number of people who the mole could be to — oh snap." Skip looked at Skylar who had a stun gun drawn on him.

"Which is why I am going to arrest you, Chasm mole," Skylar said. "Right after I stun you."

"*I* am not Chasm," Skip said flippantly, though nervously eyeing Skylar's stun gun. Skip had been stunned before, and it wasn't an experience he wanted to repeat. "That's ridiculous. Ask Amberly. She knows."

"Well, I probably should have asked her," Skylar smirked. "But unfortunately, we were pretty far along on our way to *Magellan* when we found you, a stowaway, sabotaging *American Spirit*. And with the tight beam not working, we couldn't check with her without breaking radio silence. Too bad; she might have exonerated you. But she would understand, that as captain, I had to work to eliminate the Chasm threat, so we tossed you out the airlock."

"Now wait, just a minute, you've got this all wrong," Skip said, backing up against a Wagara-patterned padded wall. "Oh, you dirt-licker. *You* are the Chasm operative, aren't you? Only you would be able to pull this off. Or me. And I know I didn't do it. *I'm such an idiot.* And now you've lured me into a quiet place, no witnesses —"

"Shut up! You are so annoying," Skylar shouted.

"And you are so arrogant, pretty boy," Skip shot back.

"You take me for an ordinary ... *boy*? A mere Chasm operative? I am a Hawk. Feeding info about our progress to my comrades on *Magellan* was easy enough. As was feeding false information to Moreno. Keeping Amberly from Moreno's response to my false reports just required some deleting. But *Magellan* can't know the *American Spirit* is coming until it is too late, and the only way to make sure that happened was to disable both the tight beams —"

Skip dove for the re-heater and tossed the heavy cooker as hard as he could at Skylar's head. Skylar easily stepped out of the way, and the he put three stun bolts into Skip.

"Owwww...." Skip slurred as he convulsed into unconsciousness.

CHAPTER SEVENTEEN

Skylar sat in his chair on the bridge of the *American Spirit*, his mind racing. Decades of training, planning and hiding in plain sight. His whole life, he had been waiting for the moment when he could bring victory to his glorious Chairman. As a teenager, he'd sworn fealty to her and the coming utopia, where he was sure he would have a bright place building perfection.

And no one ever suspected he was a Chasm Hawk until now, until it was too late.

He looked around the scarred bridge and thought about all the people who had been master of the *American Spirit* since its first visit to *Magellan* nearly seven years ago. In the last eight years, many had sat in chair he now occupied: Lars Olaf; Chasm undercover operative Järvinen; Chasm agent Sparks, Raven One, a.k.a. Kimberly Macready, April Eaton, Himari Grace, Dek Tigona, and now Skylar Trigs.

Being captain of the *American Spirit* meant you had a short life expectancy. Of the seven previous captains, only Sparks and Tigona still drew breath.

Skylar intended to remain with the living. He was a Hawk after all, the most cunning and lethal, the most elite of all Chasm ranks. He had a plan that would end *Magellan*, bring him the highest praise from the Chairman, and he would claim Amberly as his prize.

Surely, if I succeed where even the legendary Raven One has failed, the Chairman will not deny me Amberly, Captain Trigs thought. He detested the misandrist Macready and her favored position with the Chairman. He didn't know why he was jealous; Kimberly was now a floating chunk of ice somewhere in deep space. He hadn't seen the Chairman for nearly a decade, but he felt attracted to her ageless beauty after so many years. *What did the famous American diplomat say, 'Power is the ultimate aphrodisiac?'* But he knew he would never have the Chairman. Even entertaining such thoughts was blasphemous. Skylar chastised himself for having jealous emotions at all. *Amberly will be prize enough. Jealousy leads to greed, which must be purged from humanity, even from myself,* he thought.

He thought about that turncoat, Dek Tigona, who betrayed Chasm for the love of Amberly. *What a fool Dek was,* Skylar considered, *to think he could beat the Chairman and somehow keep the Macready girl for himself.* Still, as long as Dek lived, Skylar knew he posed a real threat to his success in destroying *Magellan* and winning Amberly's heart. Of course, the latter would just be a bonus, because Skylar intended on possessing the daughter of Kimberly, the enemy of Chasm, as his own personal property. Amberly Macready had forfeited any right she had for self-determination, for life even, the instant she put a bullet in her mother on this very bridge more than two years ago. Skylar would be doing redhead a favor asking the Chairman for the Amberly. *Who knows what horrors the Chairman would have for Amberly otherwise?*

Skylar's moment for glory had come.

"Snodgrass," Skylar summoned the attention of his second-in-command. "What is the status of thrusters and spooling? I want to move as soon as possible. There is no telling what damage Chasm operatives could be doing back on *Magellan*. Speed and secrecy are essential."

"I'm waiting on Chief Engineer Todum," Snodgrass said. "He's on his way to the bridge to coordinate final prep from here."

"Jefferson, tell Duke Todum to double-time it to the bridge."

"Yes, captain," the VI responded over bridge speakers.

"Is the traitor Dek on board?" Skylar looked up at Snodgrass with a hard gaze.

"Yes, sir," Snodgrass answered. "I saw to it personally. He's been returned to solitary confinement. Well, I transferred custody to Sergeant Wong. I trust Wong properly booked Dek."

"Trust is an interesting substance, XO," Skylar said. Snodgrass detected an air of condescension in the statement. "Jefferson, please ask Sergeant Wong to report to the bridge."

"Yes, captain," the VI repeated. "And captain, all hands are now onboard. We have clearance from Fuentes Station to depart."

A familiar voice that soothed Skylar's anxieties broadcast over the bridge speakers. "Captain Trigs," Amberly said. "Safe and successful travels. I'm jealous. I'd like to be going back home right now. Godspeed, sweetheart."

"Mission Commander Macready, this is Captain Trigs. Acknowledged safe and successful. We'll be back before you know it. All my love. *American Spirit* going radio silent."

"Goodbye," Amberly said as the wired transmission cut off.

"Mr. Snodgrass," Skylar said, "take us home."

As XO, Snodgrass handled issuing the myriad of orders to get *American Spirit* underway. The gangway and hard wire connection were retracted. Light thrusters were ordered. Inertia dampeners were brought online.

The ship was free and within seconds, the basic thrusters had already put nearly a hundred kilometers between *American Spirit* and the large asteroid Sonnet.

Duke Todum arrived on the bridge.

"Duke, I'm glad you're here," Skylar said. "How are the sub-light spools doing?"

"We should be ready to begin acceleration to a cruising speed of .2c in about 30 minutes," Todum said.

"Excellent work," Skylar lauded Duke. "I know being promoted from mate to chief engineer in such a short amount of time must be somewhat overwhelming, but I am confident that as the engineer with the most experience on *American Spirit*, you are the right person for the job."

"Thank you, captain," Todum said.

Skylar produced an infopad and handed it to his chief engineer. "These are confidential vectors and approach speeds. Please execute them as soon as possible."

Todum examined the infopad. He gave an are-you-crazy look to Skylar and then looked back at the infopad to make sure he hadn't misread it. Skylar saw his apprehension. He waved the chief close to his chair, and the spoke almost in a whisper near his ear.

"Time is of the essence. We don't know what is going on at *Magellan*. Don't worry, Chief. I know what those orders will do, and clearly we are not going to allow that," Skylar whispered reassuringly. "Additional orders will follow once we are halfway to *Magellan*. Everything will make sense then. But for now, keep this to ourselves. We don't know who the mole is. She or he could be on *American Spirit* with us."

"I understand captain," Todum said. "You can count on me

to keep this secret."

"Of course, I can," Skylar said. "Now go make it happen."

Ramos was generally thought of as a kind, unassuming man. But he also had the ability to appear threatening. He was now exercising that skill on Sergeant Wong.

"I don't understand, Wong, why would the captain countermand direct authorization from Mission Commander Amberly Macready? I don't believe that he has that authority, do you?" Ramos said as he stood as tall as possible.

Wong cowered slightly. "Sorry, preacherman. I don't make the rules; I just enforce them. Skylar said no one sees Dek until he has had a chance to debrief him. So, the captain isn't being insubordinate, but rather we just have an administrative delay before you can see Dek."

"Administrative delay. That sounds suspicious," Ramos said. "I'd really like to talk with Dek. It's been several months."

"Listen, Dek's fine," Wong said. "I promise. Besides, why do you care so much about this traitor anyway?"

"No one is too far gone for God to forgive them," Ramos said. "Which means no one is too far gone for me to forgive them. I have forgiven Dek for his participation with Chasm. You should too."

"I don't think I could do that," Wong mused. "I don't think I can forgive Dek for the deaths of my friends. I can barely forgive Amberly."

"So, I've heard," Ramos quipped.

"Sergeant Wong, report to the bridge, double time," Jefferson's VI voice sounded over the ship intercom. Wong looked at Ramos and sighed. The Marine took off at a fast pace to the bridge.

"I'll just wait here," Ramos said, and sat down on a bench outside the brig reception area. Once he saw Wong was out of earshot, he pulled out his infopad and called Midas.

"Midas," Ramos spoke quietly, "I'm worried something is wrong. Eli still hasn't let me see Dek, and he's been summoned to the bridge."

"I see," Midas said. "May be nothing. Still, let me come to your position. Where are you?"

"I'm in the brig lobby."

"On my way."

Wong arrived at the bridge and saw Snodgrass sitting in the command chair. "Where's the captain?"

"Skylar said to meet him in the captain's conference room," Snodgrass explained. "That's just pass the captain's quart—"

"I know where it is," Wong snapped at the XO, "... sir."

Wong wondered if he was in trouble as he quickly walked down the executive officer hall. Perhaps Skylar, as a protective beau, was going to punish him for when he drunkenly assaulted Amberly at Rick's Cafe back on *Magellan*. Amberly herself had forgiven Wong, and even asked her to be her security chief. But perhaps her new love was not as forgiving. Out here, out of communication with Fuentes Station, Amberly was unable to keep Skylar from executing some form of justice.

Wong heard a strange tapping, like a busted steam pipe, that interrupted his thoughts. The sound stopped, and he made a mental note to tell engineer Todum to check it out. He now stood in front of the door to the conference room. *I shouldn't be worried*, Wong thought. *The captain is a good man, loyal to Earth and a reasonable public servant.* Wong pressed the door chime, and the door slid open.

"Come in, Eli," Skylar was seated at the end of the conference table. The room was dimly lit. "Take a seat."

Wong did as he was instructed. "How can I help, captain?"

"I have very special request," Skylar said. "But first you must promise me that you can keep this completely confidential. You may only discuss this with Mission Commander Macready once we return, because these are her secret orders."

"I understand, sir," Wong said.

"Amberly clearly has feelings for Dek, and she knows that those feelings could compromise the mission, and if I may be vulnerable to you, our upcoming marriage," Skylar said, oozing faux authenticity in every word. "You and I know that North should not have given Dek clemency, and we should have executed him with Johnson and the others."

"Yes," Wong agreed. "I love North like a brother, but I was

shocked when he let that tool Dek keep his life."

"As was I," Skylar agreed. "But we didn't know about the continuing threat, about these Hawk agents. Dek could rally this crew against me, free our Chasm prisoners again, and then use the *American Spirit* to assault *Magellan* again. We must not let him."

"Of course, captain," Wong said. "You know that as head of security, my Marines will protect your –"

"No, no, my friend. You misunderstand," Skylar put his hand up to stop Wong from continuing. "Amberly has ordered us to terminate Dek Tigona. She knew she could never do it herself, that it would be easier if we took care of this uncomfortable deed for her."

Wong was stunned silent.

"Will you take care of Dek Tigona for us? Bring justice to the lost?"

"Yes, of course," Wong regained his composure. "It's just that…"

"You know in your heart it is the right thing to do," Skylar said. "We can let Anderson, Jindal, Twig and the others finally rest in peace."

"How and when?" Wong looked down at the table.

"Every moment Dek lives, the risk of him compromising our mission increases. Take him near an airlock, stun him, and send him on his way. Can you do that?"

"If I know I have your backing, I shall," Wong said. "Skylar, your dedication to the home planet is inspirational."

"I know where my loyalties lie, Eli. Report back to me when you have completed Amberly's orders, and I will announce Amberly's orders, and that those orders have been carried out, to the crew."

Wong left the dimly lit conference room into the hall servicing the executive suites. He had wanted Dek's head for so long, he was ready and willing to carry out the execution. He was glad that Macready had finally come around to see Dek for the evil person he was, but the clandestine nature of this execution made Wong uneasy.

As he made his way for the elevator that would take him to the brig, Wong noticed the knocking sound again. *Some busted pipe can't be good*, he thought, as he pulled his infopad from an arm pocket and sent a maintenance report to Todum. Wong checked the charge on his stun gun as he entered the elevator.

Wong was surprised and frustrated to see both Ramos and Midas waiting in the brig reception. He ignored them and spoke straight with the Marine guard on duty. Wong had four Marines he knew were loyal to him and would not be tempted to support any coup attempted by Dek. These were the only Marines assigned to guard the rogue.

"Private, please bring me prisoner Dek Tigona," Wong said, and then a little more loudly. "Captain Trigs wants to see him."

"Yes sergeant," the private replied and then he disappeared through the door into the cell bank.

"What does Skylar want with Dek?" Midas asked Wong.

"That's classified," Wong replied, looking away.

"You're full of dirt," Midas replied. "What? Is he going to beat up Dek and warn him to stay away from his girl?"

"What does Amberly know?" Ramos asked calmly.

"Well, as mission commander, I assume she is privy to classified information," Wong replied cautiously. Then he looked at Ramos. "Ramos, when Dek is brought out, you can have two minutes to speak with him. But not alone."

"Great!" Ramos said, surprised that he was going to get to check in with Dek after no contact for these past few months. "But why?"

"Because, as you have pointed out before, Mission Commander Macready gave permission," Wong said.

"And I am grateful," Ramos said, rubbing his balding brown head. "But when will I have a chance for an extended conversation with Dek."

"Preacherman," Wong said, "You are a man of God, so I won't lie to you. I don't see any guarantees of you having an opportunity to have another conversation at all."

"I see," Ramos muttered.

The door to the cell block slid open, and Dek stepped out, wearing a smartly pressed khaki jumpsuit, his hands cuffed behind his back. Dek saw Ramos and smiled. The Marine guard pushed Dek all the way through the door.

The Marine held out his infopad to Wong. "Transfer

authorization, please present exposed skin." The infopad did a nearly instant DNA scan from epidermis cells, and the guard's VI replied, "Security Chief Wong's identity confirmed. Transfer of custody complete."

Wong looked at Ramos. "Two minutes."

"What is going on?" Dek asked.

"We're headed back to *Magellan*. Amberly made Skylar captain," Ramos explained.

"Her new fiancé?" Dek asked.

"Yes. But that's not the problem. Tight beams are down on both station and ship, and Amberly is worried that *Magellan* might have been compromised by a Chasm Hawk."

"And she doesn't want to use an open radio signal because it could tip off Chasm of our little operation?"

"Something like that," Ramos said. "How have you been? I've been trying to get in to see you, but they have been keeping me away."

"Well, I'm not going to lie to you —"

"Apparently, no one ever does," Ramos interrupted.

"It's been pretty rough. Having gotten this close to being back with Amberly again, and then realizing that she's moved on. Drinking bitterness is tempting."

"I don't know if she ever did really love you, Dek," Ramos said. "You should know the truth."

"How do you know this?" Dek said, looking slightly distressed.

"I don't have time to explain," Ramos said. "But trust me."

"Unfortunately, I believe the preacher is right," Midas offered.

Dek looked at Wong for a reaction. "I don't understand anything that goes on in that woman's head," the security chief admitted. "Time's almost up."

"I've been praying," Dek said to Ramos. "And I think I am hearing God talk back to me."

"The hope of a desperate man? Or someone who actually has slowed himself down enough to harmonize with the Almighty?" Midas offered.

"Midas, not now," Ramos said, and then turned back to Dek. "Listen, keep praying. I am almost certain when we get to

Magellan, they will execute the other Chasm exiles for the attempted mutiny. I don't think I can do anything for them. Snodgrass and I will make a direct appeal to the governor and Moreno for clemency for you. Maybe God will move their hearts to mercy."

"No. It's my time. Maybe it's best for me to go back to God," Dek said. "I've made my peace with my sins. I've realized that Amberly had become almost an idol for me. God had to take her away from me so I could see. If we wouldn't have come back, I would have worshipped that redhead all the way to hell."

"Sweet Jesus," Ramos looked hard into Dek's blue-grey eyes. "You are a true believer now, aren't you?"

"To live is to suffer for God, to die is gain," Dek said. "Deep down don't we all just want to see the face of God?" Ramos suddenly embraced Tigona with a powerful hug.

"Don't be in such a hurry," Midas advised.

"All the same, Dek, we are going to work for your release," Ramos said. "I've never been a big fan of the death penalty. I'm a fan of grace."

"Let's go," Wong said stiffly, working to eliminate any trace of emotion from his voice.

"Maranatha, Dek." Ramos said.

Wong pulled on Dek.

"I will always be grateful to God for you," Dek called out as Wong tugged him into the corridor. "I will always pray for Amberly. Make sure she knows that."

The door slid closed and Dek Tigona was gone.

Midas looked up at Ramos and whispered so as not to be overheard by the Marine guard. "People lie *to me* all the time. I'm an expert at smelling falsehoods. Make no mistake. They are going to kill him. Wong is going to do it right now."

"Are you sure?" Ramos asked under his breath.

"No. But let's follow them and find out."

"And what can we do about it?"

"Start praying we'll think of something when the time comes."

Dek looked across at Wong as they walked down past a series of life filters.

"You know, Wong," Dek said, "unless you guys remodeled the *American Spirit* over the last few months, we're going away from anywhere where Skylar would be, unless he volunteered for recycler duty."

"We're not going to see the captain," Wong said. "We're going here." He stopped them in front of the outer door used for the disposing of unrecyclable waste.

"I see," Dek said as he eyed the interior airlock door nervously. "So, this is it. Is this just your idea, or is Skylar trying to eliminate the competition?"

"This order comes directly from the Mission Commander," Wong said. "I'm sure because of your past relationship, she wasn't strong enough to oversee the deed herself. Justice is finally coming. Justice for Commander Anderson. Jindal. Synder. Topez. Chasm butchered them all. Deep in her heart, Amberly knows you deserve to die."

Wong keyed open the airlock.

"I agree I deserve death," Dek said, "but I can't believe that Amberly ordered my execution."

"Believe what you want," Wong said, as he drew his stun gun. "It won't matter much in a few minutes."

"You don't want to do this," Dek dispassionately appealed to Wong. "There has to be a better way."

"Begging for mercy?" Wong scoffed and drew his stun gun.

"I see how it is then," Dek said.

"Into the airlock. Once I close this door, I've programmed it to eject the trash in two minutes. That's my grace to you. Say whatever prayers you want to say."

"And if I refuse to go in there?"

"What do you think this stun gun is for," Wong said. "You were right. Your time has indeed come. If there is a supernatural maker, say hi for me."

"I am ready," Dek whispered, as he backed into the airlock. Once inside, he knelt on both knees, and bowed his head and said no more.

"Dek Tigona, by the authority of the Mission Commander, you are sentenced to death for violation of the terms of your exile. Your previously clemency has been revoked. With no valid clemency, I now legally condemn you."

The interior door slid closed, and a computer voice informed Dek the exterior airlock would open in two minutes.

Wong leaned his head on the closed door, and began to cry, overwhelmed with emotion. Here at the end, he realized he had not been seeking justice, but had in reality given himself over to revenge. He felt painfully hollow.

A shriek from down the hall forced him to snap to attention.

"Ramos?" Wong called out.

"The fool cut me," Ramos yelled from around a corner. "Help me."

Wong ran down about 10 meters from the airlock. He found Ramos clutching his side, with a growing pool of blood flowing out from an incision near just above his waist.

"What happened?"

"Midas and I followed you, because we suspected you might be going to kill Dek," Ramos said in a pained voice. "We were right! Midas pulled out that knife," Ramos pointed to a bloody utility knife a few meters away, "and he asked me to help him jump you before you could do it. I told him violence was not the answer, and I was about to warn you when he stabbed me. I guess he was a coward, because as soon as I yelled out, he ran."

"Midas did this to you?"

"Yes, if you hurry you can catch him," Ramos said.

"I'll get him, but first I need to get you some medical help," Wong said. He looked down the hall another 10 meters and saw an emergency first aid kit. Wong went to grab it and returned to Ramos. He opened the kit, took out the wound spray, and applied the congealing antibiotic foam to Ramos' gash.

"Can you walk?" Wong asked.

"I think so," Ramos replied as he slowly stood.

"Good. Get yourself to the sick bay," Wong directed.

"Wait, you're not going to take me?" Ramos protested.

"No, I need to check something," Wong said. "Also, what you saw was classified. Disclosing classified information could be seen as treason, so I'd keep your mouth shut if I were you."

Ramos nodded, and started hobbling in the direction of sick bay.

Wong turned and walked back over to the airlock. The exterior door had opened and closed, and the airlock repressurized. He opened the interior door and saw nothing.

Dek Tigona is a floating piece of space garbage, Wong thought. *It's about time. Now my comrades can rest in peace.*

Wong punched a direct communication with Captain Trigs on his infopad. He dictated a message for Skylar.

"It's done."

Wong went to go find Midas before the old man could cause any more trouble.

CHAPTER EIGHTEEN

Skylar was in his conference room when he received Wong's communique. He smiled, knowing the Chairman would be pleased to learn of Dek Tigona's demise.

All he had to do now was divert blame and finish prepping a runabout with enough supplies to survive a long trip back to Fuentes Station. Once there, he was confident he could manipulate Amberly, soon to be his wife, with his cover story, while secretly transmitting a message to the Chairman to come rescue him. *The Chairman will come for me*, Skylar thought, *because I will have destroyed* Magellan, *and I will have the daughter of Raven One*. It would take years for Chasm to rescue him, but he would make due with Amberly's company to divert him until then.

Skylar sent a message to Wong to meet him on the bridge, and he stepped out of the conference room to head to the command deck. On the way, he felt he should go check on his former subordinate.

As he approached his quarters, Skylar noted that his door was unlocked – and he was certain he left it locked. *I left Skip was unconscious in the closet. Did he manage to escape?* Skylar thought. He put his hand on his sidearm and touched open the door.

He didn't expect to find his first officer in the room.

"Captain," the XO said with steel in his voice. "Good. I'm glad you've come. I need you to explain some things for me."

"How dare you enter my quarters without permission, Snodgrass? Just because you have access, doesn't mean you can come in here whenever you want," Skylar demurred. "Highly inappropriate. Perhaps a demotion is due."

"My apologies. Sergeant Wong reported what he thought was a broken steam pipe knocking in the executive suite," Snodgrass responded, but not defensively. "Engineer Todum was going to check it out, but I told him that I was heading to my quarters next door, so I'd see if I could find it."

"And what did you find?" Skylar murmured. His eyes were fixed on Snodgrass and the sidearm still holstered on his hip.

"I found the source of the banging just as you were walking

in," Snodgrass said flatly. Then he threw open the closet door and in the same motion drew his stun weapon against his captain.

Skylar drew his weapon in an insant.

In the closet, a bound and gagged Skip struggled. His eyes were red and his forehead was bloodied from banging on the wall.

"Careful, Snodgrass," Skylar said, as they circled each other with weapons drawn. Skip renewed his fruitless struggling. "Mutiny is punishable by death."

"If you have an explanation," Snodgrass said, "now's the time."

"Isn't it obvious," Skylar hissed. He was silhouetted by the freestanding bronzed lamp behind him. "I found Skip on board trying to assassinate me."

"Why would Skip want to kill you?" Snodgrass asked evenly. "You are friends."

"He knew I figured it out. He's the only one who could be doctoring the transmissions," Skylar explained. "He is the Chasm Hawk. Skip is the mole. So, I lured him in here and apprehended him."

"Why didn't you tell us? Why didn't you tell Wong?" Snodgrass demanded as he maneuvered himself between Skylar and the door.

"Because I don't know who else is Chasm. I don't know who to trust," Skylar said. "If his confederates knew he'd been compromised, they'd probably come to kill him to keep him from talking."

Skip was flailing wildly, but he could not communicate through his restraints.

"Well, that all makes sense," Snodgrass said, and he partially lowered his weapon.

"I am glad you see reason," Skylar said, "but I don't know now if I can trust–"

"It makes sense," Snodgrass interrupted him, "except for your secret order to Duke that would ram us into *Magellan* at one-fifth of light speed. And the fact you were preparing a runabout as a life boat, no doubt for yourself, coward."

Skylar didn't have a lie prepared to cover that fact.

"*You* are the Hawk," Snodgrass said as he lifted his weapon again.

"Bah!" Skylar shouted as he simultaneously unloaded several ineffective, random rounds from his gun, while simultaneously dropping to the floor. Snodgrass fired in return, and he managed to nick Skylar in the hand, causing the secret agent to drop his gun. In the moment it took Snodgrass to re-aim, Skylar had grabbed the lamp post and thrust it into Snodgrass' knee. The older man fell, and Skylar sprung to his feet. He swung the lamp repeatedly into his XO's head, splattering blood over everything. Snodgrass yelped and threw his arms up, but Skylar kept swinging and batted them out of the way.

Skip struggled to get free, horrified, desperate to save Snodgrass. But he was expertly bound, unable to escape the closet.

At some point, Skylar figured Snodgrass was unconscious, but he kept swinging. After a few minutes, Skylar saw that the XO was no longer breathing.

The captain then dropped the lamp to the floor and looked at Skip in his closet. Skips eyes were wide, pupils dark with terror, and he remained as still as possible.

"I'll be back for you," Skylar said as he closed the closet. Skylar knew time was of the essence now. Killing someone so violently had rattled him.

Pull yourself together, Skylar, he thought.

Either he was going to get complete control of the situation, or Skylar was going to fail. And Chasm Hawks did not fail. He looked at himself in the mirror, wiped off the blood splattered on his face, washed his hands, and headed for the bridge.

Less than five minutes later, Skylar entered the bridge at full steam. His presence was immediately felt by the half-dozen officers populating the various duty stations. Most of these women and men were new bridge officers appointed by Dek during the return to *Magellan* space, after many senior officers had been killed in the failed Chasm coup. The oldest was Todum, at 29 years old. The youngest was Ensign Elizabeth Hawkins, just 19, who was barely proficient enough in basic communications technology to be a bridge comms officer. Most the crew just called her Betsy.

"Ensign," Trigs said, "please bring up the ship wide intercom. I have a troubling announcement to make."

"Sir," Betsy acknowledged, looking down at her comm board so that her short purple hair fell over her face.

The main bridge door slid open again, and Sergeant Wong stepped in, flanked by two armed Marines.

"Reporting as ordered, sir," Wong told Skylar.

Skylar stood from the command chair, stepped up to Wong, extending his hand.

"Your sidearm, please?" Skylar asked for Wong's gun.

"Sir?" Wong was confused.

"Sergeant, just hand me your weapon. That's an order."

Wong reluctantly pulled his pistol from its holster, emptied the ammo on the floor, and then handed the gun, butt end to Skylar. He looked at the captain with distrust. Skylar set the gun on the captain's chair.

"Private," Skylar addressed one of the Marines flanking Wing. "Under the authority granted to me as captain, I am ordering you to arrest Sergeant Wong."

"What?" said a shocked Wong. "What's the charge?"

"The murder of Dek Tigona."

The bridge erupted into a chorus of gasps. Until now, the officers had been content to wait out to see how *Magellan* would deal with the injustice of Dek's further incarceration. Dek's leadership had assured their survival, and this survival had won loyalty to Dek.

"No!" Todum fought back tears. "Wong, how could you!"

"I... didn't... no, wait..." Wong stuttered.

"You couldn't wait for the tribunal, could you? Your blood lust was too great," Skylar joined in the bridge crew's anger. "And in killing Dek, you could punish Amberly — who you once assaulted because of her alleged ties to Chasm, and so you could get revenge. Biometrics show Tigona was checked out earlier today into your custody, and now he is no longer onboard."

"I don't understand, you said this was an order from —"

"What's more, I've just received a report that we have an eyewitness, Pastor Ramos."

"You told me that Amberly had ordered Dek's death!" Wong said, then he looked around the room. "This is a set up. I don't know why Skylar wanted Dek dead. Maybe he was jealous because Amberly liked Dek, but this was a setup."

Skylar made a show of suppressing a snicker as the Marine private began to zipcuff Wong.

"Why, Skylar? What did I ever do to you?" Wong couldn't understand how he had fallen so quickly from grace.

"If only your crimes ended there, Sergeant Wong. I have additional sad news," Skylar addressed the rest of the bridge officers. "Where is the XO?"

"How should I know?" Wong said. "Wait… is he…?"

"Dead. You should know," Skylar said. "At first, I thought you killed him before you killed Dek, to cover your tracks. But now I think he may have confronted you after the fact, and you panicked. Isn't that so?"

"No. That isn't true."

"You killed him before, then?"

"No. No," Wong reeled.

"You drunken butcher!" Besty shouted at Wong.

"I didn't kill the XO. I wasn't ordered to kill Snodgrass," Wong desperately choked out. "I only killed Dek. He was in violation —"

"Sounds like a confession to me," Duke said. "Looks like we don't need an eyewitness account from Ramos. Let's toss him out, now!"

"I'm sure that the sergeant will be seeing the outside of an airlock soon enough," Skylar said as the Marines grabbed Wong.

The sergeant struggled against the Marines. "Damn you, Skylar! You dirty liar. You are a dirt licking liar! Liar!"

"The best justice is a swift justice," Skylar said. He pointed at Betsy, who activated the comms, and the he addressed the ship. "*American Spirit*. This is the captain speaking. Our XO Snodgrass has been brutally murdered, and former captain Dek Tigona was airlocked by a vigilante. Sergeant Eli Wong has been arrested and charged with both crimes. Chief Engineer Duke Todum will be taking the responsibilities for both security and the XO duties in the interim. I know many of us lament the loss of Tigona, but we must—"

As the door slid open to allow the Marines and Wong to exit, three people stood waiting to come onto the bridge: Midus, a seriously beat up Skip and a quite living Dek Tigona.

Besty screamed.

"You're alive?" Wong was shocked.

"No… how," Skylar reached for his sidearm, but it wasn't there. In his haste, he had not recovered the weapon from the floor of the captain's quarters.

"Simple distraction, really. Sorry, Wong, I didn't stab Ramos," Midas said. "He did it himself while I freed Dek from the airlock."

"See, I haven't killed anyone! Dek is right here! He's *right here!*" Wong demanded.

"What the hell is going on here?" Todum demanded. "Where is Snodgrass? Is he alive?"

"No, he's dead! I saw Skylar beat him to a bloody pulp with my own eyes," Skip said. "Skylar stunned me and tied me up, and when the XO confronted him, Skylar murdered him. He's been sabotaging our comms. He's the Chasm Hawk! He's launching the *American Spirit* straight into *Magellan* to finish what he started! He's going to kill us all!"

"Dirty hell! It's true," Todum shouted. "Skylar ordered us on a collision course! I told the XO, and now he's dead."

The whole bridge erupted into a shouting chaos. Skylar produced a serrated knife and grabbed Betsy from behind, holding the knife over her throat.

"Nobody move or I slit her throat!" Skylar shouted.

The bridge became quiet.

"Easy, Skylar," Todum said, putting his hands up. "Don't do anything rash."

"Don't do anything rash?" Skylar shouted as he quickly grabbed Wong's gun from his chair. "You imbecile. Everything the Chairman has done for the last 20 years has been precisely calculated. I am just one of a dozen contingencies to carry out her will."

Skylar pushed Betsy to her knees near where the Wong had let his ammo fall to the floor. He picked up the ammo with the hand that held the gun, his other hand with the knife pressing slightly into Hawkin's neck. In one quick motion, he flung the knife out of his hand and slid the cartridge into the gun, now pointed at the kneeling officer's head.

"Todum, Dek, Skip," Skylar said with gravely intensity, "come kneel next to Betsy or I'll blow her head off. You have five seconds. The rest of you, clear the bridge. That's an order." Skylar needed to control the bridge to remain in control, but couldn't do it with so many other people on the bridge. Eventually, they would rush him when they realized he couldn't shoot them all. He could control these four and would have to find a way to compel them to help, now that he'd lost his cover.

The engineer, communications officer, and the revolutionary knelt next to Betsy, who was now sobbing. The rest of the bridge crew looked around at each other for a hint of what to do next. The captain was the enemy; the first officer was dead.

"Go ahead," Dek reassured the bridge crew. "I've got everything under control."

Skylar chuckled.

The others left the bridge. Once the main door was sealed, Skylar tapped Todum on the head with his gun. "Go lock it. And the underdeck hatch, too. Keep your hands where I can see them."

"Yes, sir," Todum said through gritted teeth and he moved to follow Skylar's instructions. "If Eaton were here, she would have kicked your ass and made you her bit —"

"Shut up, fool," Skylar commanded. "She's not here. In fact, I'm pretty sure it was one of my fellow Hawks that ended her tenure as captain."

Todum used the manual latch lock on the bridge door that had been installed after the last Chasm assault on the bridge. He then moved to secure the lower deck hatch.

"So now I have a problem," Skylar said. "We're more than a month out from *Magellan*. I need a hostage to keep me safe, and a functioning bridge crew to get us there. And I have to keep the rest of the crew off the bridge. You will all help me."

"Why should we help you, asshole?" Skip demanded. "You are just going to kill us all."

"Because you don't want to see the color Ensign Hawkin's brains. And I will let you live."

Skylar knew Skip had a valid point. Soon, perhaps in moments, the Dek, Skip and Todum would realize that too, and rush him, even if it risked all their lives. He needed to convince Dek to help him now. He needed to bring Dek *back to the right side of history*. His plan had been working so well, if only that idiot Wong had been able to actually kill Tigona. Now his options were limited, and an unlikely alliance with Dek was his only way out.

"Dek," Skylar said in a tone sounding more like his cover personality that wooed Amberly and less like a Chasm Hawk, "you can redeem yourself now in the eyes of the Chairman. This crew trusts you. Help me figure out how to complete our mission — *our* mission — brother, to end *Magellan* and break away from the old, corrupt ways."

"I don't trust you, and you don't trust me," Dek said. "I don't see how we could make that happen."

"Believe in Chasm, believe in the Chairman like you once did," Skylar begged. "If we can trust each other, we can fulfill our destiny, survive and take our rightful place among the Chasm elite and be honored forever."

Dek slowly stood up, hands up and faced Skylar. "I have to see your eyes," Dek said. Skylar's gun moved from behind the head of the sobbing Betsy to being aimed at Dek's chest.

"Do you know the book of myths you now read?" Skylar asked. "The one that charlatan Ramos peddles?"

"Yes, what of it?"

"The people in that 3000-year-old book, they are immortal on Earth. Moses. David. Mary. Jesus. Remembered forever. Unlimited glory. On Arara, we — you and I — will be the saints."

Todum finished securing the hatch and stood up next to the floor portal, facing Skylar.

Skylar continued, "New holy books will be written about us, and what is going on here and now. Our names will be praised and our deeds will be sung about by the children of Arara for millennia. You are the new prodigal son. Come home."

Dek considered the truth of Skylar's words. "And if I don't help you?" Dek asked.

Skylar took the opportunity to answer Dek and thin his opposition. He could run the bridge with just Hawkins, Skip and Dek. Skylar demonstrated his lethal aim by putting a bullet through Todum's skull. The engineer's lifeless body dropped to the floor. Betsy shrieked.

"I don't want to force you. But I will kill everyone eventually, including you. Our fate is sealed and bound together. Either we all die together, or you and I escape."

Hawkins was trembling with fear, and Skip was trying to calm her.

"I want your answer now, Dek," Skylar said, his Hawk tone returned. He pointed the gun back at Betsy's head. "If you delay, she dies. I'll tell you what. This woman is attractive. I'll let you have her while we are in the runabout to Fuentes Station. You can save your life and hers if you like."

Dek glanced around the room, trying to figure out his next move. For most of his life, he had always believed himself the ultimate survivor, that he was smart enough to pull himself out of the fire just in time, every time. Or, he wondered, did he still have an unfulfilled cosmic purpose?

And then he found the detail which gave him a sliver of hope. Skylar's dropped knife had come to rest about a meter between him and Betsy. But there was no way he was going to be able to reach down and grab it before the skilled Hawk would fill him with bullets.

"I tell you what, Dek. I know you want the redhead, too. Now I am not going to give her up, assuming the Chairman allows me keep her, but I'd be willing to share her from time to time. Her genetics are from rare stock, and I'm sure the Chairman would want her to be a prolific mother of the next generation of Aranan perfection."

The thought of Skylar exploiting the only woman he ever loved, the woman he still loved, pushed him over the edge. He gave a great cry and leapt into a slide tackle way too far away to reach Skylar.

The Hawk was confused, and hesitated as he moved his gun away from Betsy and unloaded two bullets at the moving Dek. The first hit Dek in the forearm and the second in the collarbone. Then Skylar saw Dek's intention.

Dek's forward facing leg hit the hilt of the knife resting on the floor. The kick sent it flying forward at great speed just a few centimeters over the floor with such force it lodged through Skylar's shoe, severing his large toe and digging into the rest of his foot.

Skylar screamed in pain and dropped his gun. Blood was spurting from his foot. Dek forced himself to stand up through the pain of the two gunshot wounds. He threw himself on Skylar and knocked the Hawk to the ground. Dek tried to get his hands around Skylar's throat, but he couldn't get his injured arm to move as he fought to keep from passing out from the pain.

Skylar pushed Dek off, and exhibiting a secret strength, grabbed him by both shoulders and threw him back to the ground with a painful thud. Dek struggled to stand, but his searing nerves combined with blood loss made him too disorientated to stand.

Skylar pulled the knife out of his shoe, and knelt next to Dek and pinned him to the floor, and poised the knife to lacerate Dek's throat.

"Forgive him," Dek choked, and closed his eyes. "As I have been forgiven."

"What the dirty freak are you talking about?" Skylar said. "No matter. Just so you know, I'll find an appropriate lie to make Amberly hate you." Skylar said as he drew his knife back for the final kill.

"Stop or I'll blow your brains into a million pieces, you Chasm sonofabitch!"

Skylar looked up and saw Skip, with the gun pointed directly at his head.

"Drop the knife and lie down on your belly," Skip commanded. "Do it now! I am seriously stressed out here, and I may shoot you anyway!"

"There are others who will see the will of the Chairman done," Skylar said as he complied with Skip's commands. He fumed at his former subordinate. "Worm! You will taste death at the hands of Chasm before the end."

"Not today," Skip said. "I can't believe I set you up with Amberly. Betsy, go unlock the door."

Skip kept the gun trained on Skylar's head, as Betsy unlocked the door. The Marine guards were waiting and stormed in with bullet proof armor and assault rifles.

"Arrest this man as a prisoner of war and Chasm conspirator," Skip said, pointing at Skylar.

"On whose authority?" one of the Marines asked.

Dek struggled to sit up, bleeding from two bullet holes. "Mine. Dek Tigona, captain of the *American Spirit*."

The top-ranking crew of the *American Spirit* stood in a phalanx-like formation, packed on the observation deck. In the front row of the assembled were Captain Tigona, Ensign Hawkins, Lieutenant Skip, several other senior officers and Midas. The remaining crew and passengers were assembled on the hangar deck, where they watched the proceedings via vid screen.

"If you don't believe in life after death, that there is something greater than the visible, I have little solace to offer you, except perhaps that the death of Executive Officer Snodgrass and Chief Engineer Todum at the hands of evil was not empty, but rather in the line of duty and service to Earth. Theirs was not a senseless sacrifice," Ramos offered. "But I believe that there is more to this life that what the eyes can see, and we have a great hope in the good news of eternal redemption. Someday those with faith will see the face of our maker. Godspeed and amen."

From the large windows of the observation deck, the gathered crew could see two caskets ejected into space.

"What do we do now?" Skip asked Dek as the crowd began to disperse.

"We go back to Fuentes Station and help Amberly finish her mission," Dek said.

"She'll need all of us now, the poor girl," Midas said. "She thought confronting you was going to be hard. Wait until she finds out that her fiancé was Chasm all along. She doesn't deserve all this emotional trauma. That poor girl is wounded. You best give her plenty of space, captain."

"That's if she doesn't throw me back in jail again," Dek sighed. He turned to face Skip, Ramos and Midas. "Whatever happens to me, you three must take care of Amberly. Do you understand? She's more special than any of you could understand. The Chairman was very connected to Kimberly. Based on what Skylar said, my guess is the Chairman will want to exact her revenge on the woman who shot her favored Raven One. Or she has some other plan for our mission commander."

"We'll keep her safe," Skip promised. "And North and the *Magnus* will defeat Chasm and its Chairman. You'll see."

"We must not underestimate the Chairman again," Dek pondered aloud. "I hope North succeeds, for Amberly's sake. But if he doesn't, let's make sure Amberly's mission does. For all our sakes."

"Don't you worry, Dek," Skip smirked. "North will win."

L.S. ROEBUCK

EPILOGUE ONE

Fuentes Station, on the asteroid Sonnet, in orbit around Spencer Minorum, December 5, 2604, 26 months after the Battle of Magellan, and two days after the Battle of Marquette.

Kora accompanied her sister to the Fuentes Station makeshift brig. She knew Amberly would need her support for the two hard visits Amberly felt she must make.

"I can sit with you when you when meet with them," Kora offered to her little sister.

"I'd like that," Amberly smiled weakly in reply, "but this is something I must do alone."

"Do you think this is goodbye?" Kora said. Amberly didn't have an answer. Kora shrugged at Amberly's non-response and hugged her. "Have Verne message me when you are done, just so I know you are okay," Kora said as she turned back down the hall. Amberly walked into brig's foyer.

Boro, one of the two Marines on duty, saluted the mission commander.

"Who would you like first?" the Lt. Boro asked.

"Prisoner Tigona," Amberly said, as she sat down on a simple aluminum chair next to a similarly constructed table, the only décor in the foyer. Boro nodded to the private, and the Marine disappeared in the cell bank.

Within a few minutes, the Marine returned with Dek, hands zipped together in front of him. Dek smiled when he saw Amberly, and he sat in the chair opposite her.

"I thought you were going to be Ramos," Dek said. "But this is a pleasant surprise."

Amberly blushed despite herself. She was still attracted to Dek, who was much less a mystery now to her than he was when they first met more than two years ago. Her mouth was dry and her palms were damp. This was the conversation that she never wanted to have, but she knew it was a conversation she must have.

"I've come to tell you how sorry I am," Amberly said.

"Don't worry. I understand why I need to be incarcerated for the time being. I am confident the tribunal won't toss me in the airlock."

"Oh, not about you being under arrest again," Amberly said. She took a deep breath. She paused and looked directly into Dek's blue-grey eyes. "I'm sorry I lied to you, back on *Magellan*."

Dek took a moment to hear Amberly, considering her words. What she said didn't surprise him, but hearing her say it make him take stock of his own feelings.

"It was a beautiful lie." Dek smiled tenderly. "It's what I wanted to hear. I wanted to believe that you could love me —"

"Dek Tigona, I *could* love you," Amberly said quickly. "I just wasn't sure that I did — that I do."

Dek eyed Amberly's ring finger, now missing one shard ring. "And Skylar?"

"Oh, Dek. I honestly don't know my own heart. I didn't know it when I was 19, and know it even less now. I'm just someone who has had to grow up so fast who wants to slow it down for a while," Amberly put her right hand on Dek's. "I don't really know who Skylar Trigs is. I'm not in love with his Chairman-cult obedience side. I was definitely in love with his patriotic, *Magellan*-serving, selfless leader side. But that wasn't real."

"That Hawk was in so deep, who knows what was real," Dek said. "I can't imagine he survives the tribunal."

"Well, the basis of my love for him was a lie," Amberly explained, "and when I found out it was a lie, it cut deeply. After what North did to me, I never thought I would be hurt so bad again. I was wrong."

"Amberly," Dek said, "I'm sorry I brought you into all this."

"I've forgiven you long ago," Amberly said, starting to tear up. "But I realized that the same thing Skylar did to me, the same lie he made to me, I guess I made that lie to you. It hurts, deeply. And now I've only begun to realize how badly I hurt you. I'm so deeply sorry."

"Amberly, grace rules the day. We can forgive each other, and move on," Dek said. "I wanted the lie to be true, but I don't want to live in a lie. Even for someone as magnificent as you. I am glad to know where I stand."

"Well, I hope you stand as captain of the *American Spirit* when the tribunal is over," Amberly said, as she stood. Dek did the same, and Amberly quickly moved around the table and kissed the rogue on the cheek. "Hopefully, I'll see you soon, *captain*."

Dek smiled as the duty Marine took him away.

Lieutenant Boro returned to the room. "Prisoner Trigs refuses to see you. Do you want us to force him?"

"No. Did he say why he won't see me?"

"No, Amberly," Boro said. "He doesn't seem angry or defiant. He's moved inside of himself."

"Will you take him a message?" Amberly asked.

"Of course."

"Tell him I'm sorry," Amberly said. "And I forgive him."

Amberly was happy to be receiving messages from Moreno again. With Skylar's sabotage reversed, secure tight beam communication with *Magellan* had resumed. Amberly watched the recorded message from the waypoint Marine Commander. Moreno had established a military tribunal on the *Magellan* to decide the fate of unwitting conspirator Staff Sergeant Eli Wong, returned exile Captain Dek Tigona, and Chasm Hawk Skylar Trigs.

Testimony had been recorded at Fuentes Station and transmitted via tight beam to *Magellan* and then reviewed by the secret tribunal. The trial took a week because the tribunal had a round of follow-up questions for the witnesses, which had to be transmitted back to Sonnet, and then the responses of those questions, transmitted back to *Magellan*.

"Sweet Amberly, Thor and I are sorry for all you have been through. We never thought leading this mission would take such a personal toll. You've already born so much betrayal," recorded Moreno said in words filled with empathy. "I can only hope by having the tribunals here, we've spared you some of the pain of having to see your fiancé prosecuted."

Amberly had never gone through the motion of officially ending her engagement. In her heart, she wanted to believe that this was all a bad dream. She had been betrayed by so many who loved her and whom she had loved. Of course, she betrayed North first, but that didn't make his denunciation of her any less painful. She wanted to wake up from this nightmare and find that she hadn't been fooled by Skylar. That she was madly in love with a good man about to start a happily ever after, safely tucked away in her home on *Magellan*. By day, she'd get lost in her research, and he'd be off making speeches. By night, they'd relax together and watch old Earth movies while drinking real tea. But she knew now that sort of happiness was just a fantasy. At least for her. Fate, or God, or the randomness of the universe had some other, much lonelier path for her.

For all the many ways her mother was wrong, maybe she was right when she warned Amberly that having a lifelong commitment to a spouse was a fool's errand.

"Unfortunately, you will have to carry out the sentencing as mission commander. I've included the sentences in an authenticated data packet so you can be sure there is no mistake." Moreno continued. "I await your next progress update, when we have put this unfortunate business behind us and focus on your primary mission. And I absolutely cannot wait for the day when you return to us, so we can have tea together again. Be well. Moreno out."

The image of Moreno faded away, and Amberly told Verne to deactivate the personal monitor in her quarters.

She resisted the urge to cry; there would be time enough for that later.

She fished through her wardrobe for her white-and-green Science Corps uniform – her most appropriate outfit for this solemn occasion. After dressing, she grabbed her infopad and headed for the gardens to transfer from Fuentes Station to the docked *American Spirit*, where the sentencing would be held.

The small gathering of court officials, legal representatives and Marines were assembled at the same airlock chamber where Dek had almost been spaced several months earlier. Trot Wilder commanded the Marines now. The accused were lined up side-by-side in front of the interior airlock door under heavy guard.

"I've confirmed the authenticity of these verdicts and sentences," Skip announced to the proceedings. He handed an infopad to Wilder, who read the verdicts. Tigona, Wong and Trigs all stood silently, under guard. Wong had legal counsel seated next to him, but both Tigona and Trigs had waived their right to representation.

"Staff Sergeant Eli Wong has been found guilty of conspiracy and malfeasance. He is hereby stripped of all rank, dishonorably discharged from Marine service, and subsequently assigned to work detail on Sonnet mining operations and house arrest until the Fuentes Station mission is concluded," Wilder read.

Wong looked like he was going to say something in his defense, but then his lawyer tapped him gently on the shoulder and Wong seemed to calm down.

Wong's attorney spoke, "Let the record show my client did not admit guilt and never knowingly committed conspiracy against Earth or waypoint."

"The record is noted," Wilder said and then looked at his group of Marines. "Please escort Wong and confine him to his quarters."

Wong shot an angry look at Skylar Trigs. "I hope they give you the airlock, Chasm scum." Wong spit on the ground in front of Trigs, and then pointed at Dek. "You too, traitor."

Two of the Marines took Wong away.

Amberly's brother-in-law cleared his throat and continued reading, "Captain Dek Tigona is found innocent of additional violation of terms of his exile. Furthermore, the tribunal recognizes Mission Commander Macready's appointment of Mr. Tigona as the captain of the *American Spirit*. However, captain, please be advised that the original terms of exile are in force, and should you set foot on *Magellan* proper, your life is subject to forfeit. The prisoner is free to go."

Dek smiled, relief washing over his face, and he walked to where Amberly, Ramos and Midas were standing. He shook the men's hands, then faced Amberly and gave her an awkward hug. She returned the squeeze, but the embrace reminded her that she didn't know how to relate to Dek now.

She was glad to have him around because of his immense talent and powerful leadership, and she was glad he no longer actively wooed her. But she knew she had broken his heart and betrayed his trust. She could see the scars every time she looked in his eyes, his proclamation of forgiveness notwithstanding.

"Congratulations, captain," Amberly offered a sincere smile. "Now get your crew ready. We have a lot of work to do."

"Maybe we can discuss the supply schedule over dinner?" Dek said as he stepped away from the airlock door, a hint of that familiar roguish smile on his lips as he stepped away from the airlock door.

Skylar watched the exchange silently, wearing sorrow on his face.

Then Trot started to read the final sentence. "The honorable Skylar Trigs, member of the *Magellan* council, is found guilty of high treason, conspiracy against waypoint and first-degree murder."

The word "guilty" though expected, still added a new layer of heaviness to the mood of the group. In spite of what Skylar had done, no one, except perhaps Eli Wong, was in a hurry to see capital punishment in action again. But Amberly knew there was no other course of action. In theory, she could grant him clemency, but on what grounds?

Trot continued, "For his crimes of conspiracy, Mr. Trigs has been formally censured and ejected from the council. His *Magellan* and American citizenship have been revoked, and all his assets have been confiscated by the tribunal. For his crimes of murder, Trigs has been sentenced to work prison for the rest of his natural life. The sentence for murder, however has been superseded by the sentence for treason, which is death by expulsion into space, to be conducted immediately."

For most in the small group, Trigs was hard to read. Today, he didn't seem like a crazy member of a utopian terrorist cult, but just like a normal man who got caught up in the wrong cause, remorseful and full of regrets — but resigned to his fate.

Trot Wilder nodded and a pair of Marines approached Skylar.

"Wait," he semi-shouted. The Marines stopped. "May I have a vape smoker before I have to go?"

Midas, standing in the back of the group, fingered his smoker and frowned. "He can have mine." Amberly stepped over to Midas and took the stick device.

"Thank you, Midas, truly," Skylar said.

"I hope your utopian dream was worth it," Amberly said, as she gave him the smoke stick. At the same time, she handed him her engagement shard ring. "I would have chosen to love you forever."

He held onto her hand for a fleeting moment that seemed like a blessed eternity, then released before she had a chance to withdraw it.

"Really? You would have loved me?" Skylar asked, with a bittersweet desperation in his voice. "Or are you just saying that so I'll feel better the last few moments of my life?"

"Does it matter?" Amberly asked, no longer able to hold back her own tears. She reached out and ran her fingers ever so briefly though his golden hair. "Goodbye, Skylar."

Amberly turned and walked away. She didn't have the strength for what was coming next. "It wasn't worth it, Amberly Macready," Skylar called out after her. Amberly paused, but didn't turn around. She didn't want him to see her crying. She continued walking.

"It wasn't worth it!" he shouted again.

Heartbroken, Amberly rounded the corner and slipped out of sight.

The Marines guided Skylar into the airlock. Standing near the interior door, Ramos offered a brief, quiet prayer.

"Thank you," Skylar caught the eye of the preacher, the last human he would see, as the interior door closed.

The airlock was cold and dimly lit by stars through small window on the exterior door. Skylar turned away from the window out of fear, then he briefly panicked because he was worried he would not have time to light the smoke stick. He powered it up, and put the filter end to his lips and began to inhale the tasty fumes. He calmed himself, controlled his breathing, took a few more drags, and then held the smoke stick in place with his lips.

Skylar turned from the windowless interior door to face the vastness of space on the other side of the exterior window. A VI voice was offering warnings, but he had tuned that out. Instead he focused on the symbol of love he held in his hands. He held up the ring and smiled as the shard crystal caught and refracted light from the stars.

In seconds, he imagined a full life with Amberly, conjuring up a farmstead on Arara, playing with their children, a boy with curly red hair and a girl with straight blonde hair. They had brilliant green eyes and innocent smiles, and they loved him and their mother.

Amberly was older now, but still the most beautiful woman he had ever seen. She looked up from the children, came over to Skylar, and gave him a brief, sweet kiss. She took his hand, and they both watched the children playing in the grassy fields.

"I love you, Skylar."

"I love you, too."

He looked down at her hand and saw her wearing the ring. And then he was just holding the ring. And Amberly wasn't there. He was alone, smoke fumes swirling around his head.

He saw the stars, closed his eyes, took another pull from the vape and waited patiently for oblivion.

A second later, the exterior door obliged him, opened, and Skylar Trigs was sucked into space.

Amberly lay quietly on her bed, trying to clear her mind from her grief, letting her heart decompress. The tears were no longer flowing, though a few slowly escaped her eyes. She had to pull herself together to complete the mission. Her greatest fear was that all she had sacrificed, all that she had lost, the pain she had suffered, would be in vain if Chasm were to win.

The door chime rang. Amberly knew it was her sister.

"Verne, let Kora in," she instructed her VI.

She heard the front door open, and her sister call out. "Hello? Amberly?"

"Back here," Amberly replied.

Kora entered the bedroom, holding her son, and looked at her sister with compassion. She sat beside Amberly and set Alroy down on the bed. Amberly saw her nephew and smiled. She remembered what she was fighting for.

Alroy looked at his aunt and crawled over to her, unceremoniously grabbing a fistful of her short hair.

"I'm so sorry about Skylar," Kora said. "In the end, I think he was undercover so long, he had almost forgotten that he was Chasm. Some of him was real."

"Maybe," Amberly said. "I remember when we spaced Johnson. He was spewing venom and swearing allegiance to Chasm to the very end. Not Skylar. He showed regret. Remorse. Almost like he wanted to become what he pretended he was. When other Chasm defectors were facing the end, they kept blathering about the common good and how their lives didn't matter. Not Skylar."

"If you want to forgive him, it's okay," Kora prompted. "You don't have to be angry."

"Somewhere, somehow, Mom is laughing at me. She's mocking me from the other side," Amberly closed her eyes and pictured her mother's face and dark raven hair. "She would have been horrified that I was engaged. It's like she planted Skylar to lead me on, and then break me, so she could say, 'That's what you get for falling in love with a man.'"

"You can forgive Mom, too," Kora said.

"Have you?"

"Sure," Kora smiled at her sister and took her hand. "I can't afford to be bitter when I have to show this little man all the galaxy has to offer."

"Mom would have said that it was wrong for me to want a family," Amberly mused. "She would have said that I am selling myself short. Distracting myself from becoming the smartest scientist in all the waypoints. Is it wrong for me to want someone?"

"No. I don't think it's wrong to want someone. I think it's a really powerful thing to get married and really take on life with someone. We were created for relationship."

Amberly was quiet for a minute, thinking.

"And now that Dek is back in the picture ... and really built ..." Kora added.

"What-the-waypoint, Kora!" Amberly exclaimed, pushing her sister off the bed. "*Too* soon."

Kora smiled mischievously and the girls settled into silence again. Alroy patted Amberly's stomach and babbled. Then, Amberly covered her face with her hands and looked at Kora through her fingers. "Seriously, he looks really good, doesn't he?"

"What-the-waypoint, *Amberly*!" Kora mocked, laughing out loud as she leaned over and scooped Alroy up off the bed.

Amberly was grateful for her sister's presence. The weight of everything she carried felt a little lighter, now.

"Well, I just wanted to stop by and remind you that I love you," Kora said as she scooped up her toddler. "Trot and I are having dinner with Skip and Lydia at the mess. You want to join?"

"Thanks, but I think I just want to be alone for a while," Amberly rolled over on the bed. "And Kora, I will forgive Skylar."

"Good for you," Kora said as she moved for the door. "May God rest his soul."

When Amberly heard her sister leave, she rolled on her back and looked out the viewport at the symphony of space rocks, which along with Fuentes Station, orbited Spencer Minorum.

I still have my friends, Amberly thought. *Lydia, Skip, Trot, my dear sister, Midas, the Dinos. So many people here, now, to support me. But I don't have North. And he has no one.*

Amberly sat up and ordered her personal display panel on. "Verne, show me pictures of North."

The first image that appeared was a snapshot at Rick's at her birthday party. She looked at her 18-year-old self with her arm around North's waist and on his other side, Kora. Skip stood next to Kora with his normal sour expression. Lydia had jumped behind them, sticking her tongue out. She wanted to go back to this point in time, before Chasm, with her friends living halcyon days keeping *Magellan* running between deep space ship visits.

She did some quick math in her head. *Magnus* had been running silent for more than two years now. North would be at *Marquette*. Amberly wondered what was going on, what adventures and dangers North was facing. And assuming *Magnus* was heading on to Arara, would he stay there, find himself a kind woman, settle on the family farm and have the life Amberly said she didn't want?

If I can forgive Skylar and even Mom, maybe North can forgive me, Amberly thought. *Maybe. Only one way to find out.*

Amberly rummaged through a keepsake box and pulled out her encryption key. She didn't know the exact location of *Magnus*, so using the tight beam was not an option. But she could broadcast the message on an encrypted channel. The *Magnus* would already be at Arara by the time North received the message, 1.5 light years from *Magellan*. It would probably take years for someone to decrypt the message without North's key.

I'm going to risk it, Amberly thought. *What's the point of being mission commander if you can't bend the rules a little*? Amberly knew Skip would be more than willing to help her send this clandestine message when he knew it was for North.

"Verne, begin voice recording."

"Yes, Amberly," Verne said. "I'm sure North will be pleased to hear from you."

"Hey, North, it's Amberly," she spoke sweetly as she stared at the photo of her friends at Rick's. "There is so much to tell you and so much I can't say, because you know, Chasm could eventually get this.

"But first, I want you to know I think you must be praying for me, because when I was all alone, looking at Viapos, after you left, I thought I could feel you. I didn't want to believe it because, well ... I was really hurt by what you said before you left, what you ... did. You shut me out when you left. And then I met someone."

Amberly relayed the events of the last year to North. Alroy's birth. The fight with Wong. The rescue of the *American Spirit*. A secret mission of which she couldn't relay the details. Dek's return. Her engagement. Skylar's betrayal. His execution.

"So, now, I'm alone again." Amberly swallowed hard, eyes moist, the emotion of it all welling just under the surface. "And I feel that feeling I haven't felt in so long, that somewhere between *Magellan* and the shiny star Viapos, my friend North was praying for me.

"I better wrap this up. Give my half-crazy, so-called sister Sparks my best. I sort of miss her, too.

"Before I go, I guess I wanted to tell you that I've learned two things since we were last together. First, I've learned to forgive. I've forgiven Sparks. I forgave Dek, even Skylar. I've forgiven Mom. And I'm hoping – and asking – that someday you'll to forgive me, too.

"Besides that, I've learned that there is nothing I want more than for you to come home. Do you hear me? If you have a choice, please come home, North. I'll be waiting."

EPILOGUE TWO

U.S.S. Magnus, in flight to Waypoint Magellan, June 2, 2605, six months after the Battle of Marquette.

Rhodes smiled, took a bite of protein ration and chased it with a swig from her bitter caffeinated drink that tasted nothing like coffee. She reclined back in a booth table at the Officer's Lounge with her favorite three people: North, Sparks and little Nora.

"Nora is getting pretty proficient with that spork," Sparks observed. Her rescuers on *Magnus* didn't know her actual age, but the pediatrician estimated she was approaching three years old. Dr. Hershey believed that Nora Ryder-Olana would eventually catch up with the other children her age, but her development was retarded from the malnutrition during her desperate escape from the destruction of *Waypoint Corez* onboard the *Iron Star* with Ryder, and the now deceased siblings, Arvin and Olana.

Not knowing if Nora had a family name or not, Capt. Obadiah gave Nora the last name Ryder-Olana, in honor of the women who saved her. After Ryder's betrayal, some wanted to scrub the Chasm's officer's name from Nora's, but Obadiah noted that you shouldn't try to erase history just to make oneself feel better.

Sparks also stood up for the memory of Ryder. She did save Nora, after all.

Nora's care responsibilities had been passed around for many months until a pair of engineers who had married somewhere between *Waypoint Balboa* and *Waypoint Coronado*, Linda Navarro-Smith and Inon Smith, adopted her. Rhodes adored the girl, and often babysat, taking Nora on outings.

Nora scooped a glob of green vita-paste and took a bite. She set the spoon down, pushed her messy brown hair out of her face, wrinkled her nose and looked like she was going to cry. Then she spit the vitamin rich foodstuff out onto the table.

"Don't do that, Nora," Rhodes said loud enough for everyone in the lounge, and some people down the hall, to hear. "Eat it. It's good for you."

"Yucky!" Nora shouted, and threw her spork down. She grabbed a sippy cup of artificially-flavored orange drink and tipped it to her mouth.

"Looks like she is picking up your temperament – and volume," North joked. Sparks considered the girl.

"Do you think we'll ever be moms?" Sparks asked Rhodes. Sparks took in Rhodes visually, nearly 19, almost jealous of her youthful beauty. Rhodes had grown her dark brown hair out, and it reminded Sparks of Raven One's dark mane.

"I'm too young to think about that," Rhodes replied as she looked up from Nora to Sparks. For a while after the Battle of *Marquette*, Rhodes found it hard to look at Spark's burn-scarred face, but now Rhodes was accustomed to the slight disfigurement. "Besides, I am busy enough running comms and trying to get this little monster to eat something healthy."

The medical team did their best to cosmetically salvage Sparks' attractive mug, but *Magnus* did not leave with the advanced skin regenerative technology available on Earth. Even worse, Sparks had several cancers develop from the radiation exposure of from the nuclear blast.

The cancers were removed, but the treatment left Sparks unable to walk more than a few steps. She had lost about a third of her muscle mass, but had been recently been focusing on therapy to rebuilt her strength and stamina.

"Well, after seeing how cute Nora is, I think I'd like to be a mom," Sparks said. "No reason I shouldn't bless future generations with my hot genes."

North rolled his eyes. After the blast, he had temporarily lost his sight, but his burns were much less severe and eventually his skin healed itself, replacing the damaged cells with new ones.

"We'll, I'm stuffed," North said, and turned to Sparks. "You ready to go on our walk? Let's get out of here before Rhodes tries to make me eat my vita-paste."

Sparks started to gather dishes from the table.

"Oh, don't worry about those," Rhodes pressed. "I'll take care of them. You guys enjoy your walk."

"Thanks," Sparks said.

"Do you have watch duty tomorrow?" Rhodes asked North.

"The morning shift," North said.

"Well, I'll see you in then," Rhodes smiled.

North slid the hoverchair that Sparks was sitting in out from the open end of the booth table, and pushed it towards the door. Using the inverse technology that powered the artificial gravity, the chair could be self-propelled, but Sparks liked the intimacy of being pushed around by North, and he obliged her.

Magnus had one garden spot, a greenhouse observation deck in the deep aft of the ship. The corridor to access the greenhouse was narrow, and Sparks' wheelchair could not fit through the door. This was not unexpected, and true to his routine, North gently lifted sparks from the chair, and carried her broken body in his strong arms through the greenhouse, and sat her down on bench that faced the viewport into space. Even though they were a light year away, the brightest star was still Viapos.

North sat with Sparks for several hours. Sometimes they had engaging conversation, but sometimes they just rested silently. Sparks had been thinking about her maternity discussion with Rhodes, and it made her wistful and pensive.

"I'm glad to be headed back to *Magellan*," North broke the silence as he studied the star around which Arara orbited, "but I am sad we're getting further away from the beaches of Lewis Island. I'd like to go there again."

"That would be nice," Sparks said. "Nice and boring."

"Oh, you know you'd love it," North returned the tease.

"Well I guess it would be peaceful," Sparks admitted. "But who am I to complain. I'm a survivor, and I'm alive. And this peace right here isn't bad." She patted North's muscular arm, then rested her head on North's shoulder.

After a few moments, Sparks lifted her head. "North, I'm tired. Would you mind taking me home?"

North placed one arm under Sparks' torso, and the other under her knees and lifted gently.

North set Sparks down so that she was sitting on the edge of her bed in her studio quarters.

"Would you mind handing me my sleeping gown?" Sparks said. North grabbed the gown off of Spark's vanity, and also, knowing she would ask, grabbed an oral cleanser for her.

"Oh, and would you grab my toothbr–"

North smiled and handed her the cleanser.

"Can you start the zipper for me?" Sparks glanced over her shoulder.

North pulled the zipper on her black jumpsuit down to her lower back, and then faced away.

Sparks struggled a bit to complete the change, but was able to slip into her sleeping gown.

"Okay," she said. North turned around.

"Goodnight, Sparks," North flashed his perfect smile.

"North, stay the night," Sparks blurted, then spoke more slowly. "Please be with me."

"Sparks, I'm sorry. I don't think –"

"It's because I'm ugly now," Sparks blurted again. She knew North wasn't that shallow, which is one of the reasons she desired him. But she felt ugly. And she wanted to believe she could still be loved. And if not North, there wasn't anyone. "I'm sorry, North. I shouldn't have —"

"Shhh…" North sat down next to Sparks and leaned in and kissed her gently for several moments. Sparks felt like the most beautiful woman on *Magnus*.

"I'm sorry I can't give you more," North said. "I wish I could. It's because of —"

"Amberly. My sister. It's okay, North, I understand."

"She's not —"

"Really my sister. I know, I know. Look at us. We're finishing each other's sentences. How disgusting is that?" Sparks back peddled with levity.

"You're alright, kid," North winked at Sparks as he stood up to leave.

"Goodnight, North. I'll see you for lunch tomorrow?"

"No, I have a date with the *other* psycho ex-Chasm femme fatale on this ship."

Sparks eyes lit up. She enjoyed sarcastic smack North. They looked at each other knowingly for another moment, then North left.

As he walked back to the XO quarters, North felt as broken on the inside as Sparks looked on the outside. He hadn't been praying as much as he used to, but he wondered if maybe providence hadn't brought him and Sparks together.

By the time they arrived at *Magellan*, North calculated more than four years will have passed since he left the waypoint. Why was he sifting through the Amberly baggage? He burned that bridge pretty well when he left on the *Magnus*.

North compared Amberly to Sparks in his mind's eye as he began to undress to shower. *In many ways, Sparks and I have more in common...*

His thought was interrupted by a message from Condi.

"North, we received an encrypted message directed to you, which was surprising considering the radio silence orders surrounding our mission. Comm officer Rhodes does not have a matching encryption chip — she said she returned it to you — so I couldn't tell you who it was from or what is says."

Amberly!

North tore through his footlocker to produce the encryption key Amberly had sent to him before he left *Magellan*. He had used it once before to warn Amberly about the Hawks.

North physically plugged the key into his infopad.

"Condi, decode and playback the message."

North wished there was video with the message, but still it was good to hear Amberly's voice. He felt helpless as he heard about Amberly's trials. He felt jealous at the mentions of Skylar and Dek.

As Amberly talked about forgiveness, North felt as if he was being put back together, as if somehow life went from tasting bitter to tasting sweet.

"If you have a choice, you come home," Amberly said, "I'll be waiting."

Nothing will stop me, Amberly. Nothing, North pledged.

EPILOGUE THREE

Chasm's Utopia battleship, June 8, 2605, .9 light years from Waypoint Magellan, six months after the Battle of Marquette.

The Chairman waited patiently for the news. She sat almost perfectly still in the command chair on the bridge of a fully repaired *Utopia*.

The engines had been upgraded and tested. They could propel the ship faster than six-tenths of light speed. Fully repaired, *Utopia* was now the fastest vessel ever created, and she might actually be able to overtake *Magnus*. But the Chairman had to make sure that Project Brimstone was in place.

Patience was perhaps the Chairman's greatest strength. But she was not immortal, and the delays in the creation of the chasm between Earth and Arara had cost years of her life.

She had been waiting for months since *Marquette* left its anchorage and moved into Arara's orbit. The ultimate high ground, *Marquette* had been transformed into an orbit-to-surface weapon with the ability to obliterate any resistance to Chasm's new control of Arara from an untouchable position.

Unable to fight back, the Earth-loyal Araran government had been be forced to surrender unconditionally to Chasm.

"Madam Chairman," the comm officer spoke up, clearly trying to preserve her professional decorum in the face of great news. "*Marquette* tight beam reports Operation Brimstone is a complete success. Governor Paito sends his compliments and wishes us good hunting."

Competing with the virtue of patience in the mind of the Chairman was her thirst for revenge — to punish those who had already slowed down her ascension. The combination of patience and vengeance made the Chairman particularly lethal.

"Navigator, prepare rapid spool up. Please transmit to fleet go orders," the Chairman smiled. She looked out at the gleaming fleet of dual-hull warships, four in total, that matched the *Utopia's* lethal form. She imagined waypoint after waypoint, destroyed by her Dark Armada. They would not return to Arara, but bring a clear, destructive message when they reached Earth: the child has supplanted the parent, and now the parent must die.

Once *Utopia* had completed its mission at *Magellan*, however, the Chairman planned on returning to Arara to oversee the engineering of a perfected humanity. Eternal peace and equity for all. She would, however indulge herself with one spoil of war.

I will savor revenge on Amberly Macready for taking away my Raven One, the Chairman thought. *And when I bring her back to Arara, there will be no end to her pain. She will suffer for the greater good.*

Follow the continuing stories of the brave men and women of humanity's waypoints in The Dark Armada, *the next exciting novel in the Project Waypoint Series from Shadowlands Press. Sign up for e-mail news and announcements online at ShadowlandsPress.com*

To report errata and other mistakes found in this edition, please e-mail us at editor@ShadowlandsPress.com.